dave roman
astronaut academy
Re-Entry

:01

First Second

New York

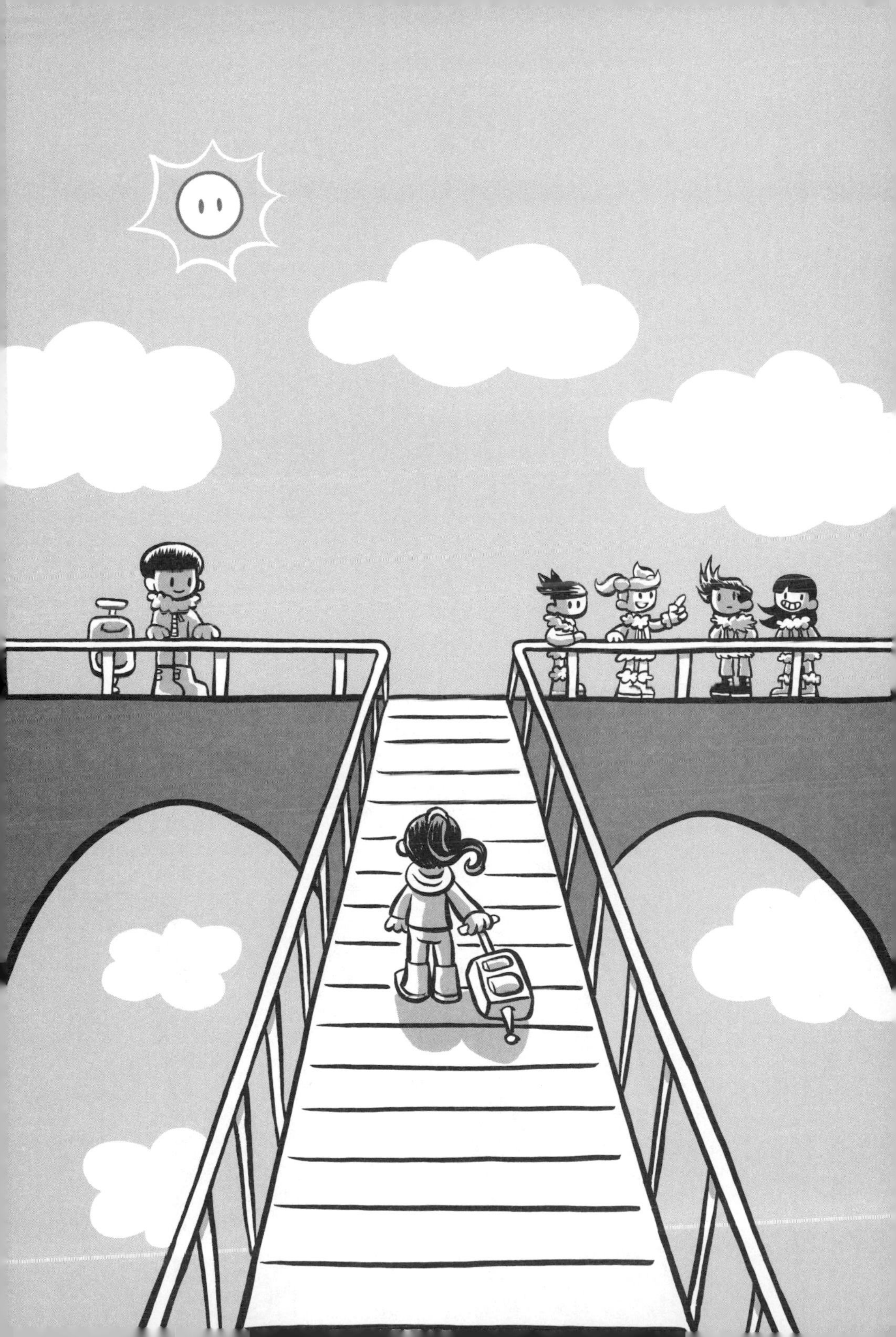

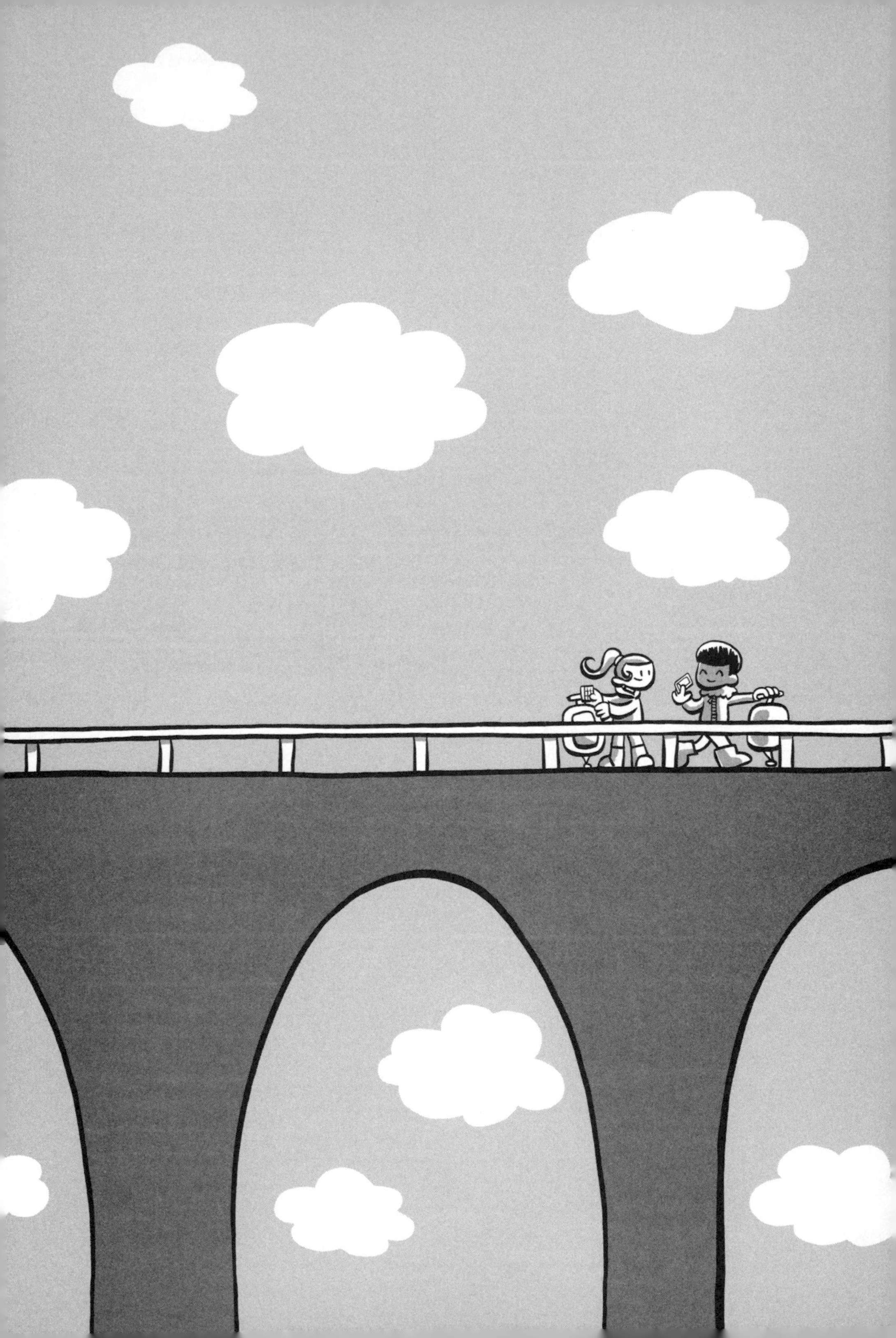

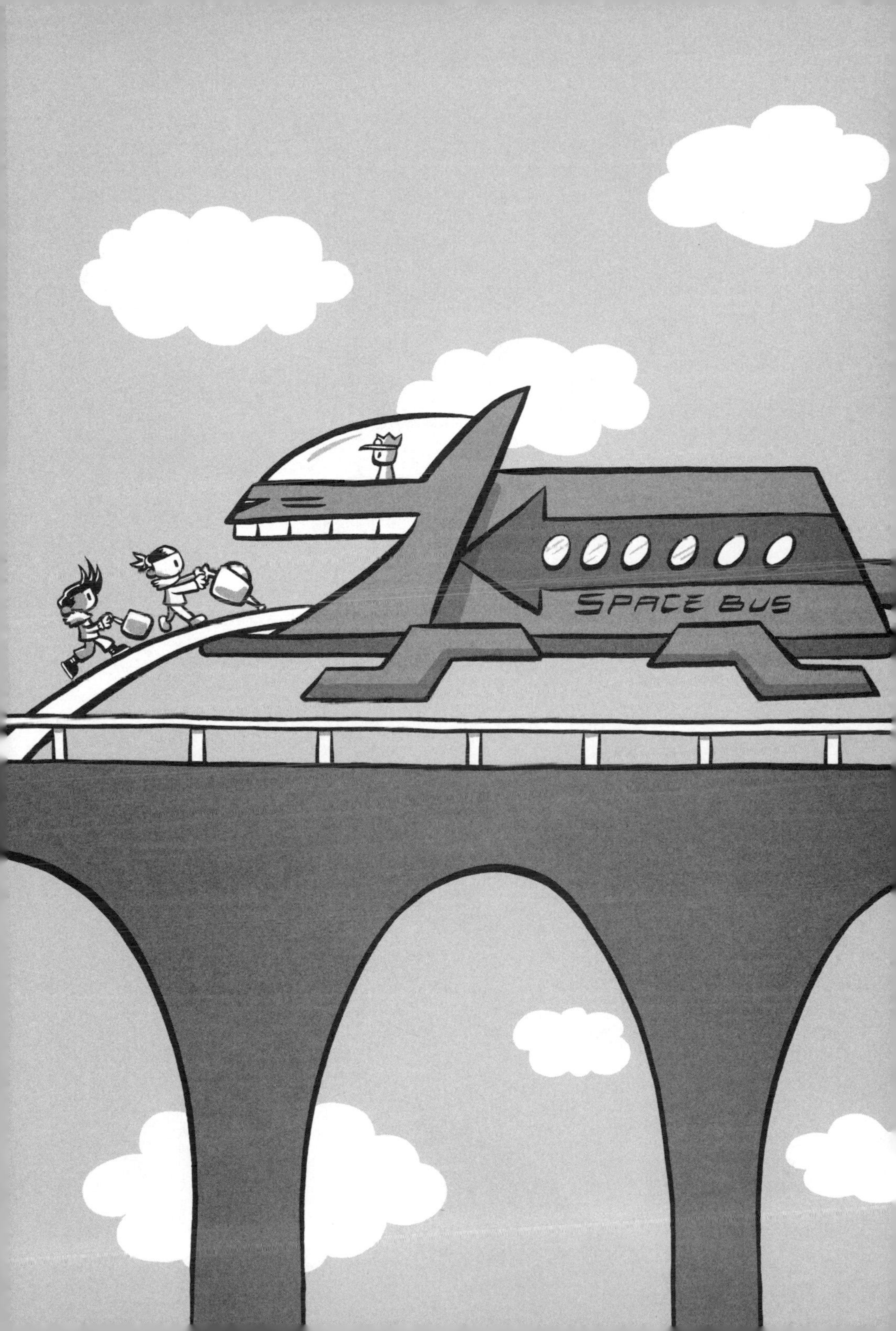
SPACE BUS

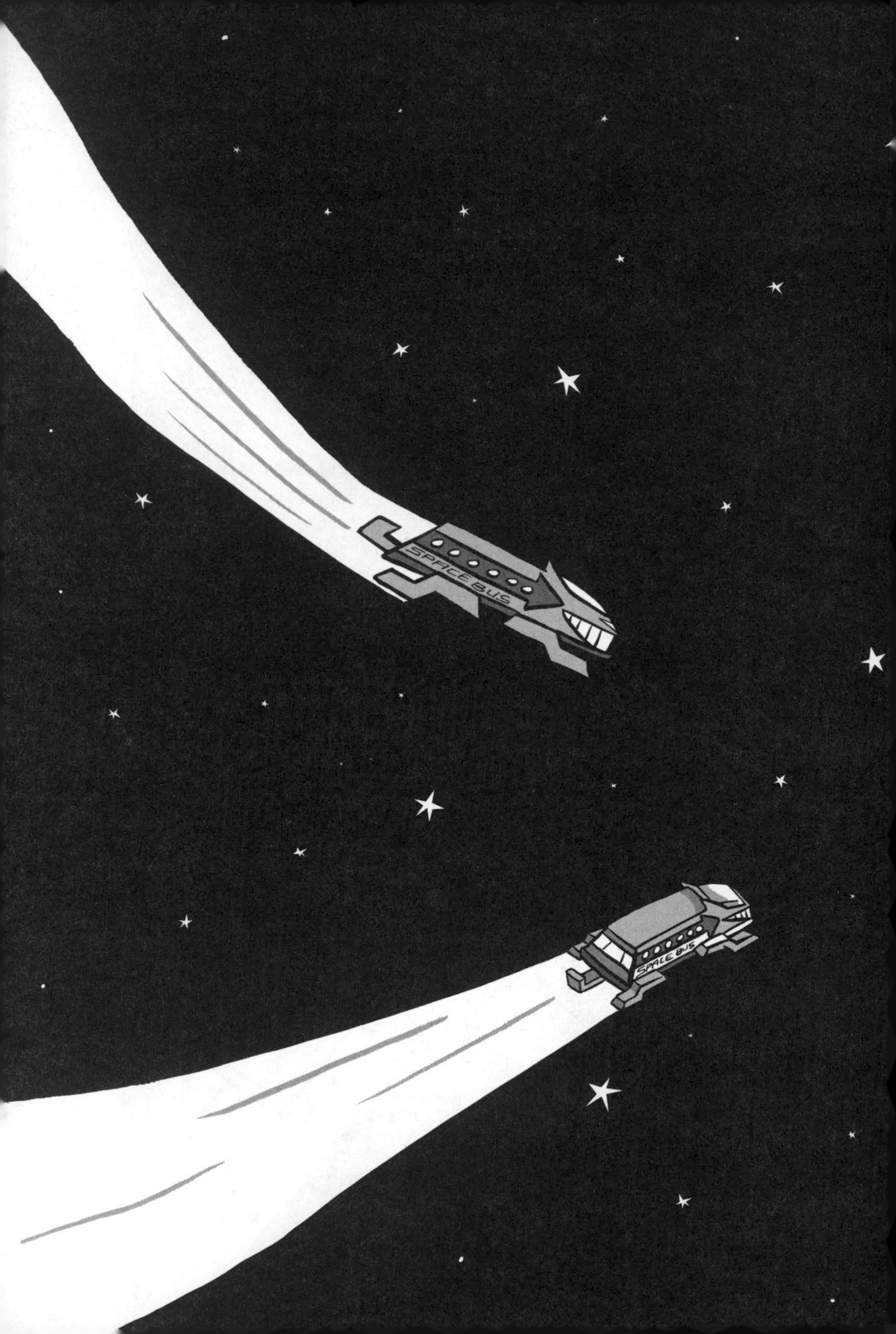
SPACE BUS
SPACE BUS

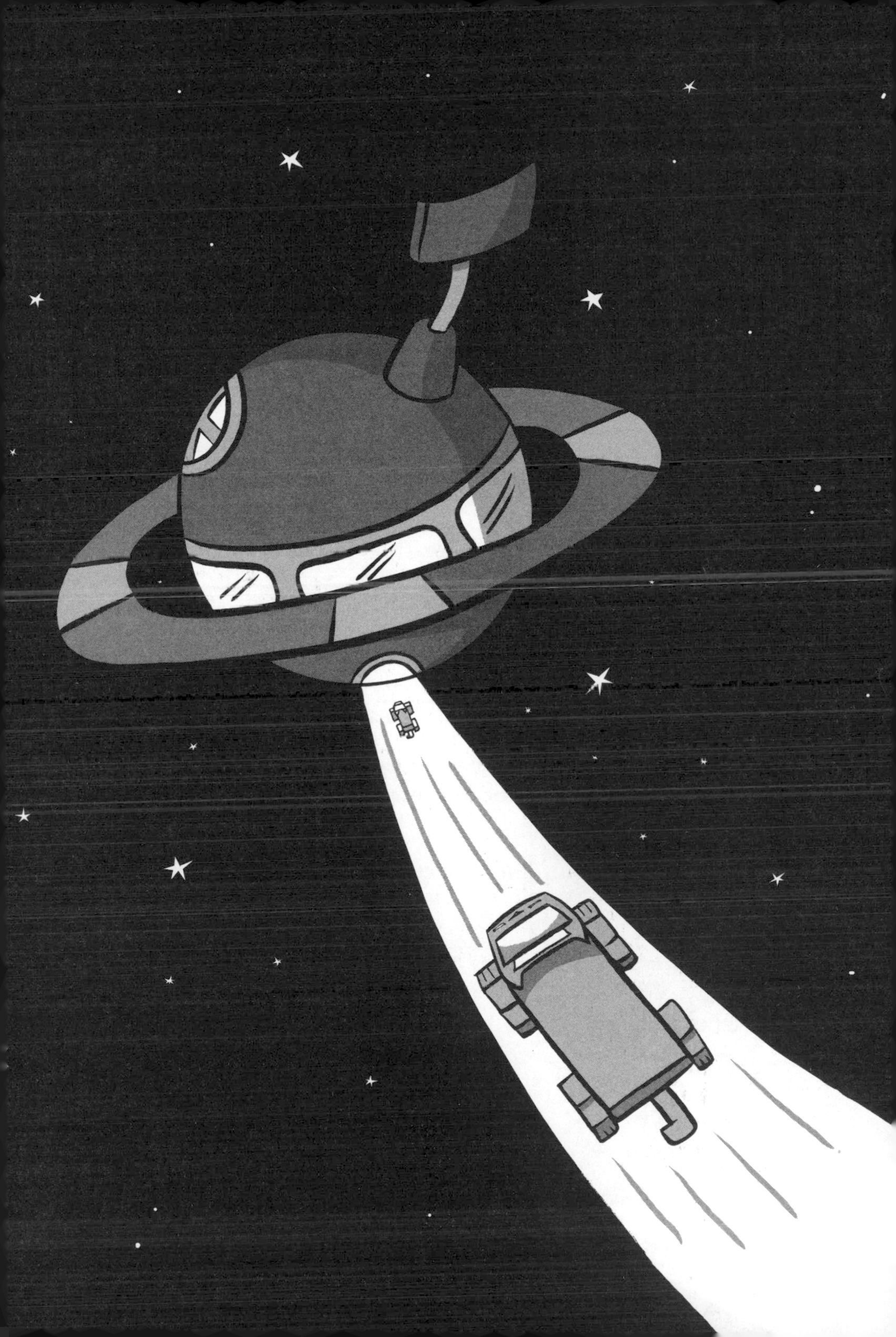

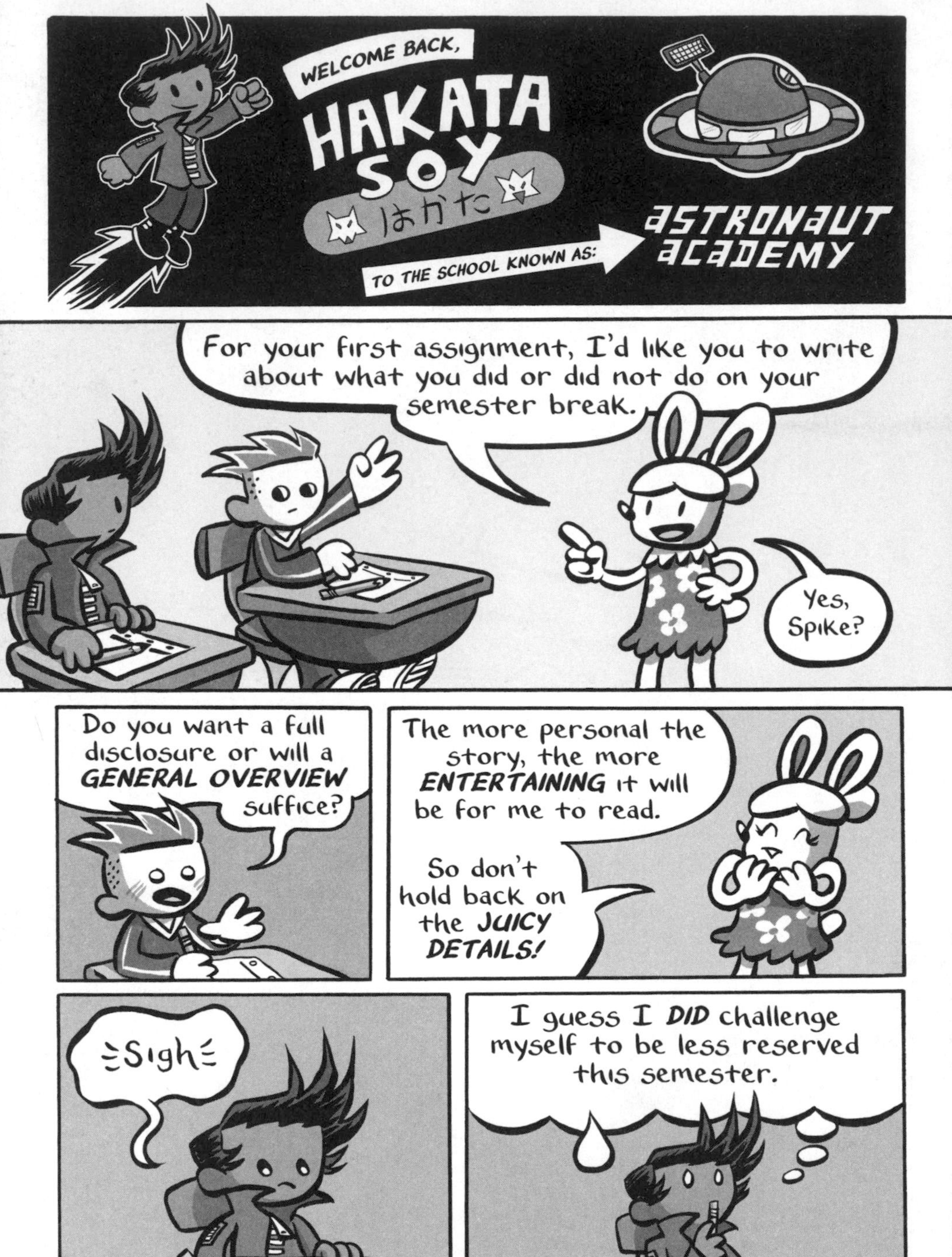
WELCOME BACK,
HAKATA SOY
はかた
TO THE SCHOOL KNOWN AS:
ASTRONAUT ACADEMY
For your first assignment, I'd like you to write about what you did or did not do on your semester break.
Yes, Spike?
Do you want a full disclosure or will a GENERAL OVERVIEW suffice?
The more personal the story, the more ENTERTAINING it will be for me to read.
So don't hold back on the JUICY DETAILS!
Sigh
I guess I DID challenge myself to be less reserved this semester.

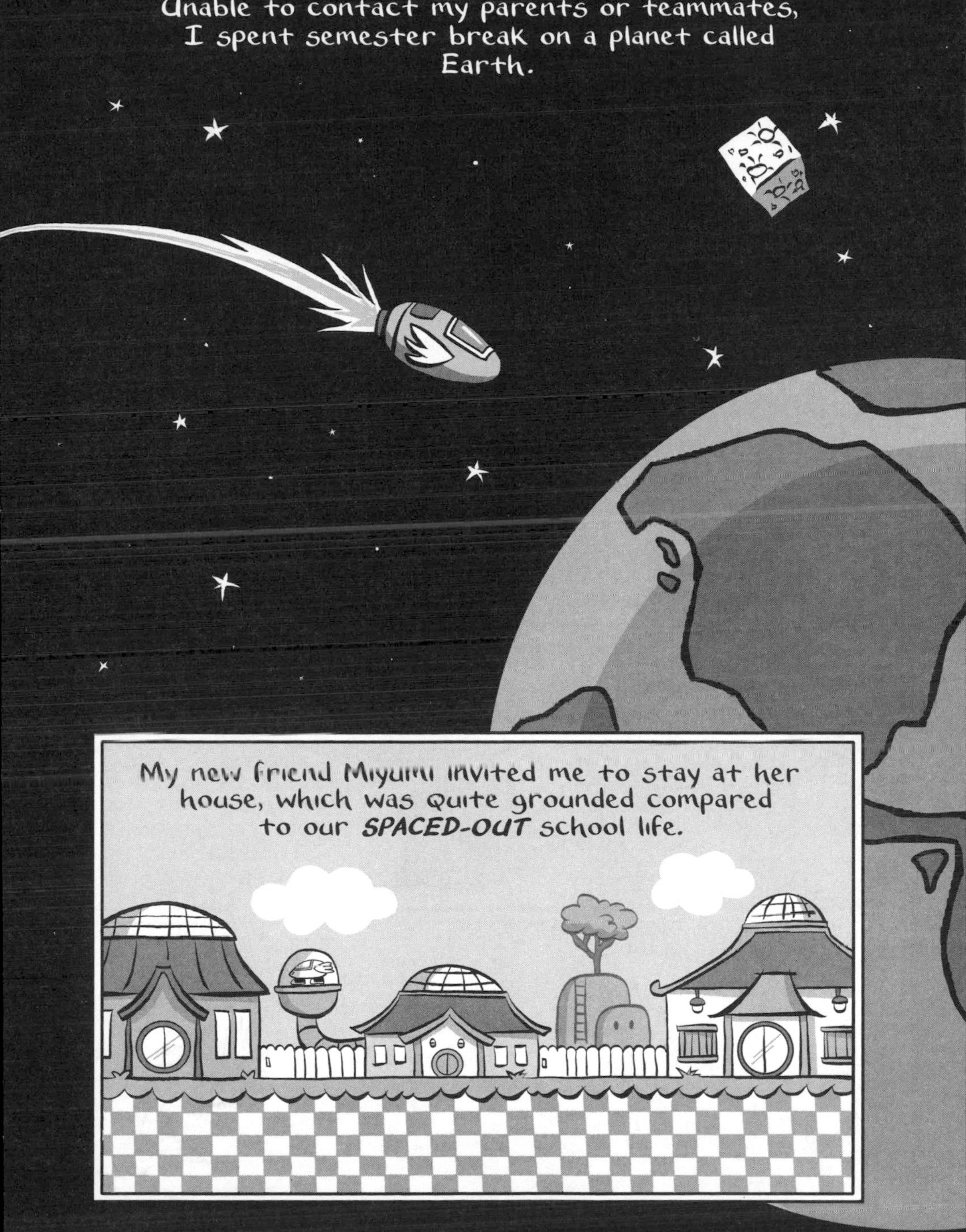
Unable to contact my parents or teammates, I spent semester break on a planet called Earth.
My new friend Miyumi invited me to stay at her house, which was quite grounded compared to our SPACED-OUT school life.

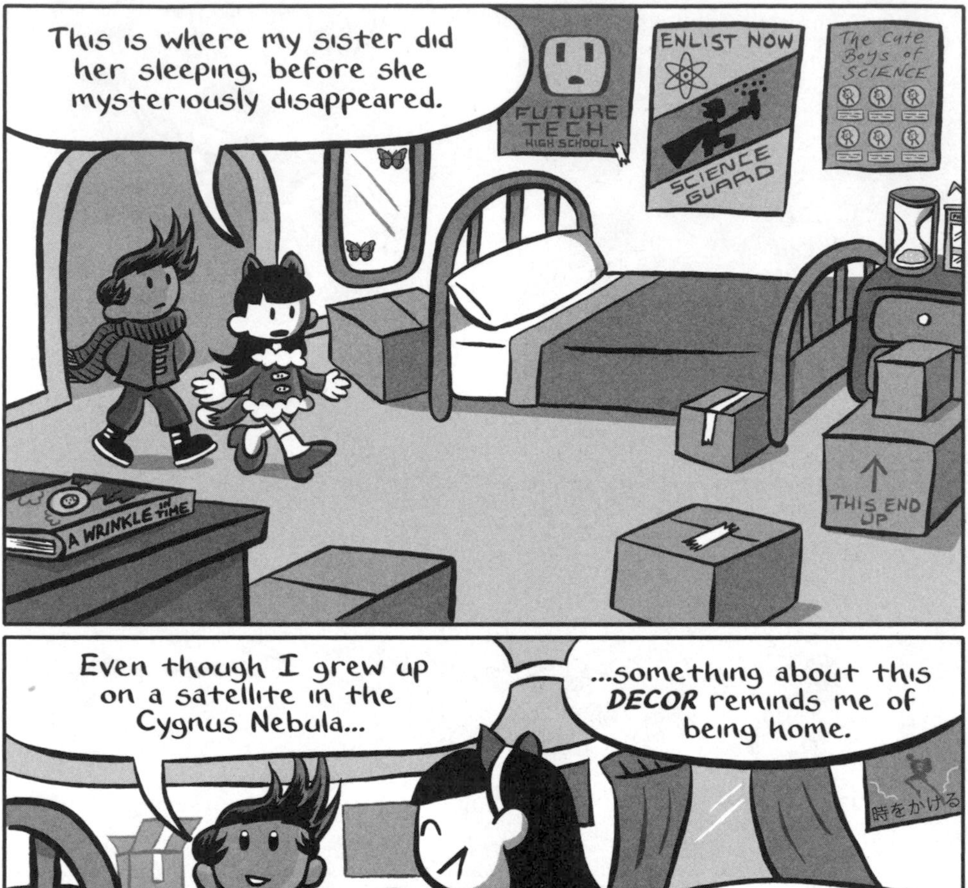
This is where my sister did her sleeping, before she mysteriously disappeared.
FUTURE TECH HIGH SCHOOL
ENLIST NOW
SCIENCE GUARD
The Cute Boys of SCIENCE
A WRINKLE IN TIME
THIS END UP
Even though I grew up on a satellite in the Cygnus Nebula...
...something about this DECOR reminds me of being home.
時をかける
Then you won't mind a relaxing sit, while I check for fresh towels.

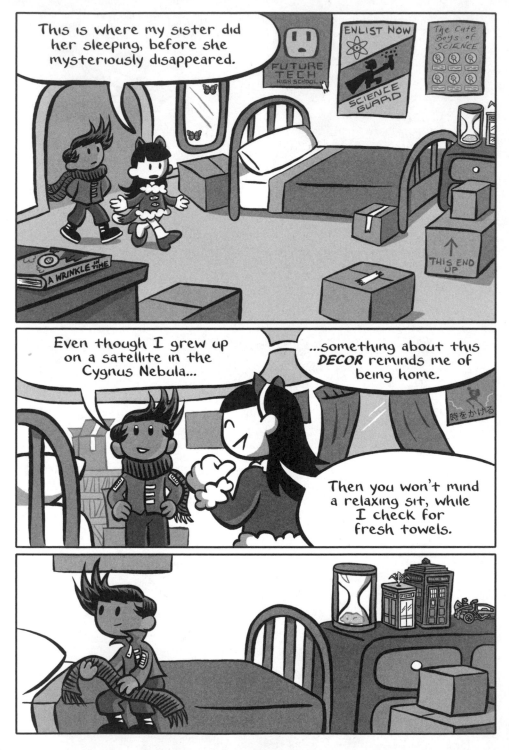

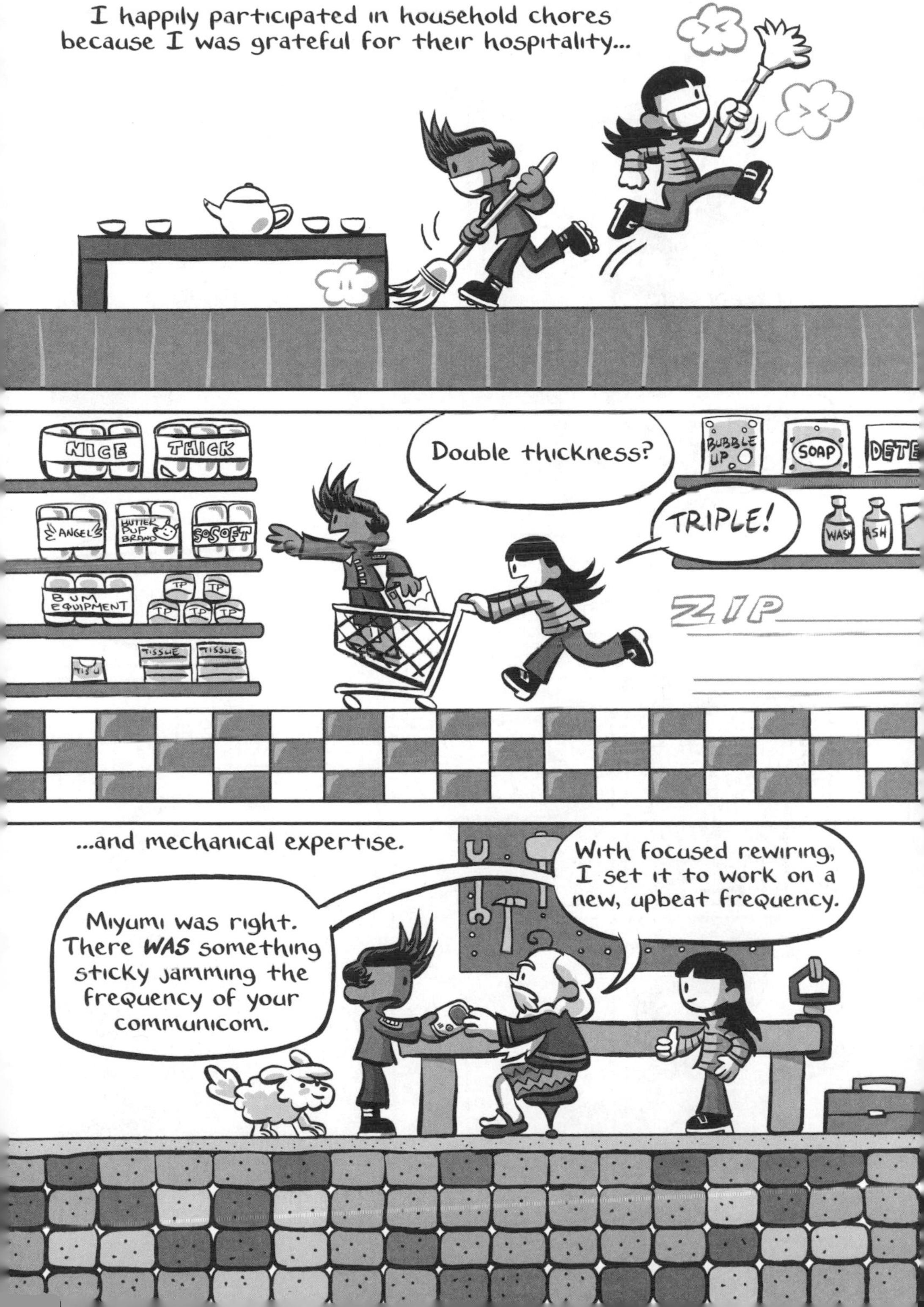

I happily participated in household chores because I was grateful for their hospitality...
NICE
THICK
ANGEL
BUTTER PUP BRAND
SO SOFT
BUM EQUIPMENT
TP
TISSUE
Double thickness?
BUBBLE UP
SOAP
TRIPLE!
WASH
ZIP
...and mechanical expertise.
Miyumi was right. There *WAS* something sticky jamming the frequency of your communicom.
With focused rewiring, I set it to work on a new, upbeat frequency.

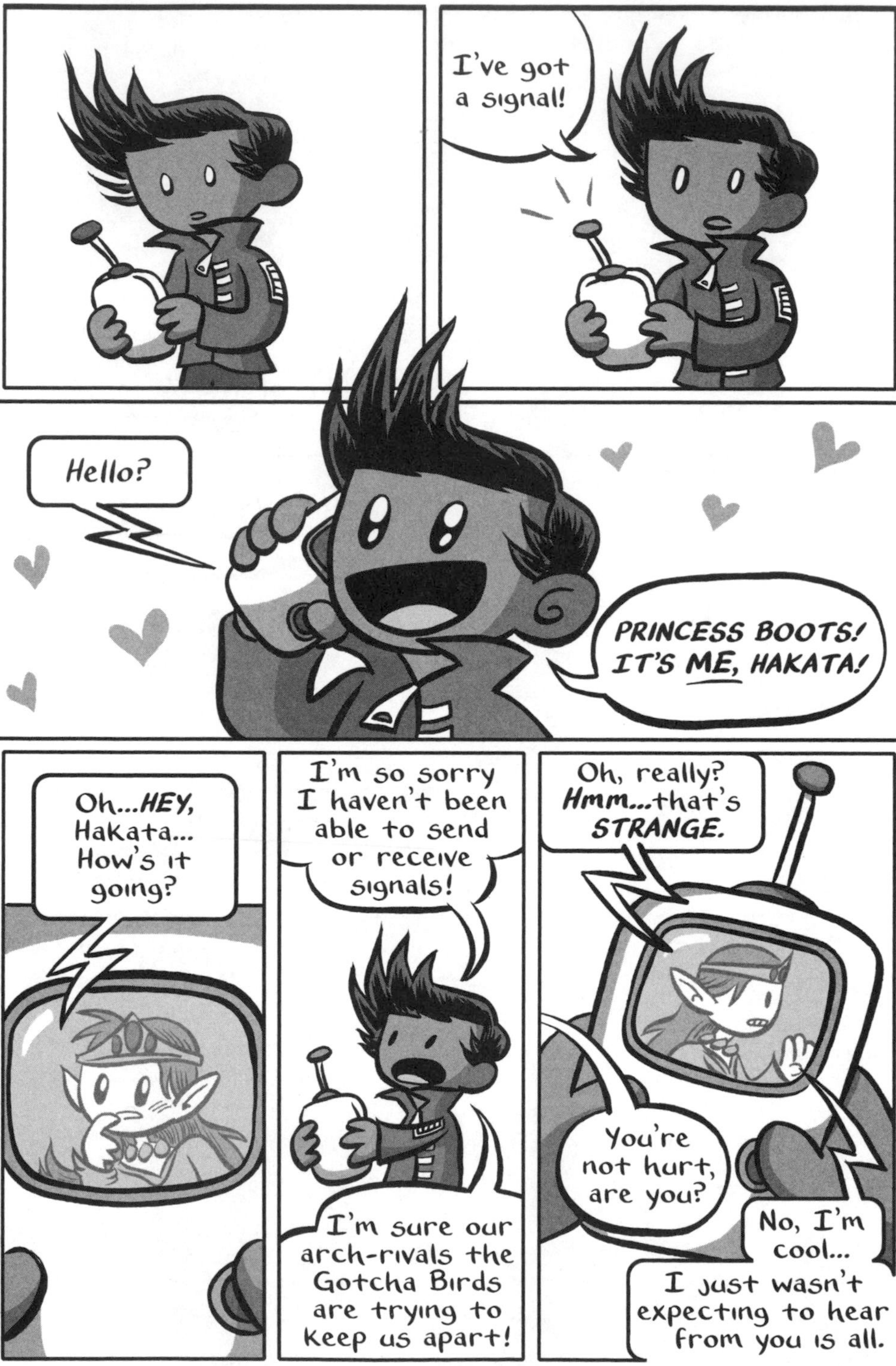
I've got a signal!
Hello?
PRINCESS BOOTS! IT'S ME, HAKATA!
Oh...HEY, Hakata... How's it going?
I'm so sorry I haven't been able to send or receive signals!
I'm sure our arch-rivals the Gotcha Birds are trying to keep us apart!
Oh, really? Hmm...that's STRANGE.
You're not hurt, are you?
No, I'm cool...
I just wasn't expecting to hear from you is all.

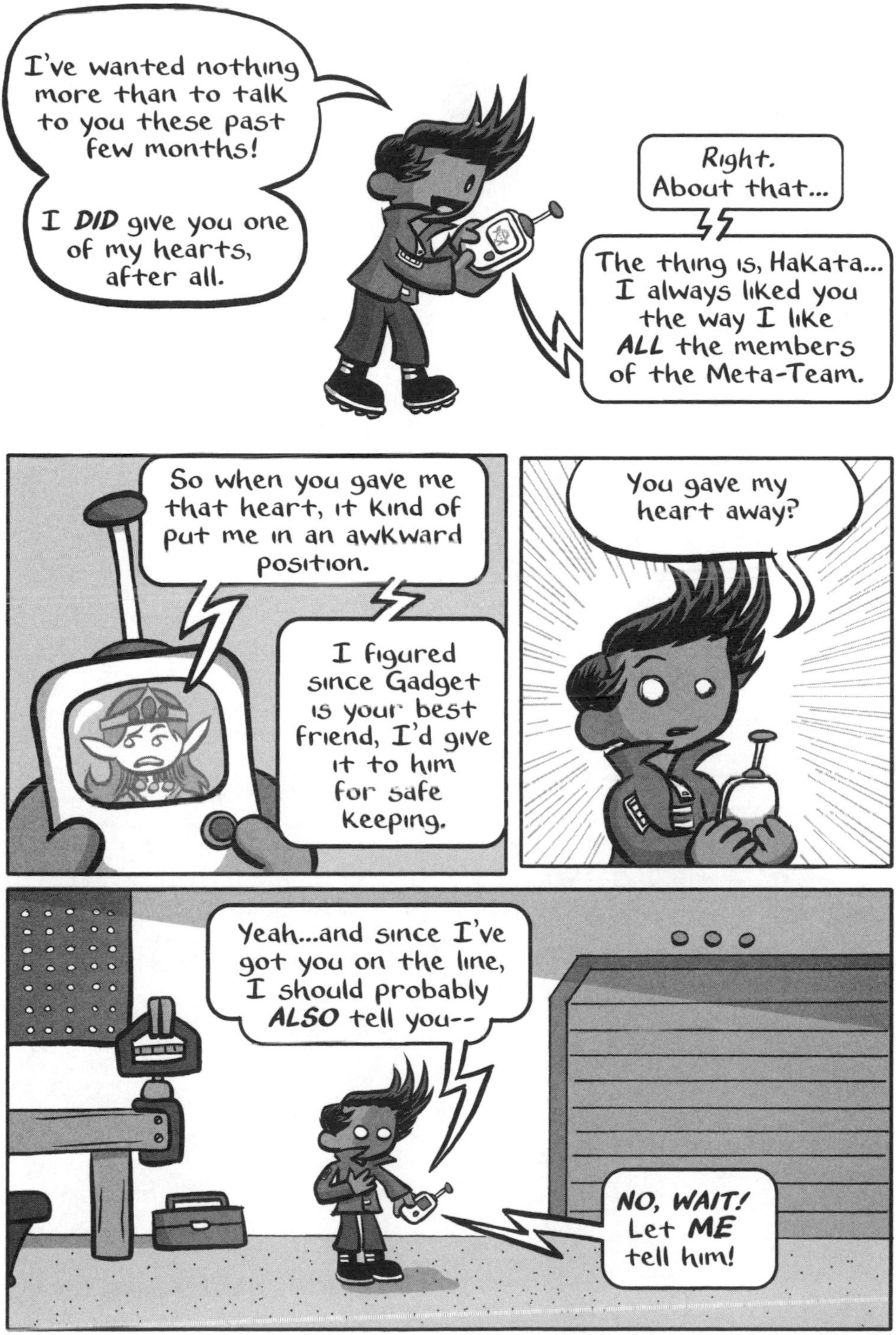
I've wanted nothing more than to talk to you these past few months!
I DID give you one of my hearts, after all.
Right. About that...
The thing is, Hakata... I always liked you the way I like ALL the members of the Meta-Team.
So when you gave me that heart, it kind of put me in an awkward position.
I figured since Gadget is your best friend, I'd give it to him for safe keeping.
You gave my heart away?
Yeah...and since I've got you on the line, I should probably ALSO tell you--
NO, WAIT! Let ME tell him!

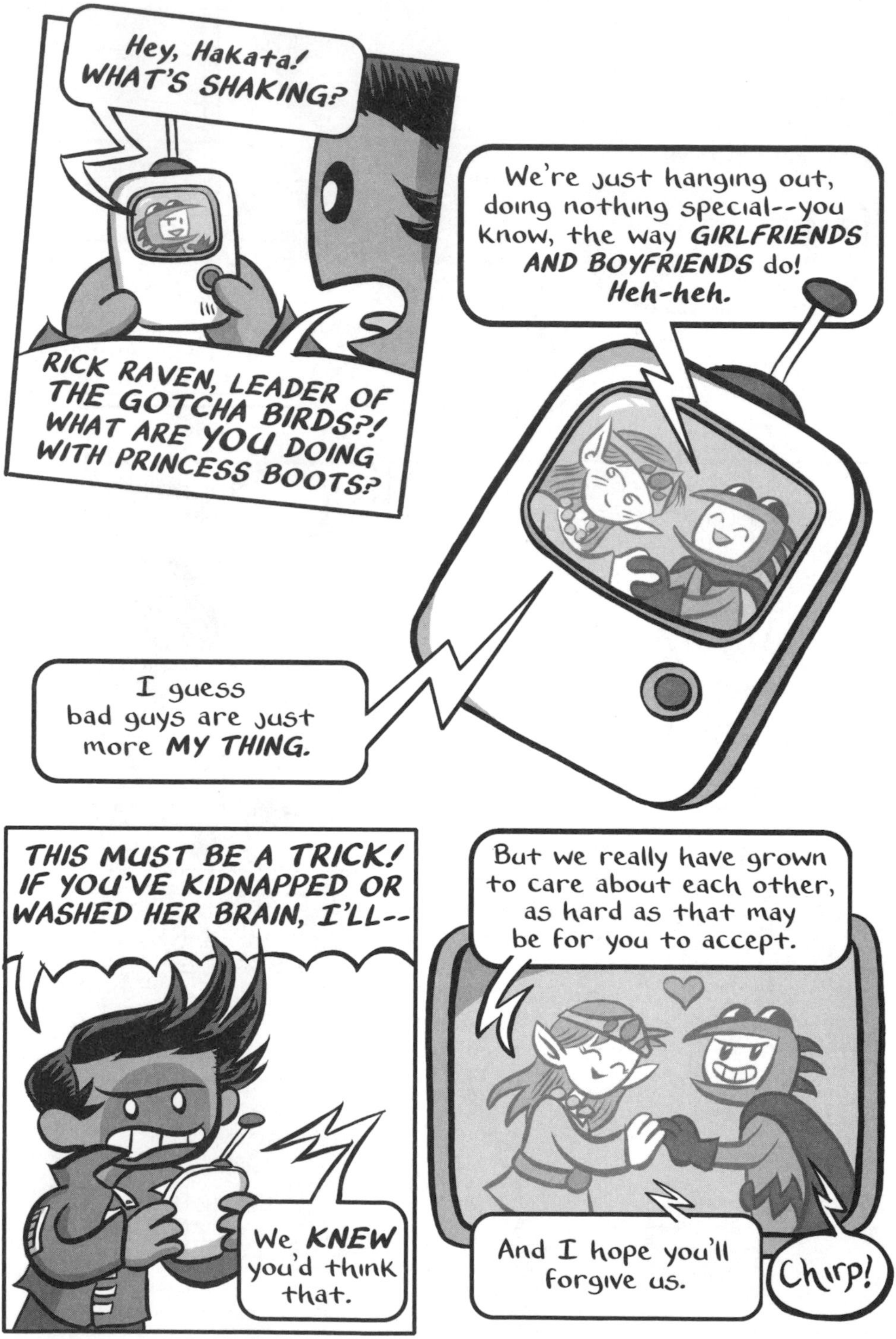
Hey, Hakata! WHAT'S SHAKING?
RICK RAVEN, LEADER OF THE GOTCHA BIRDS?! WHAT ARE YOU DOING WITH PRINCESS BOOTS?
We're just hanging out, doing nothing special--you know, the way GIRLFRIENDS AND BOYFRIENDS do! Heh-heh.
I guess bad guys are just more MY THING.
THIS MUST BE A TRICK! IF YOU'VE KIDNAPPED OR WASHED HER BRAIN, I'LL--
We KNEW you'd think that.
But we really have grown to care about each other, as hard as that may be for you to accept.
And I hope you'll forgive us.
Chirp!

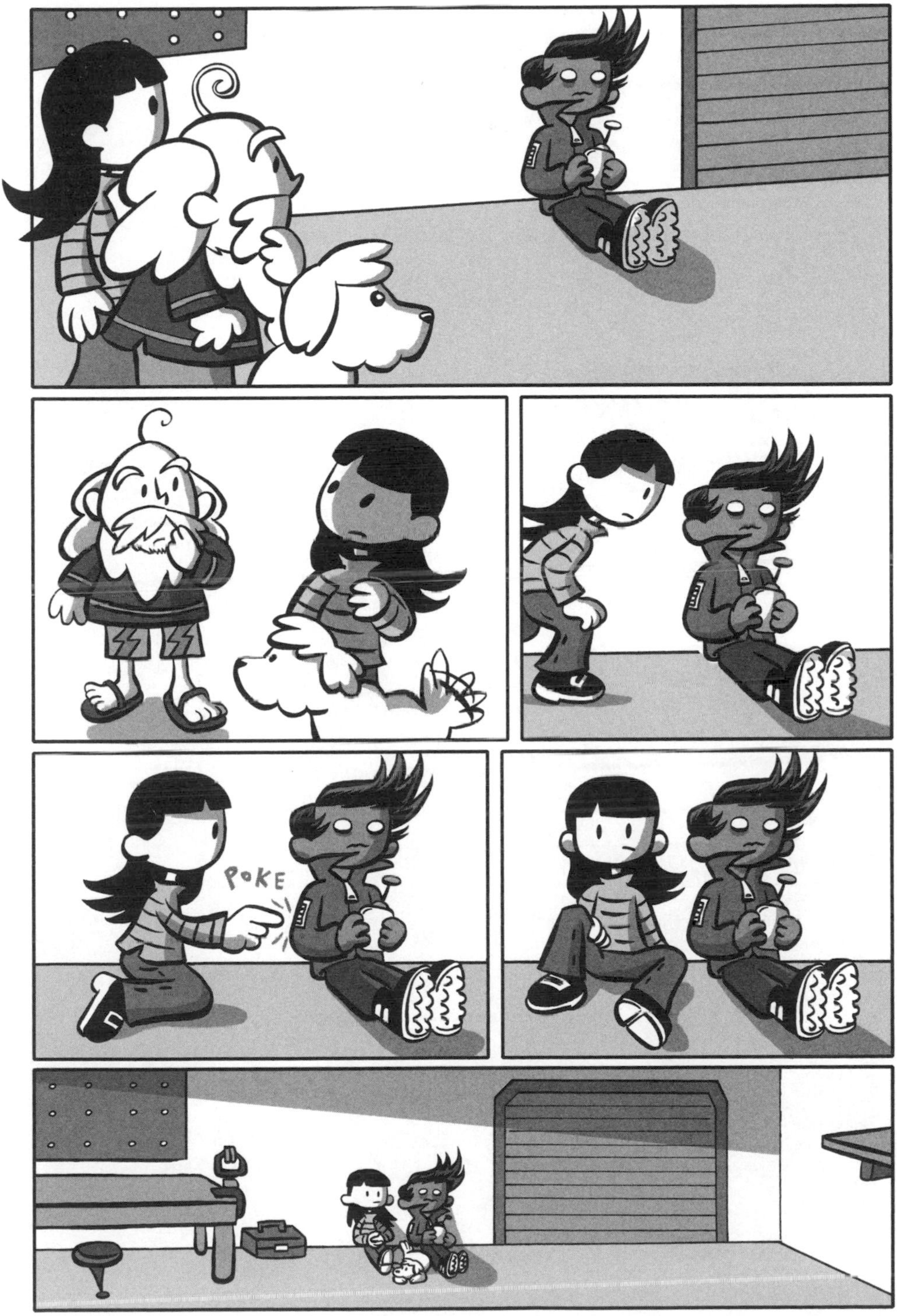
POKE

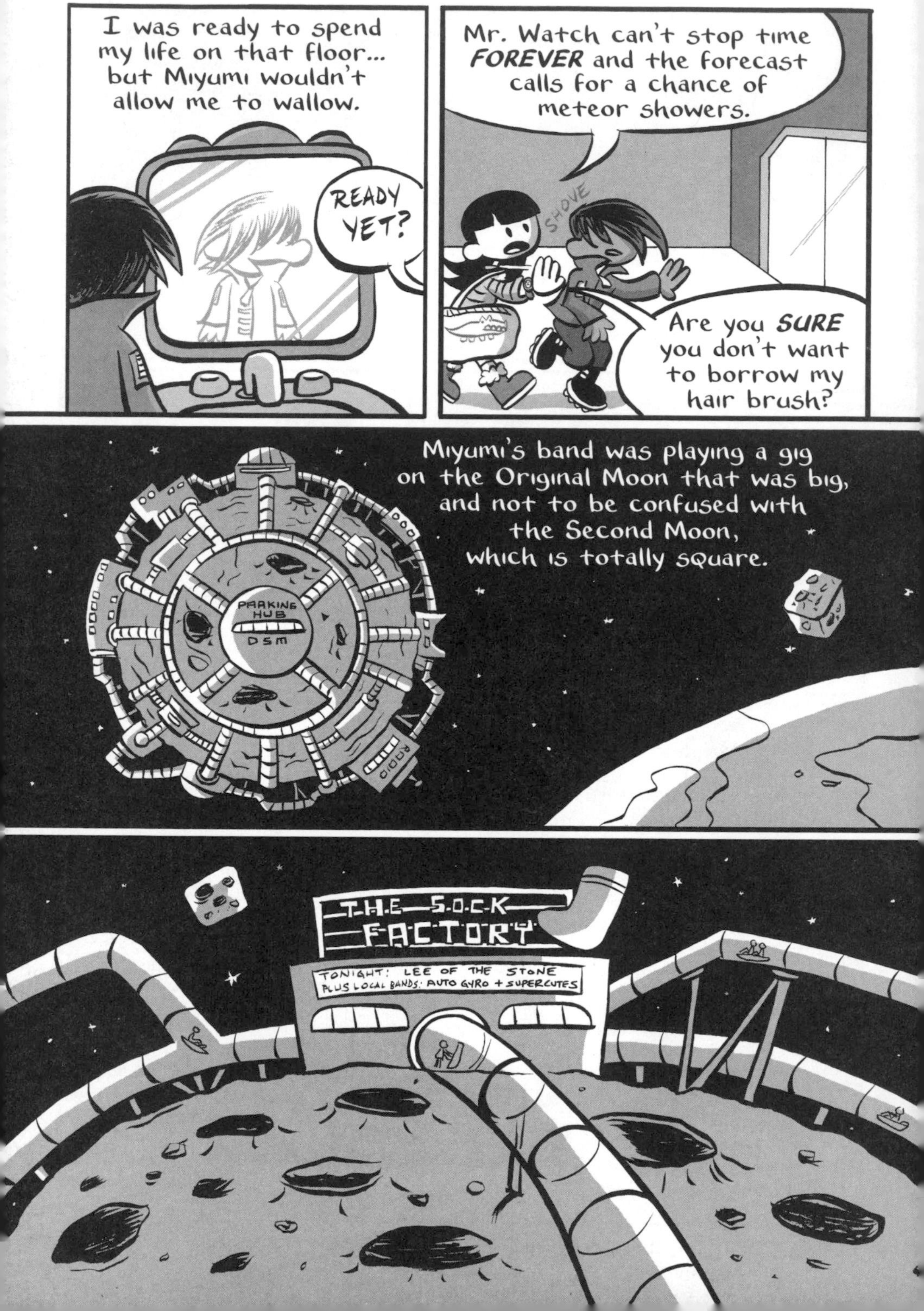
I was ready to spend my life on that floor... but Miyumi wouldn't allow me to wallow.
READY YET?
Mr. Watch can't stop time **FOREVER** and the forecast calls for a chance of meteor showers.
SHOVE
Are you **SURE** you don't want to borrow my hair brush?
Miyumi's band was playing a gig on the Original Moon that was big, and not to be confused with the Second Moon, which is totally square.
PARKING HUB
DSM
RADIO
THE SOCK FACTORY
TONIGHT: LEE OF THE STONE
PLUS LOCAL BANDS: AUTO GYRO + SUPERCUTES

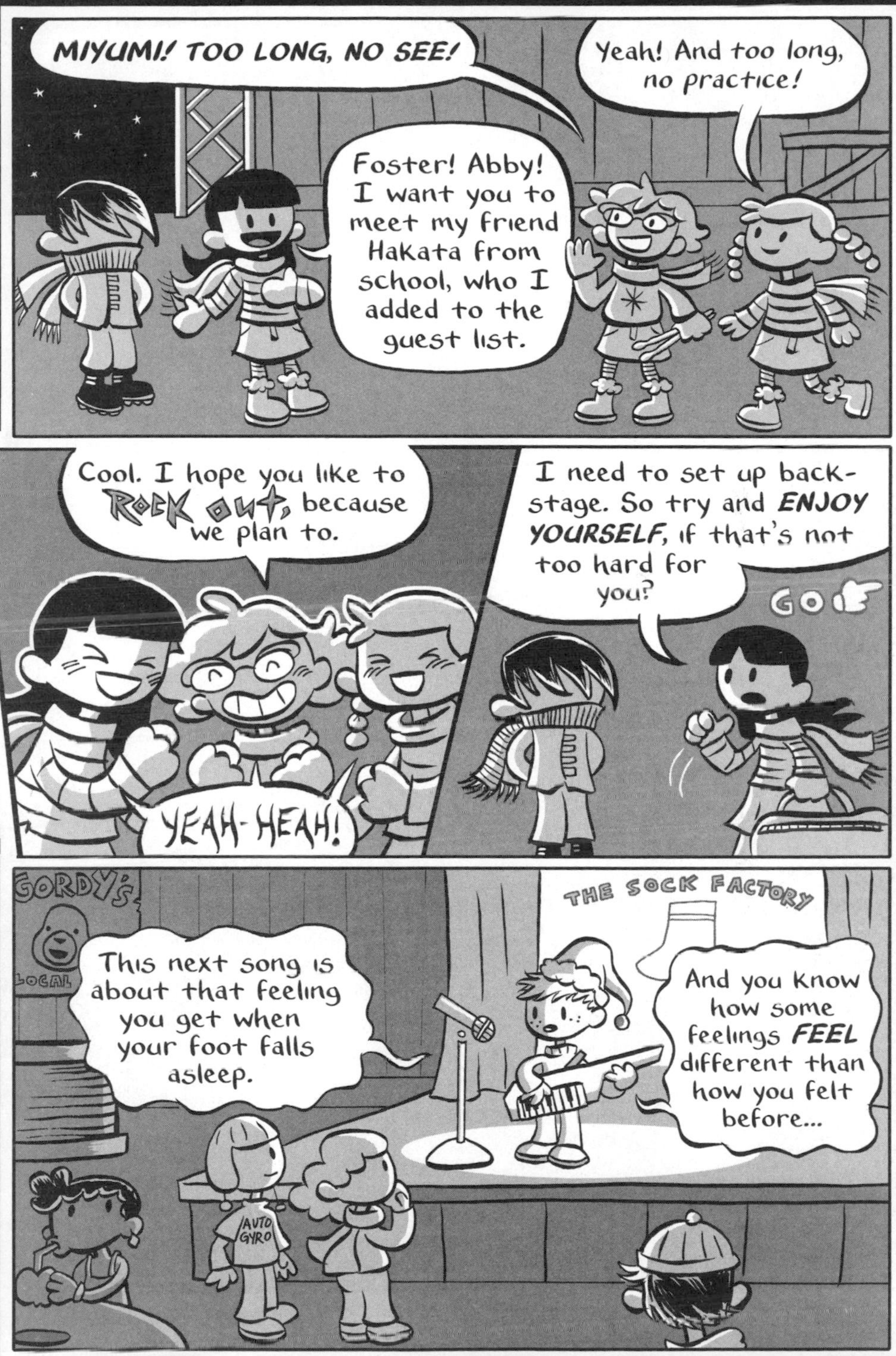
MIYUMI! TOO LONG, NO SEE!
Yeah! And too long, no practice!
Foster! Abby! I want you to meet my friend Hakata from school, who I added to the guest list.
Cool. I hope you like to ROCK OUT, because we plan to.
YEAH-HEAH!
I need to set up back-stage. So try and ENJOY YOURSELF, if that's not too hard for you?
GO
GORDY'S
LOCAL
THE SOCK FACTORY
This next song is about that feeling you get when your foot falls asleep.
And you know how some feelings FEEL different than how you felt before...
AUTO GYRO

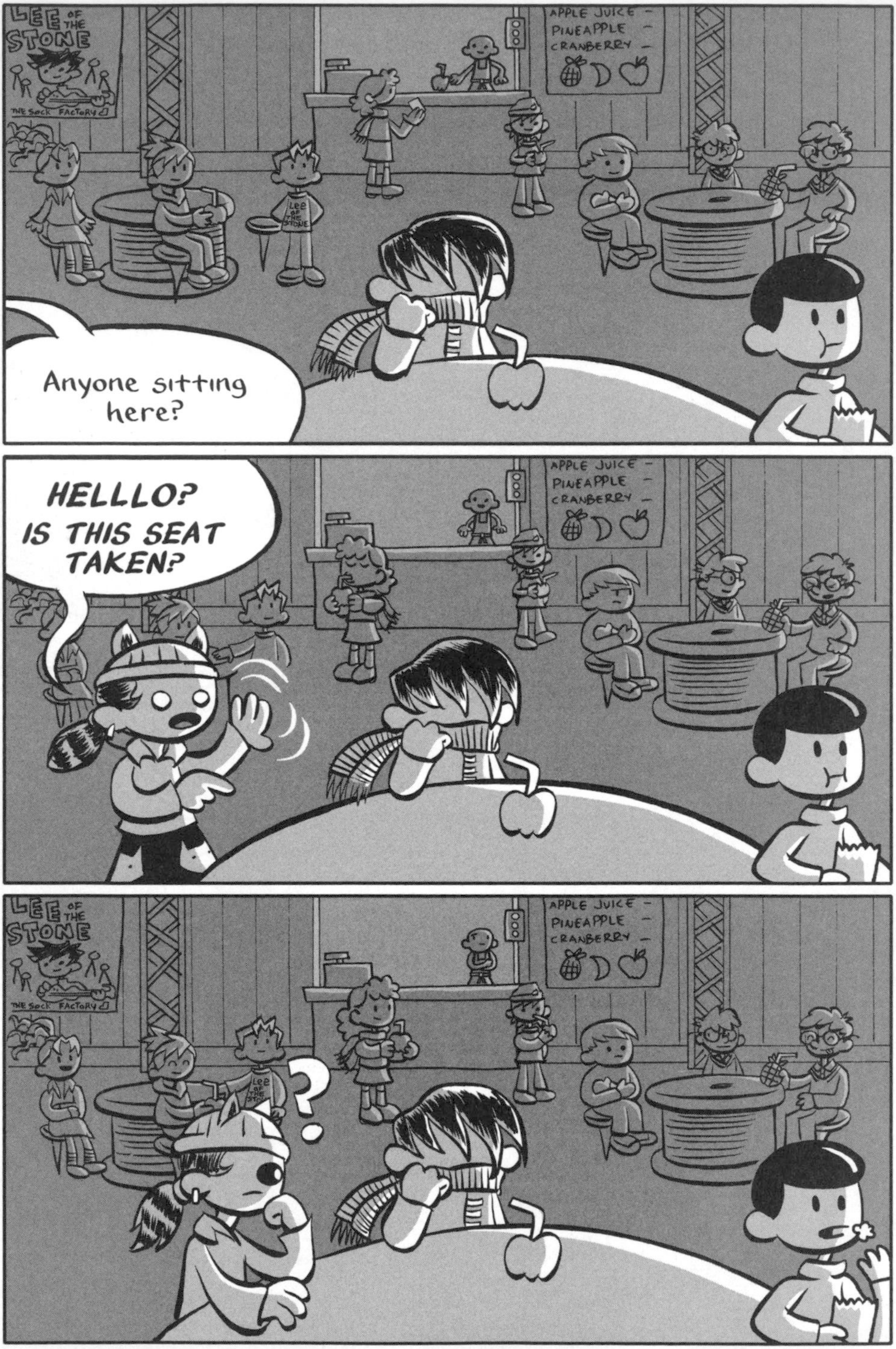
LEE OF THE STONE
THE SOCK FACTORY
APPLE JUICE –
PINEAPPLE –
CRANBERRY –
LEE OF THE STONE
Anyone sitting here?
HELLLO? IS THIS SEAT TAKEN?
?

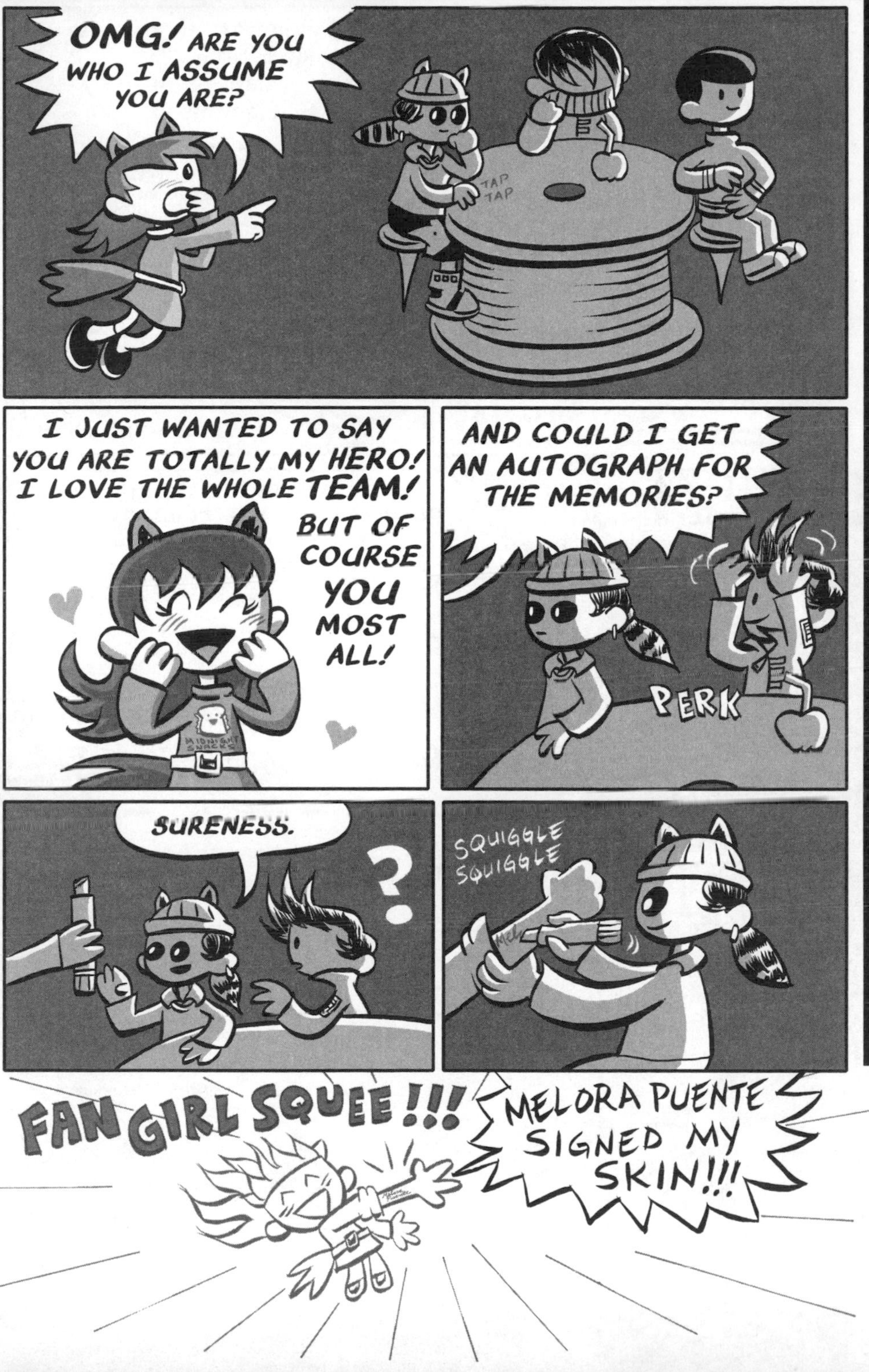
OMG! ARE YOU WHO I ASSUME YOU ARE?
TAP TAP
I JUST WANTED TO SAY YOU ARE TOTALLY MY HERO! I LOVE THE WHOLE TEAM!
BUT OF COURSE YOU MOST ALL!
MIDNIGHT SNACKS
AND COULD I GET AN AUTOGRAPH FOR THE MEMORIES?
PERK
SURENESS.
?
SQUIGGLE SQUIGGLE
FAN GIRL SQUEE!!!
MELORA PUENTE SIGNED MY SKIN!!!

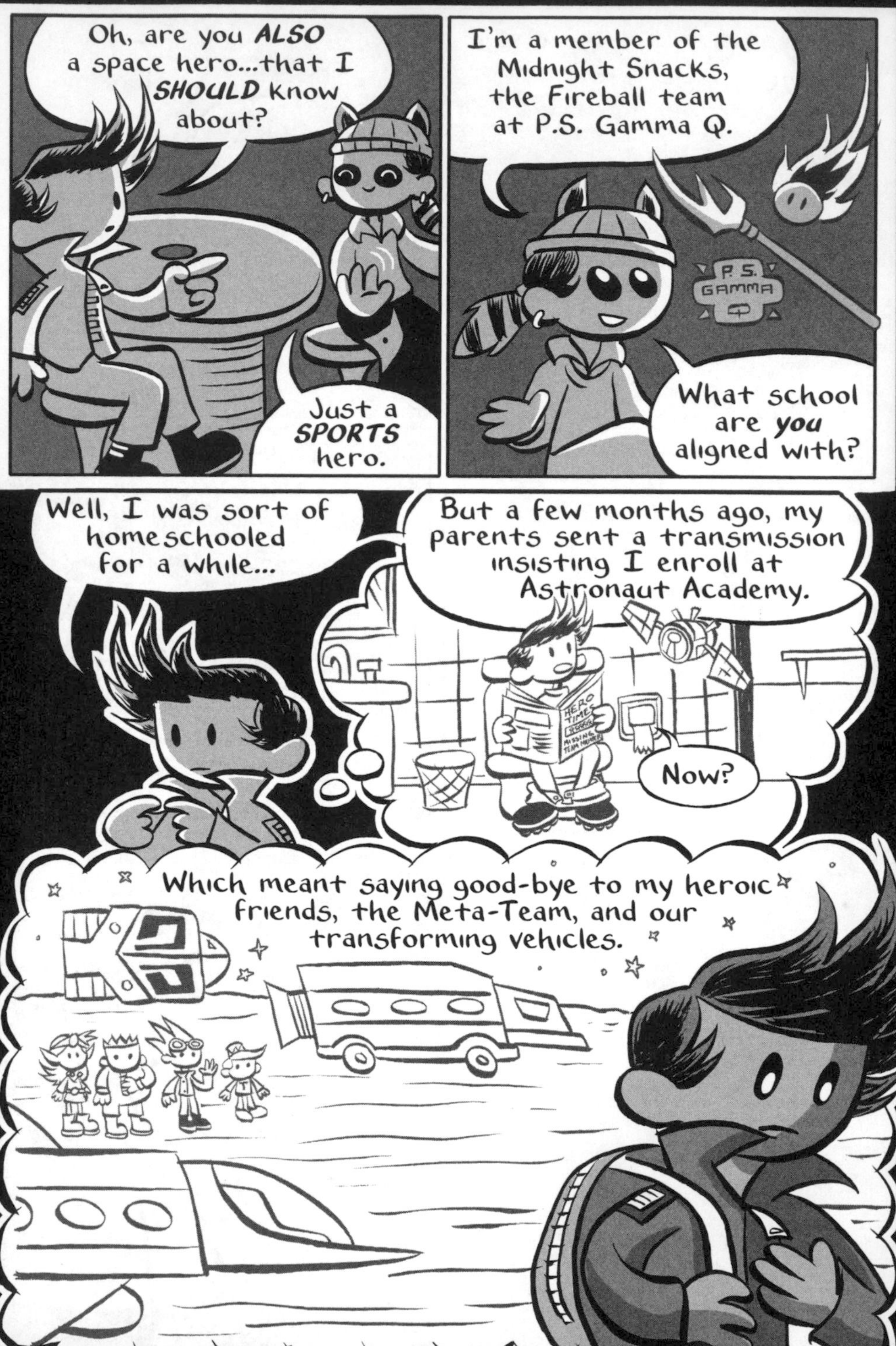
Oh, are you ALSO a space hero...that I SHOULD know about?
Just a SPORTS hero.
I'm a member of the Midnight Snacks, the Fireball team at P.S. Gamma Q.
P.S. GAMMA
What school are you aligned with?
Well, I was sort of homeschooled for a while...
But a few months ago, my parents sent a transmission insisting I enroll at Astronaut Academy.
Now?
Which meant saying good-bye to my heroic friends, the Meta-Team, and our transforming vehicles.

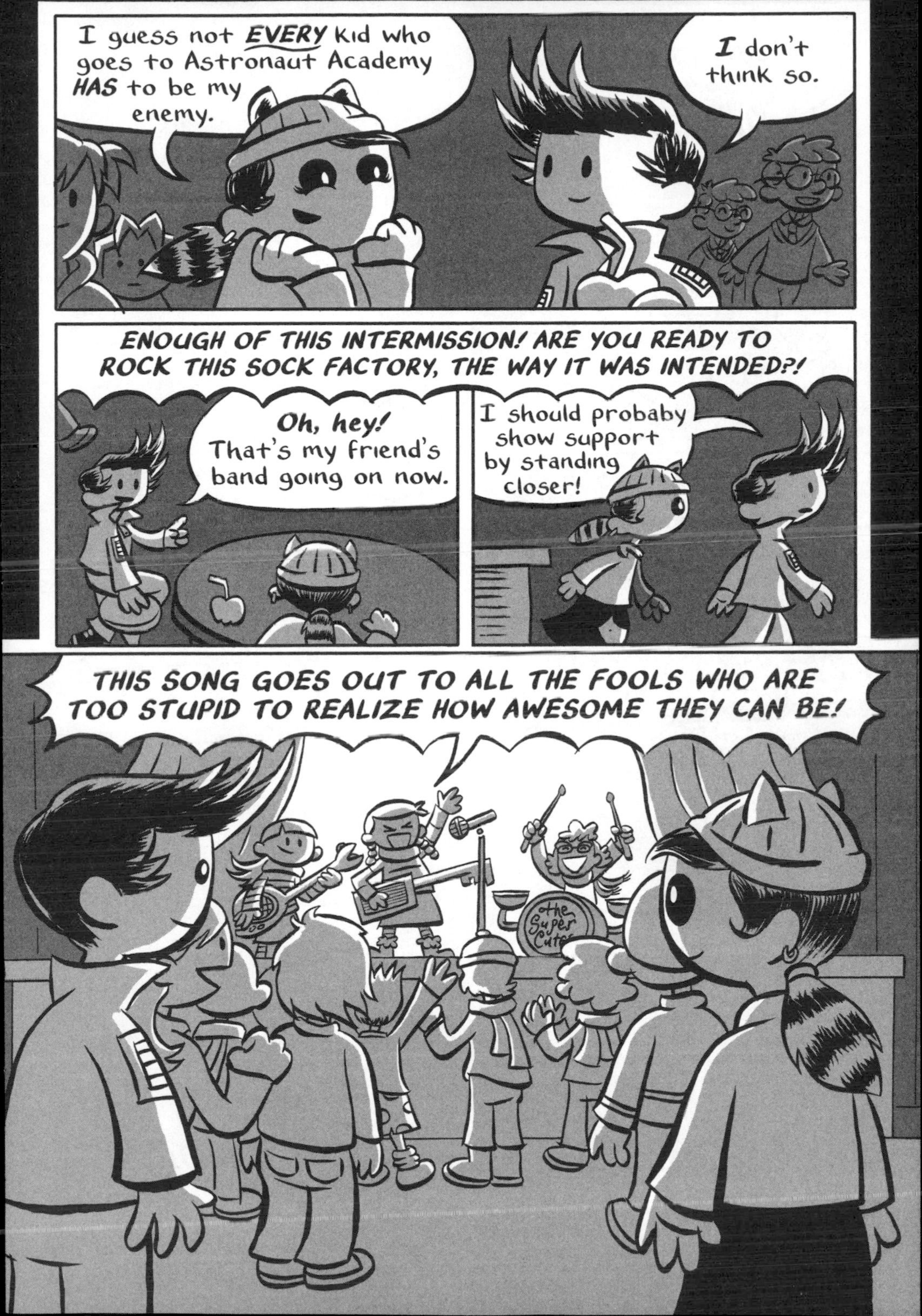
I guess not EVERY kid who goes to Astronaut Academy HAS to be my enemy.
I don't think so.
ENOUGH OF THIS INTERMISSION! ARE YOU READY TO ROCK THIS SOCK FACTORY, THE WAY IT WAS INTENDED?!
Oh, hey! That's my friend's band going on now.
I should probaby show support by standing closer!
THIS SONG GOES OUT TO ALL THE FOOLS WHO ARE TOO STUPID TO REALIZE HOW AWESOME THEY CAN BE!
the Super Cuter

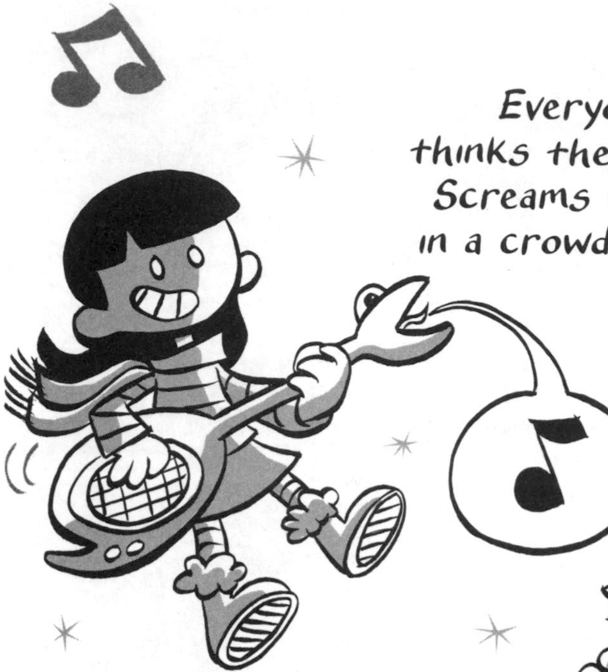

Everyone around,
thinks they're the **ONLY.**
Screams with no sound,
in a crowd for the lonely.

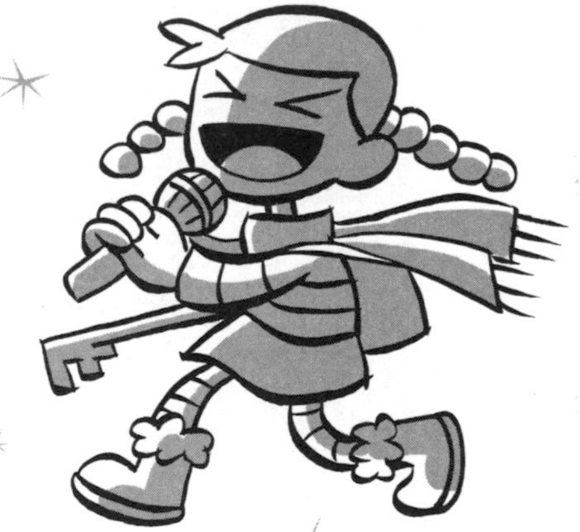

First love may be gone,
but I'm here **LIVIN'.**
Gotta keep on,
no pride in quittin'!

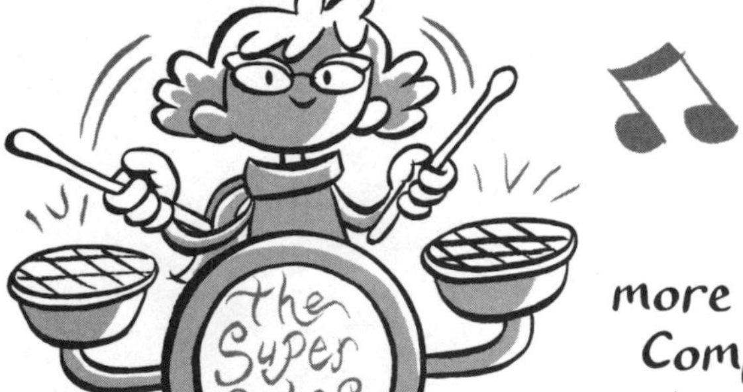
The Super Cutes

Life is a test,
more than one **SOLUTION.**
Complacency may rest,
but productivity is...
REVOLUTION!

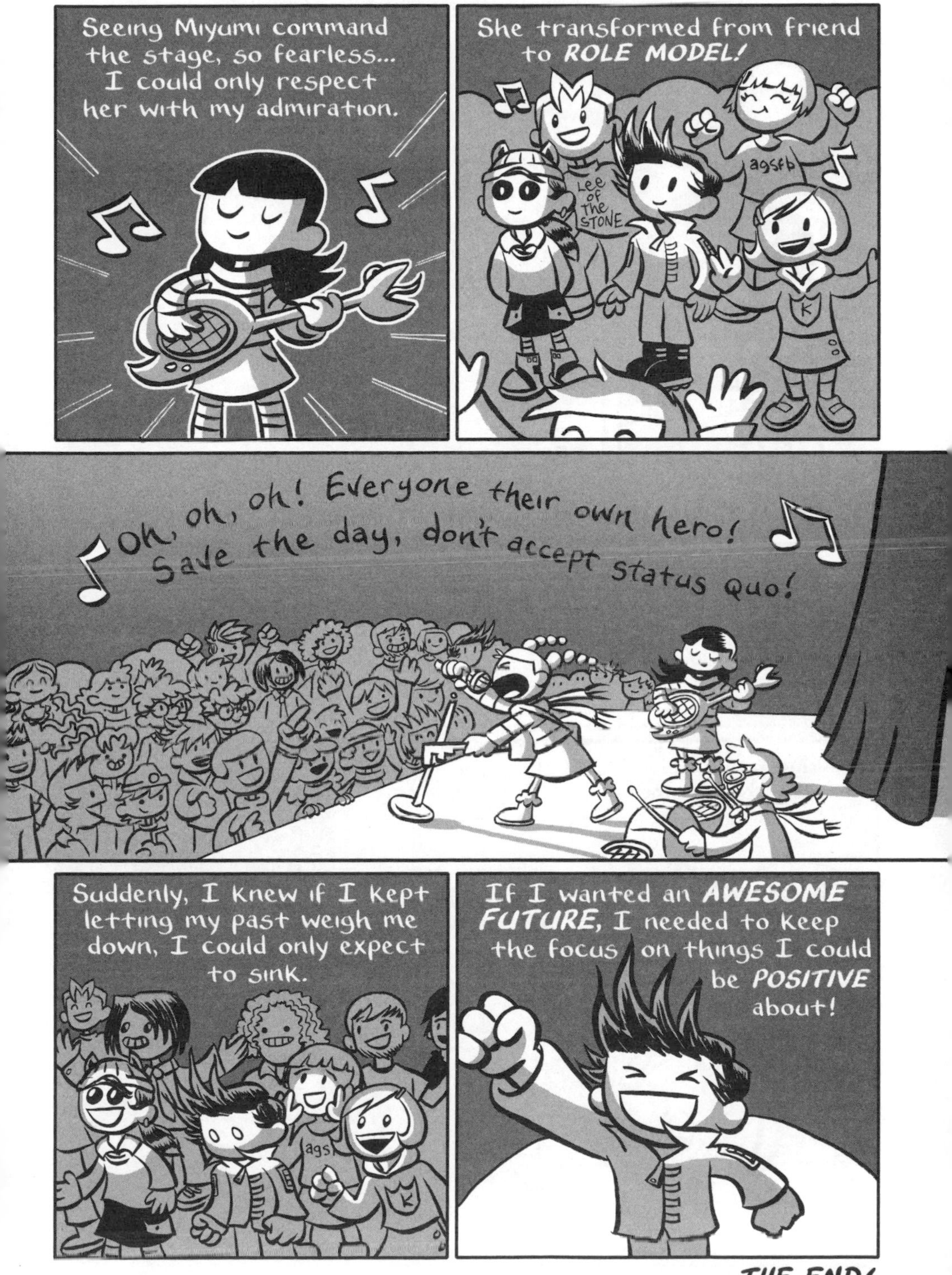

Seeing Miyumi command the stage, so fearless... I could only respect her with my admiration.
She transformed from friend to ROLE MODEL!
Lee of the STONE
agsfb
Oh, oh, oh! Everyone their own hero! Save the day, don't accept status quo!
Suddenly, I knew if I kept letting my past weigh me down, I could only expect to sink.
ags
If I wanted an AWESOME FUTURE, I needed to keep the focus on things I could be POSITIVE about!
THE END!

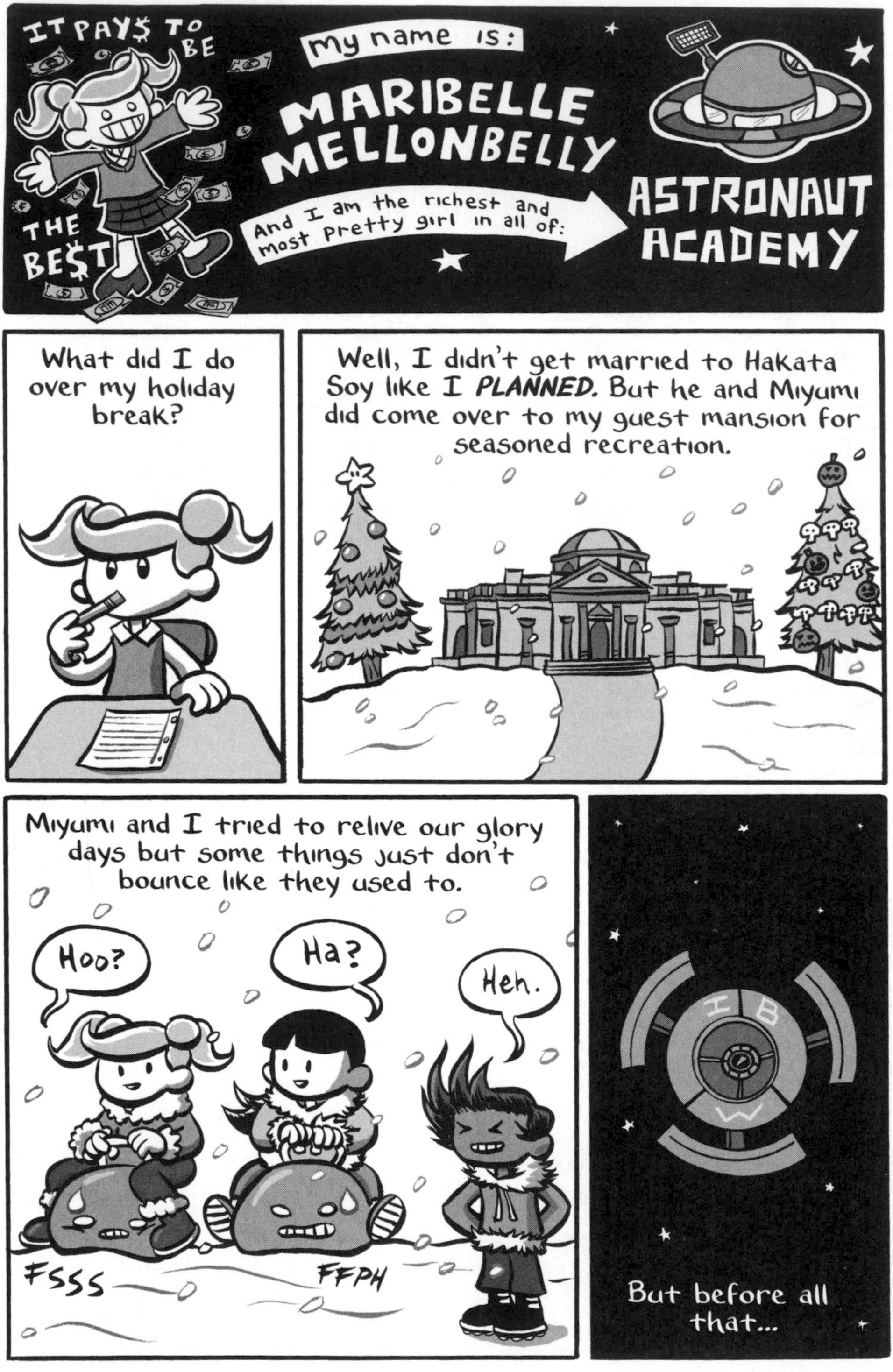
IT PAY$ TO BE THE BE$T
my name is:
MARIBELLE MELLONBELLY
And I am the richest and most pretty girl in all of:
ASTRONAUT ACADEMY
What did I do over my holiday break?
Well, I didn't get married to Hakata Soy like I PLANNED. But he and Miyumi did come over to my guest mansion for seasoned recreation.
Miyumi and I tried to relive our glory days but some things just don't bounce like they used to.
Hoo?
Ha?
Heh.
FSSS
FFPH
But before all that...

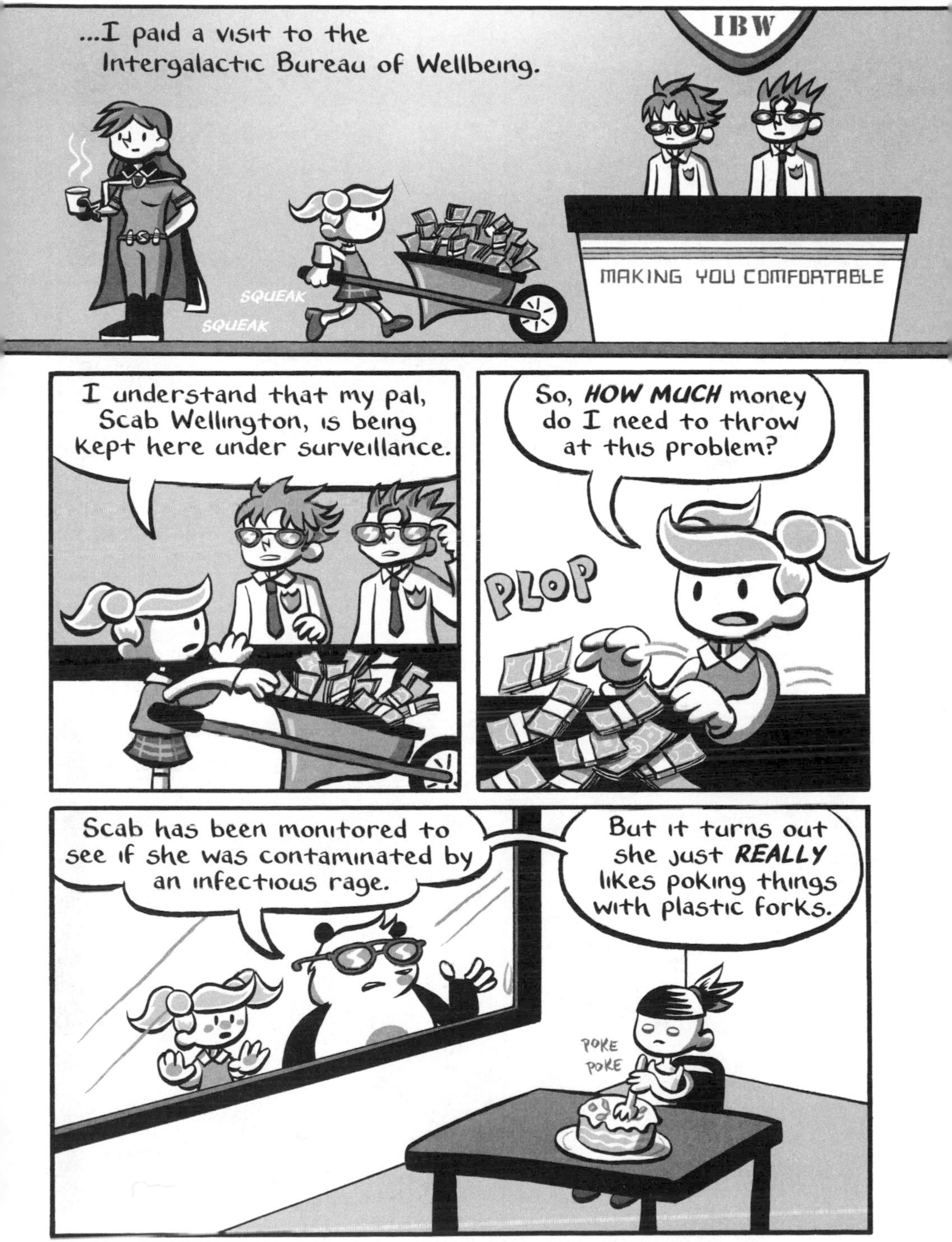

...I paid a visit to the Intergalactic Bureau of Wellbeing.
IBW
MAKING YOU COMFORTABLE
SQUEAK
SQUEAK
I understand that my pal, Scab Wellington, is being kept here under surveillance.
So, HOW MUCH money do I need to throw at this problem?
PLOP
Scab has been monitored to see if she was contaminated by an infectious rage.
But it turns out she just REALLY likes poking things with plastic forks.
POKE
POKE

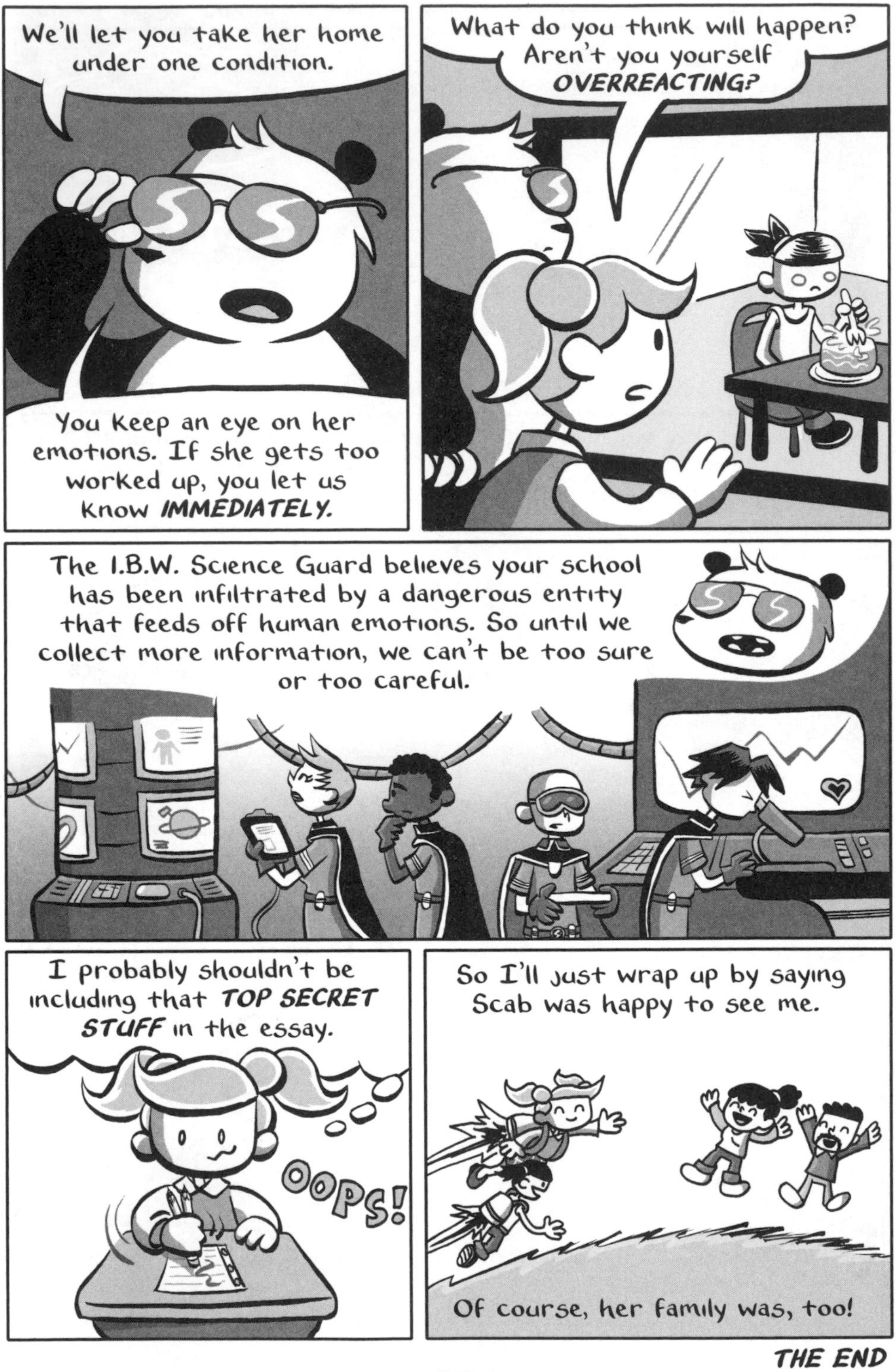
We'll let you take her home under one condition.
You keep an eye on her emotions. If she gets too worked up, you let us know IMMEDIATELY.
What do you think will happen? Aren't you yourself OVERREACTING?
The I.B.W. Science Guard believes your school has been infiltrated by a dangerous entity that feeds off human emotions. So until we collect more information, we can't be too sure or too careful.
I probably shouldn't be including that TOP SECRET STUFF in the essay.
OOPS!
So I'll just wrap up by saying Scab was happy to see me.
Of course, her family was, too!

THE END

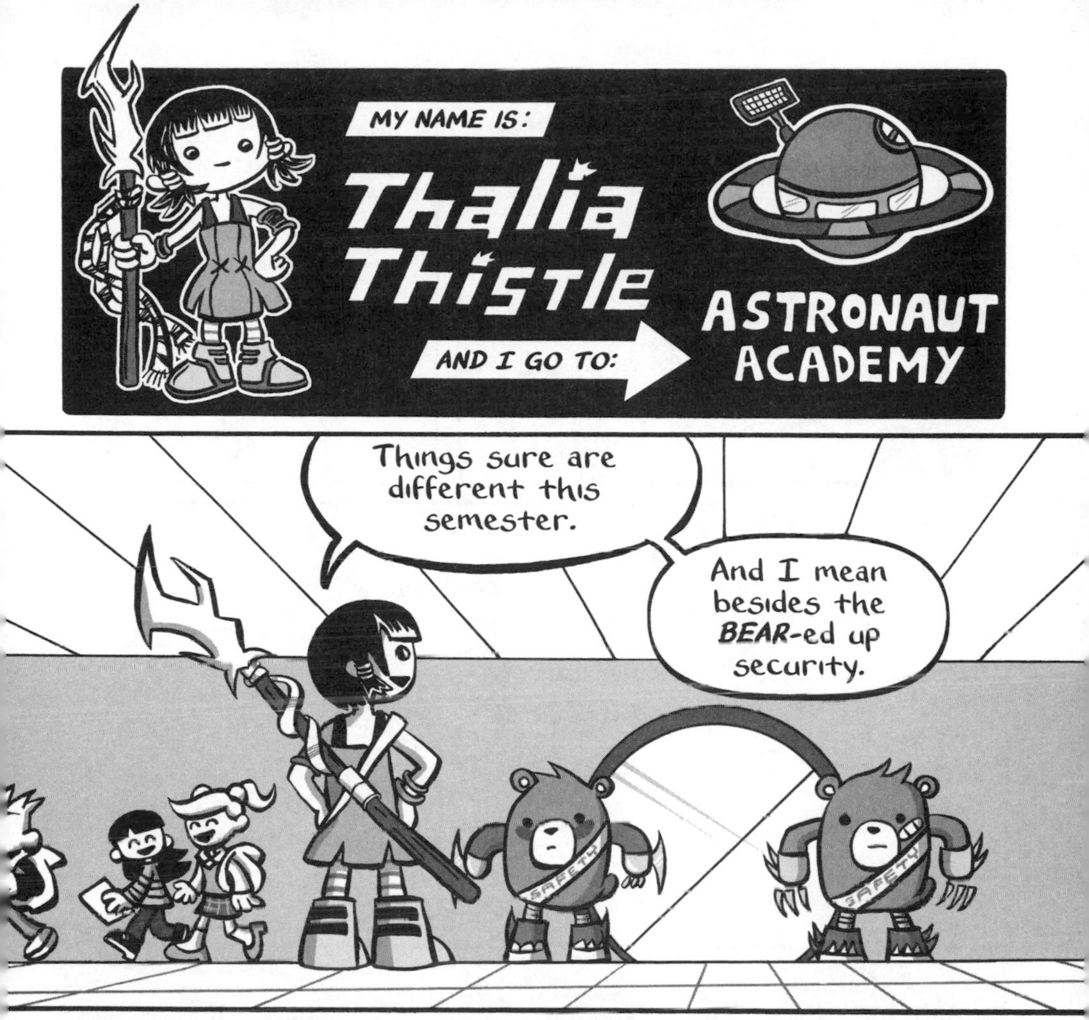
MY NAME IS:
Thalia Thistle
AND I GO TO:
ASTRONAUT ACADEMY
Things sure are different this semester.
And I mean besides the BEAR-ed up security.
SAFETY
It is also different in a way that excites me on a COMPETITIVE level.
Sorry, ma'am. But I'm going to have to inspect your weapon for dangerous attributes.
Silly old bear. This fire poker means you no harm.
Its intent is pure: HIGH SCORES ON THE FIELD!

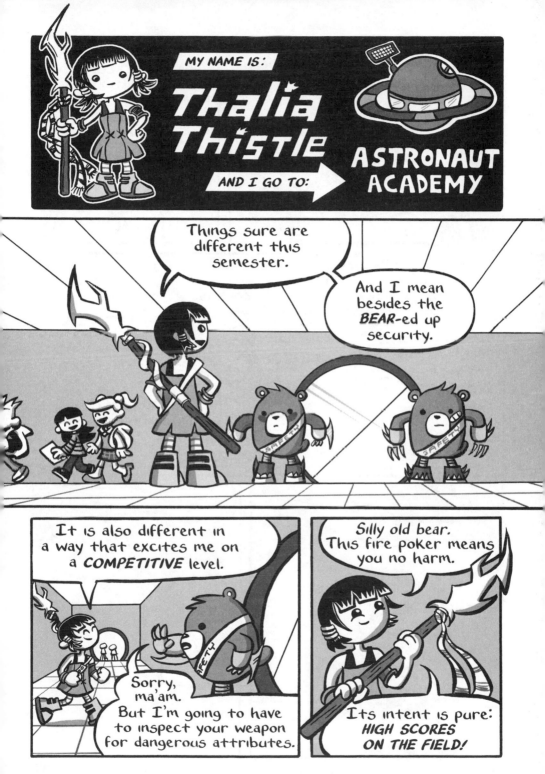

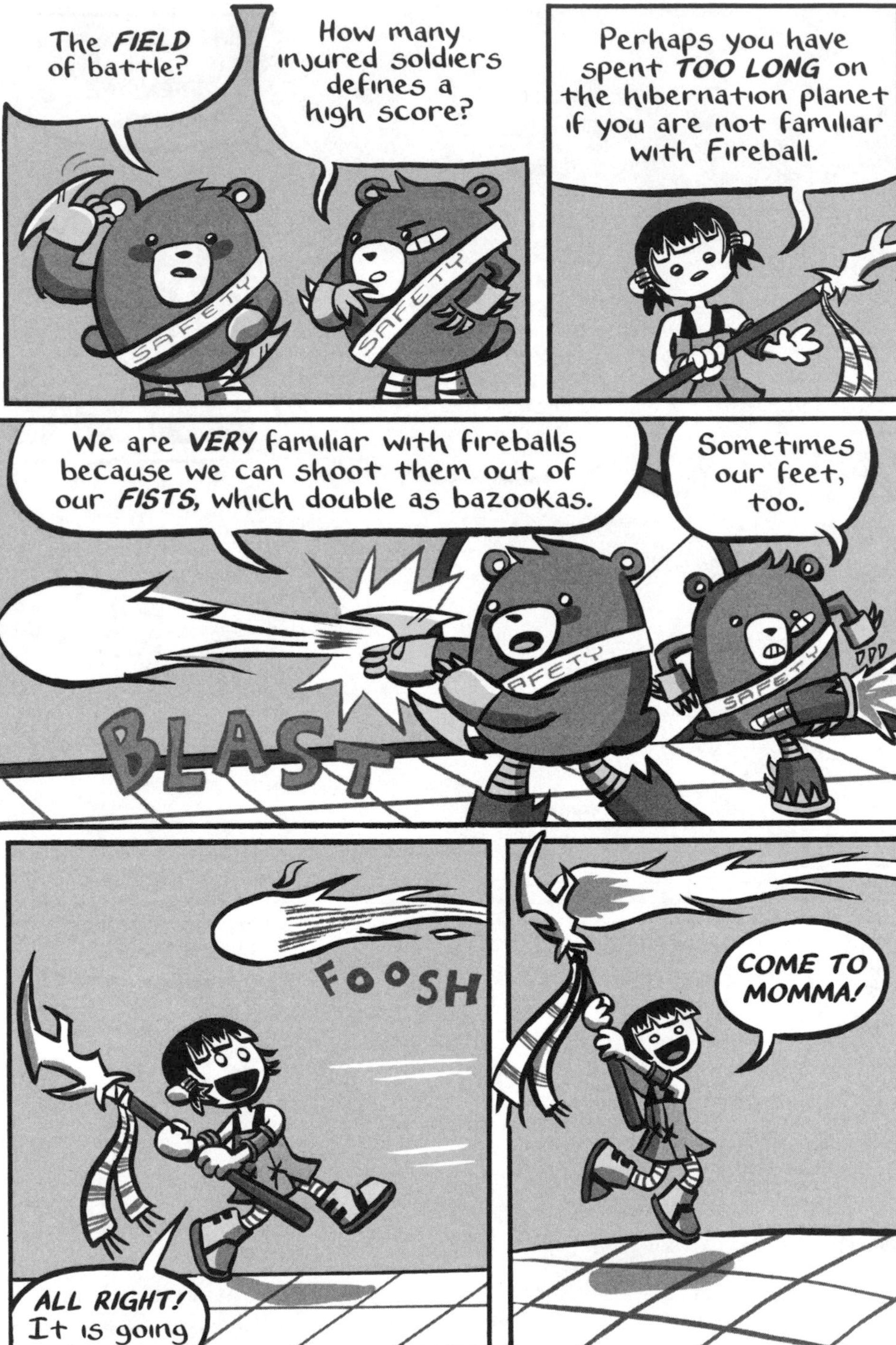
The FIELD of battle?
How many injured soldiers defines a high score?
Perhaps you have spent TOO LONG on the hibernation planet if you are not familiar with Fireball.
SAFETY
SAFETY
We are VERY familiar with fireballs because we can shoot them out of our FISTS, which double as bazookas.
Sometimes our feet, too.
BLAST
SAFETY
SAFETY
FOOSH
ALL RIGHT! It is going long.
COME TO MOMMA!

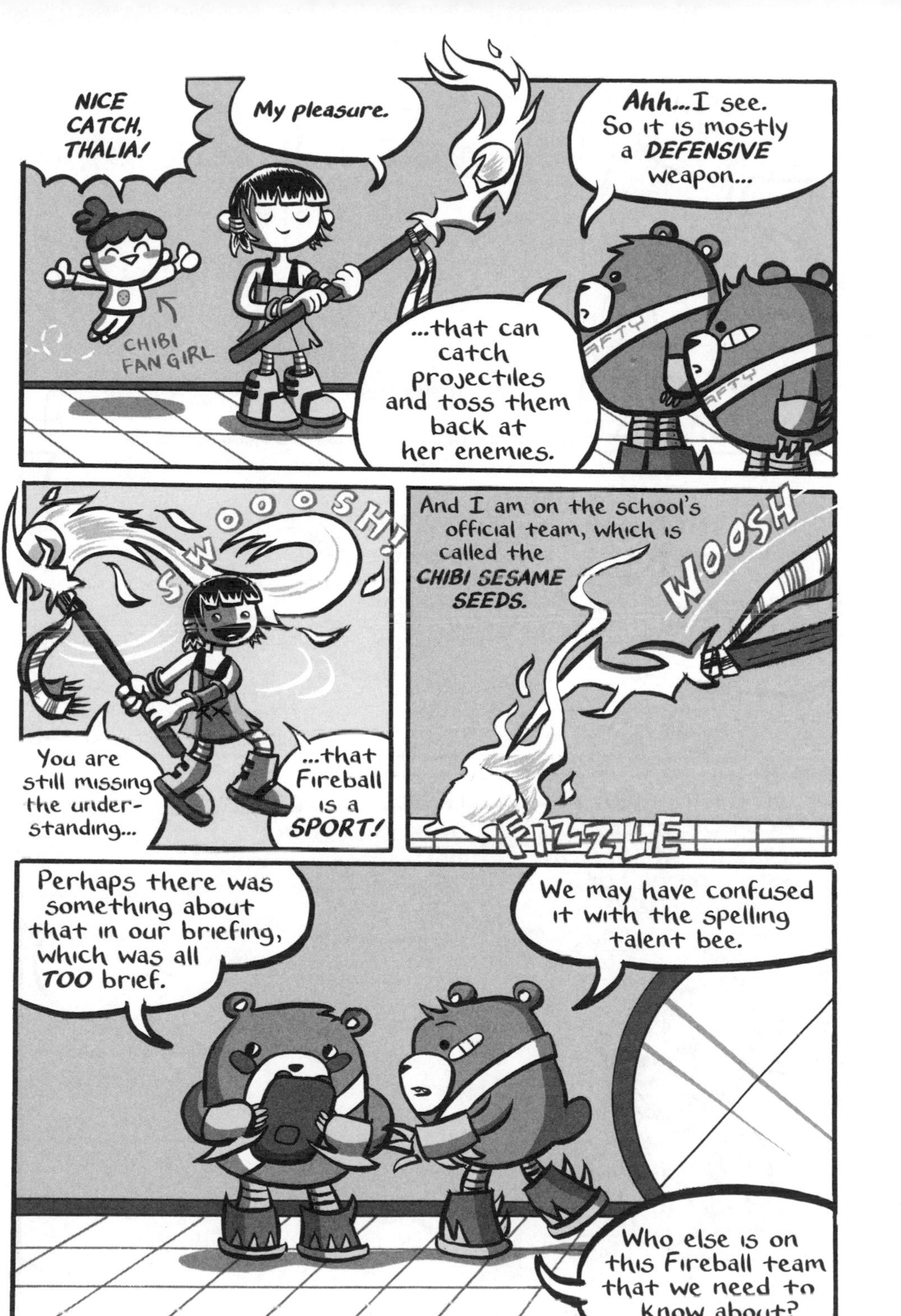
NICE CATCH, THALIA!
My pleasure.
CHIBI FAN GIRL
Ahh...I see. So it is mostly a DEFENSIVE weapon...
...that can catch projectiles and toss them back at her enemies.
SWOOOSH!
You are still missing the under-standing...
...that Fireball is a SPORT!
And I am on the school's official team, which is called the CHIBI SESAME SEEDS.
WOOSH
FIZZLE
Perhaps there was something about that in our briefing, which was all TOO brief.
We may have confused it with the spelling talent bee.
Who else is on this Fireball team that we need to know about?

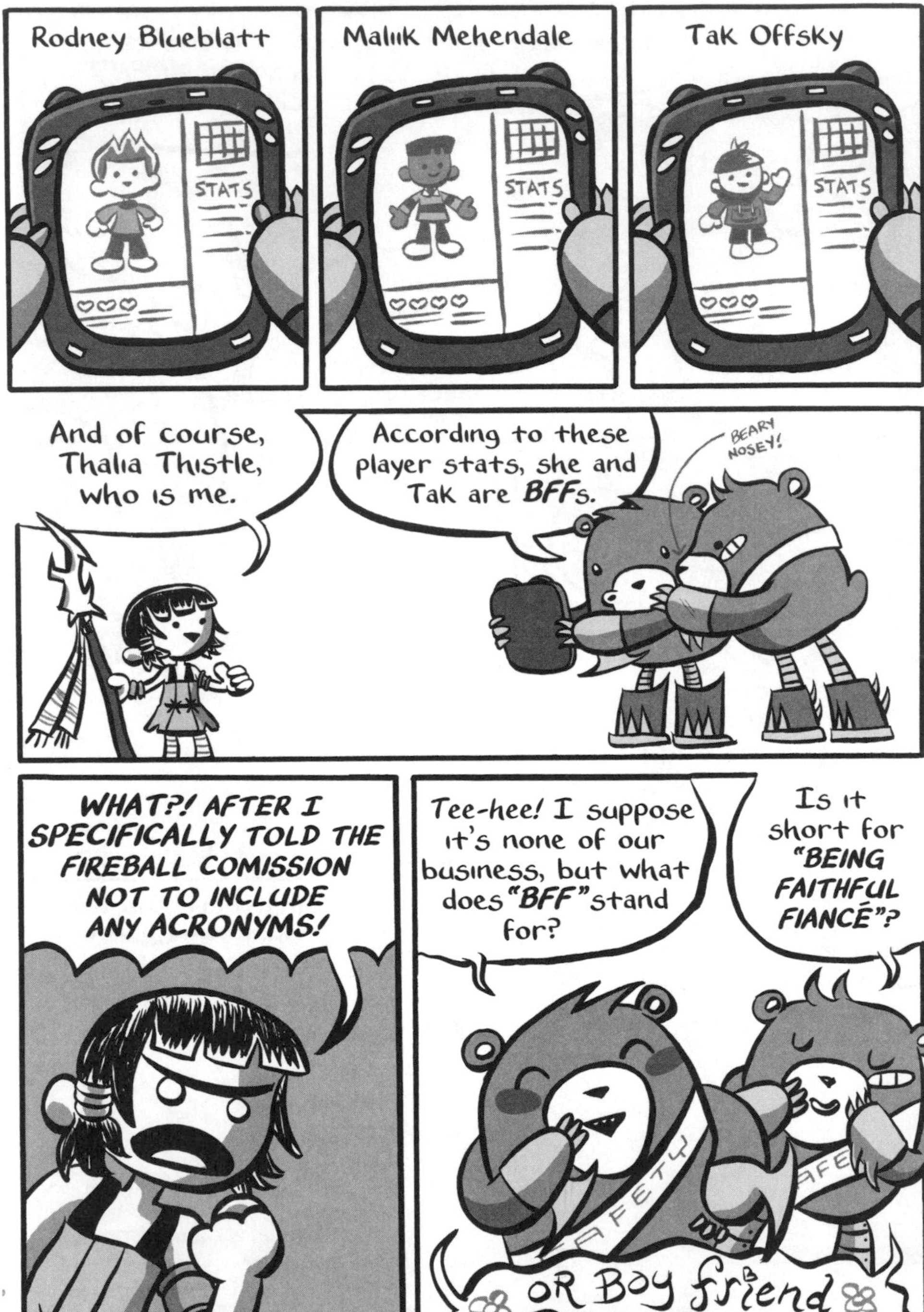
Rodney Blueblatt
STATS
Maliik Mehendale
STATS
Tak Offsky
STATS
And of course, Thalia Thistle, who is me.
According to these player stats, she and Tak are BFFs.
BEARY NOSEY!
WHAT?! AFTER I SPECIFICALLY TOLD THE FIREBALL COMISSION NOT TO INCLUDE ANY ACRONYMS!
Tee-hee! I suppose it's none of our business, but what does "BFF" stand for?
Is it short for "BEING FAITHFUL FIANCÉ"?
OR Boy friend FANTASY!

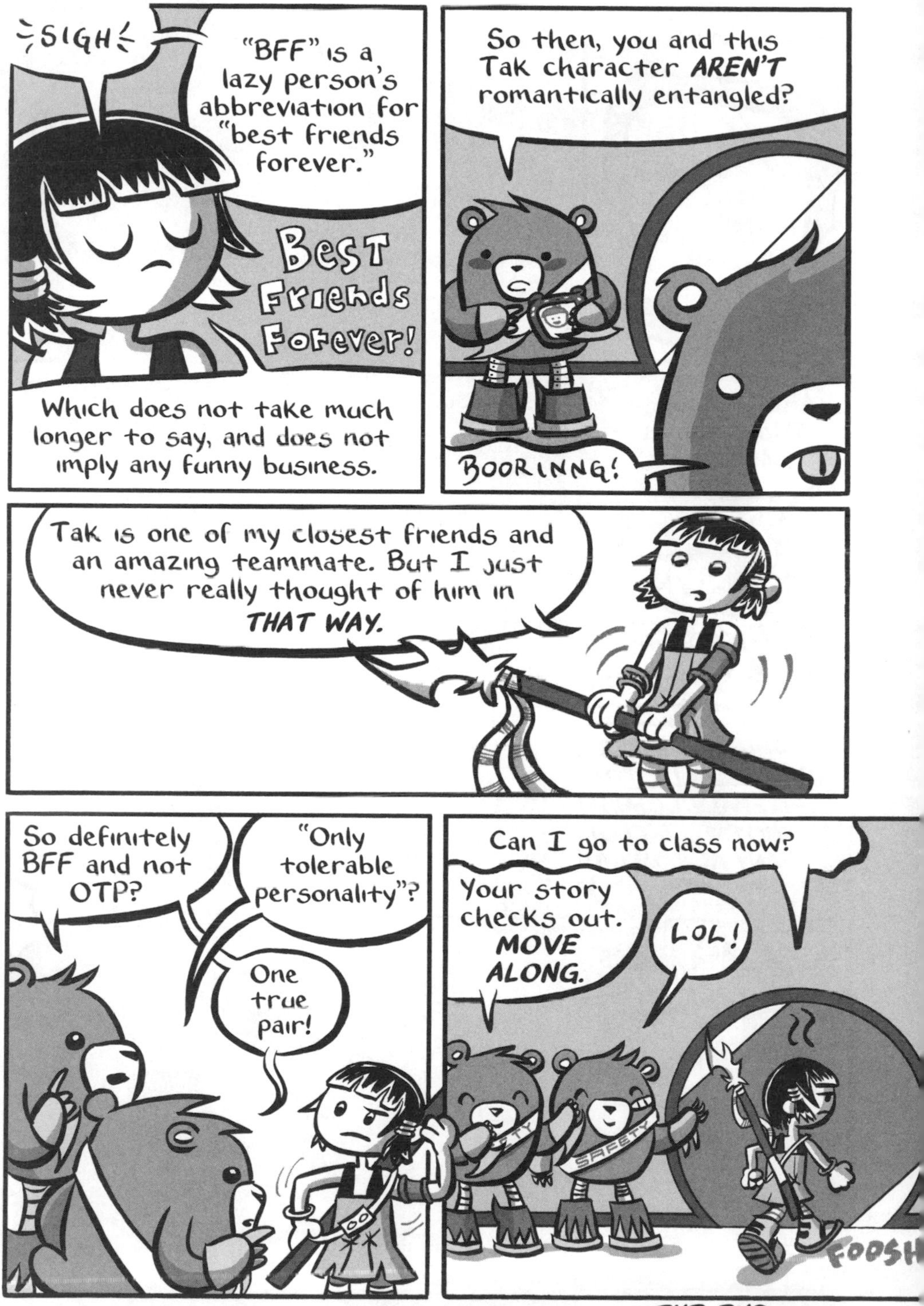
SIGH
"BFF" is a lazy person's abbreviation for "best friends forever."
Best Friends Forever!
Which does not take much longer to say, and does not imply any funny business.
So then, you and this Tak character AREN'T romantically entangled?
BOORINNG!
Tak is one of my closest friends and an amazing teammate. But I just never really thought of him in THAT WAY.
So definitely BFF and not OTP?
"Only tolerable personality"?
One true pair!
Can I go to class now?
Your story checks out. MOVE ALONG.
LOL!
SAFETY
FOOSH

THE END

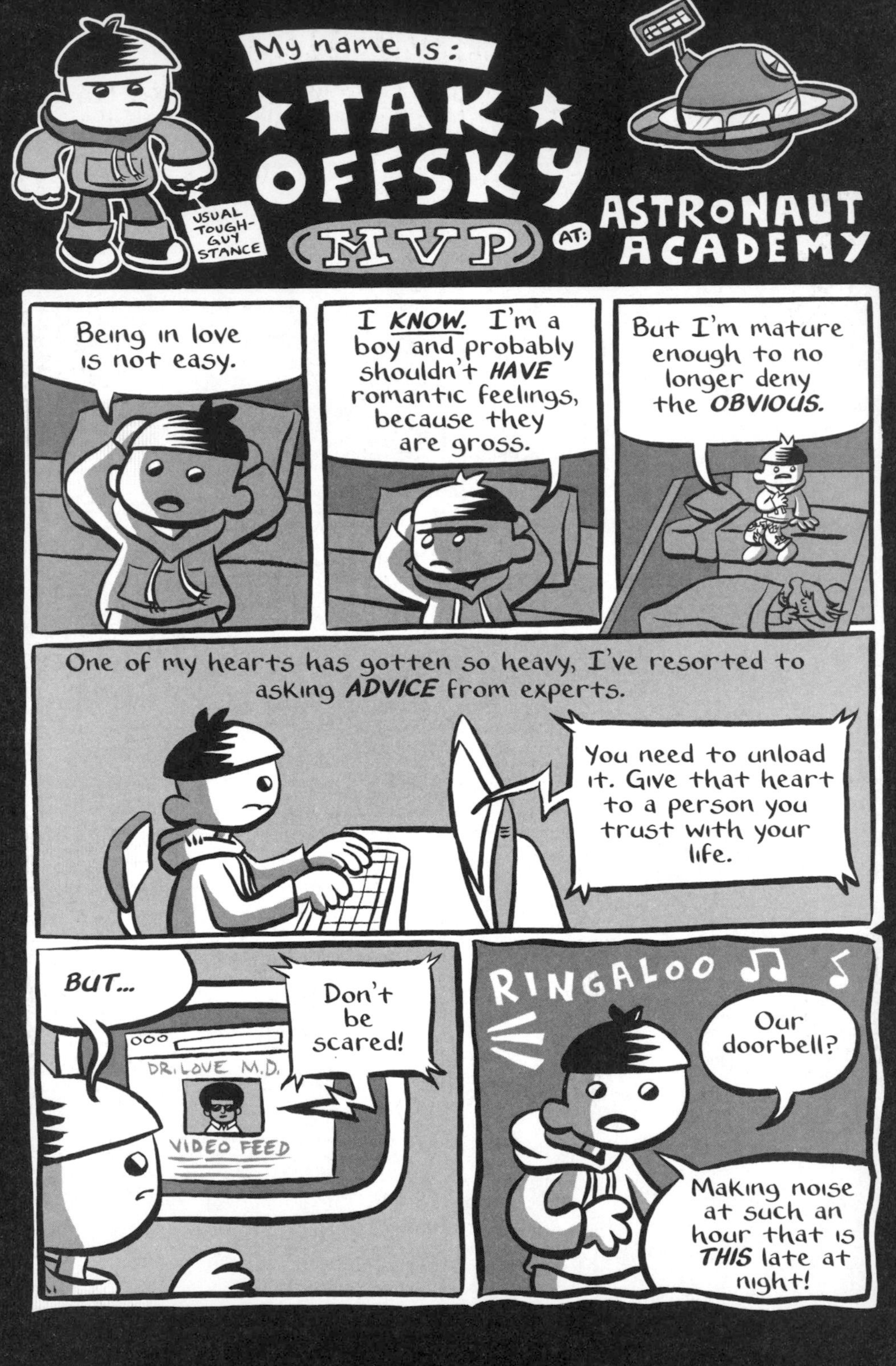
My name is:
★TAK★ OFFSKY
(MVP) AT: ASTRONAUT ACADEMY
USUAL TOUGH-GUY STANCE
Being in love is not easy.
I KNOW. I'm a boy and probably shouldn't HAVE romantic feelings, because they are gross.
But I'm mature enough to no longer deny the OBVIOUS.
One of my hearts has gotten so heavy, I've resorted to asking ADVICE from experts.
You need to unload it. Give that heart to a person you trust with your life.
BUT...
Don't be scared!
DR. LOVE M.D.
VIDEO FEED
RINGALOO
Our doorbell?
Making noise at such an hour that is THIS late at night!

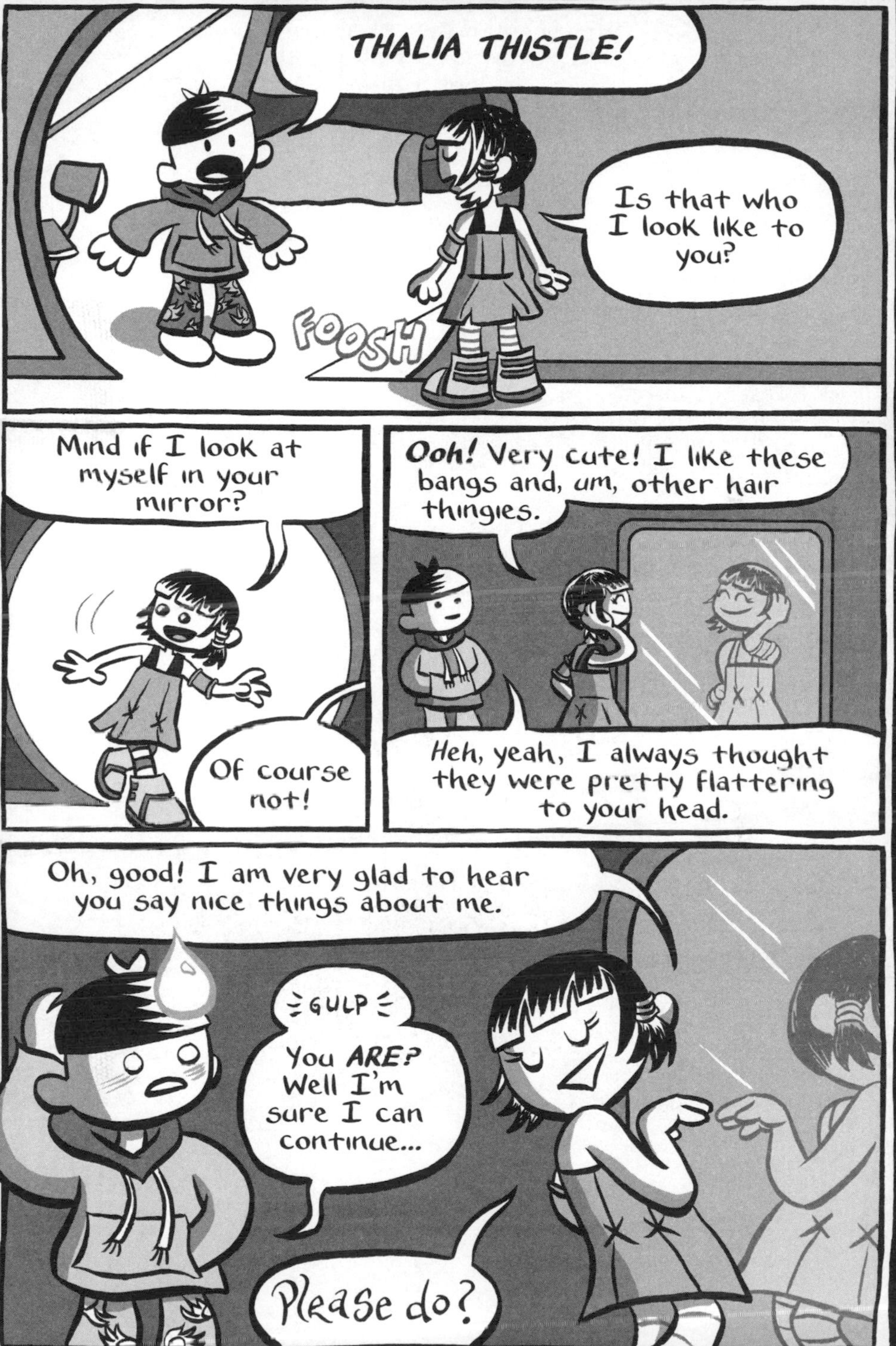
THALIA THISTLE!
Is that who I look like to you?
FOOSH
Mind if I look at myself in your mirror?
Of course not!
Ooh! Very cute! I like these bangs and, um, other hair thingies.
Heh, yeah, I always thought they were pretty flattering to your head.
Oh, good! I am very glad to hear you say nice things about me.
GULP
You ARE? Well I'm sure I can continue...
Please do?

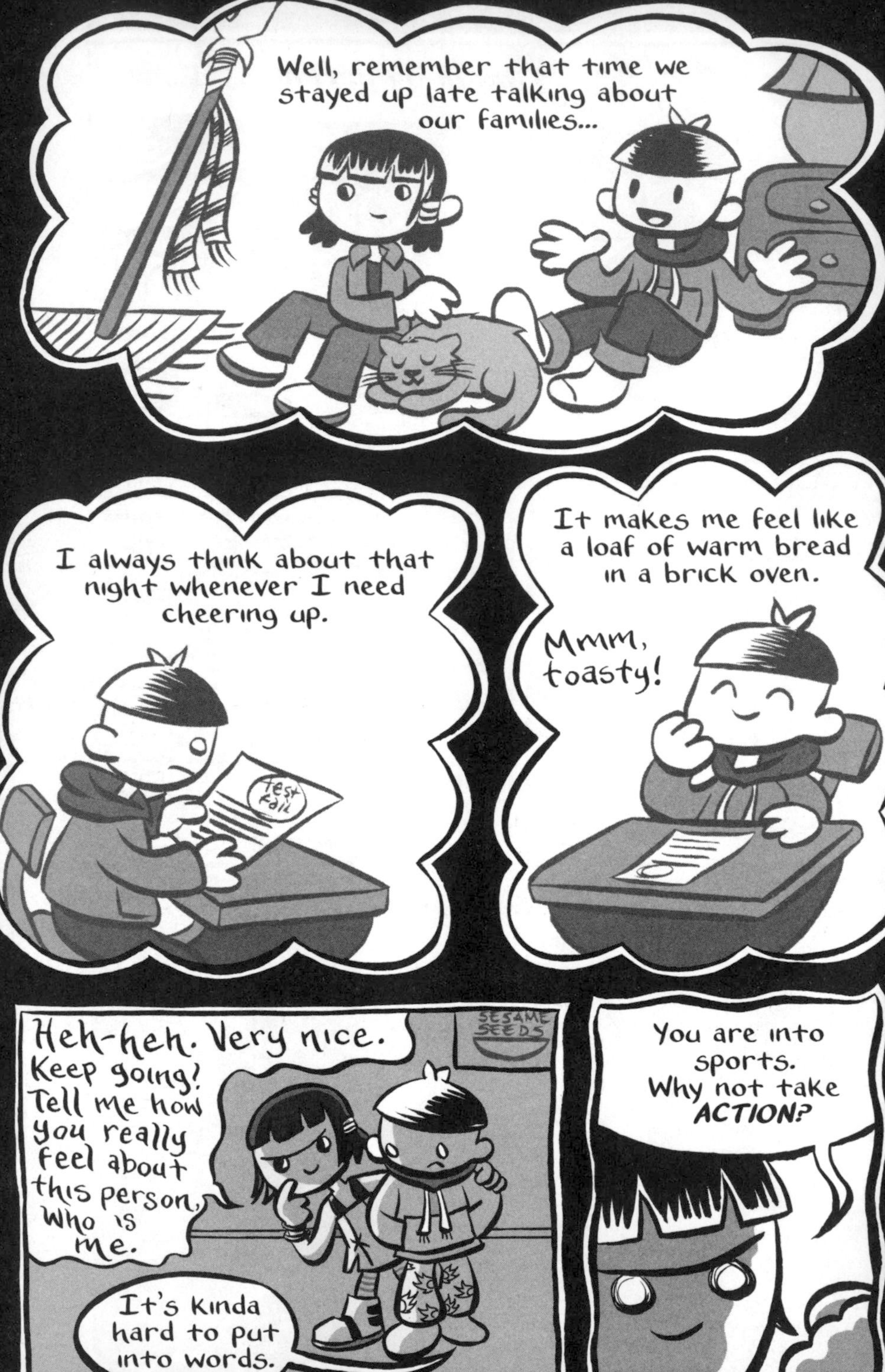

Well, remember that time we stayed up late talking about our families...
I always think about that night whenever I need cheering up.
test fail
It makes me feel like a loaf of warm bread in a brick oven.
Mmm, toasty!
Heh-heh. Very nice.
Keep going! Tell me how you really feel about this person, who is me.
SESAME SEEDS
It's kinda hard to put into words.
You are into sports. Why not take ACTION?

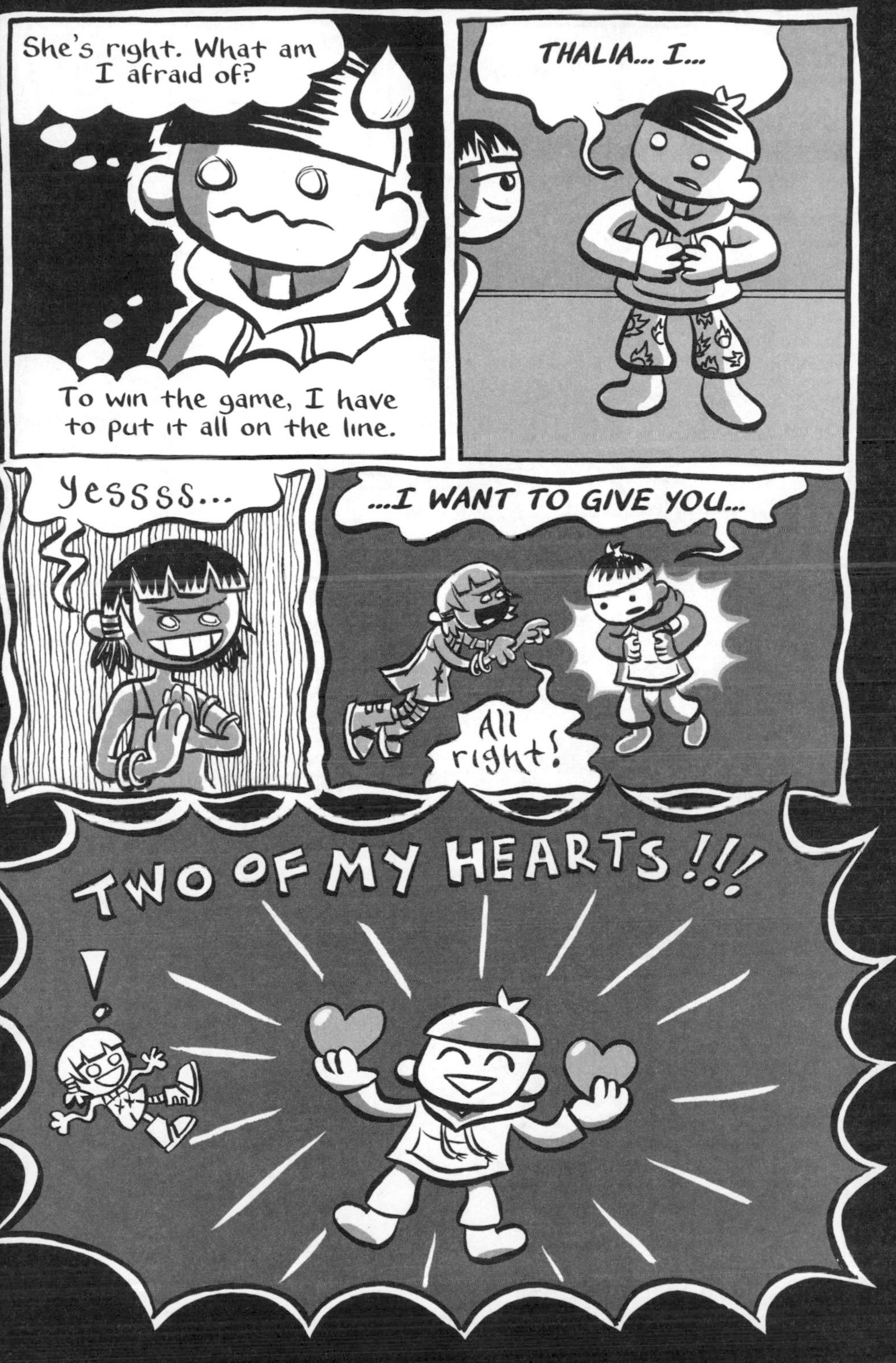
She's right. What am I afraid of?
To win the game, I have to put it all on the line.
THALIA... I...
Yessss...
...I WANT TO GIVE YOU...
All right!
TWO OF MY HEARTS!!!
!

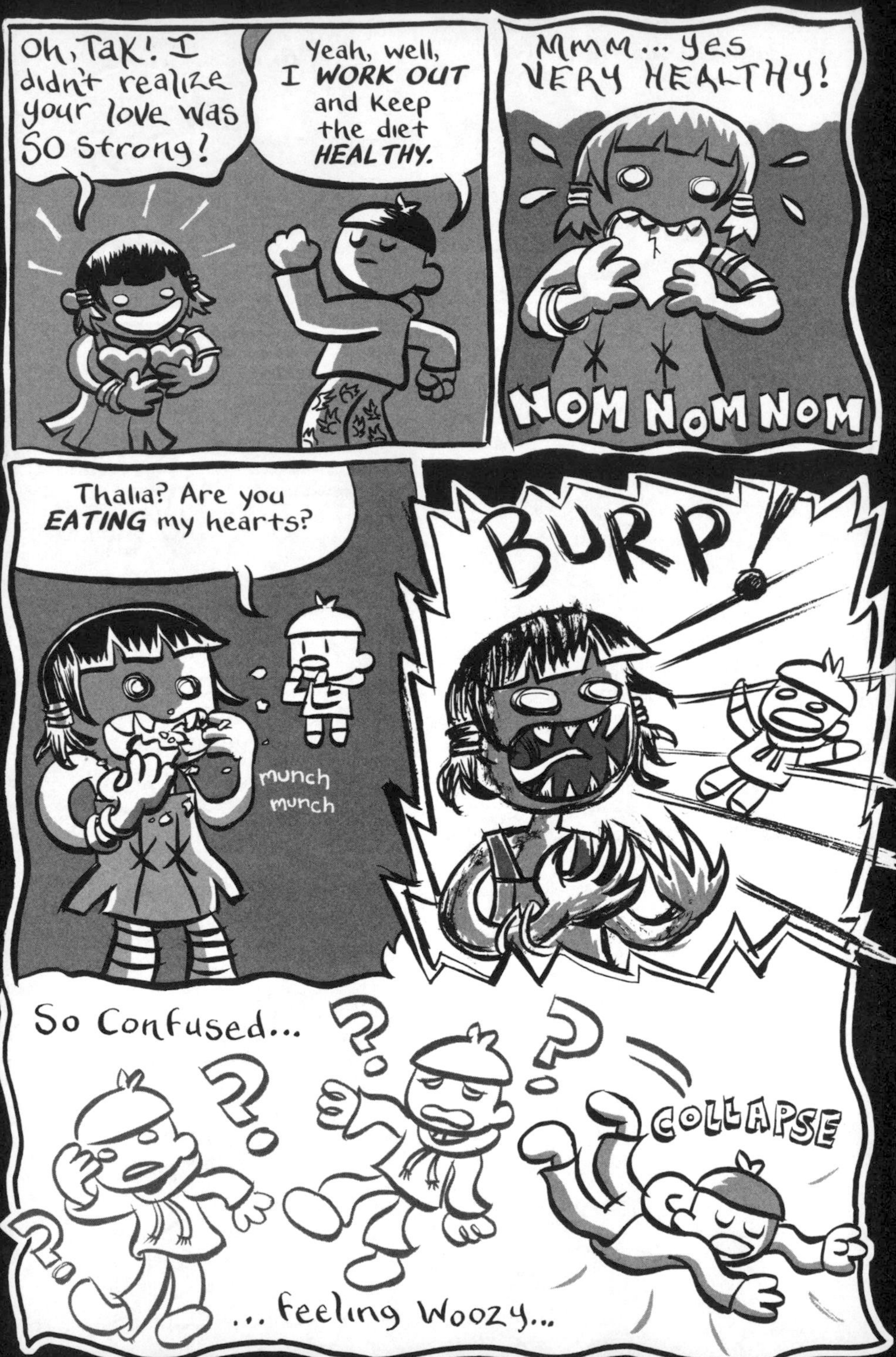
Oh, Tak! I didn't realize your love was so strong!
Yeah, well, I **WORK OUT** and keep the diet **HEALTHY.**
Mmm... yes VERY HEALTHY!
NOM NOM NOM
Thalia? Are you **EATING** my hearts?
munch munch
BURP!
So Confused...
COLLAPSE
... feeling woozy...

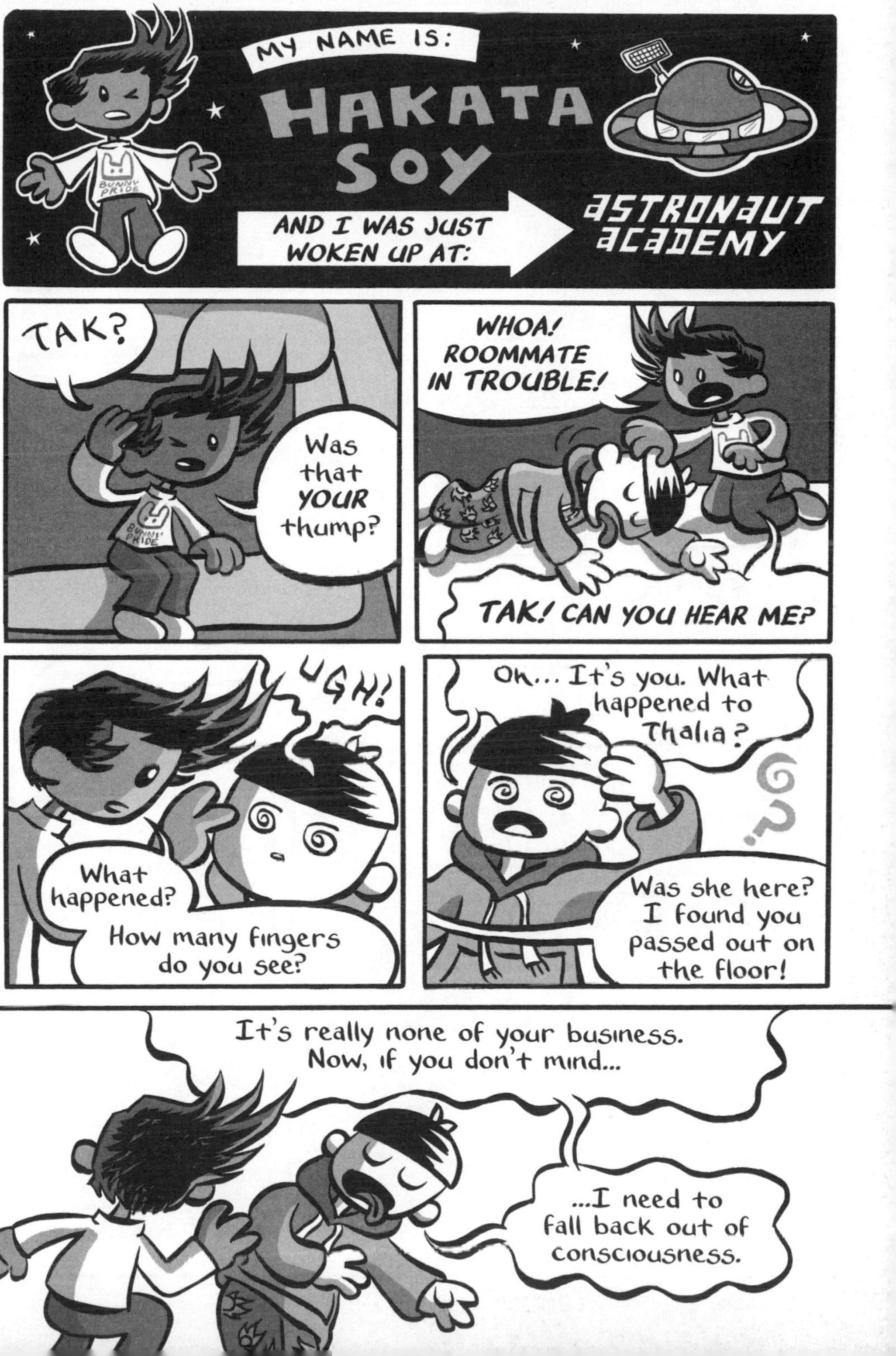
MY NAME IS:
HAKATA SOY
AND I WAS JUST WOKEN UP AT:
ASTRONAUT ACADEMY
TAK?
Was that YOUR thump?
WHOA! ROOMMATE IN TROUBLE!
TAK! CAN YOU HEAR ME?
UGH!
What happened?
How many fingers do you see?
Oh... It's you. What happened to Thalia?
Was she here? I found you passed out on the floor!
It's really none of your business. Now, if you don't mind...
...I need to fall back out of consciousness.

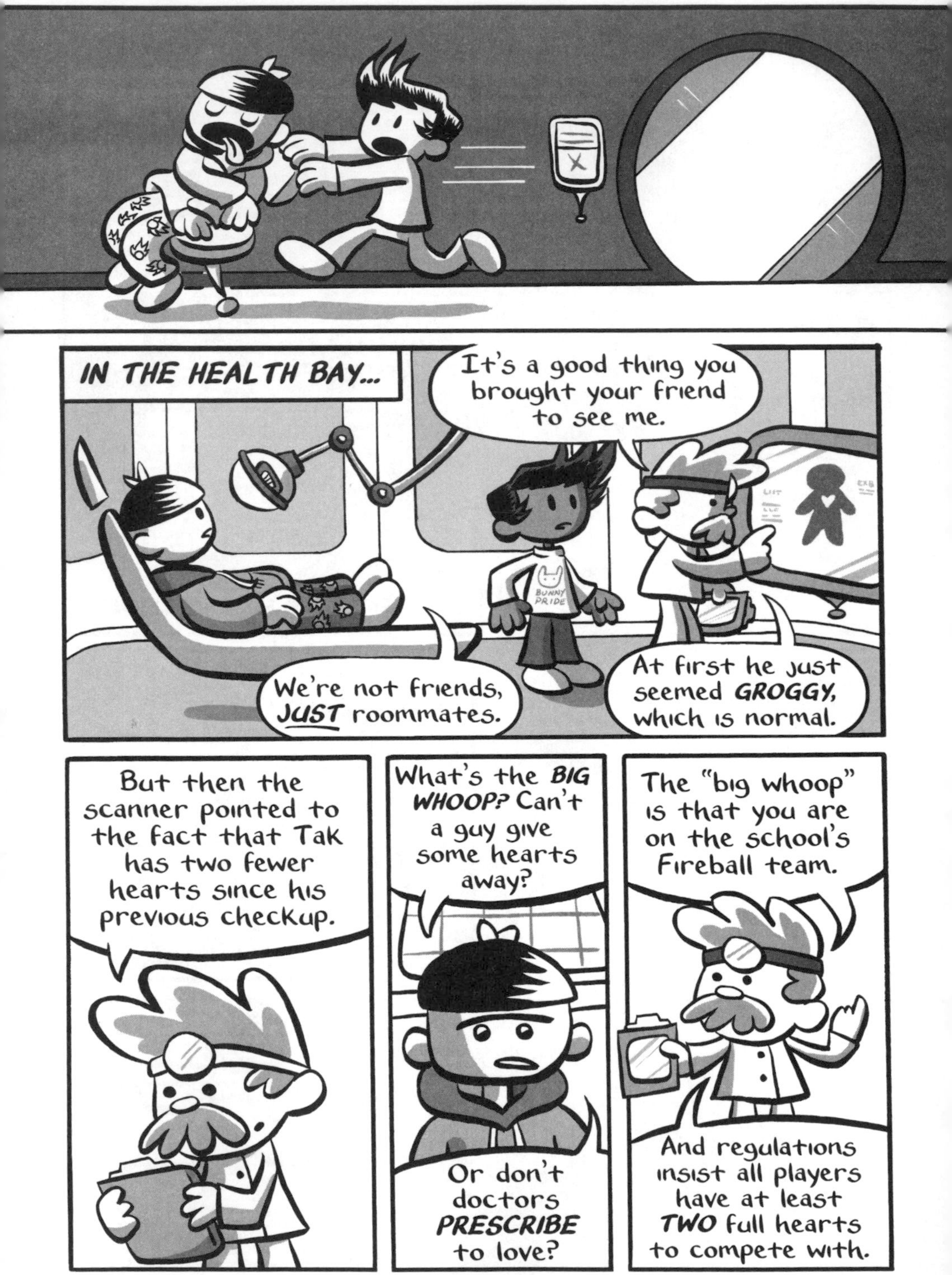
IN THE HEALTH BAY...
It's a good thing you brought your friend to see me.
We're not friends, JUST roommates.
At first he just seemed GROGGY, which is normal.
But then the scanner pointed to the fact that Tak has two fewer hearts since his previous checkup.
What's the BIG WHOOP? Can't a guy give some hearts away?
Or don't doctors PRESCRIBE to love?
The "big whoop" is that you are on the school's Fireball team.
And regulations insist all players have at least TWO full hearts to compete with.

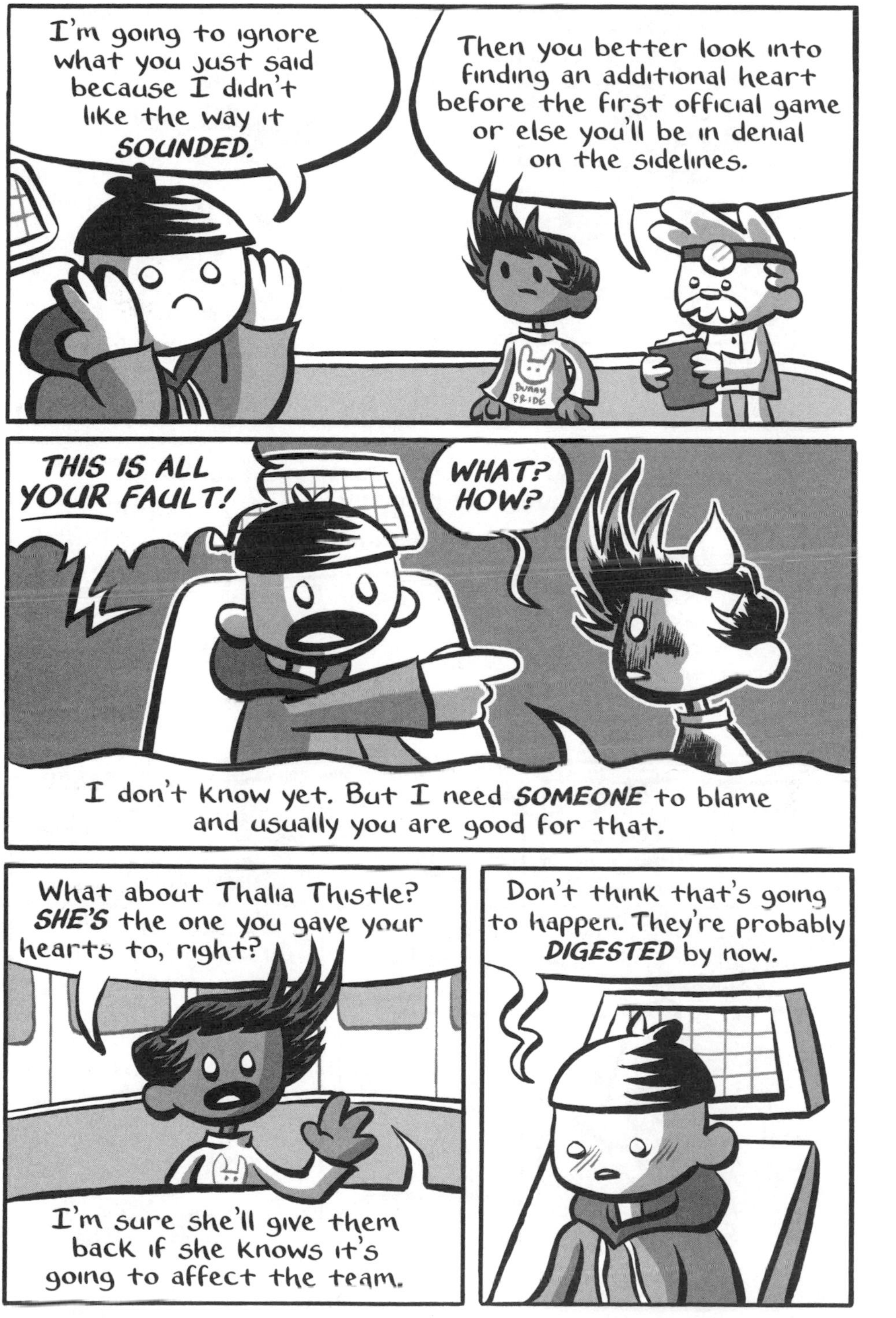
I'm going to ignore what you just said because I didn't like the way it SOUNDED.
Then you better look into finding an additional heart before the first official game or else you'll be in denial on the sidelines.
BUNNY PRIDE
THIS IS ALL YOUR FAULT!
WHAT? HOW?
I don't know yet. But I need SOMEONE to blame and usually you are good for that.
What about Thalia Thistle? SHE'S the one you gave your hearts to, right?
I'm sure she'll give them back if she knows it's going to affect the team.
Don't think that's going to happen. They're probably DIGESTED by now.

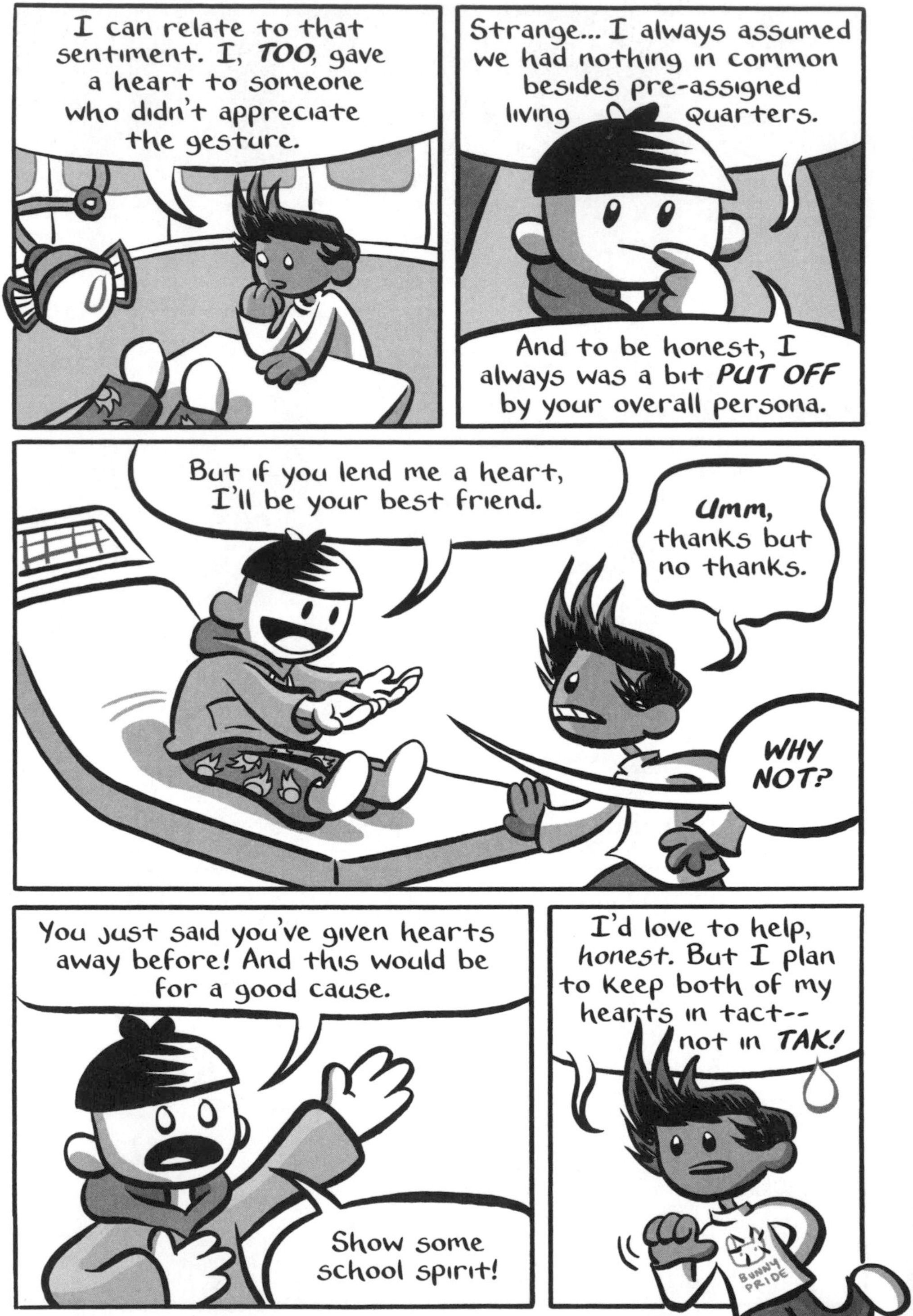
I can relate to that sentiment. I, TOO, gave a heart to someone who didn't appreciate the gesture.
Strange... I always assumed we had nothing in common besides pre-assigned living quarters.
And to be honest, I always was a bit PUT OFF by your overall persona.
But if you lend me a heart, I'll be your best friend.
Umm, thanks but no thanks.
WHY NOT?
You just said you've given hearts away before! And this would be for a good cause.
Show some school spirit!
I'd love to help, honest. But I plan to keep both of my hearts in tact-- not in TAK!
BUNNY PRIDE
THE END!

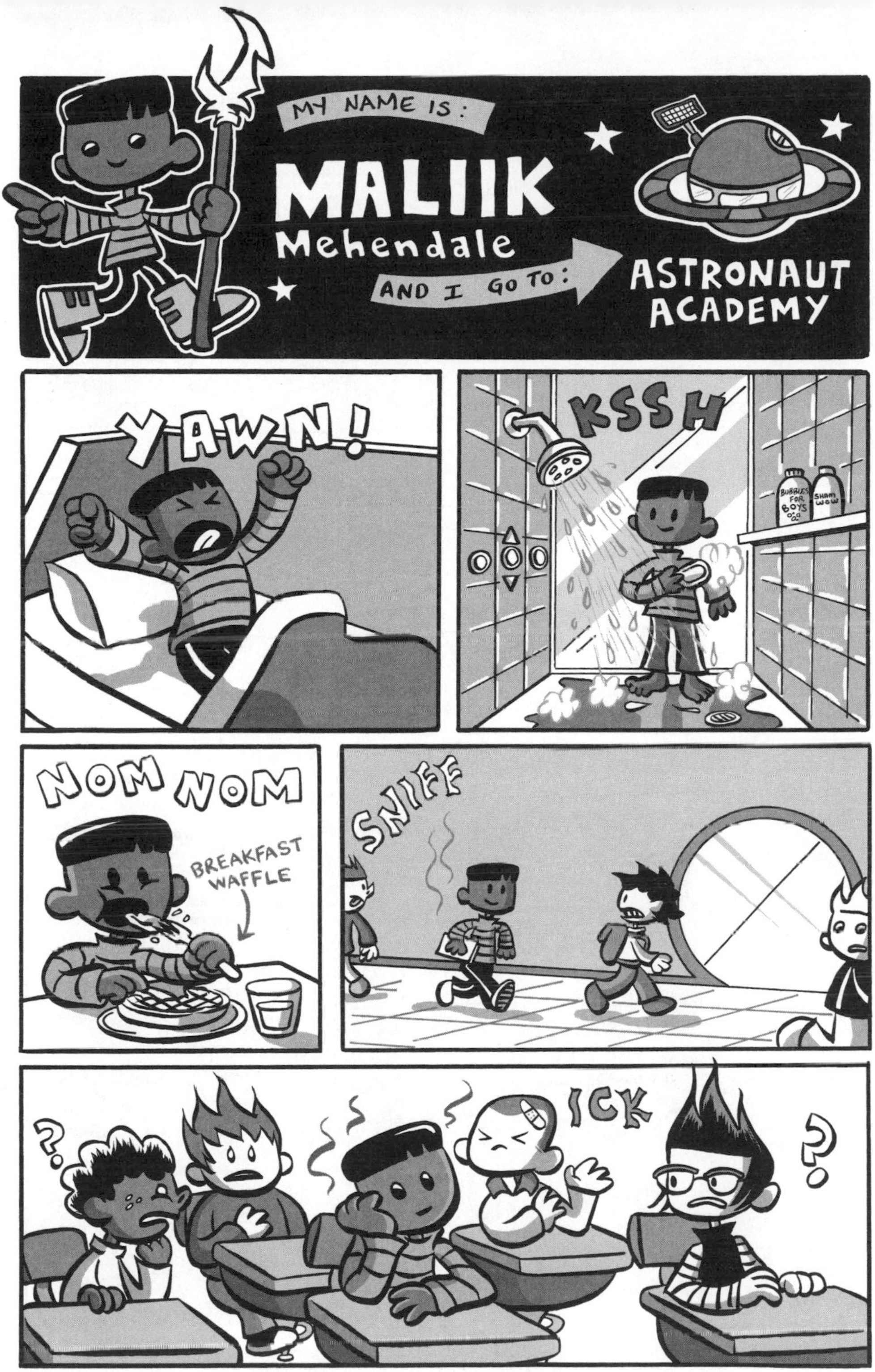
MY NAME IS:
MALIIK
Mehendale
AND I GO TO:
ASTRONAUT ACADEMY
YAWN!
KSSH
BUBBLES FOR BOYS
SHAM WOW
NOM NOM
BREAKFAST WAFFLE
SNIFF
ICK
?
?

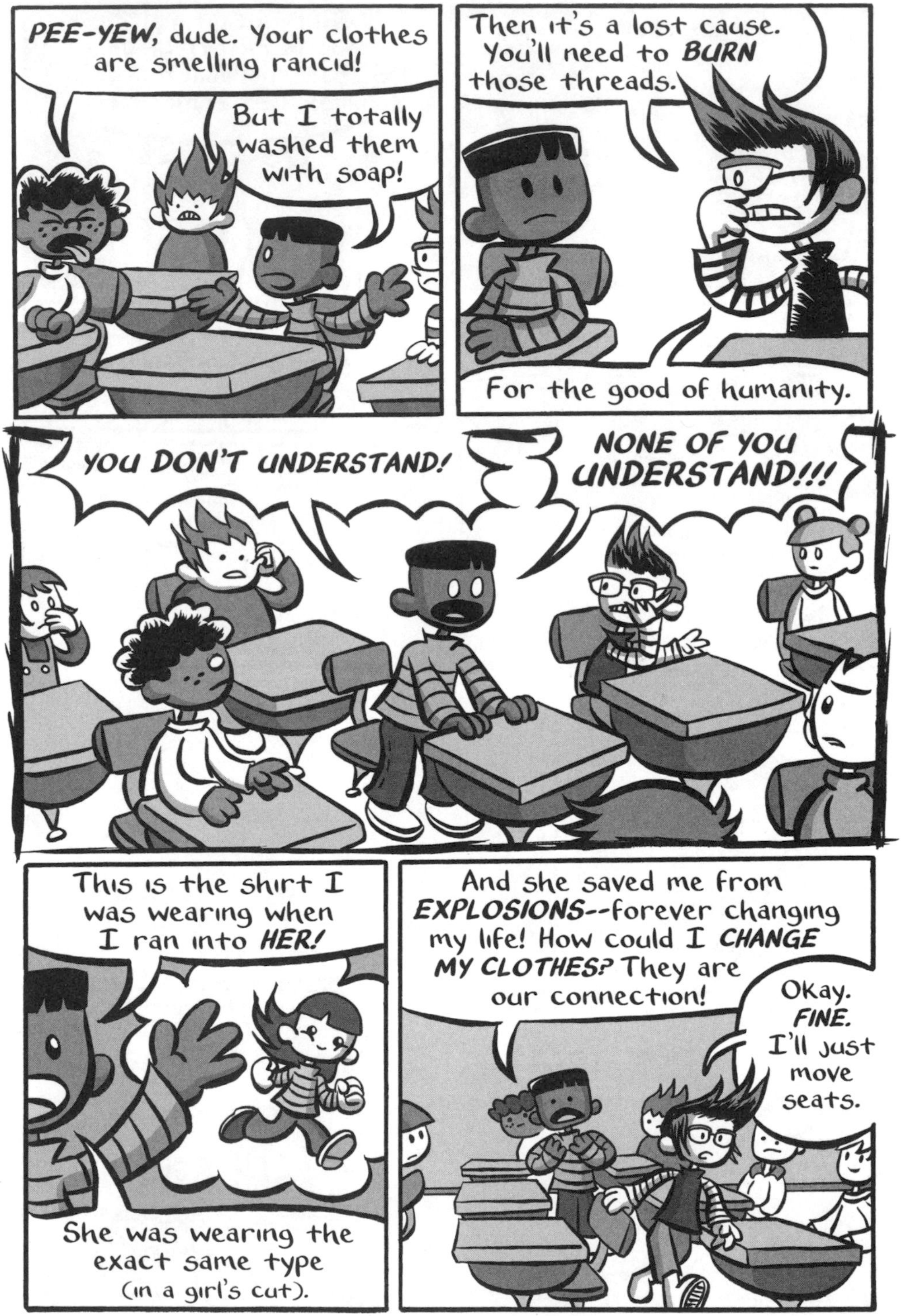
PEE-YEW, dude. Your clothes are smelling rancid!
But I totally washed them with soap!
Then it's a lost cause. You'll need to BURN those threads.
For the good of humanity.
YOU DON'T UNDERSTAND!
NONE OF YOU UNDERSTAND!!!
This is the shirt I was wearing when I ran into HER!
She was wearing the exact same type (in a girl's cut).
And she saved me from EXPLOSIONS--forever changing my life! How could I CHANGE MY CLOTHES? They are our connection!
Okay. FINE. I'll just move seats.

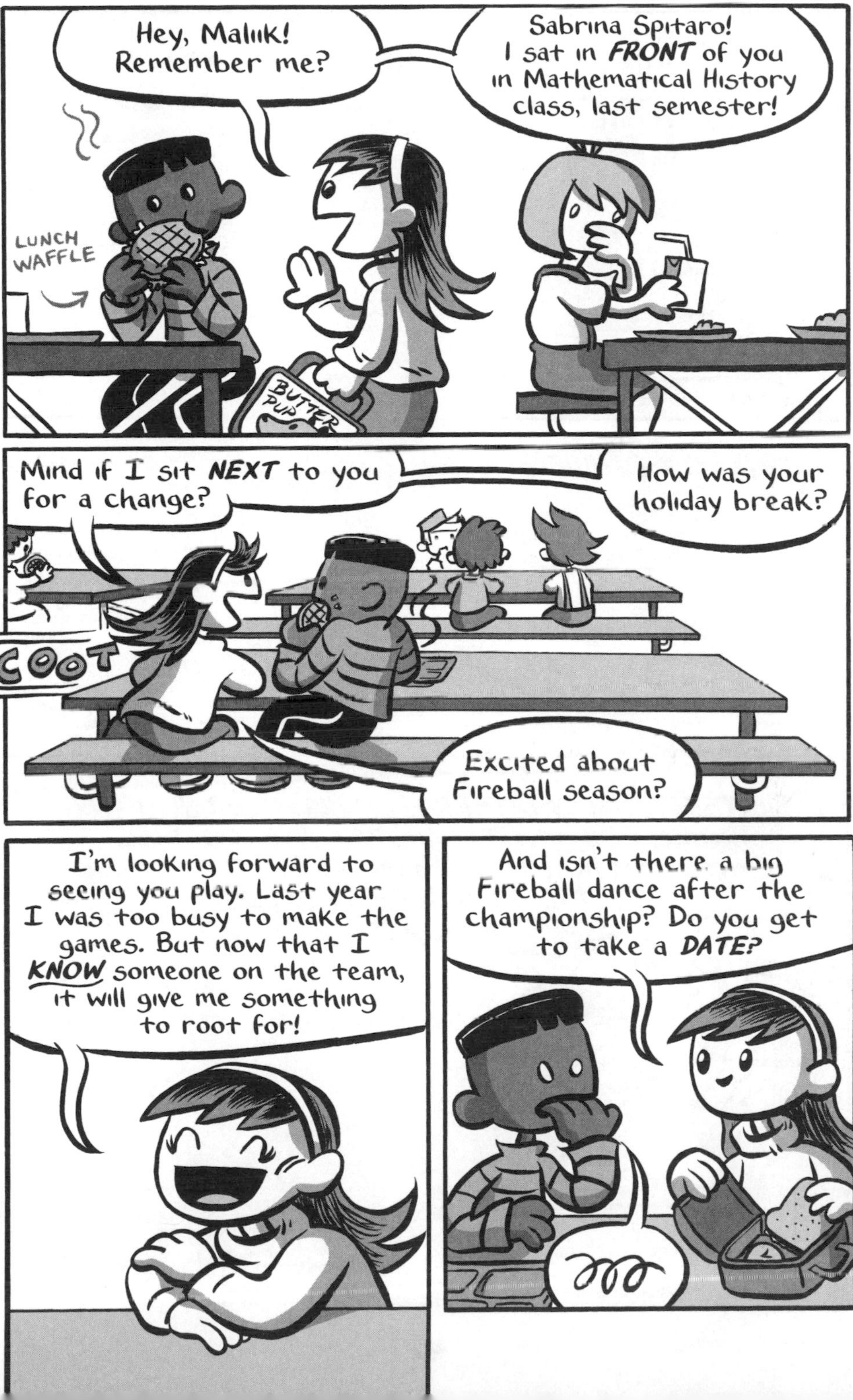
Hey, Malik! Remember me?
Sabrina Spitaro! I sat in FRONT of you in Mathematical History class, last semester!
LUNCH WAFFLE
BUTTER PUP
Mind if I sit NEXT to you for a change?
How was your holiday break?
SCOOT
Excited about Fireball season?
I'm looking forward to seeing you play. Last year I was too busy to make the games. But now that I KNOW someone on the team, it will give me something to root for!
And isn't there a big Fireball dance after the championship? Do you get to take a DATE?

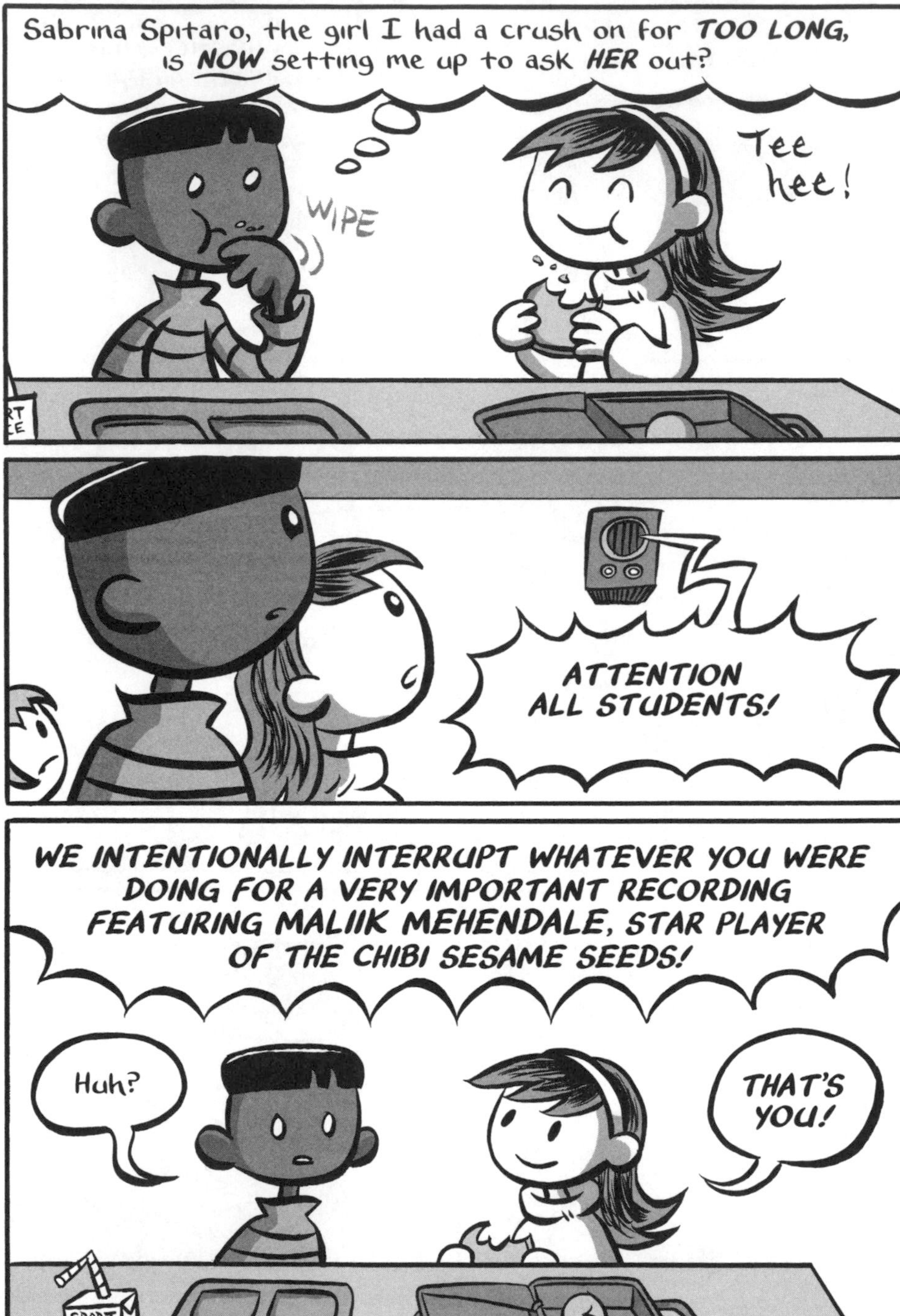
Sabrina Spitaro, the girl I had a crush on for TOO LONG, is NOW setting me up to ask HER out?
WIPE
Tee hee!
ATTENTION ALL STUDENTS!
WE INTENTIONALLY INTERRUPT WHATEVER YOU WERE DOING FOR A VERY IMPORTANT RECORDING FEATURING MALIIK MEHENDALE, STAR PLAYER OF THE CHIBI SESAME SEEDS!
Huh?
THAT'S YOU!
SPORT JUICE

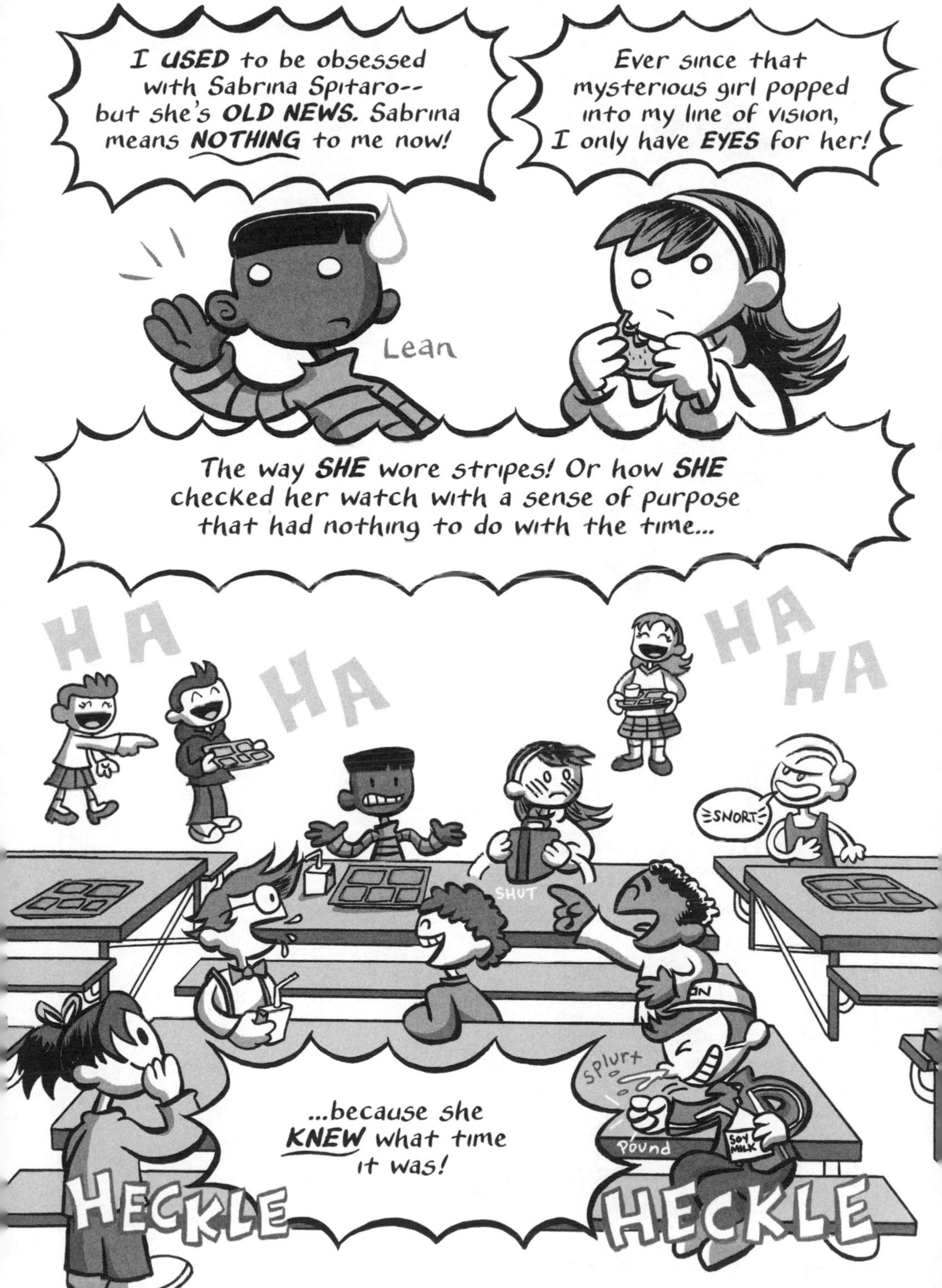
I USED to be obsessed with Sabrina Spitaro-- but she's OLD NEWS. Sabrina means NOTHING to me now!
Ever since that mysterious girl popped into my line of vision, I only have EYES for her!
Lean
The way SHE wore stripes! Or how SHE checked her watch with a sense of purpose that had nothing to do with the time...
HA HA HA HA HA
SNORT
SHUT
splurt
Pound
SOY MILK
...because she KNEW what time it was!
HECKLE
HECKLE

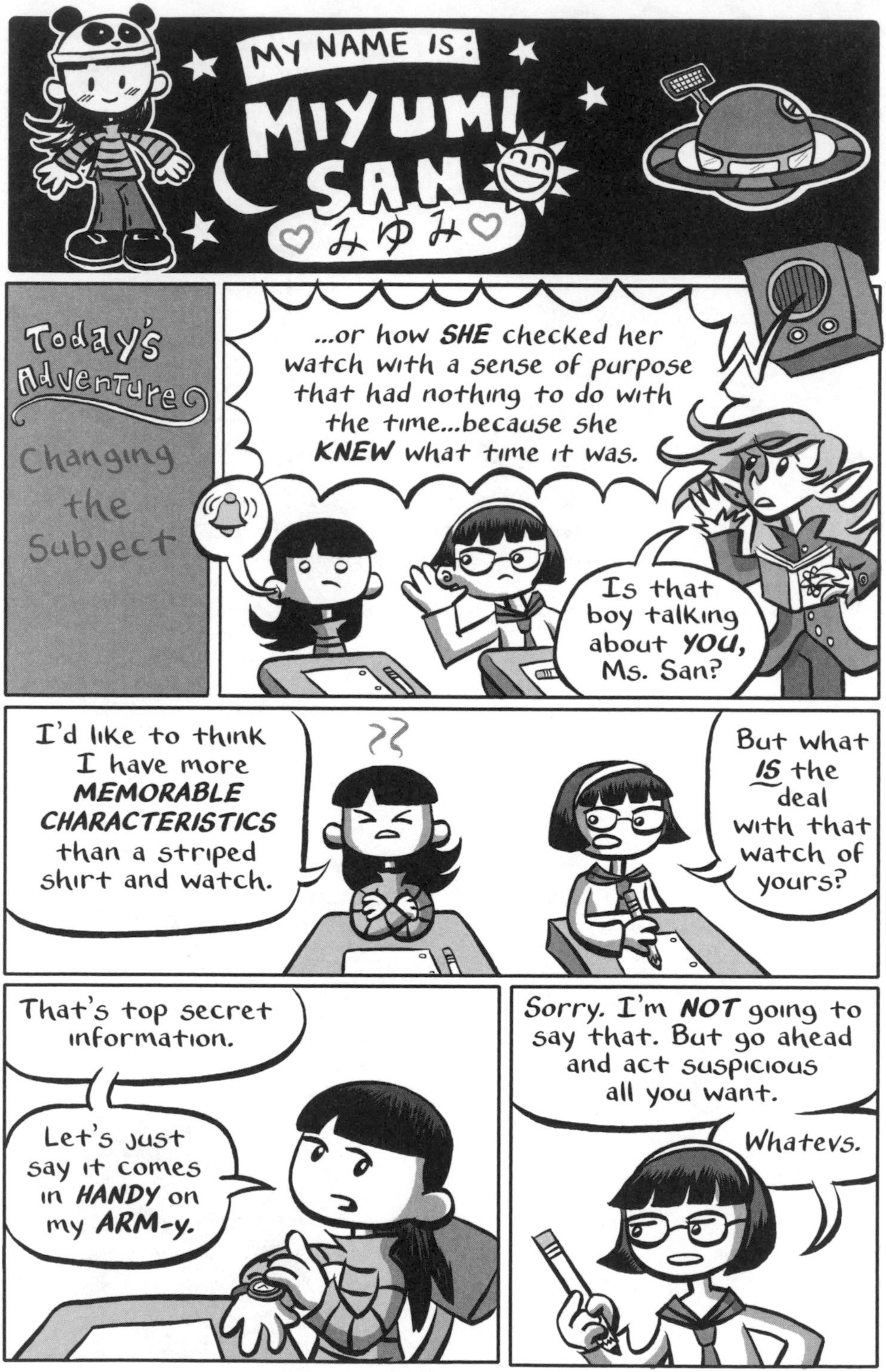
MY NAME IS:
MIYUMI SAN
みゆみ
Today's Adventure
Changing the Subject
...or how SHE checked her watch with a sense of purpose that had nothing to do with the time...because she KNEW what time it was.
Is that boy talking about YOU, Ms. San?
I'd like to think I have more MEMORABLE CHARACTERISTICS than a striped shirt and watch.
But what IS the deal with that watch of yours?
That's top secret information.
Let's just say it comes in HANDY on my ARM-y.
Sorry. I'm NOT going to say that. But go ahead and act suspicious all you want.
Whatevs.

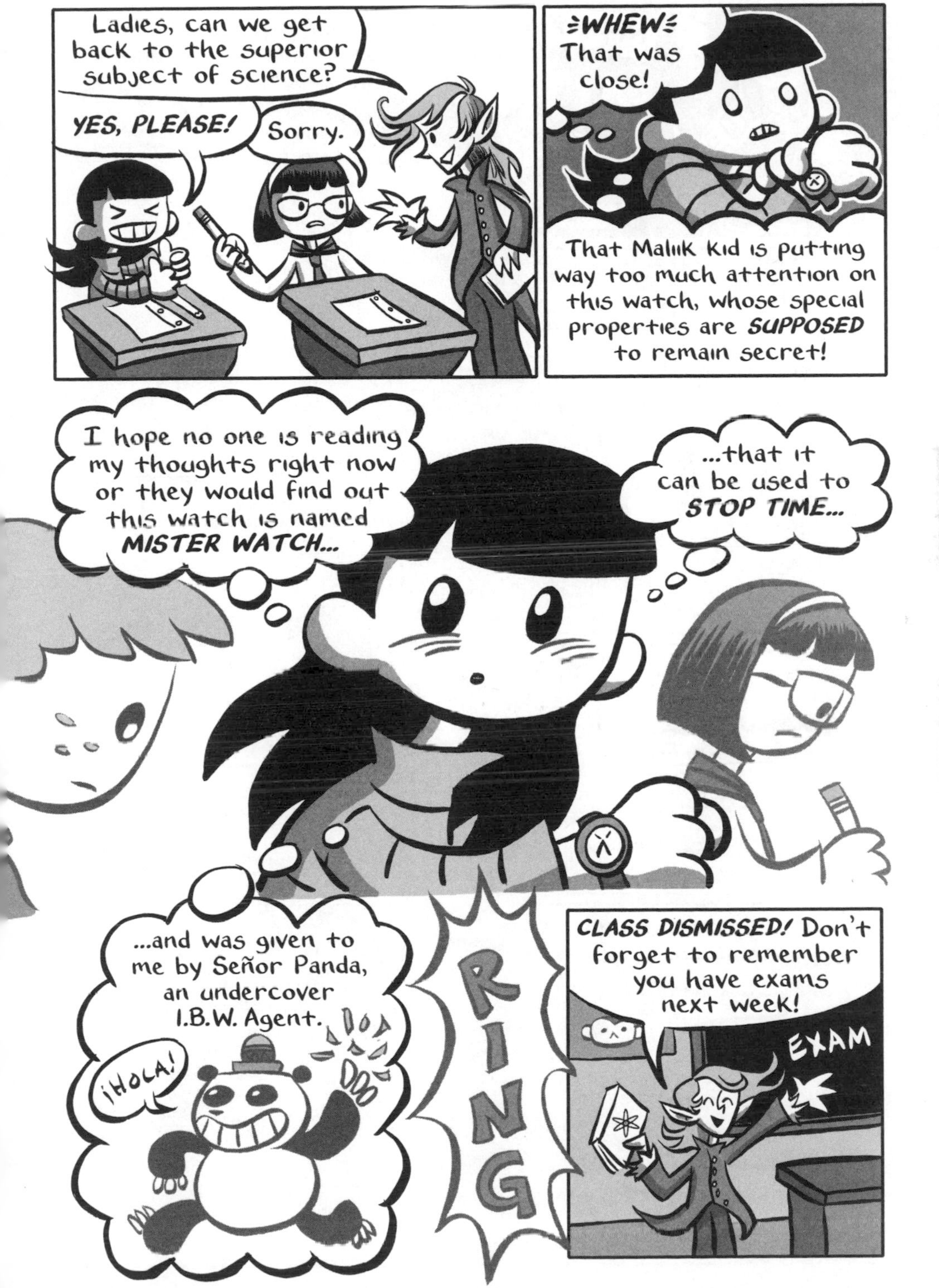

Ladies, can we get back to the superior subject of science?
YES, PLEASE!
Sorry.
≷WHEW≶ That was close!
That Malik kid is putting way too much attention on this watch, whose special properties are SUPPOSED to remain secret!
I hope no one is reading my thoughts right now or they would find out this watch is named MISTER WATCH...
...that it can be used to STOP TIME...
...and was given to me by Señor Panda, an undercover I.B.W. Agent.
¡HOLA!
RING
CLASS DISMISSED! Don't forget to remember you have exams next week!
EXAM

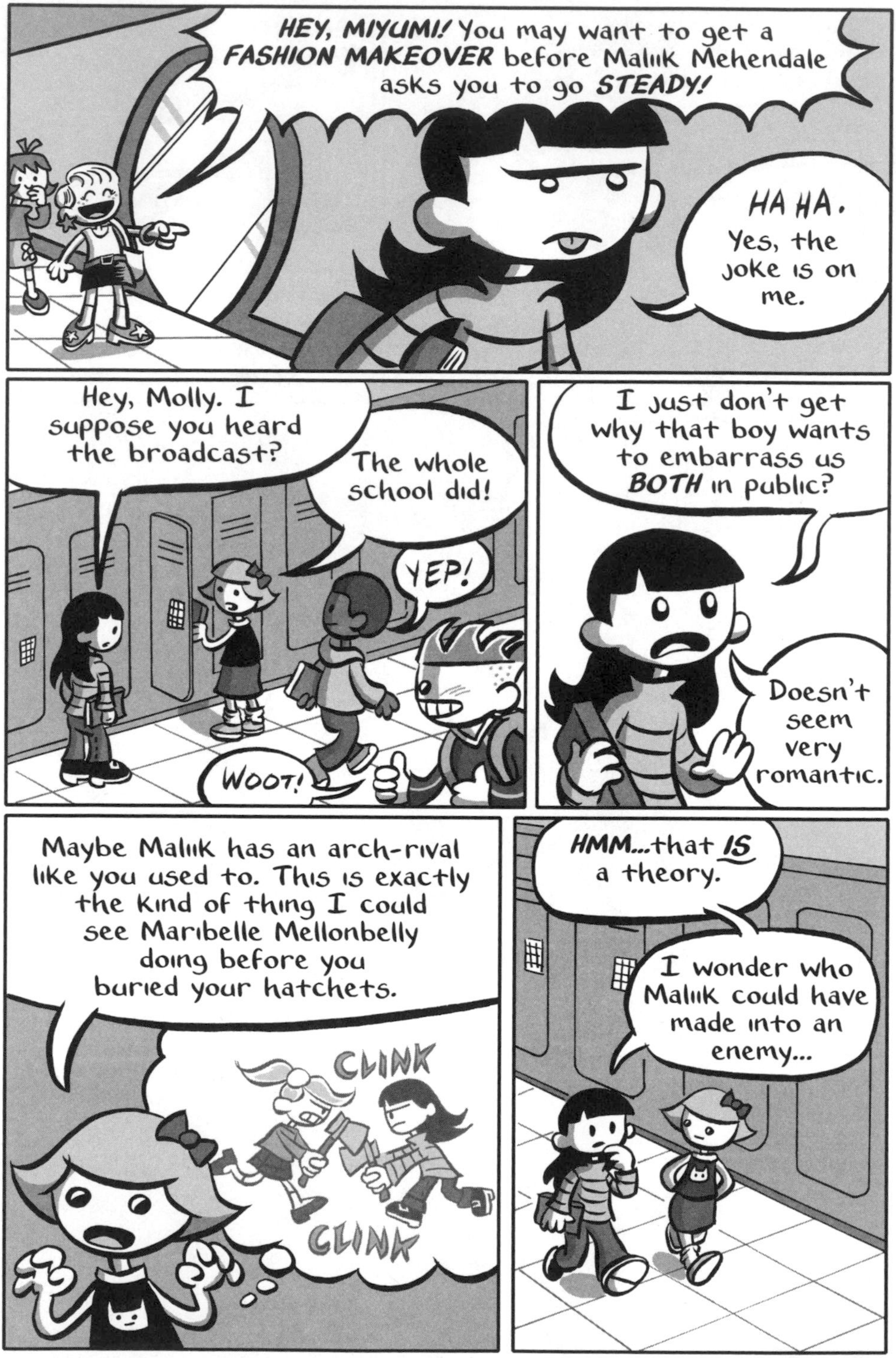
HEY, MIYUMI! You may want to get a FASHION MAKEOVER before Malik Mehendale asks you to go STEADY!
HA HA. Yes, the joke is on me.
Hey, Molly. I suppose you heard the broadcast?
The whole school did!
YEP!
WOOT!
I just don't get why that boy wants to embarrass us BOTH in public?
Doesn't seem very romantic.
Maybe Malik has an arch-rival like you used to. This is exactly the kind of thing I could see Maribelle Mellonbelly doing before you buried your hatchets.
CLINK
CLINK
HMM...that IS a theory.
I wonder who Malik could have made into an enemy...

SEGUE!

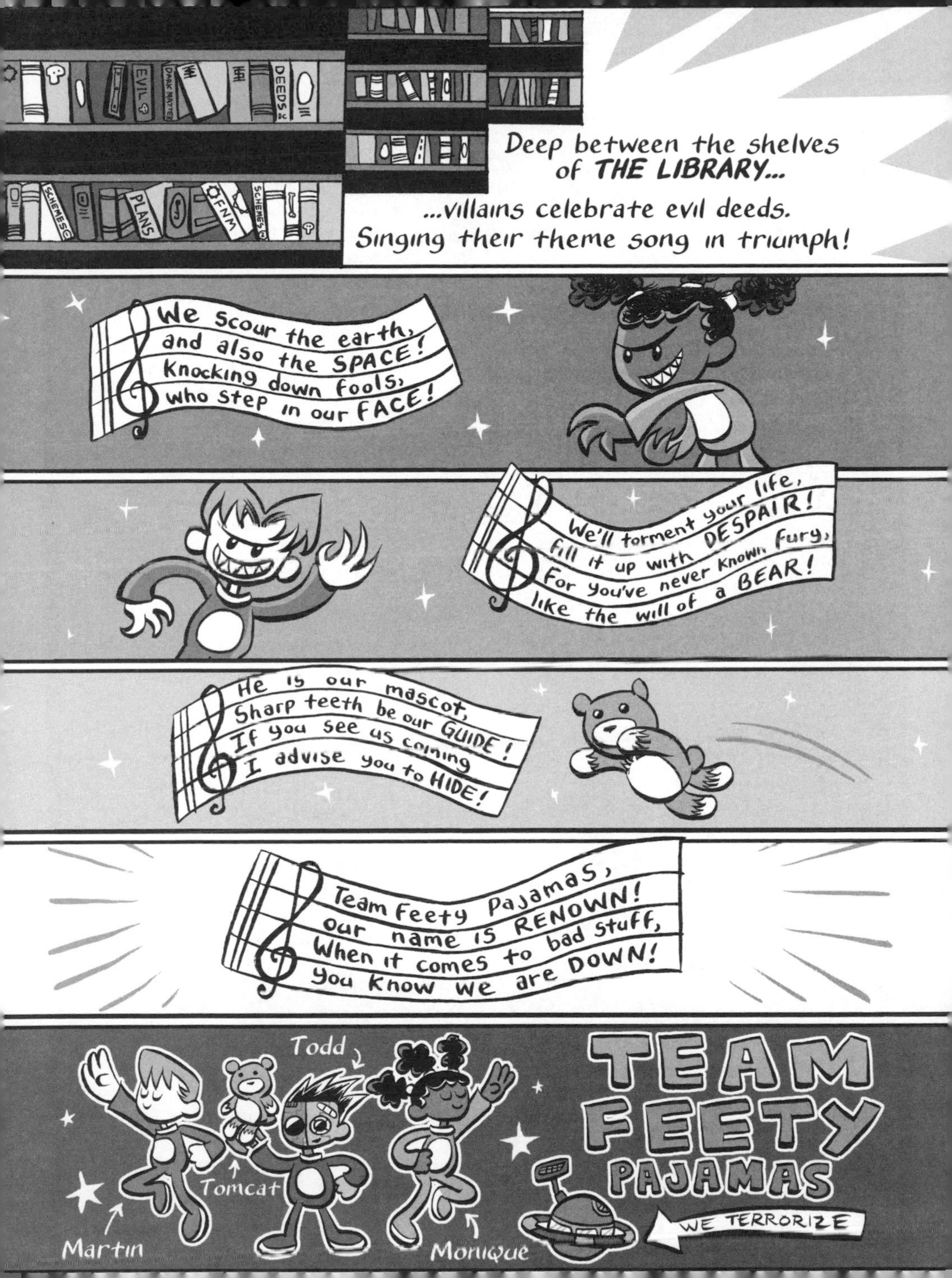

Deep between the shelves of THE LIBRARY...
...villains celebrate evil deeds. Singing their theme song in triumph!
We scour the earth, and also the SPACE! Knocking down fools, who step in our FACE!
We'll torment your life, fill it up with DESPAIR! For you've never known fury, like the will of a BEAR!
He is our mascot, Sharp teeth be our GUIDE! If you see us coming I advise you to HIDE!
Team Feety Pajamas, our name is RENOWN! When it comes to bad stuff, you know we are DOWN!
Todd
Tomcat
Martin
Monique
TEAM FEETY PAJAMAS
WE TERRORIZE

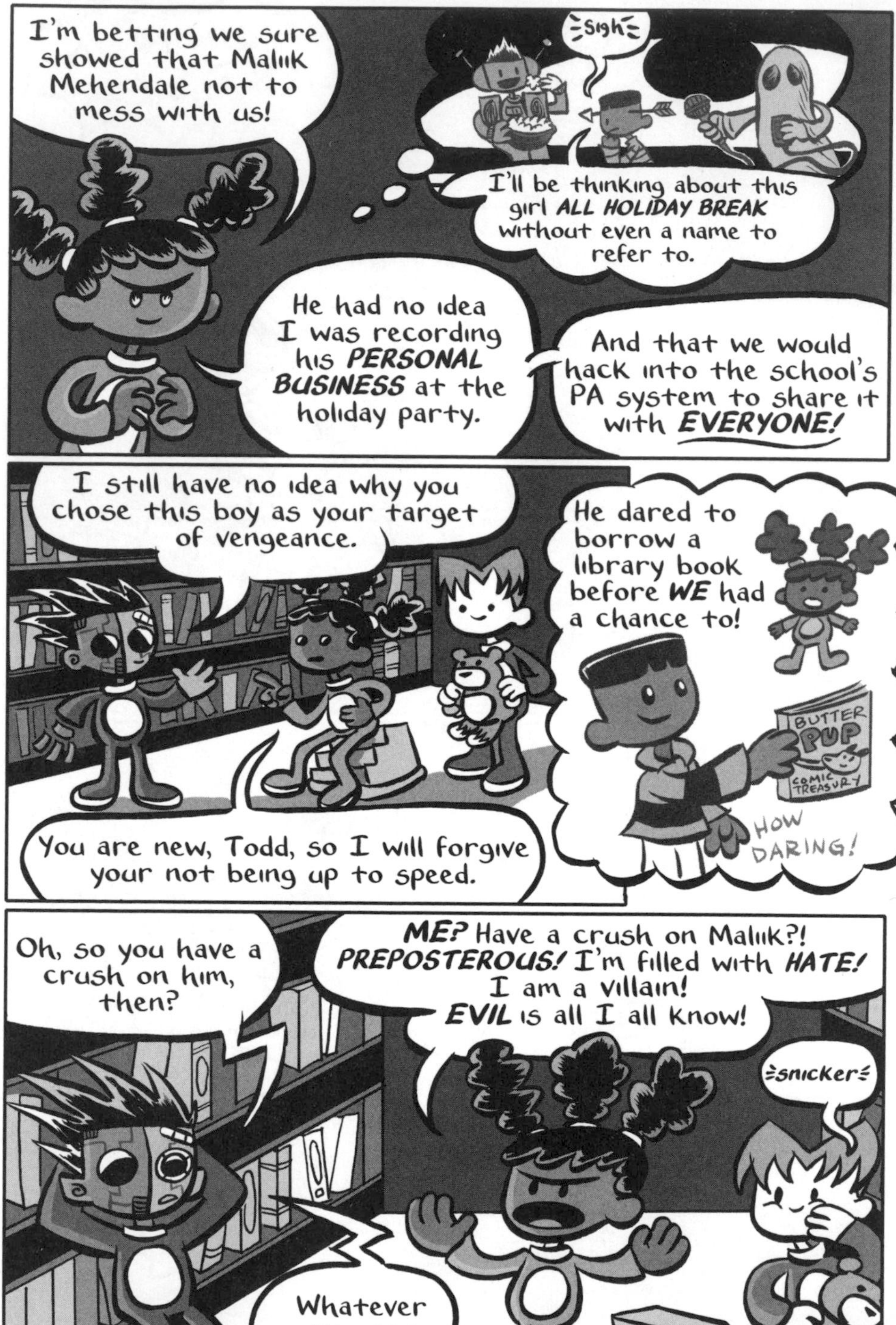
I'm betting we sure showed that Malik Mehendale not to mess with us!
Sigh
I'll be thinking about this girl ALL HOLIDAY BREAK without even a name to refer to.
He had no idea I was recording his PERSONAL BUSINESS at the holiday party.
And that we would hack into the school's PA system to share it with EVERYONE!
I still have no idea why you chose this boy as your target of vengeance.
You are new, Todd, so I will forgive your not being up to speed.
He dared to borrow a library book before WE had a chance to!
BUTTER PUP COMIC TREASURY
HOW DARING!
Oh, so you have a crush on him, then?
ME? Have a crush on Malik?! PREPOSTEROUS! I'm filled with HATE! I am a villain! EVIL is all I all know!
snicker
Whatever you say.

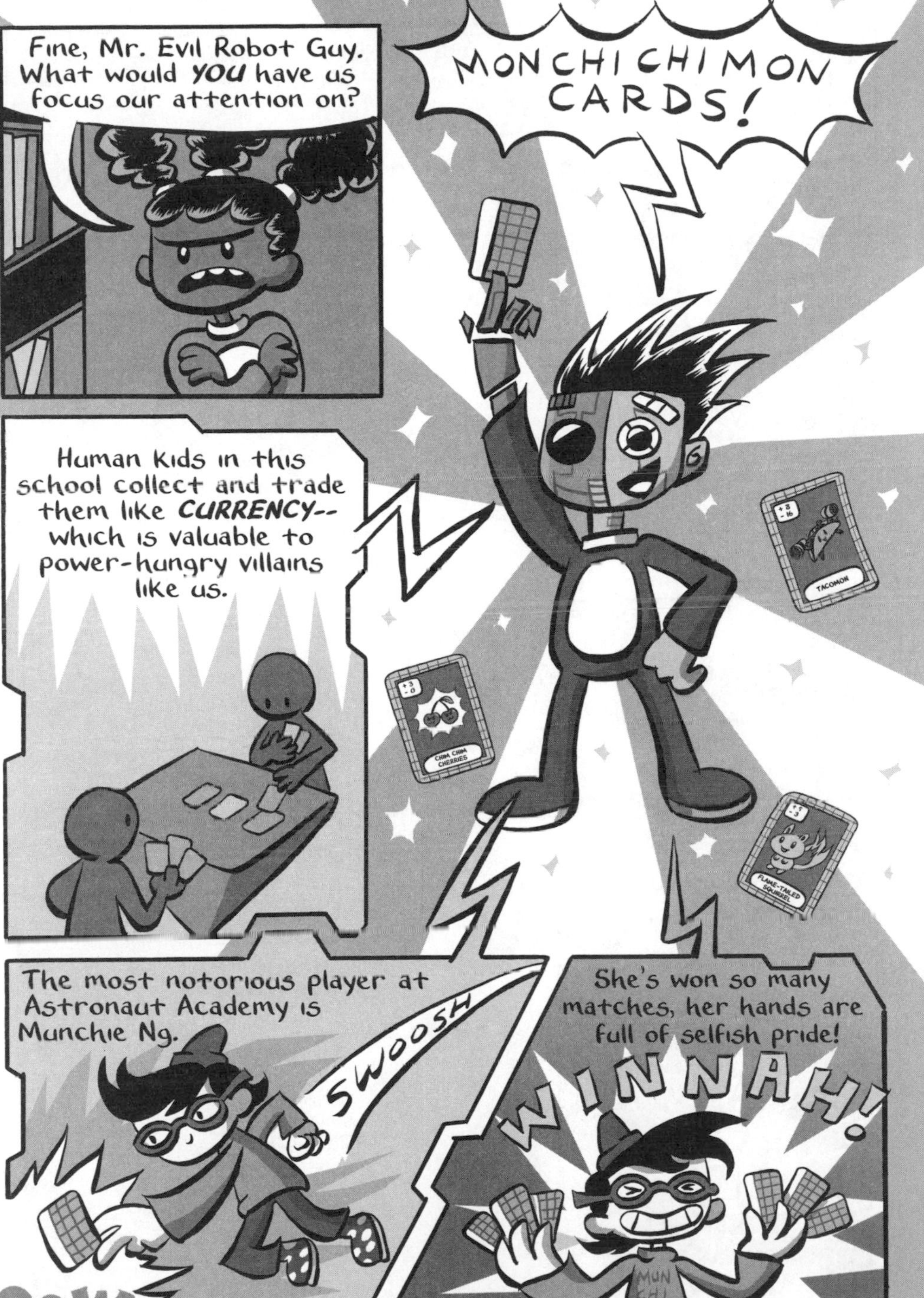
Fine, Mr. Evil Robot Guy. What would YOU have us focus our attention on?
MONCHICHIMON CARDS!
TACOMON
CHIM CHIM CHERRIES
FLAME-TAILED SQUIRREL
Human kids in this school collect and trade them like CURRENCY-- which is valuable to power-hungry villains like us.
The most notorious player at Astronaut Academy is Munchie Ng.
SWOOSH
POW
She's won so many matches, her hands are full of selfish pride!
WINNAH!
MUNCHI

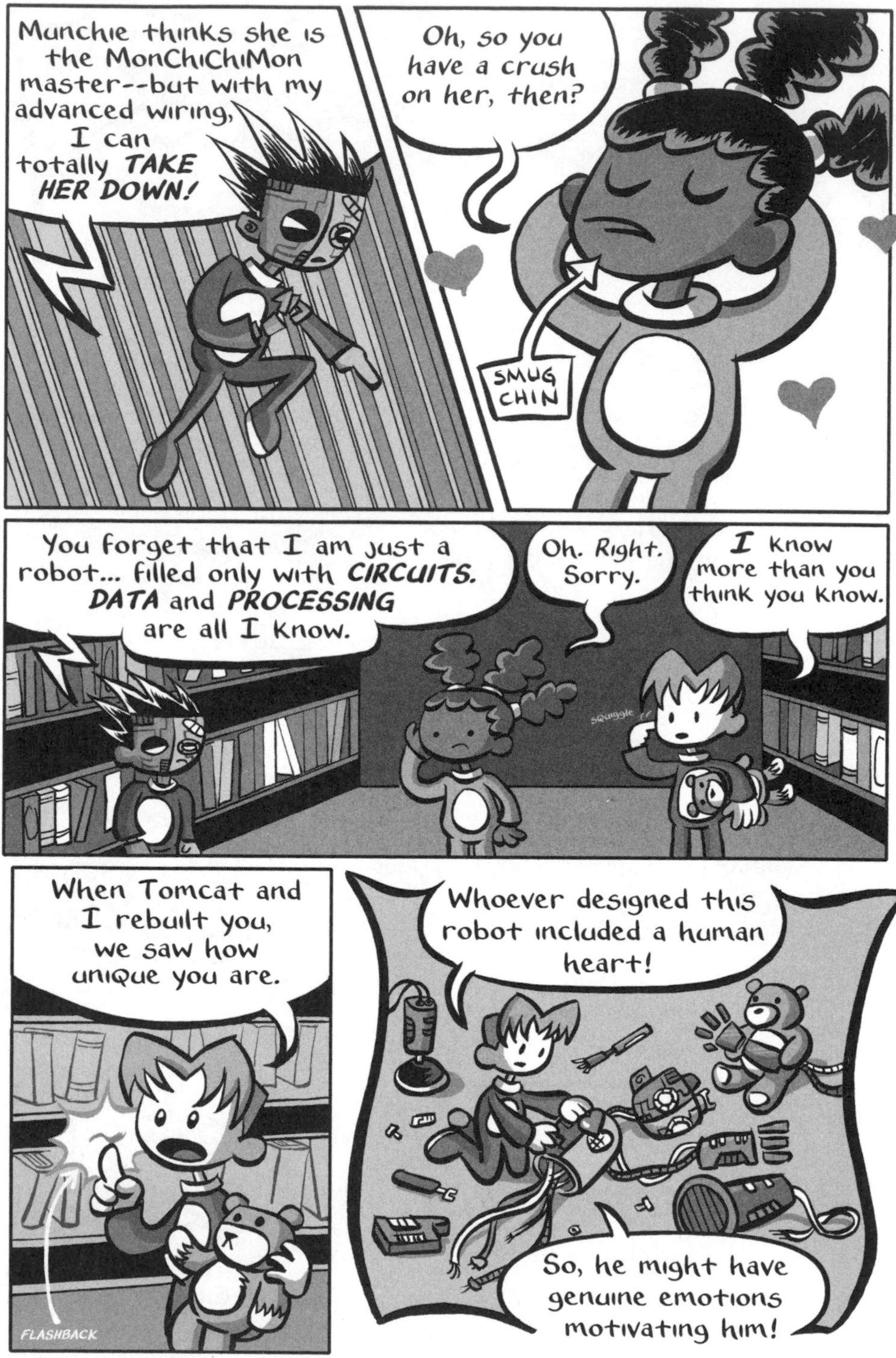
Munchie thinks she is the MonChiChiMon master--but with my advanced wiring, I can totally TAKE HER DOWN!
Oh, so you have a crush on her, then?
SMUG CHIN
You forget that I am just a robot... filled only with CIRCUITS. DATA and PROCESSING are all I know.
Oh. Right. Sorry.
I know more than you think you know.
SQUiggle
When Tomcat and I rebuilt you, we saw how unique you are.
FLASHBACK
Whoever designed this robot included a human heart!
So, he might have genuine emotions motivating him!

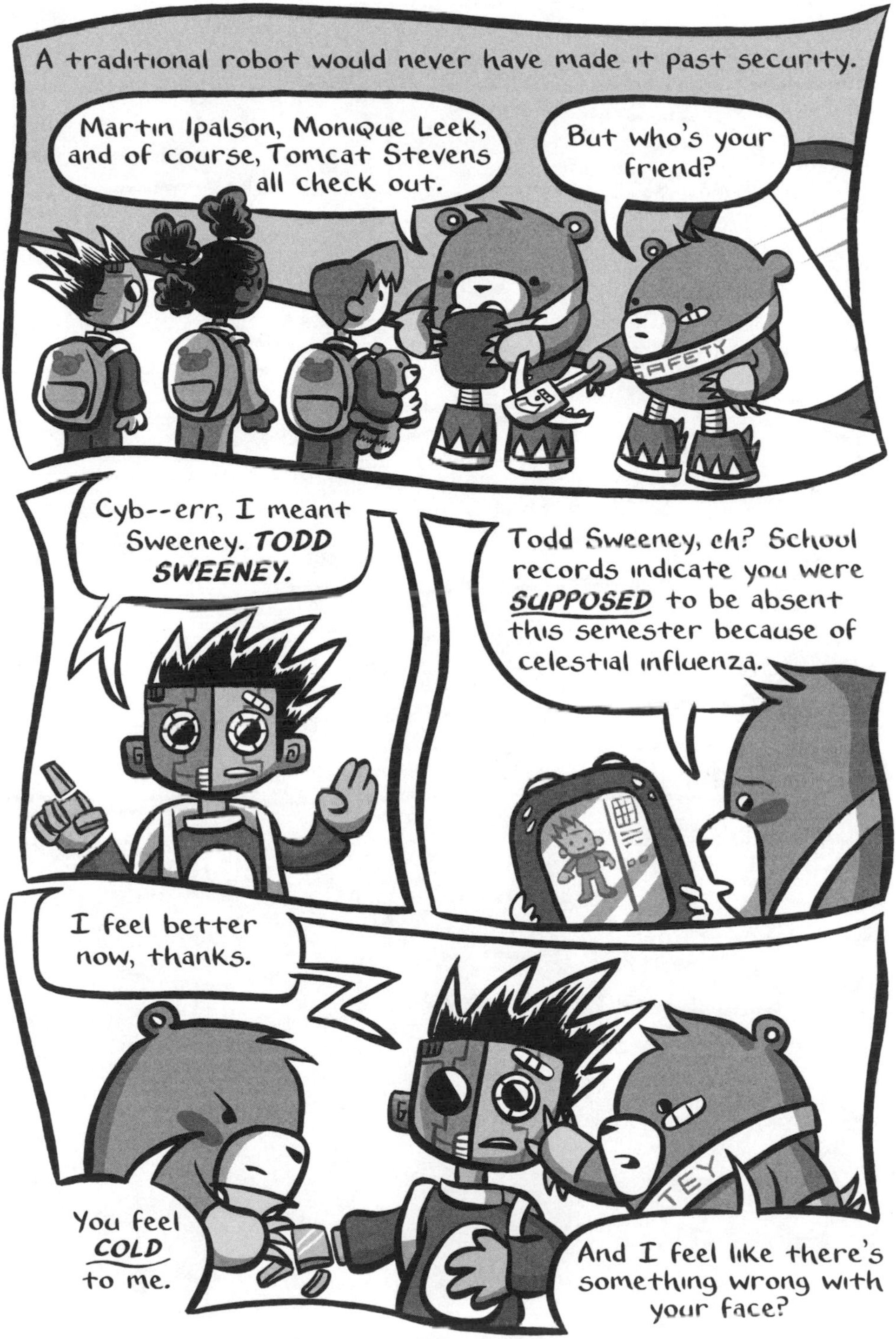
A traditional robot would never have made it past security.
Martin Ipalson, Monique Leek, and of course, Tomcat Stevens all check out.
But who's your friend?
SAFETY
Cyb--err, I meant Sweeney. TODD SWEENEY.
Todd Sweeney, eh? School records indicate you were SUPPOSED to be absent this semester because of celestial influenza.
I feel better now, thanks.
You feel COLD to me.
And I feel like there's something wrong with your face?

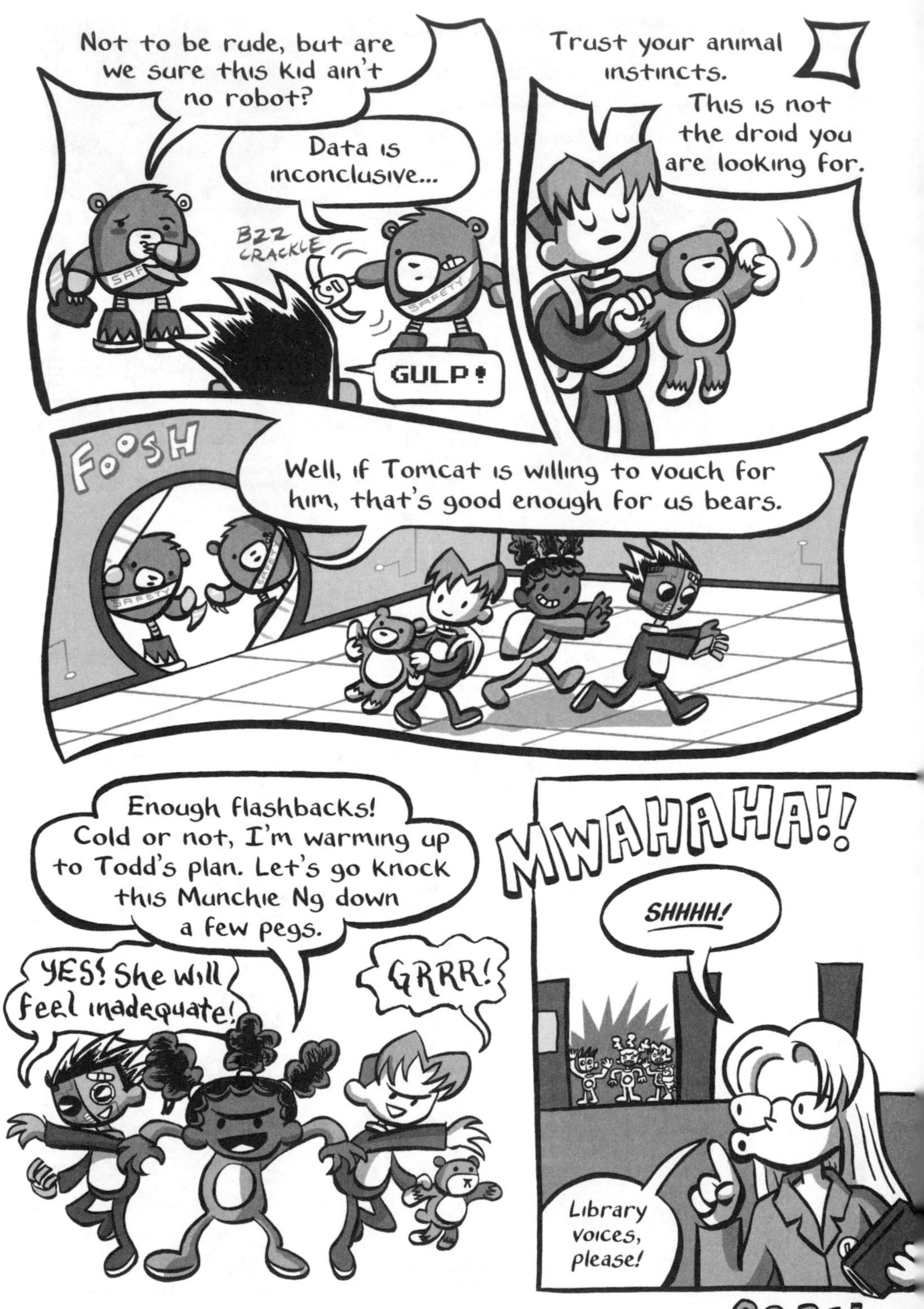
Not to be rude, but are we sure this kid ain't no robot?
Data is inconclusive...
BZZ CRACKLE
GULP!
Trust your animal instincts.
This is not the droid you are looking for.
FOOSH
Well, if Tomcat is willing to vouch for him, that's good enough for us bears.
Enough flashbacks! Cold or not, I'm warming up to Todd's plan. Let's go knock this Munchie Ng down a few pegs.
YES! She will feel inadequate!
GRRR!
MWAHAHA!!
SHHHH!
Library voices, please!
OOPS!

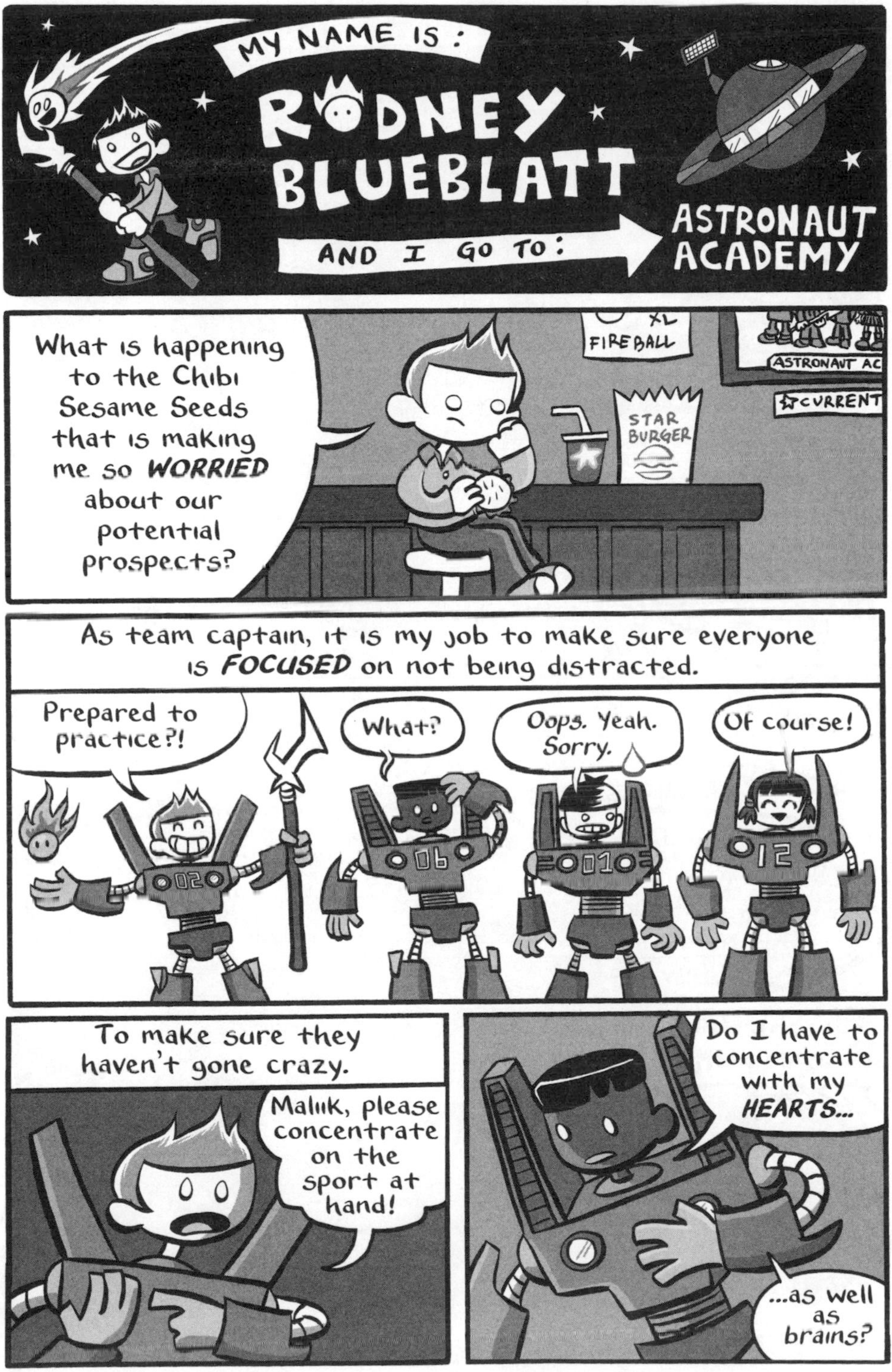
MY NAME IS:
RODNEY BLUEBLATT
AND I GO TO:
ASTRONAUT ACADEMY
What is happening to the Chibi Sesame Seeds that is making me so **WORRIED** about our potential prospects?
XL FIREBALL
STAR BURGER
ASTRONAUT AC
CURRENT
As team captain, it is my job to make sure everyone is **FOCUSED** on not being distracted.
Prepared to practice?!
What?
Oops. Yeah. Sorry.
Of course!
02
06
01
12
To make sure they haven't gone crazy.
Maliik, please concentrate on the sport at hand!
Do I have to concentrate with my **HEARTS...**
...as well as brains?

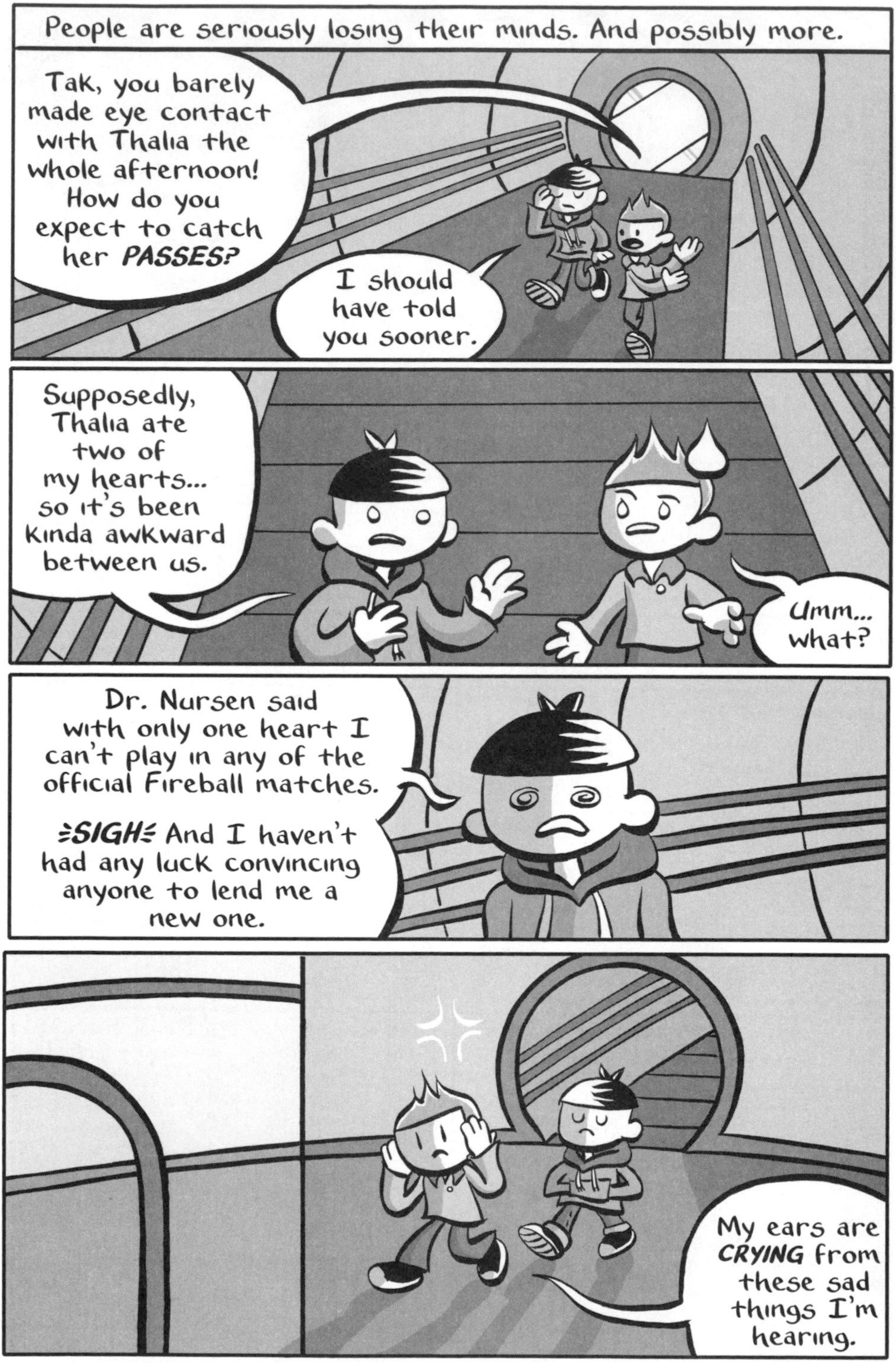
People are seriously losing their minds. And possibly more.
Tak, you barely made eye contact with Thalia the whole afternoon! How do you expect to catch her **PASSES?**
I should have told you sooner.
Supposedly, Thalia ate two of my hearts... so it's been kinda awkward between us.
Umm... what?
Dr. Nursen said with only one heart I can't play in any of the official Fireball matches.
SIGH And I haven't had any luck convincing anyone to lend me a new one.
My ears are **CRYING** from these sad things I'm hearing.

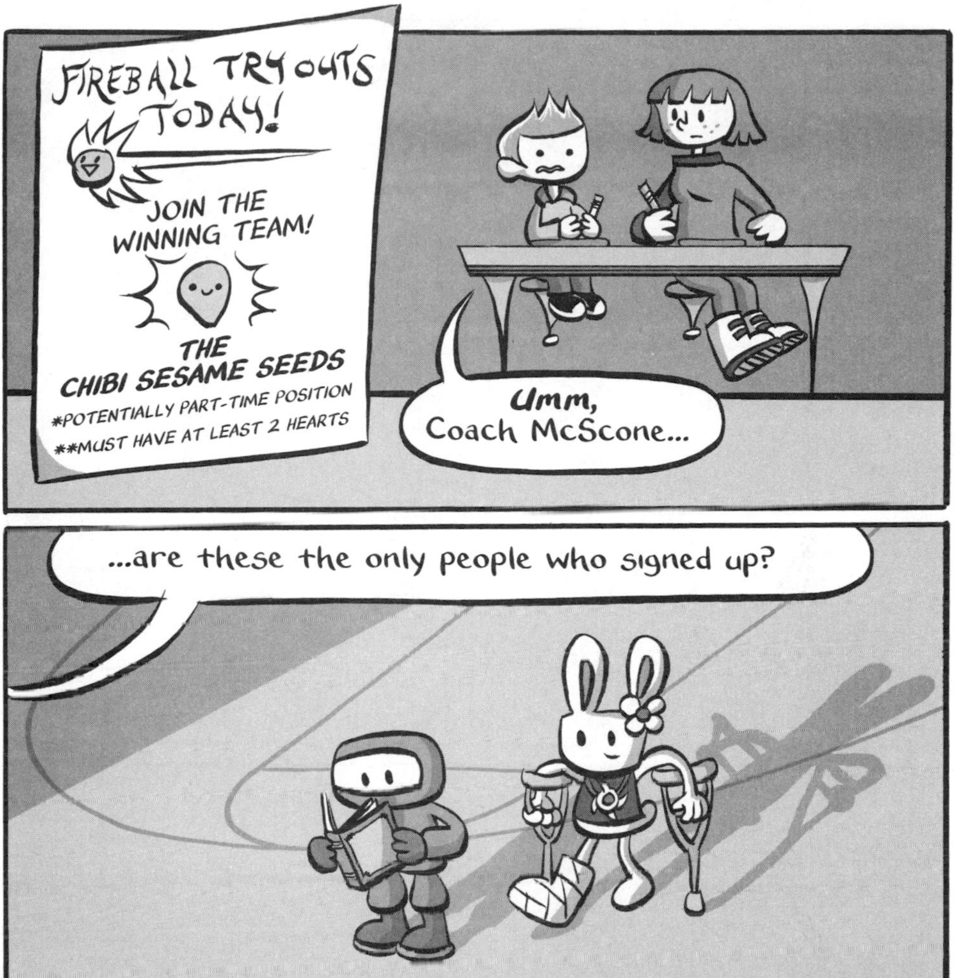
FIREBALL TRYOUTS TODAY!
JOIN THE WINNING TEAM!
THE CHIBI SESAME SEEDS
*POTENTIALLY PART-TIME POSITION
**MUST HAVE AT LEAST 2 HEARTS
Umm, Coach McScone...
...are these the only people who signed up?
Afraid so.

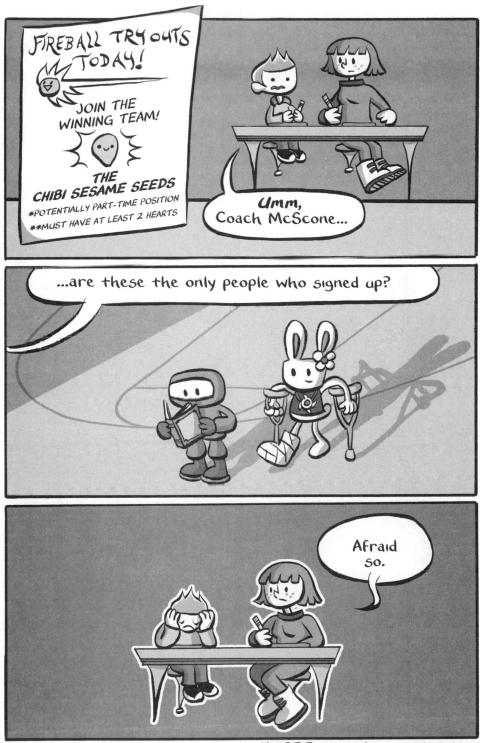

HOPEFULLY NOT THE END!

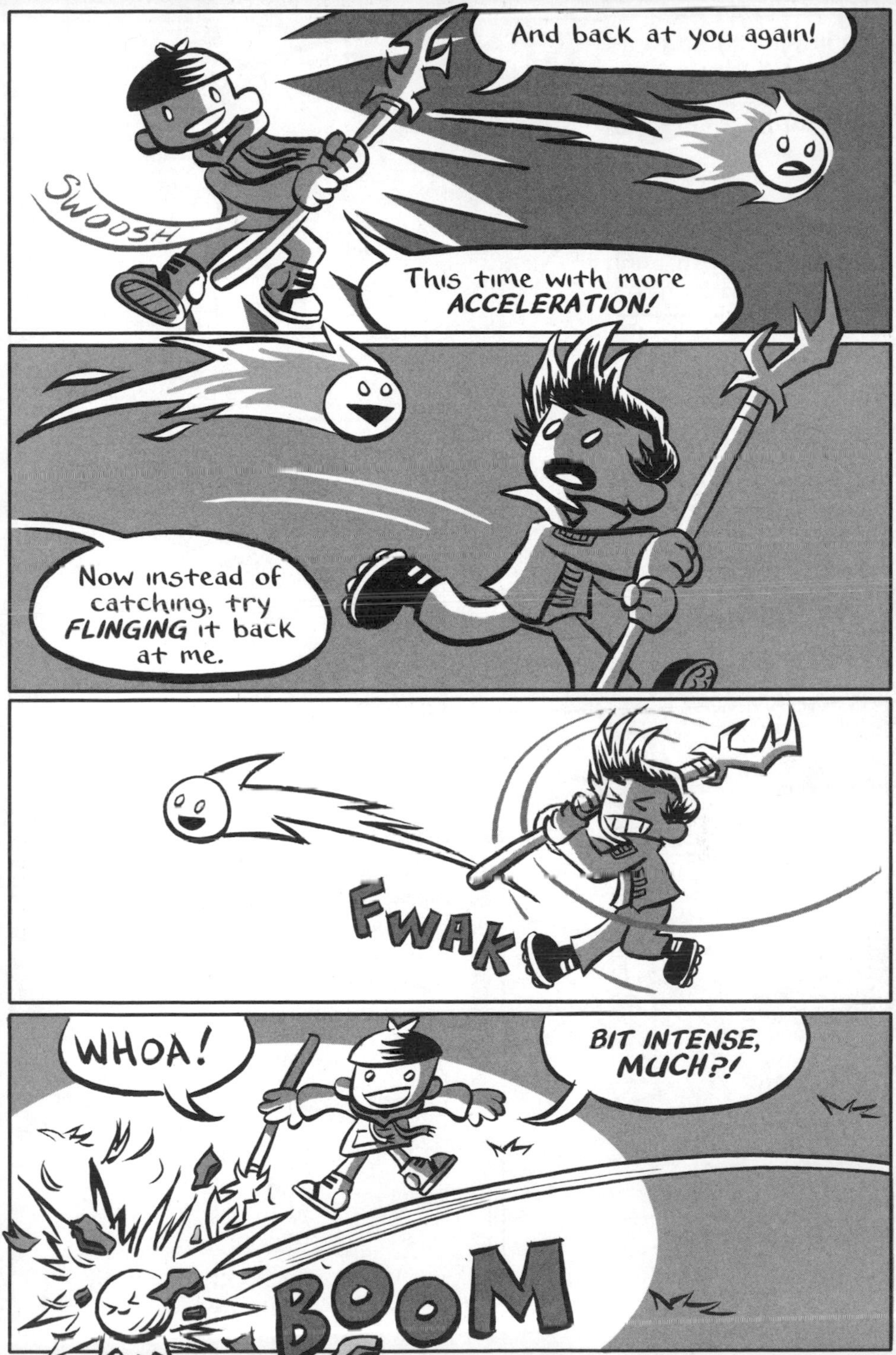
And back at you again!
SWOOSH
This time with more ACCELERATION!
Now instead of catching, try FLINGING it back at me.
FWAK
WHOA!
BIT INTENSE, MUCH?!
BOOM

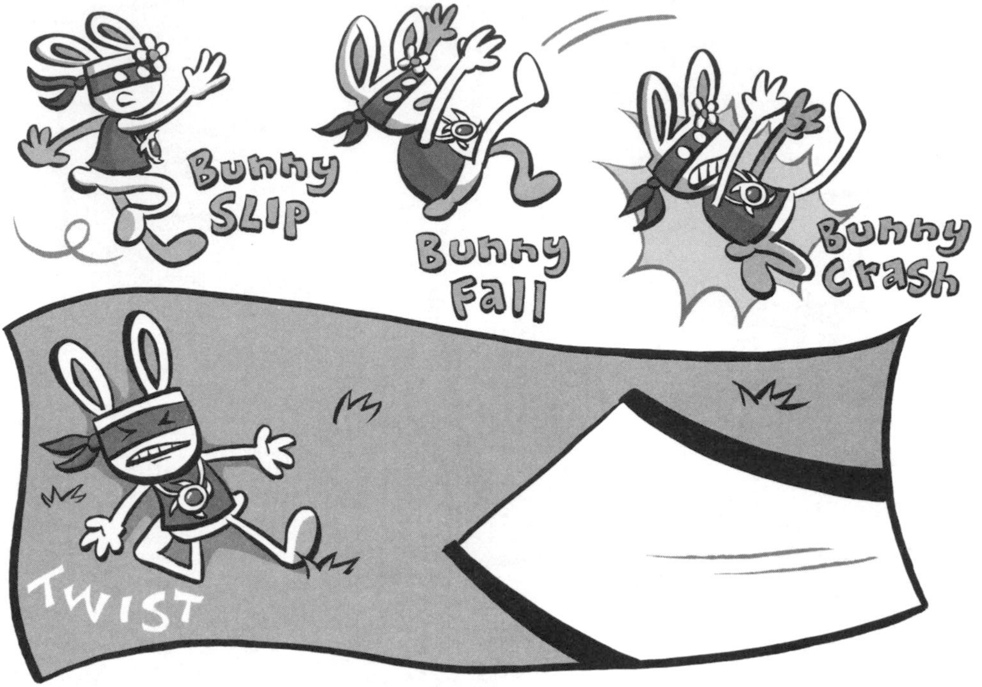
Bunny SLIP
Bunny Fall
Bunny Crash
TWIST

I debated using my medallion to call Hakata Soy.

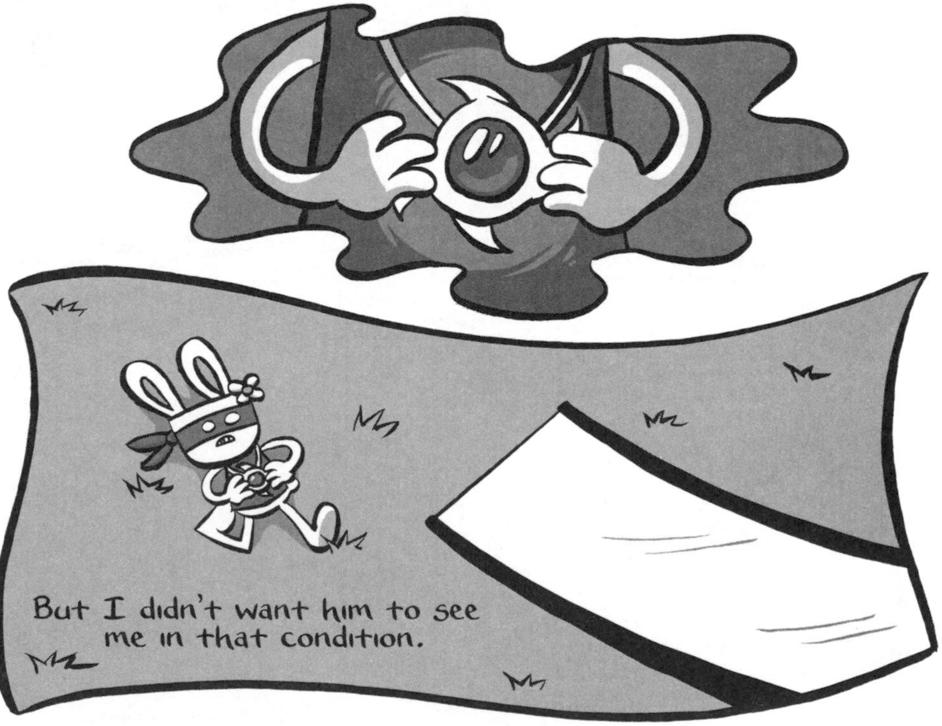
But I didn't want him to see me in that condition.

72

END!

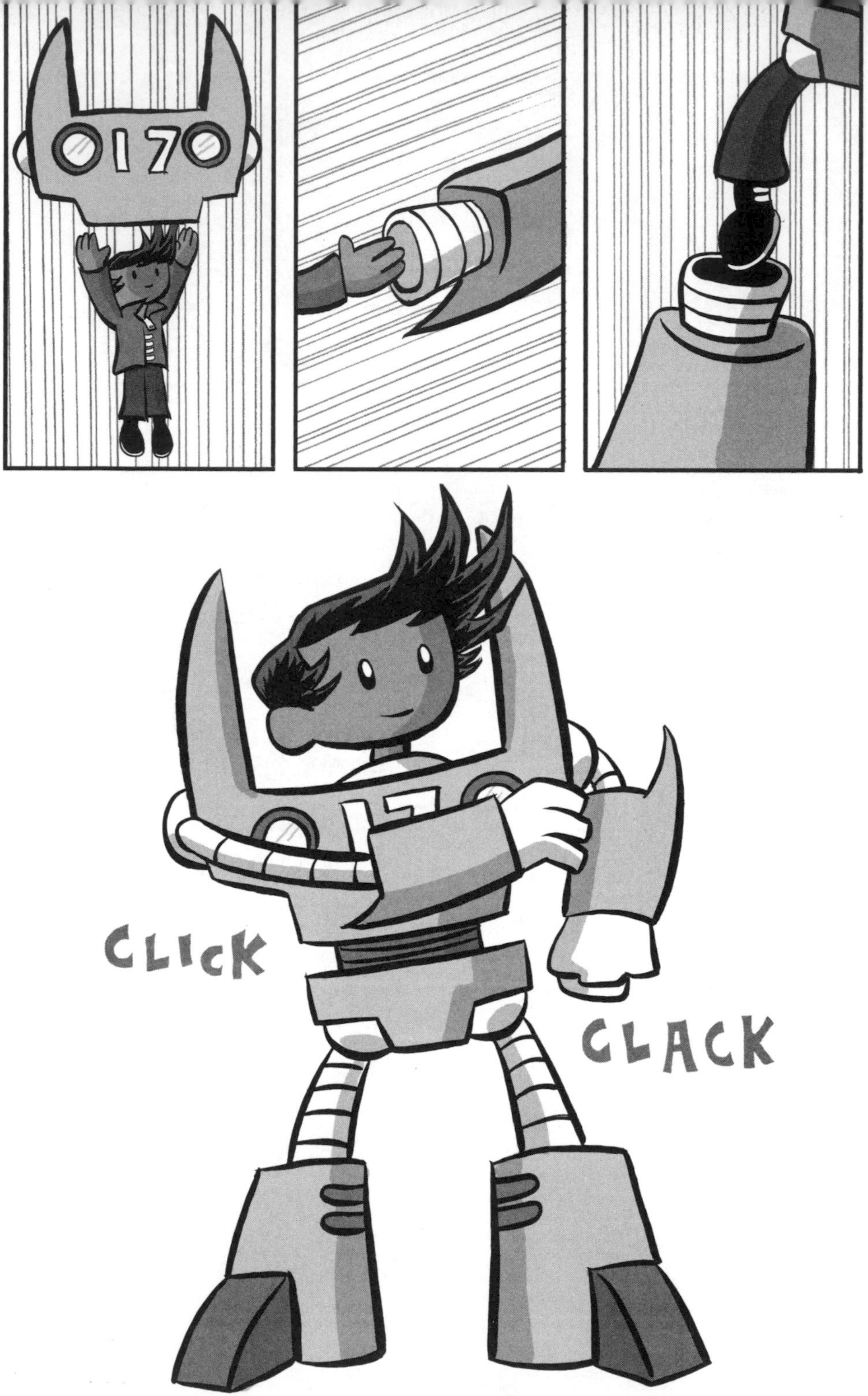
17
CLICK
CLACK

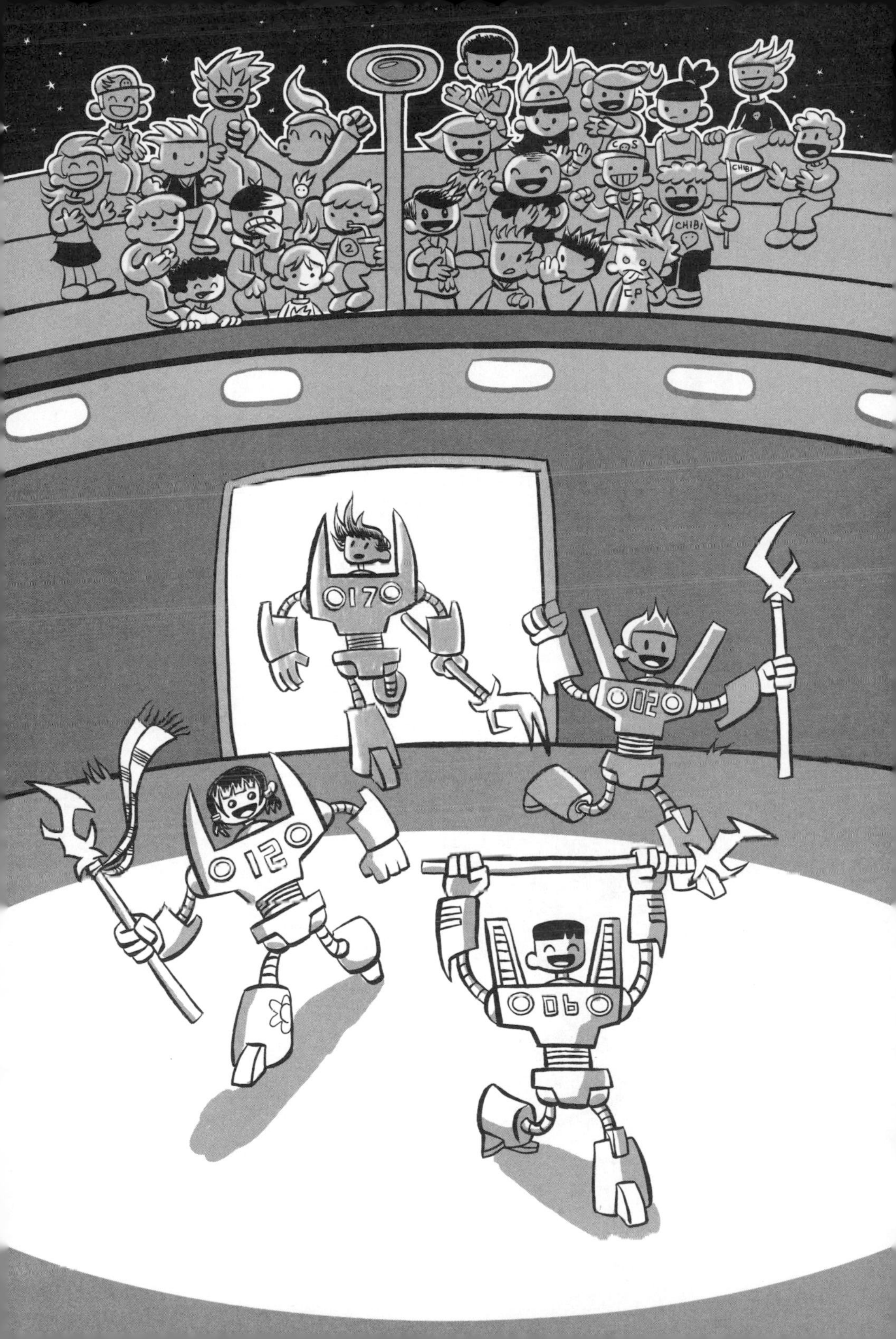
CHIBI
CHIBI

GAME ONE

ASTRONAUT ACADEMY
Chibi Sesame Seeds

VS.

COSMONAUT PREP
Super Deformed Poppy Seeds

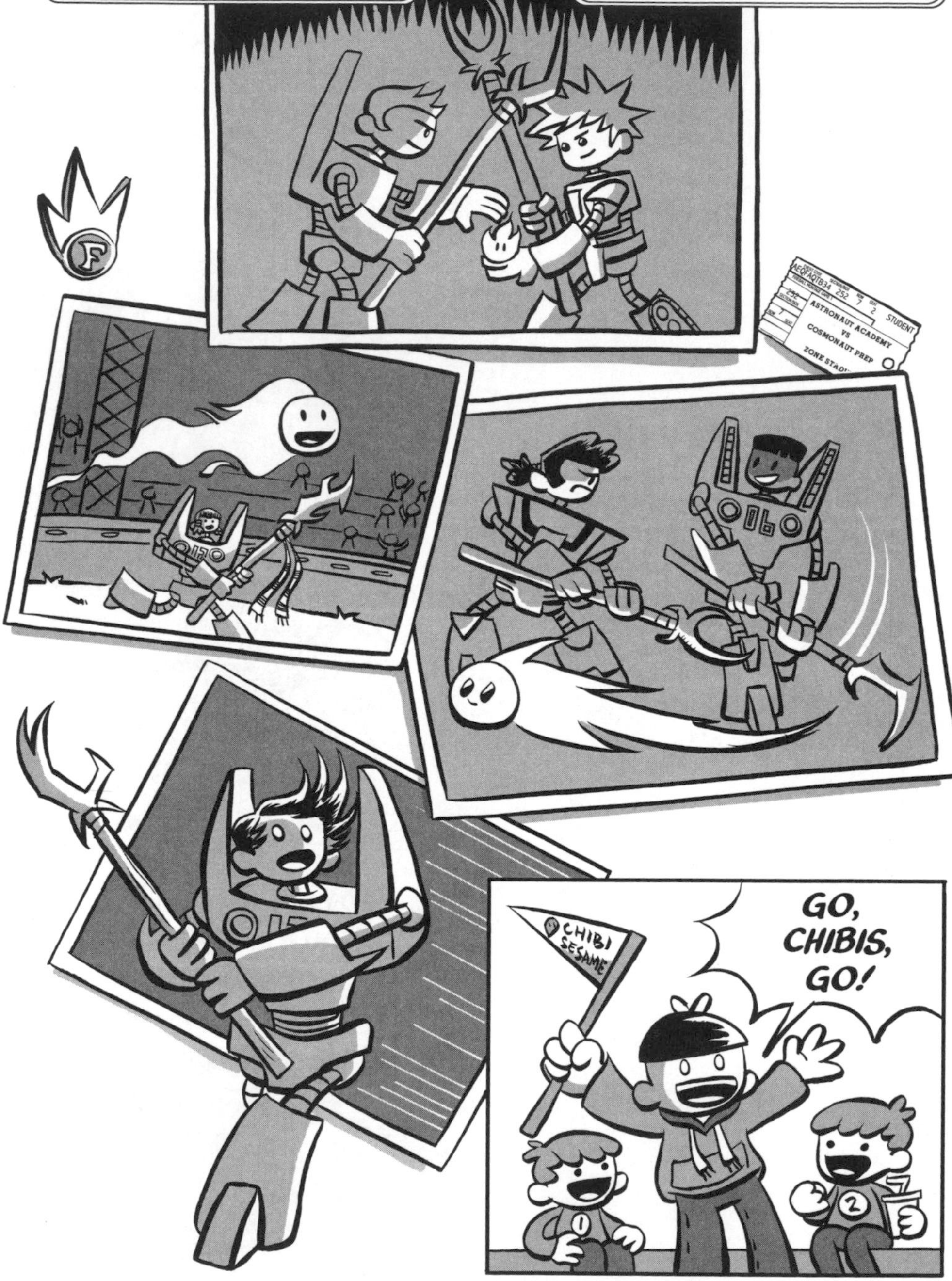
STUDENT
ASTRONAUT ACADEMY
VS
COSMONAUT PREP
CHIBI SESAME
GO, CHIBIS, GO!

GAME TWO

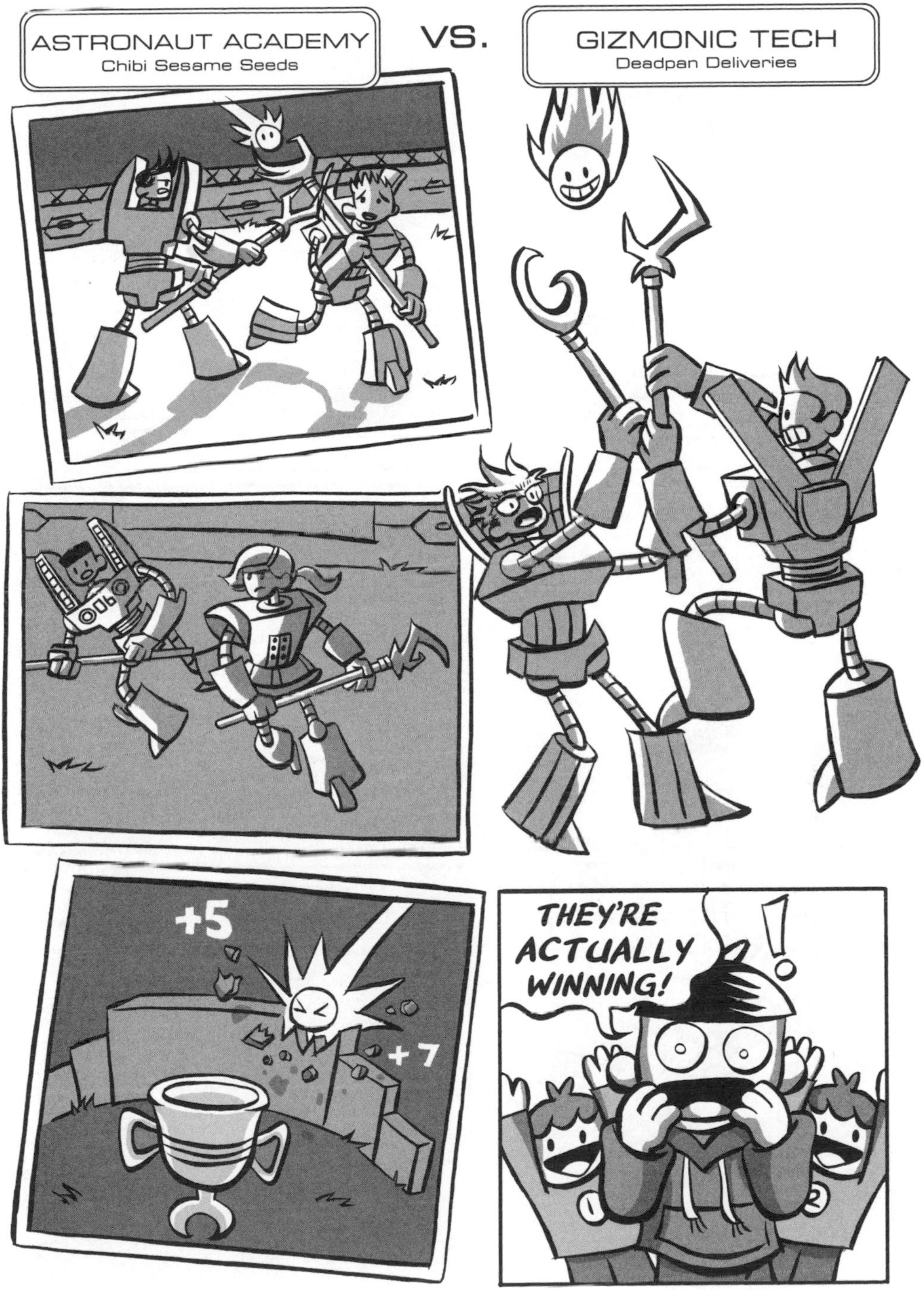
ASTRONAUT ACADEMY
Chibi Sesame Seeds
VS.
GIZMONIC TECH
Deadpan Deliveries
+5
+7
THEY'RE ACTUALLY WINNING!
!

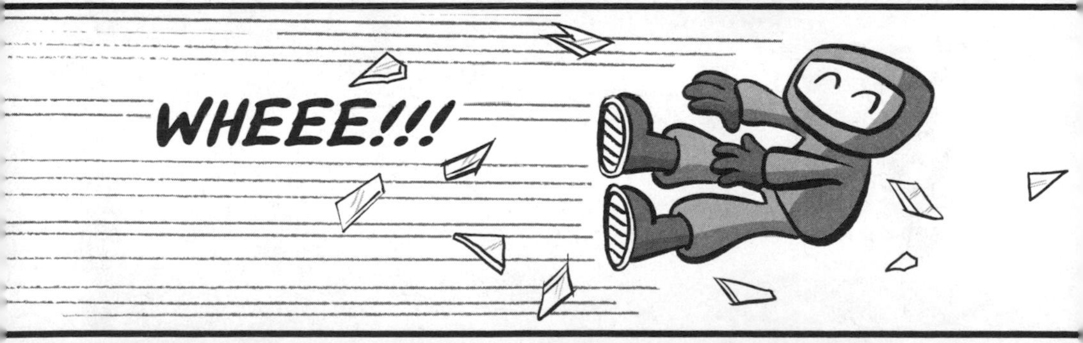
WHEEE!!!

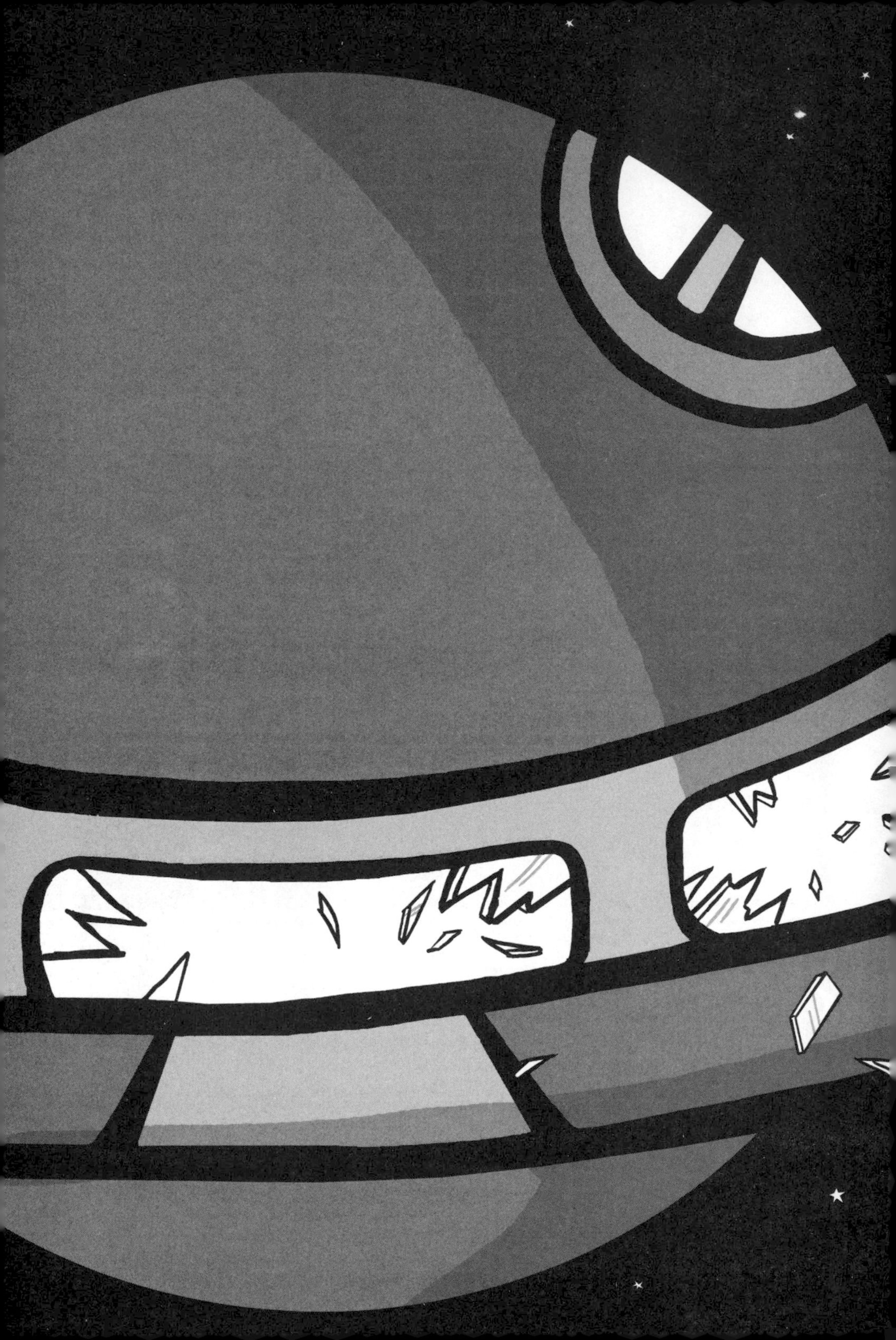

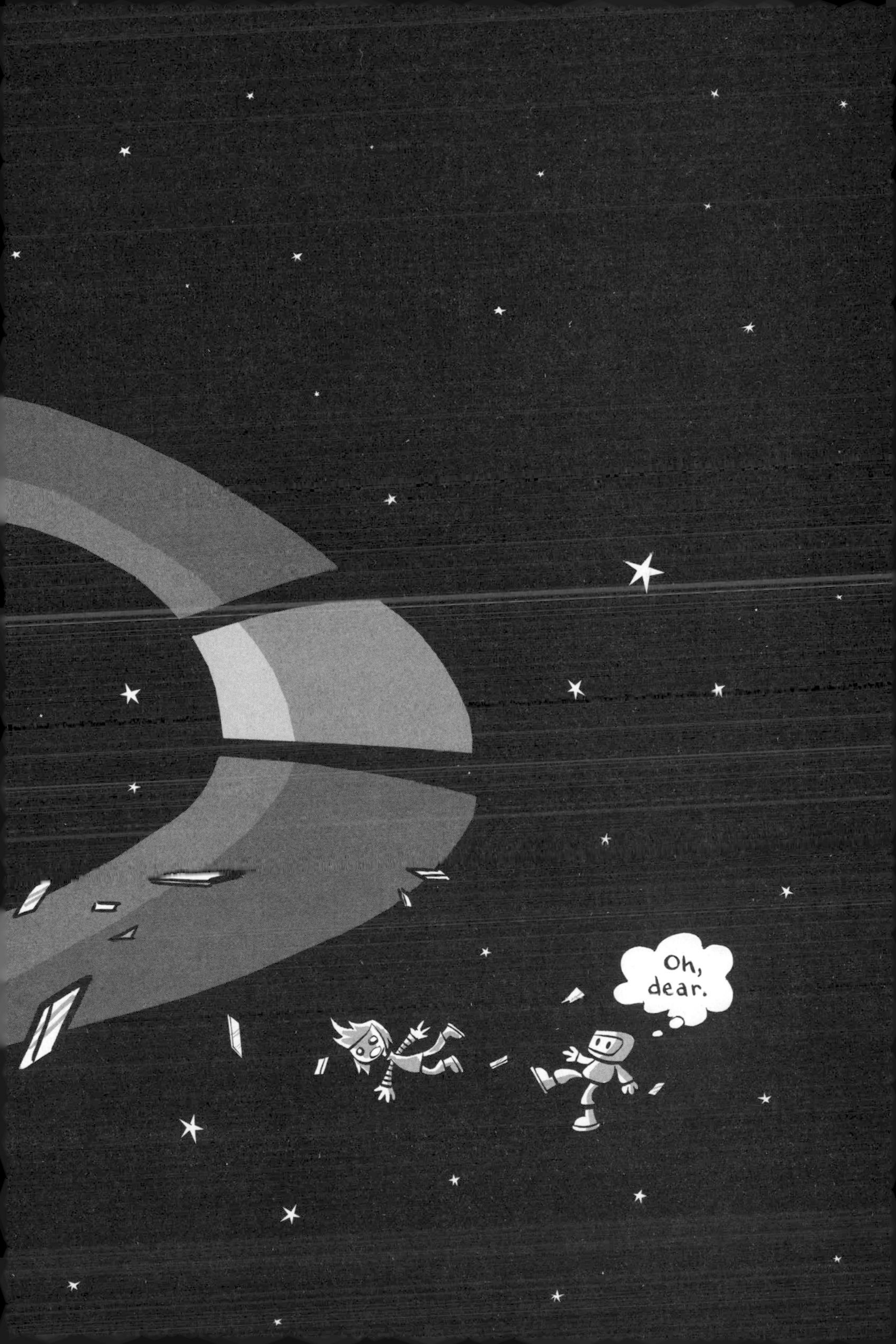
Oh, dear.

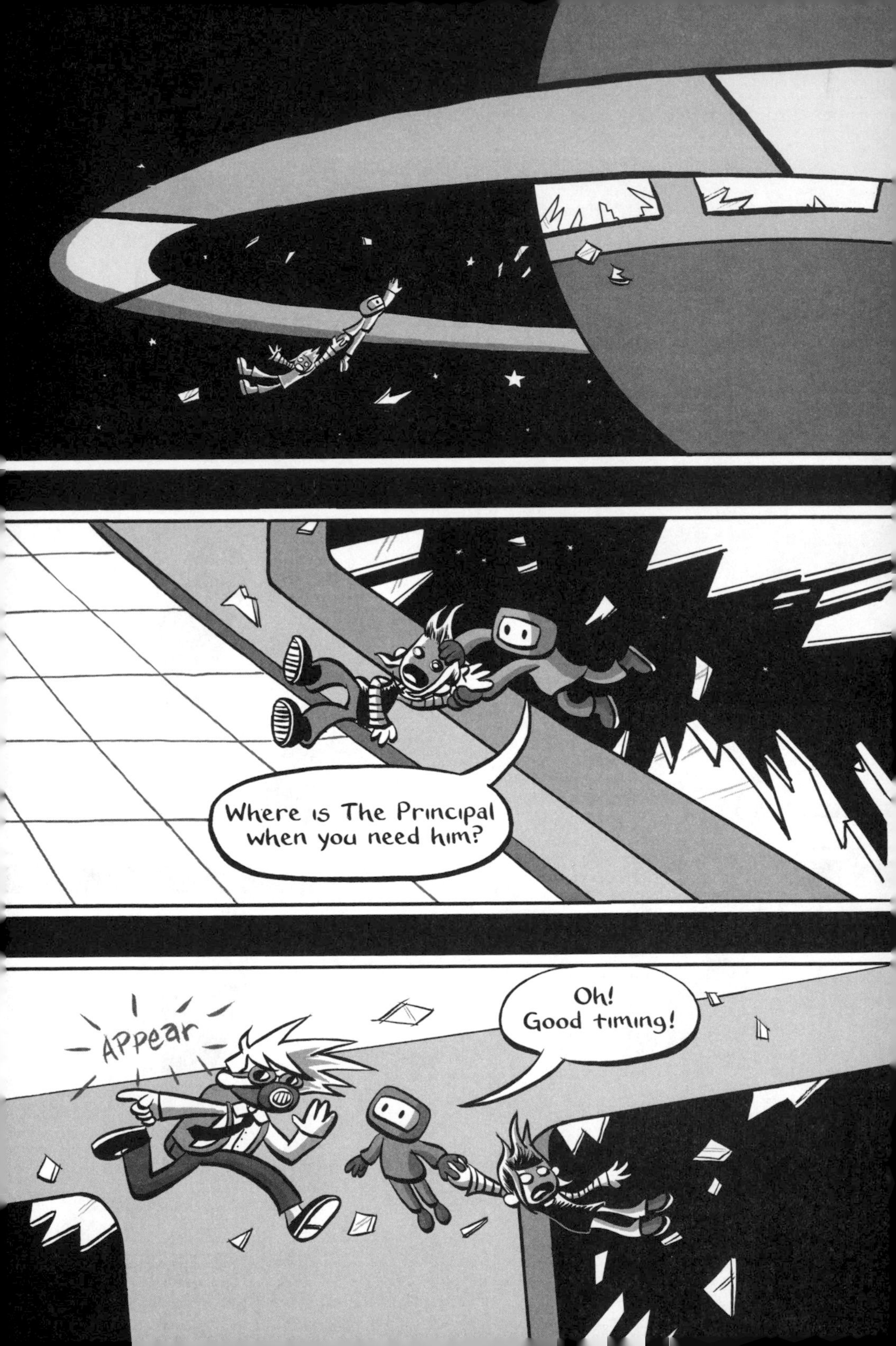

Where is The Principal when you need him?
APPEAR
Oh! Good timing!

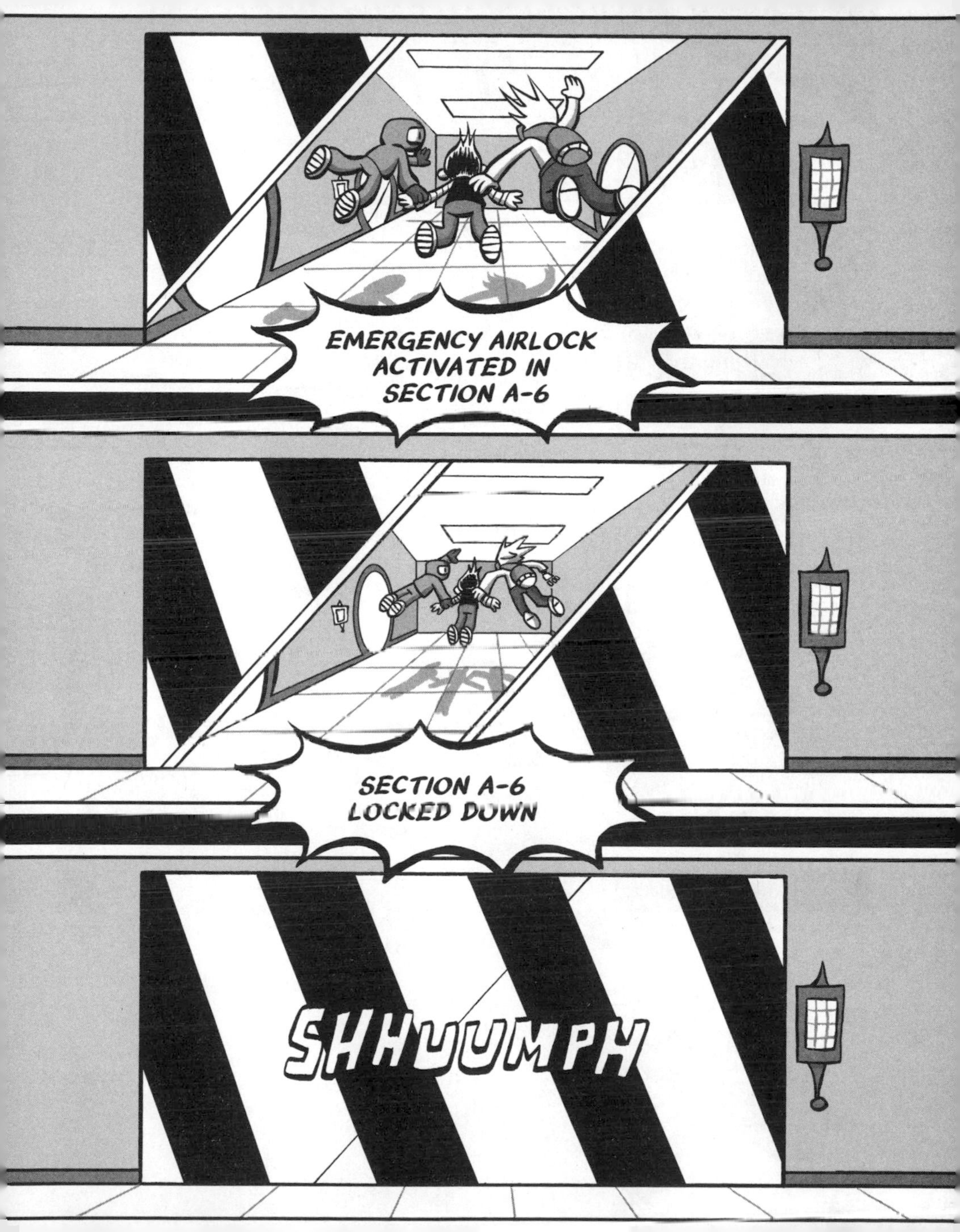
EMERGENCY AIRLOCK ACTIVATED IN SECTION A-6
SECTION A-6 LOCKED DOWN
SHHUUMPH

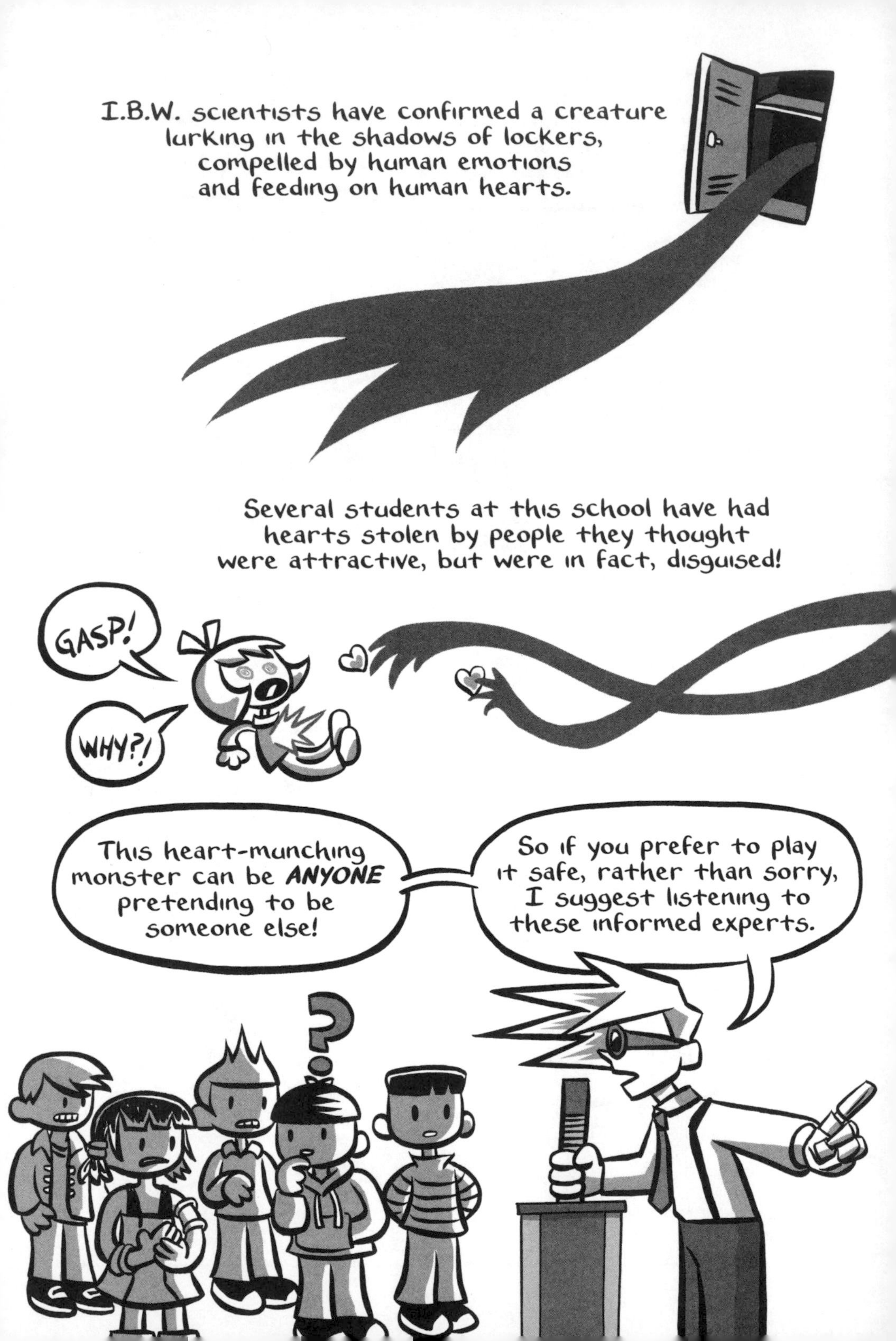
I.B.W. scientists have confirmed a creature lurking in the shadows of lockers, compelled by human emotions and feeding on human hearts.
Several students at this school have had hearts stolen by people they thought were attractive, but were in fact, disguised!
GASP!
WHY?!
This heart-munching monster can be ANYONE pretending to be someone else!
So if you prefer to play it safe, rather than sorry, I suggest listening to these informed experts.
?

¡ADIÓS!

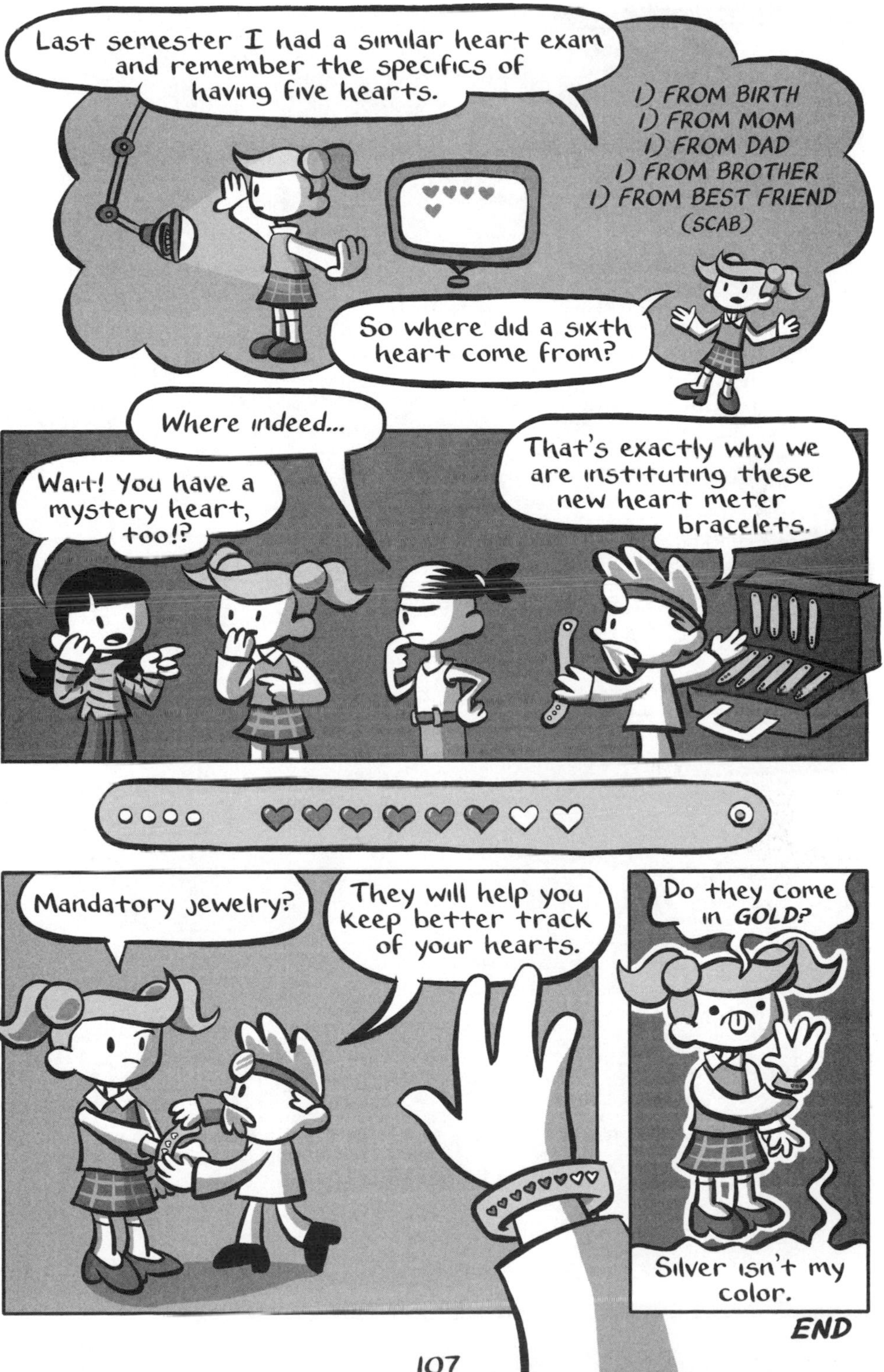
Last semester I had a similar heart exam and remember the specifics of having five hearts.
1) FROM BIRTH
1) FROM MOM
1) FROM DAD
1) FROM BROTHER
1) FROM BEST FRIEND
(SCAB)
So where did a sixth heart come from?
Where indeed...
Wait! You have a mystery heart, too!?
That's exactly why we are instituting these new heart meter bracelets.
Mandatory jewelry?
They will help you keep better track of your hearts.
Do they come in GOLD?
Silver isn't my color.
END

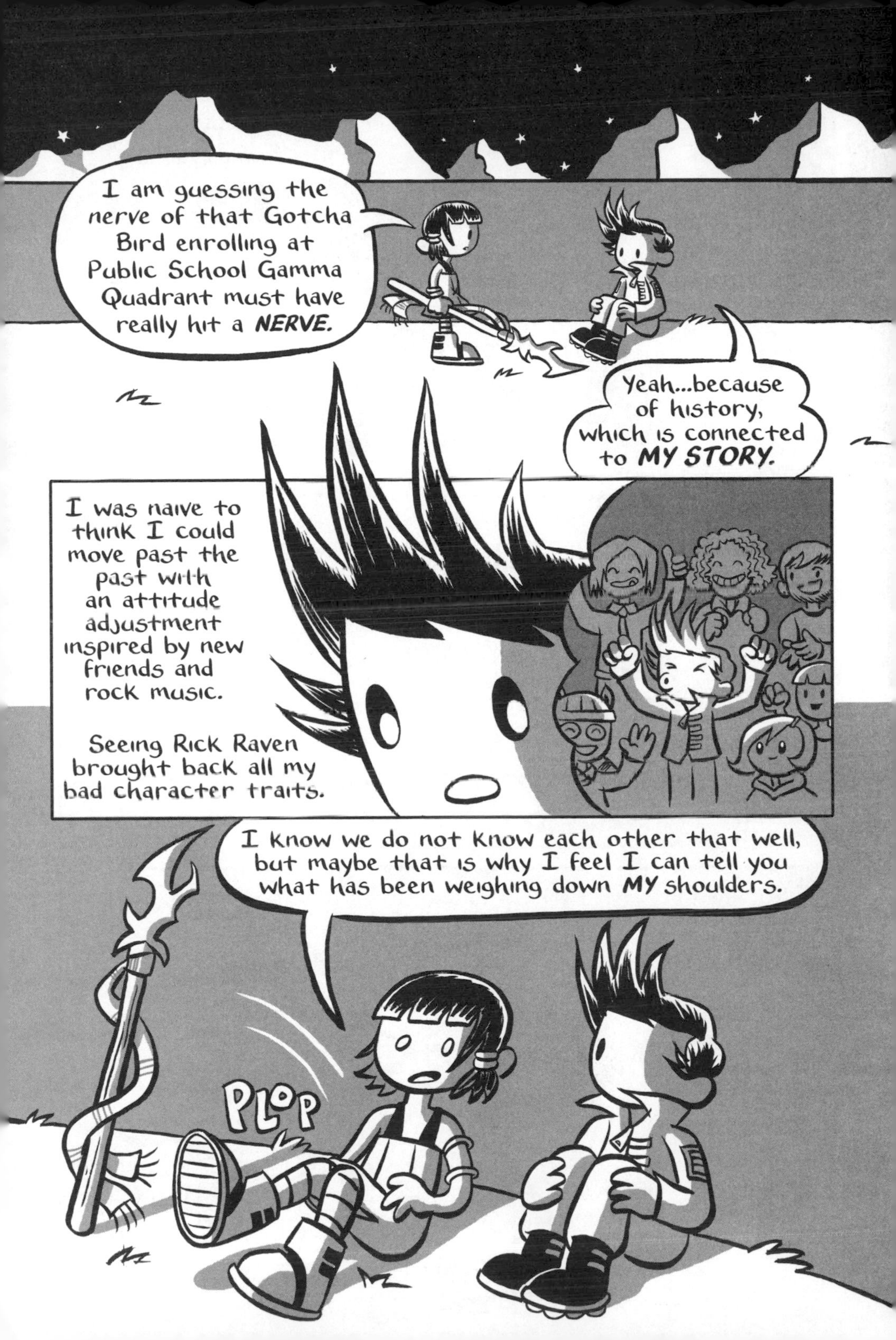
I am guessing the nerve of that Gotcha Bird enrolling at Public School Gamma Quadrant must have really hit a NERVE.
Yeah...because of history, which is connected to MY STORY.
I was naive to think I could move past the past with an attitude adjustment inspired by new friends and rock music.
Seeing Rick Raven brought back all my bad character traits.
I know we do not know each other that well, but maybe that is why I feel I can tell you what has been weighing down MY shoulders.
PLOP

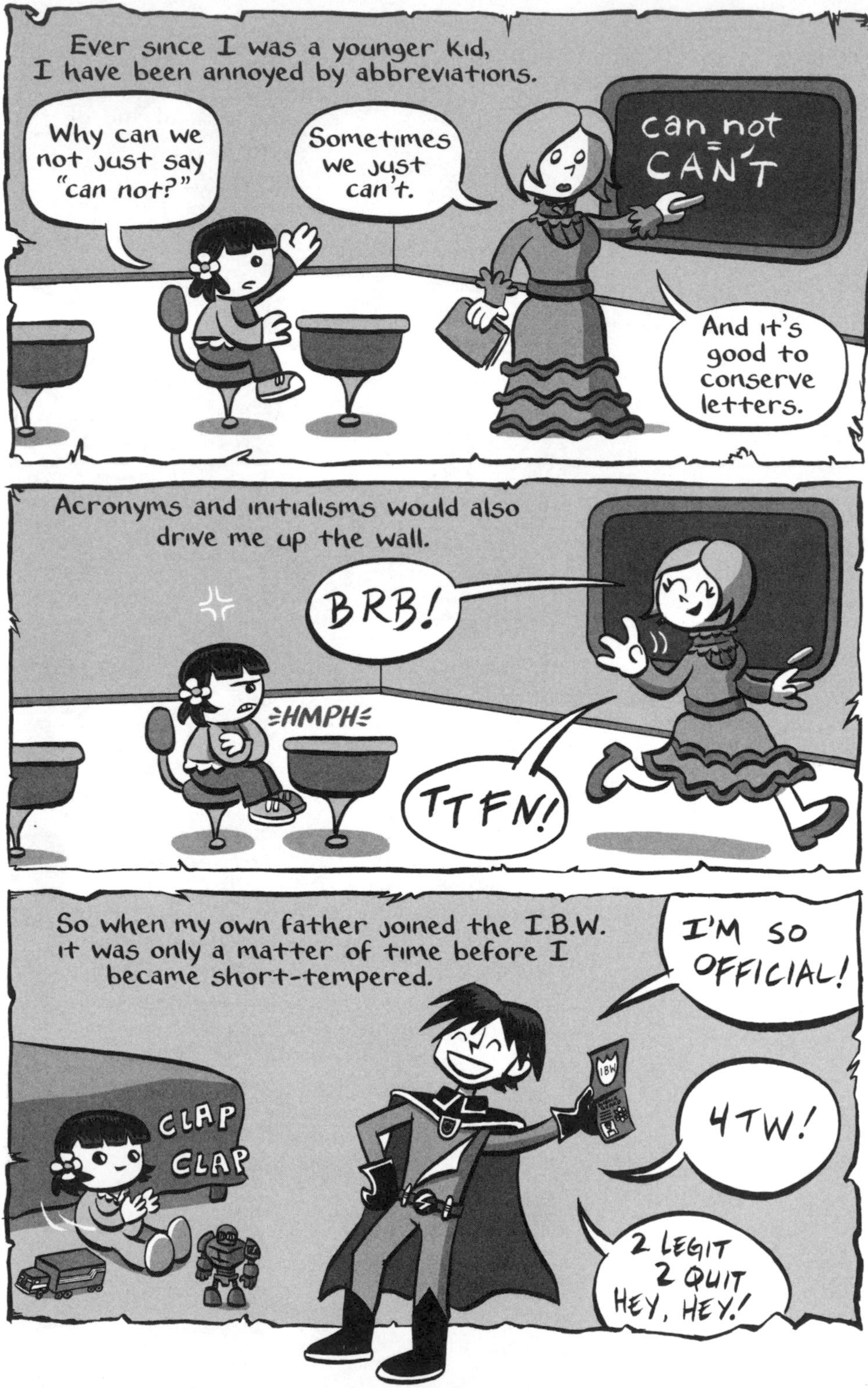
Ever since I was a younger kid, I have been annoyed by abbreviations.
Why can we not just say "can not?"
Sometimes we just can't.
can not = CAN'T
And it's good to conserve letters.
Acronyms and initialisms would also drive me up the wall.
BRB!
HMPH
TTFN!
So when my own father joined the I.B.W. it was only a matter of time before I became short-tempered.
I'M SO OFFICIAL!
IBW
CLAP
CLAP
4TW!
2 LEGIT 2 QUIT HEY, HEY!

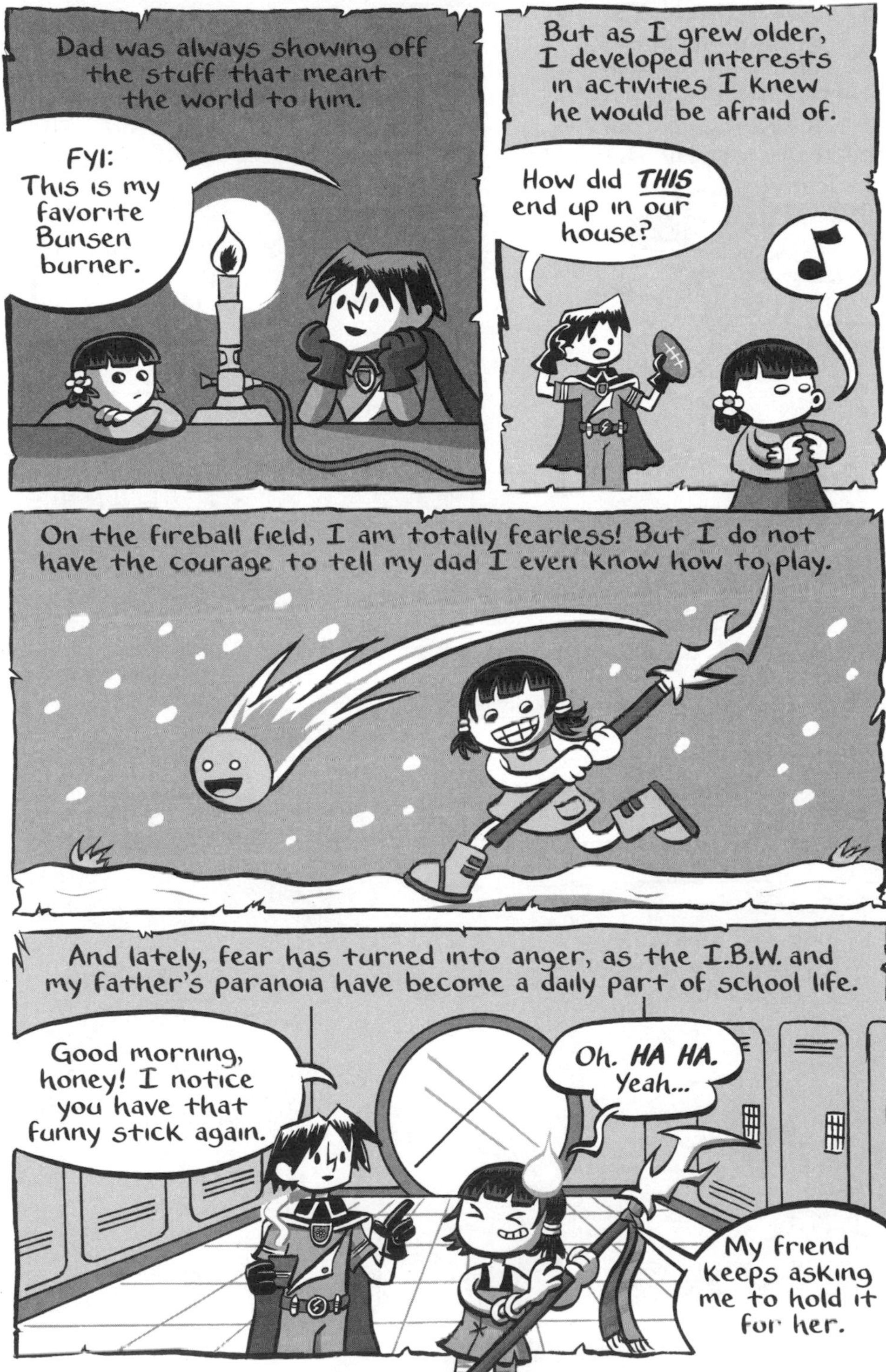
Dad was always showing off the stuff that meant the world to him.
FYI: This is my favorite Bunsen burner.
But as I grew older, I developed interests in activities I knew he would be afraid of.
How did THIS end up in our house?
On the fireball field, I am totally fearless! But I do not have the courage to tell my dad I even know how to play.
And lately, fear has turned into anger, as the I.B.W. and my father's paranoia have become a daily part of school life.
Good morning, honey! I notice you have that funny stick again.
Oh. HA HA. Yeah...
My friend keeps asking me to hold it for her.

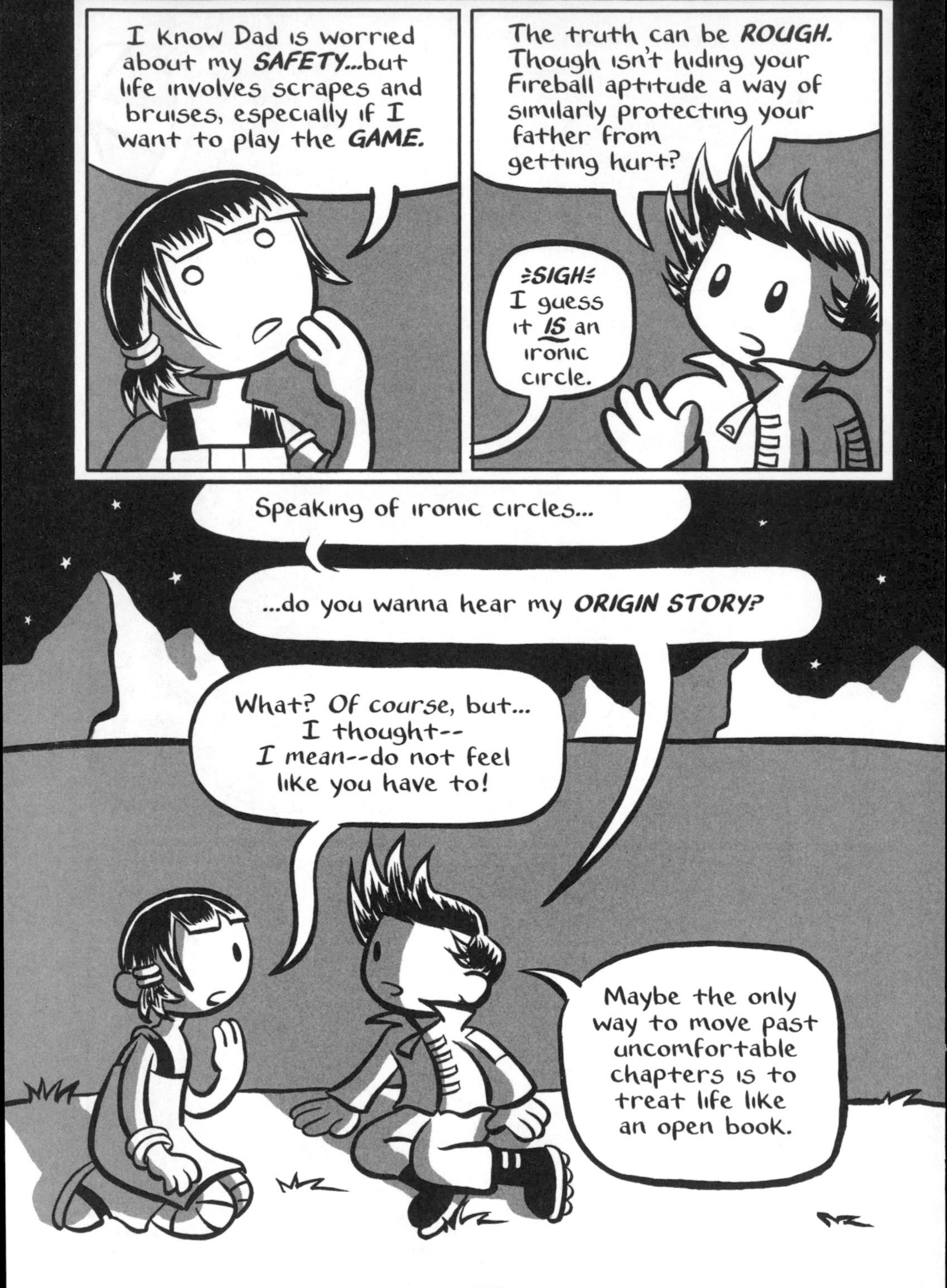
I know Dad is worried about my SAFETY...but life involves scrapes and bruises, especially if I want to play the GAME.
The truth can be ROUGH. Though isn't hiding your Fireball aptitude a way of similarly protecting your father from getting hurt?
SIGH I guess it IS an ironic circle.
Speaking of ironic circles...
...do you wanna hear my ORIGIN STORY?
What? Of course, but... I thought-- I mean--do not feel like you have to!
Maybe the only way to move past uncomfortable chapters is to treat life like an open book.

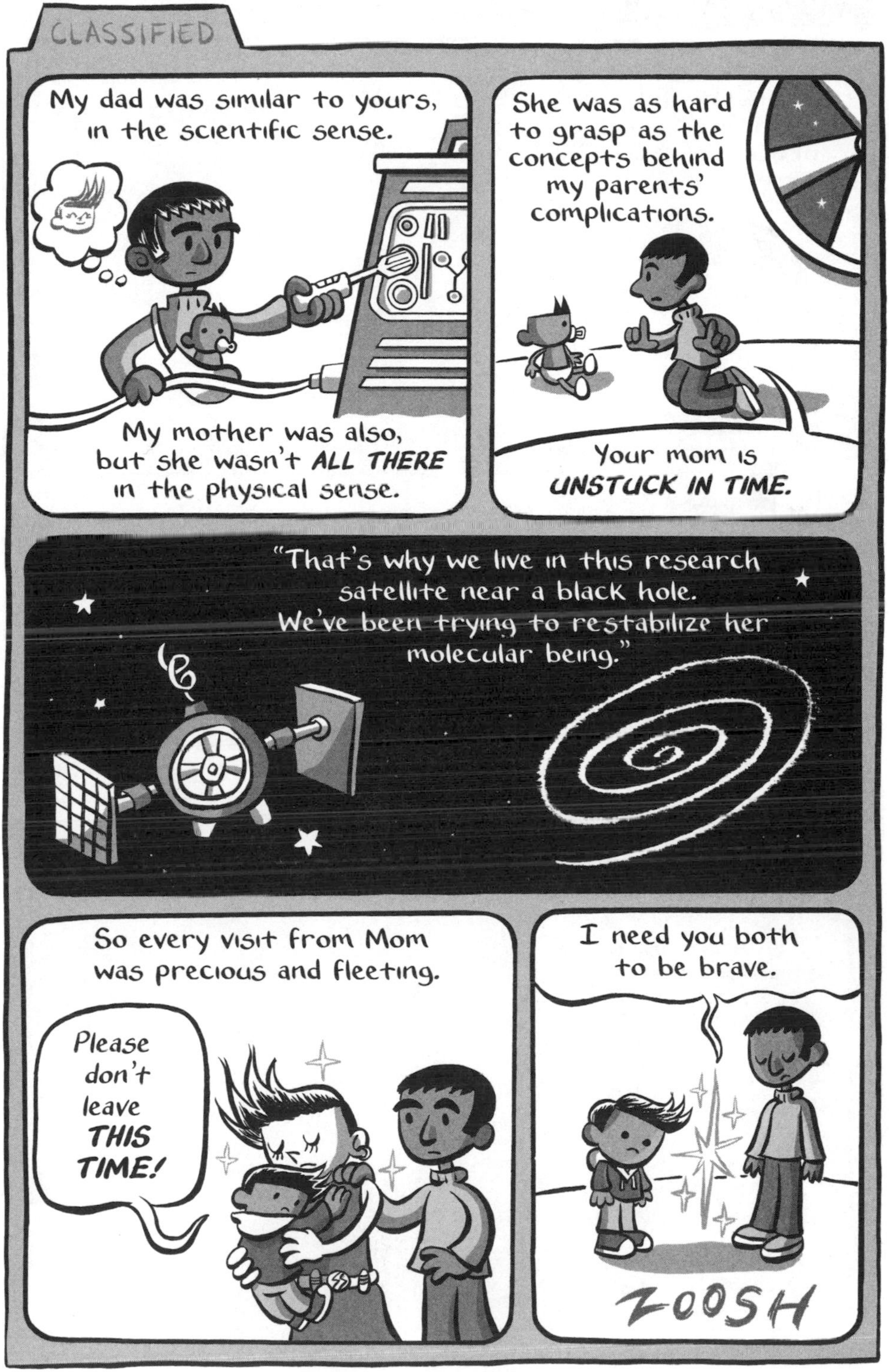
CLASSIFIED
My dad was similar to yours, in the scientific sense.
My mother was also, but she wasn't ALL THERE in the physical sense.
She was as hard to grasp as the concepts behind my parents' complications.
Your mom is UNSTUCK IN TIME.
"That's why we live in this research satellite near a black hole. We've been trying to restabilize her molecular being."
So every visit from Mom was precious and fleeting.
Please don't leave THIS TIME!
I need you both to be brave.
ZOOSH

116

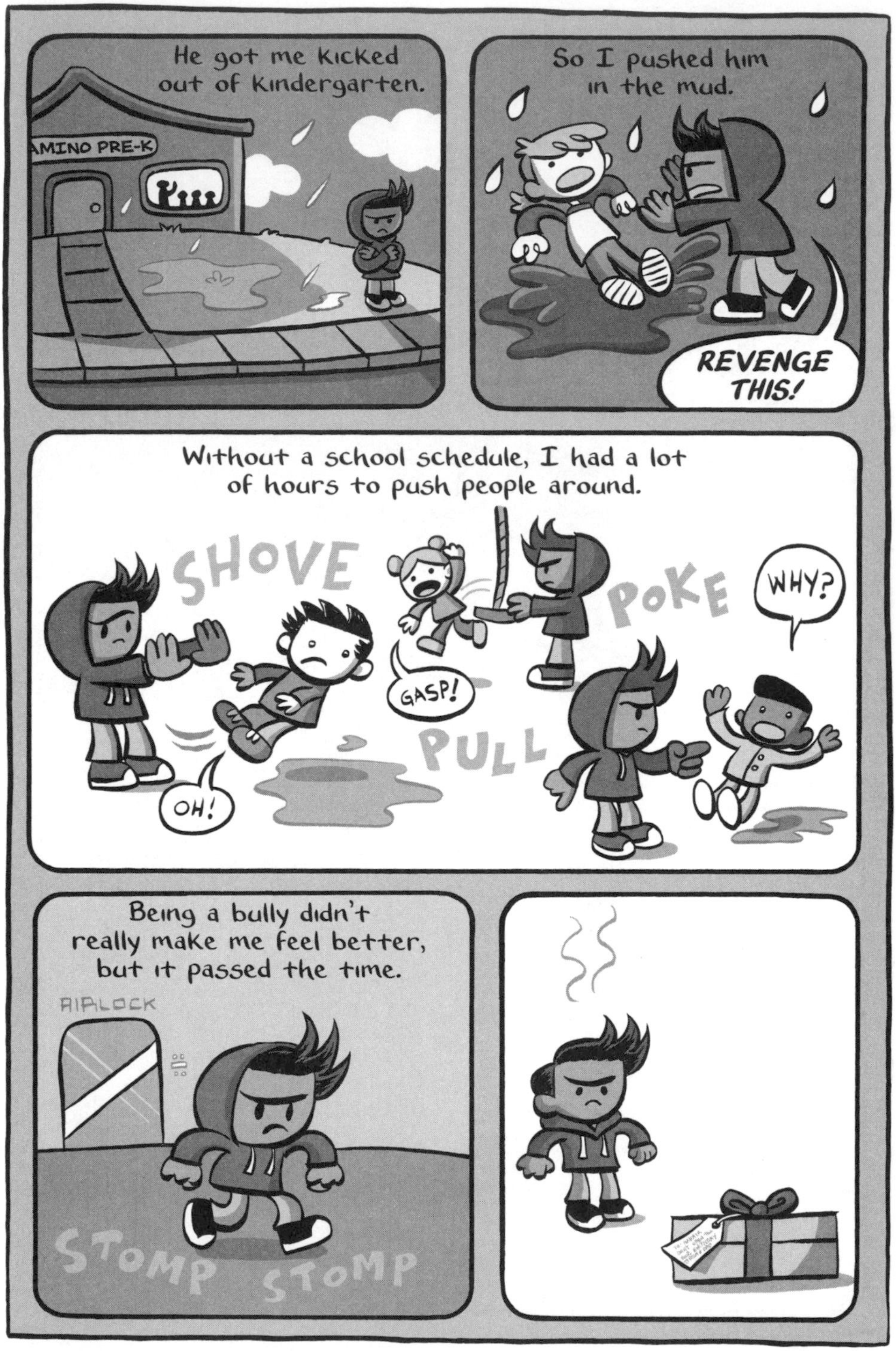
He got me kicked out of kindergarten.
AMINO PRE-K
So I pushed him in the mud.
REVENGE THIS!
Without a school schedule, I had a lot of hours to push people around.
SHOVE
OH!
GASP!
PULL
POKE
WHY?
Being a bully didn't really make me feel better, but it passed the time.
AIRLOCK
STOMP STOMP

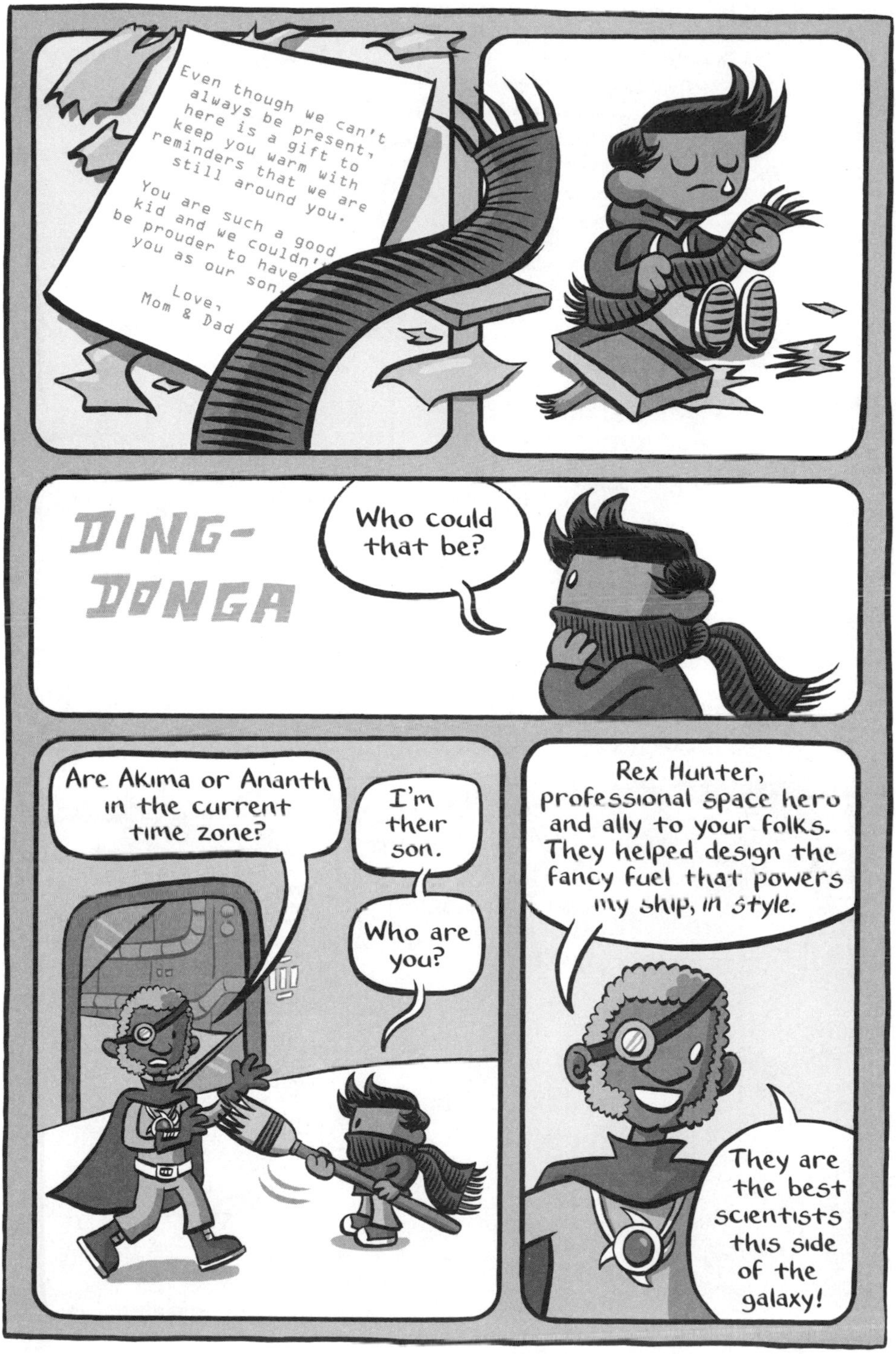
Even though we can't always be present, here is a gift to keep you warm with reminders that we are still around you.
You are such a good kid and we couldn't be prouder to have you as our son.
Love, Mom & Dad
DING-DONGA
Who could that be?
Are Akima or Ananth in the current time zone?
I'm their son.
Who are you?
Rex Hunter, professional space hero and ally to your folks. They helped design the fancy fuel that powers my ship, in style.
They are the best scientists this side of the galaxy!

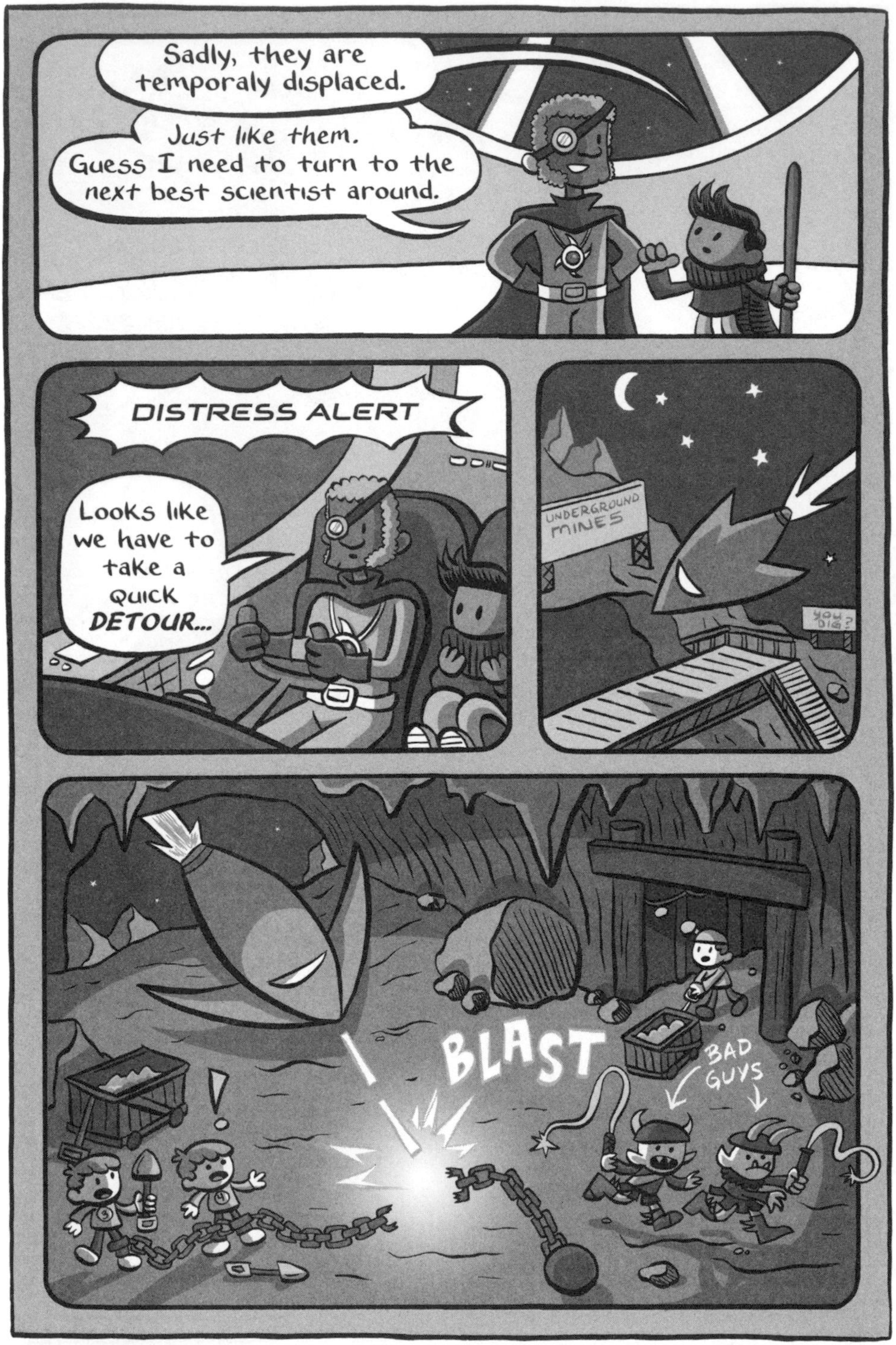
Sadly, they are temporaly displaced.
Just like them. Guess I need to turn to the next best scientist around.
DISTRESS ALERT
Looks like we have to take a quick DETOUR...
UNDERGROUND MINES
YOU DIG?
BLAST
BAD GUYS

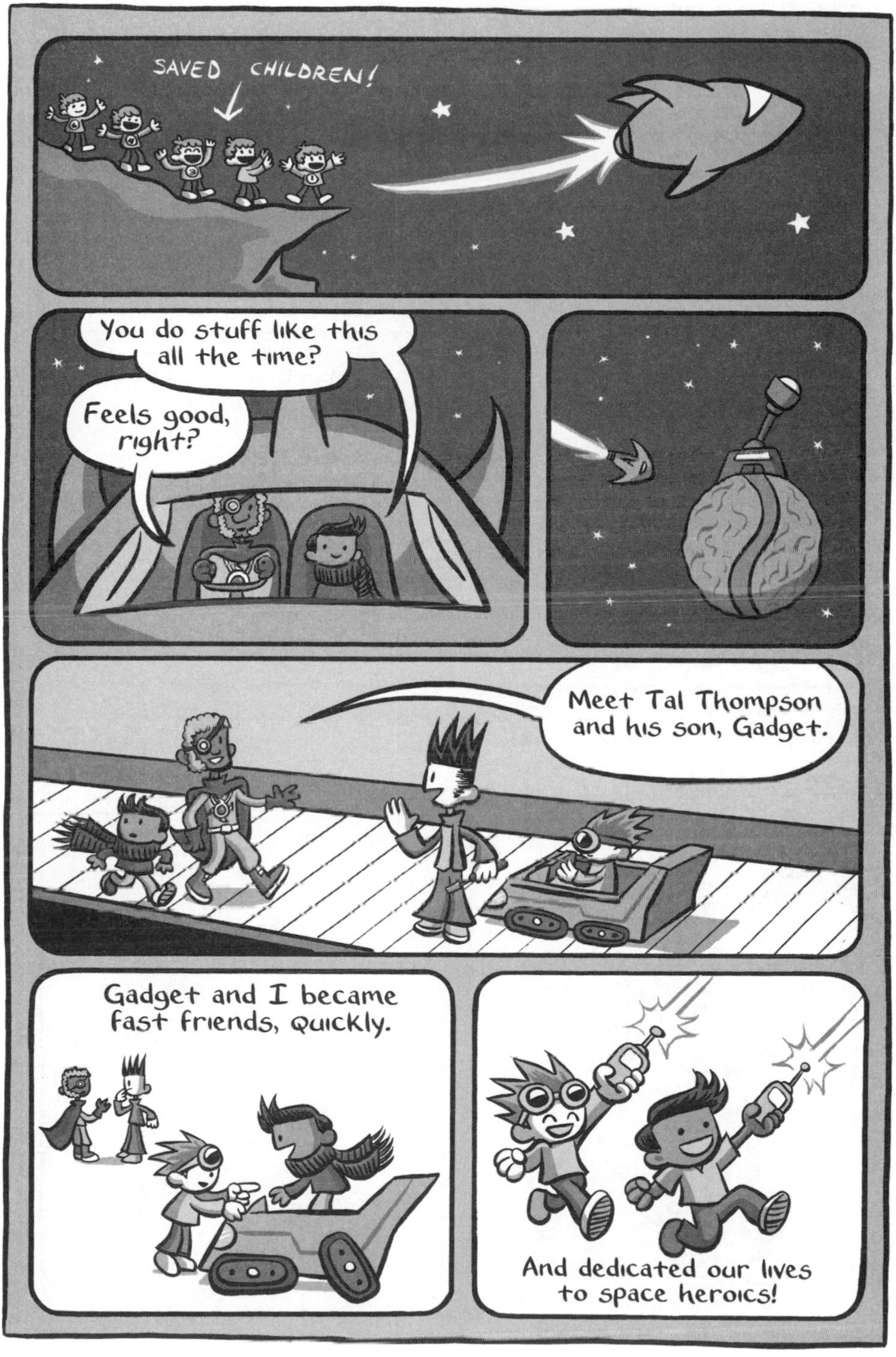
SAVED CHILDREN!
You do stuff like this all the time?
Feels good, right?
Meet Tal Thompson and his son, Gadget.
Gadget and I became fast friends, quickly.
And dedicated our lives to space heroics!

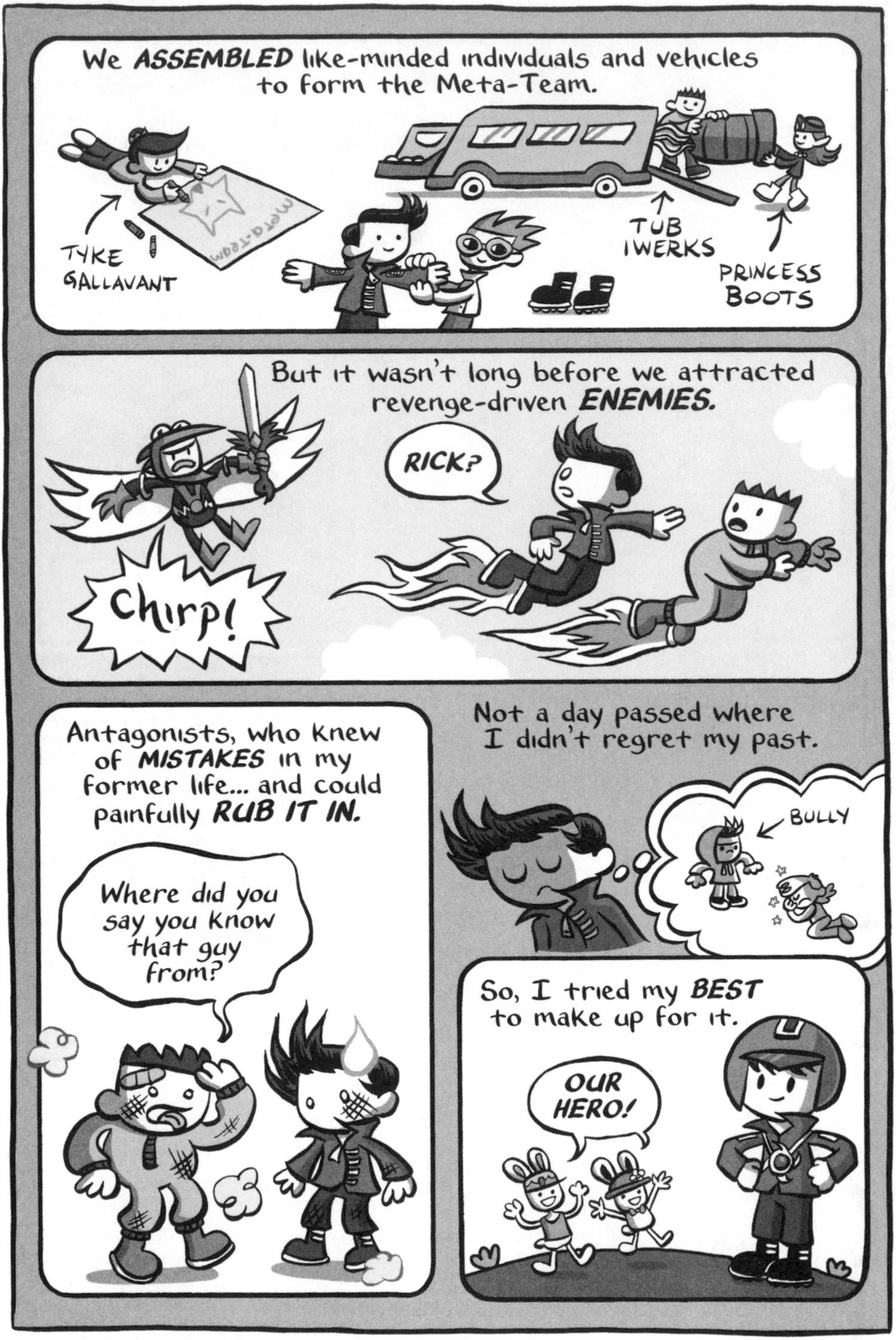

We ASSEMBLED like-minded individuals and vehicles to form the Meta-Team.
TYKE GALLAVANT
META-TEAM
TUB IWERKS
PRINCESS BOOTS
But it wasn't long before we attracted revenge-driven ENEMIES.
RICK?
Chirp!
Antagonists, who knew of MISTAKES in my former life... and could painfully RUB IT IN.
Where did you say you know that guy from?
Not a day passed where I didn't regret my past.
BULLY
So, I tried my BEST to make up for it.
OUR HERO!

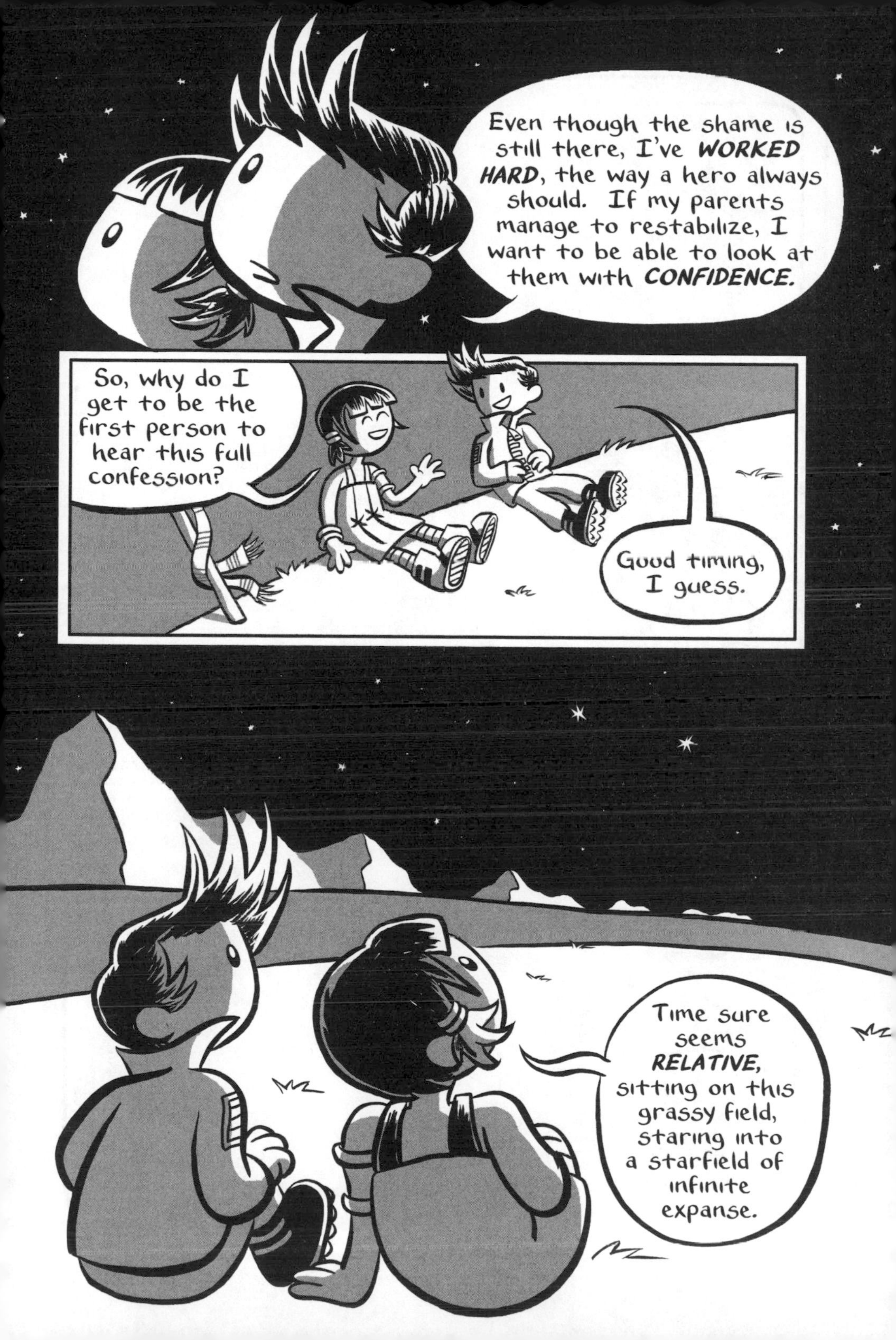
Even though the shame is still there, I've **WORKED HARD**, the way a hero always should. If my parents manage to restabilize, I want to be able to look at them with **CONFIDENCE.**
So, why do I get to be the first person to hear this full confession?
Good timing, I guess.
Time sure seems **RELATIVE,** sitting on this grassy field, staring into a starfield of infinite expanse.

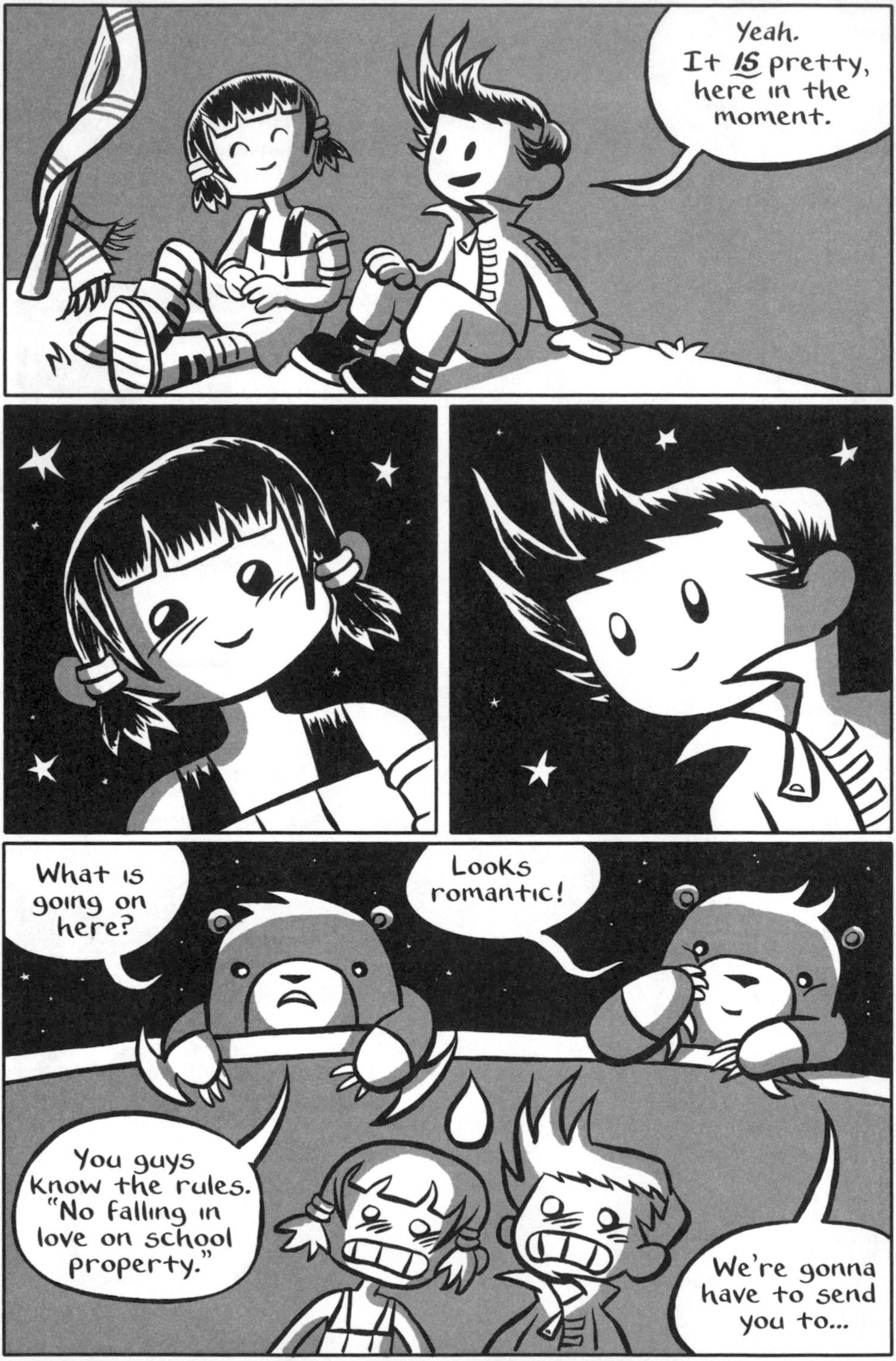
Yeah. It IS pretty, here in the moment.
What is going on here?
Looks romantic!
You guys know the rules. "No falling in love on school property."
We're gonna have to send you to...

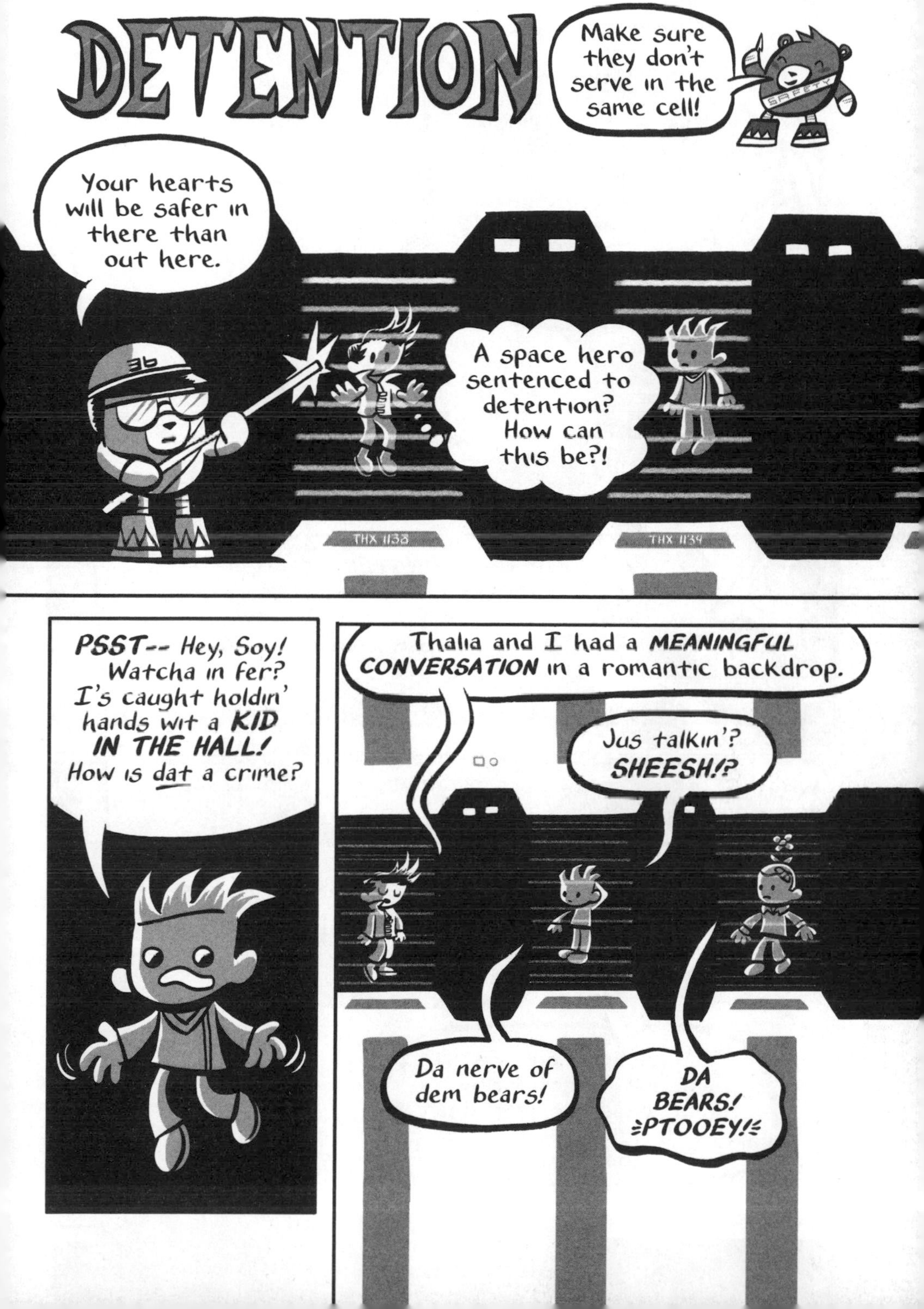
DETENTION
Make sure they don't serve in the same cell!
Your hearts will be safer in there than out here.
A space hero sentenced to detention? How can this be?!
THX 1138
THX 1139
PSST-- Hey, Soy! Watcha in fer? I's caught holdin' hands wit a KID IN THE HALL! How is dat a crime?
Thalia and I had a MEANINGFUL CONVERSATION in a romantic backdrop.
Jus talkin'? SHEESH!?
Da nerve of dem bears!
DA BEARS! PTOOEY!

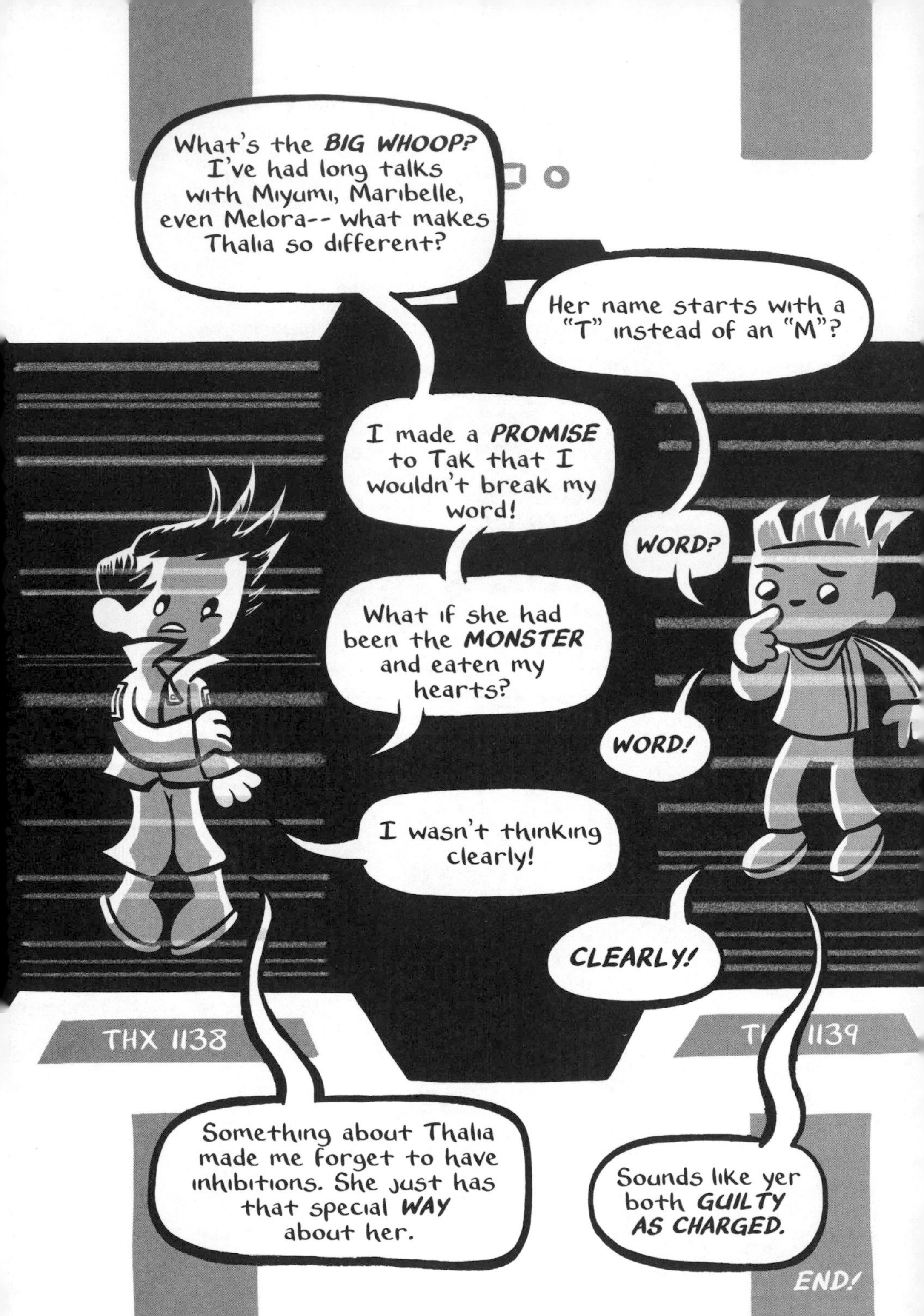
What's the **BIG WHOOP?** I've had long talks with Miyumi, Maribelle, even Melora-- what makes Thalia so different?
Her name starts with a "T" instead of an "M"?
I made a **PROMISE** to Tak that I wouldn't break my word!
WORD?
What if she had been the **MONSTER** and eaten my hearts?
WORD!
I wasn't thinking clearly!
CLEARLY!
THX 1138
Something about Thalia made me forget to have inhibitions. She just has that special **WAY** about her.
Sounds like yer both **GUILTY AS CHARGED.**
END!

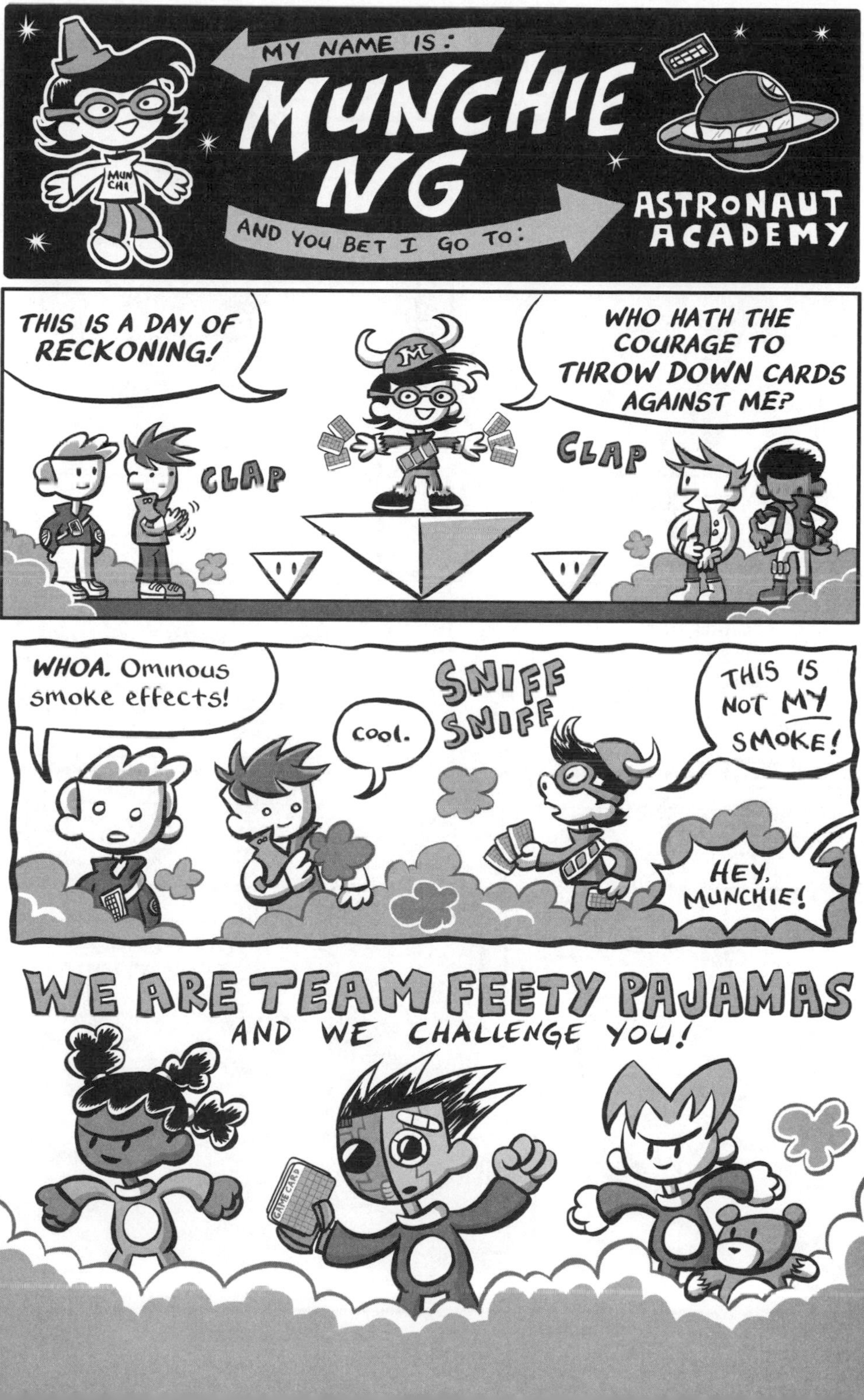
MY NAME IS:
MUNCHIE NG
AND YOU BET I GO TO:
ASTRONAUT ACADEMY
MUN CHI
THIS IS A DAY OF RECKONING!
WHO HATH THE COURAGE TO THROW DOWN CARDS AGAINST ME?
CLAP
CLAP
WHOA. Ominous smoke effects!
cool.
SNIFF SNIFF
THIS IS NOT MY SMOKE!
HEY, MUNCHIE!
WE ARE TEAM FEETY PAJAMAS
AND WE CHALLENGE YOU!
GAME CARD

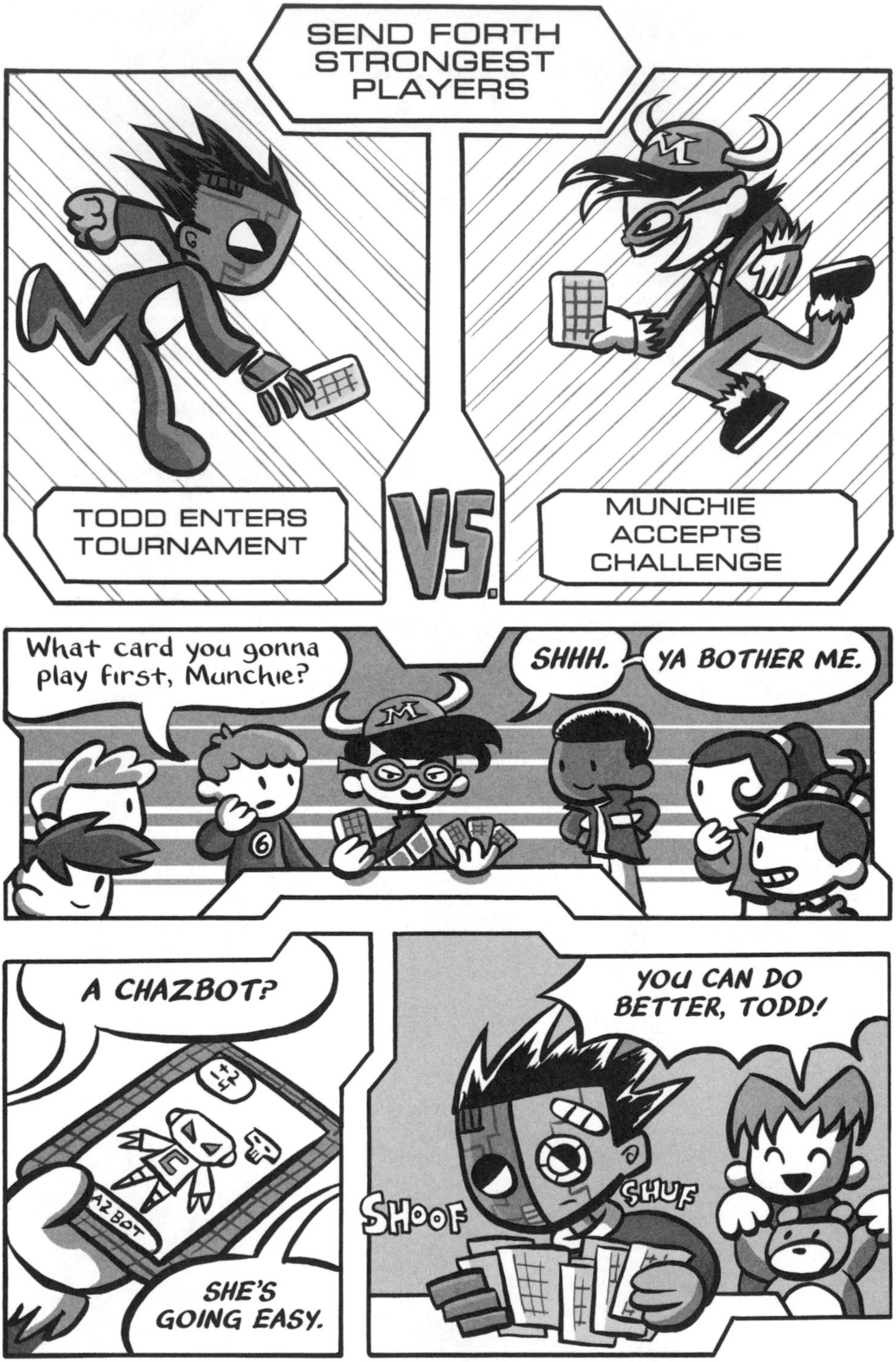
SEND FORTH STRONGEST PLAYERS
TODD ENTERS TOURNAMENT
VS.
MUNCHIE ACCEPTS CHALLENGE
What card you gonna play first, Munchie?
SHHH.
YA BOTHER ME.
A CHAZBOT?
SHE'S GOING EASY.
YOU CAN DO BETTER, TODD!
SHOOF
SHUF

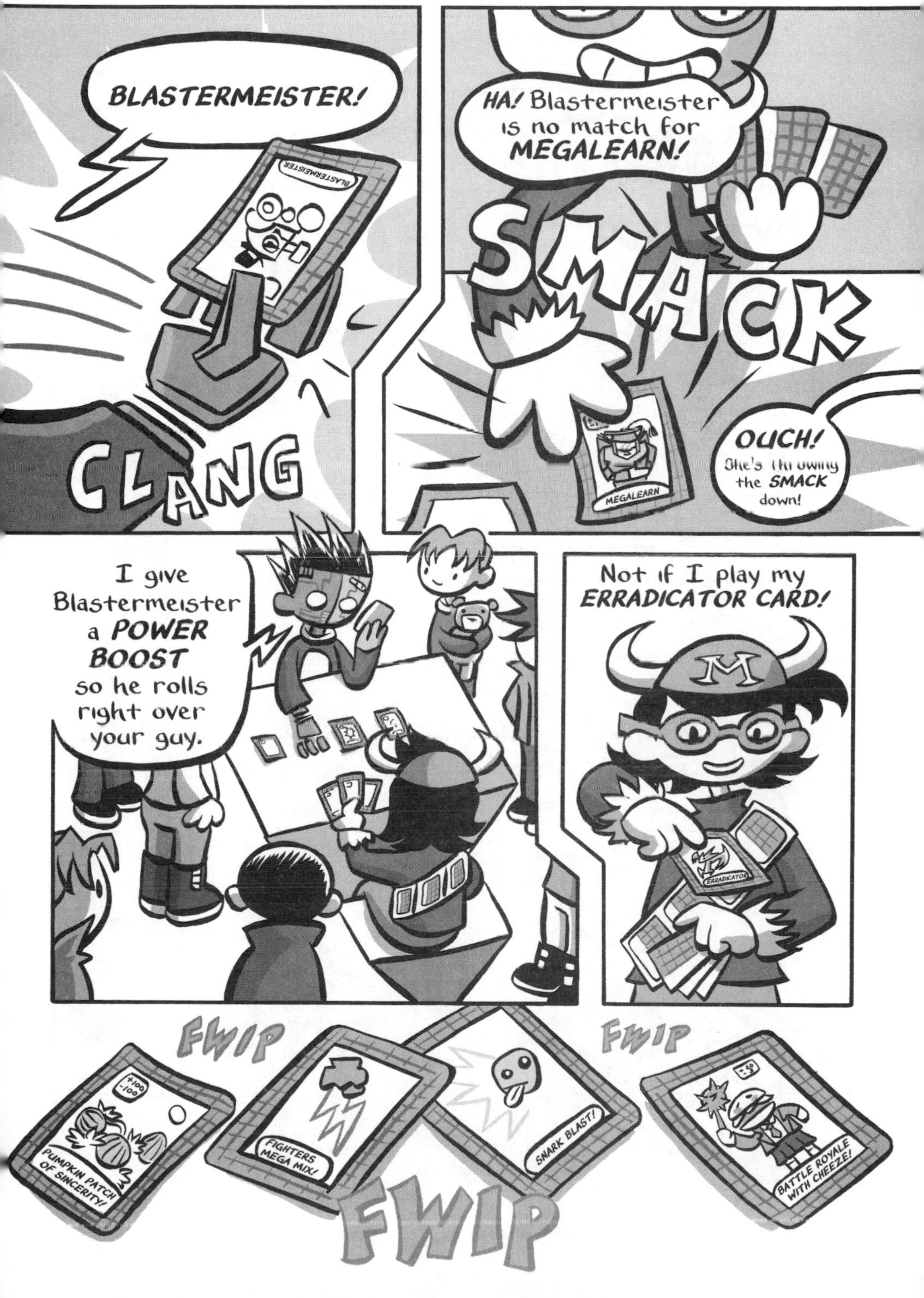
BLASTERMEISTER!
BLASTERMEISTER
CLANG
HA! Blastermeister is no match for MEGALEARN!
SMACK
MEGALEARN
OUCH! She's throwing the SMACK down!
I give Blastermeister a POWER BOOST so he rolls right over your guy.
Not if I play my ERRADICATOR CARD!
ERRADICATOR
FWIP
FWIP
+100 -100
PUMPKIN PATCH OF SINCERITY!
FIGHTERS MEGA MIX!
SNARK BLAST!
BATTLE ROYALE WITH CHEEZE!
FWIP

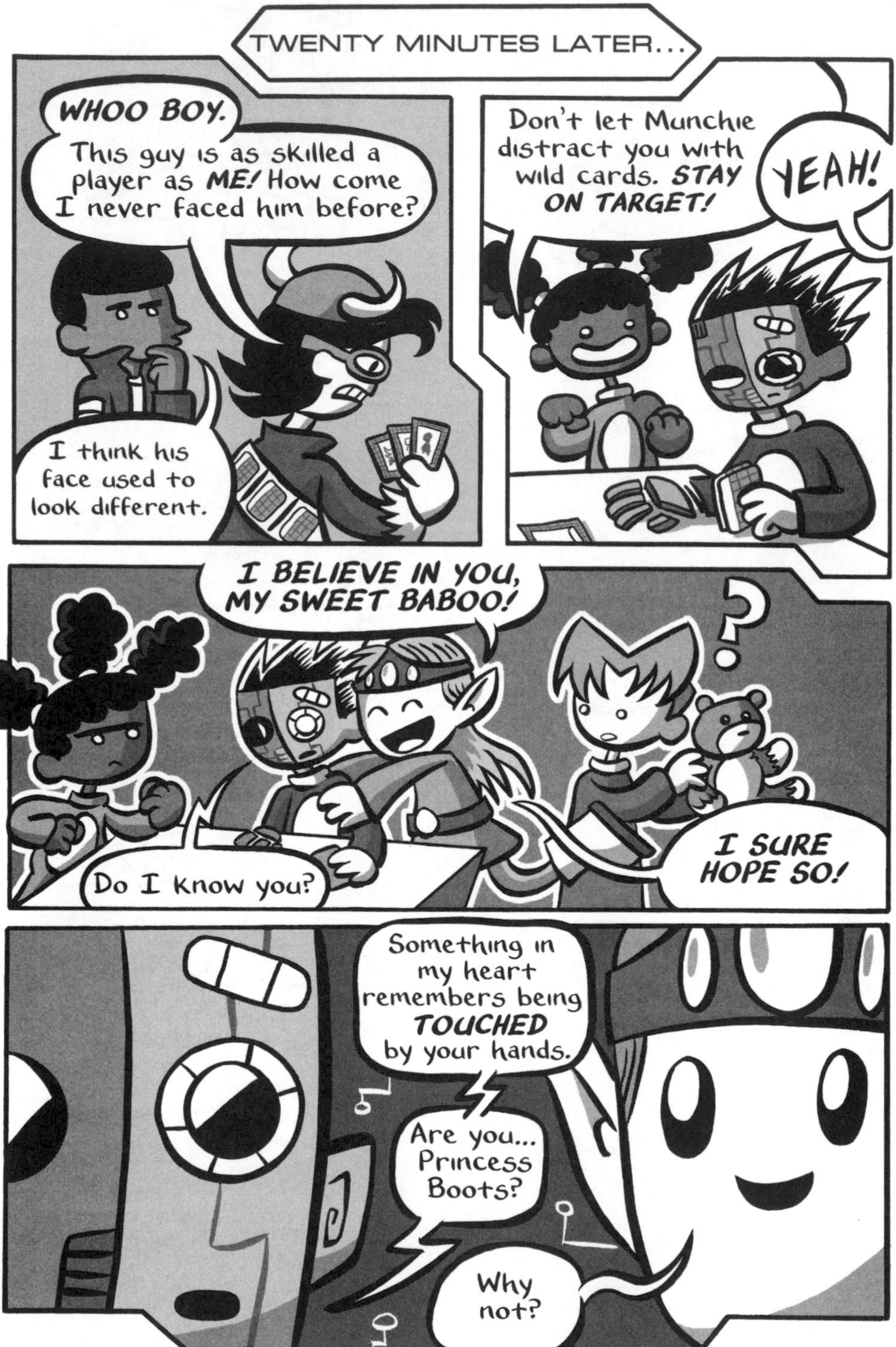
TWENTY MINUTES LATER...
WHOO BOY.
This guy is as skilled a player as ME! How come I never faced him before?
I think his face used to look different.
Don't let Munchie distract you with wild cards. STAY ON TARGET!
YEAH!
I BELIEVE IN YOU, MY SWEET BABOO!
?
Do I know you?
I SURE HOPE SO!
Something in my heart remembers being TOUCHED by your hands.
Are you... Princess Boots?
Why not?

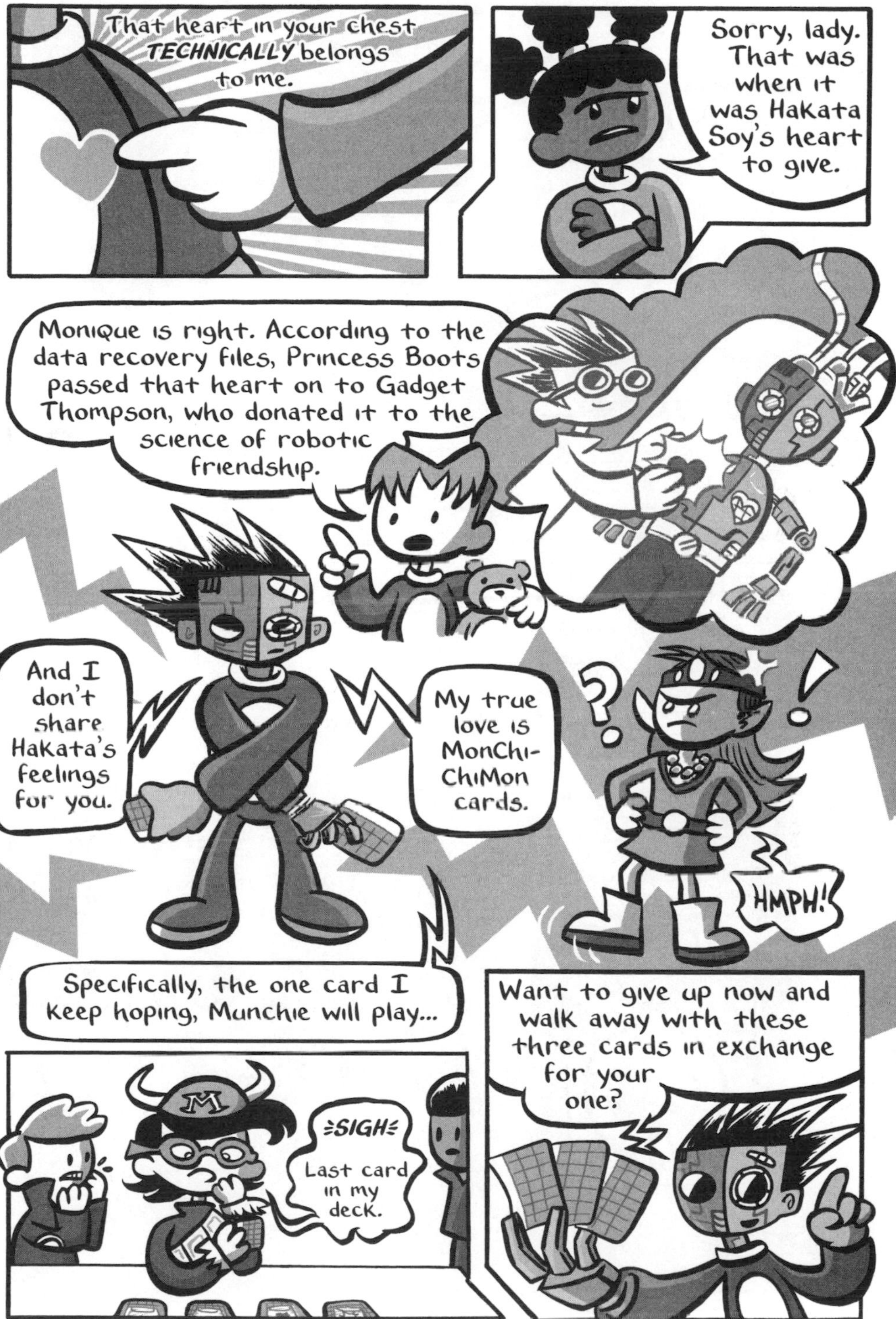
That heart in your chest TECHNICALLY belongs to me.
Sorry, lady. That was when it was Hakata Soy's heart to give.
Monique is right. According to the data recovery files, Princess Boots passed that heart on to Gadget Thompson, who donated it to the science of robotic friendship.
And I don't share Hakata's feelings for you.
My true love is MonChi-ChiMon cards.
HMPH!
Specifically, the one card I keep hoping, Munchie will play...
Want to give up now and walk away with these three cards in exchange for your one?
SIGH
Last card in my deck.

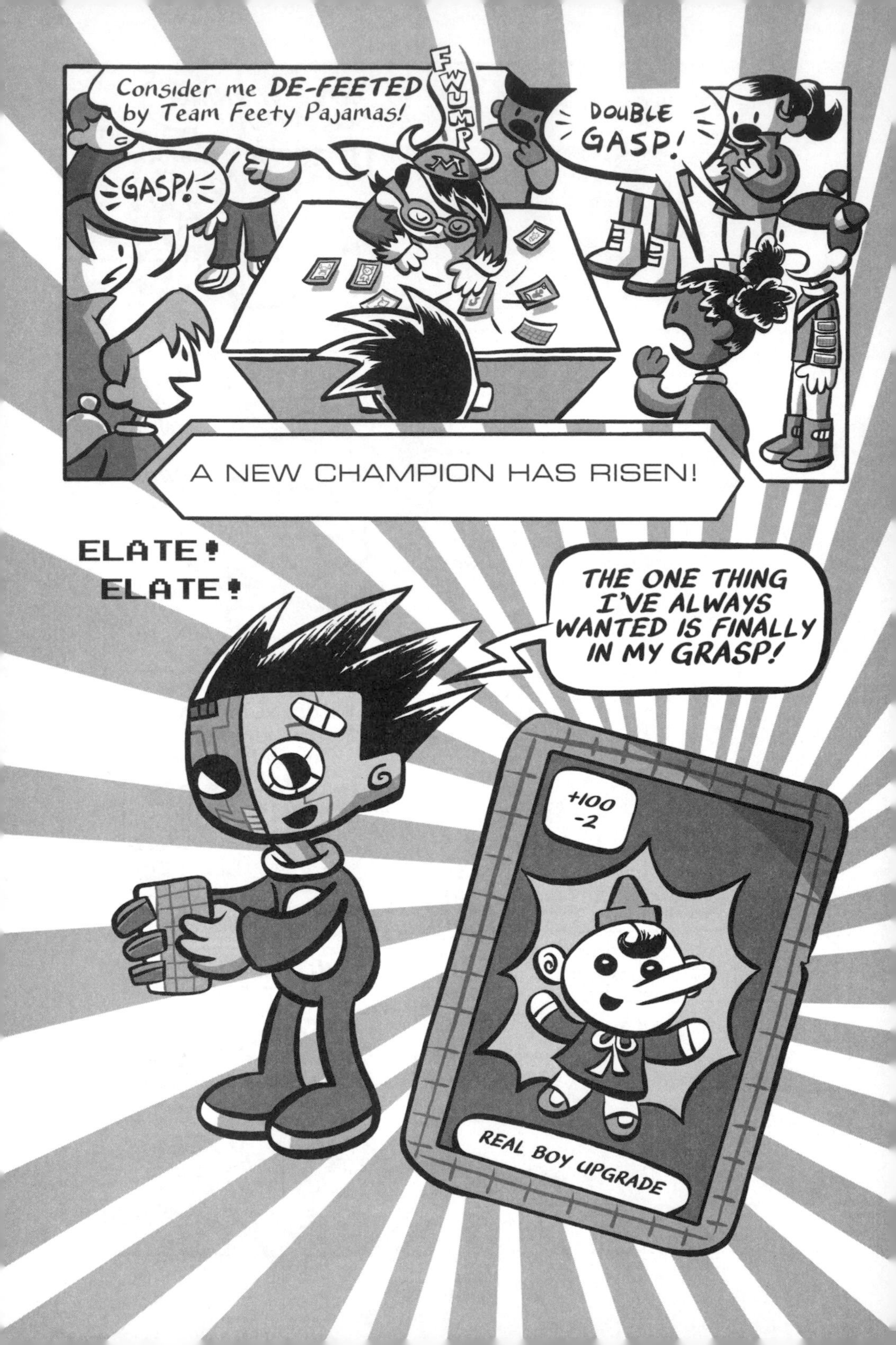
Consider me DE-FEETED by Team Feety Pajamas!
FWUMP
GASP!
DOUBLE GASP!
A NEW CHAMPION HAS RISEN!
ELATE! ELATE!
THE ONE THING I'VE ALWAYS WANTED IS FINALLY IN MY GRASP!
+100 -2
REAL BOY UPGRADE

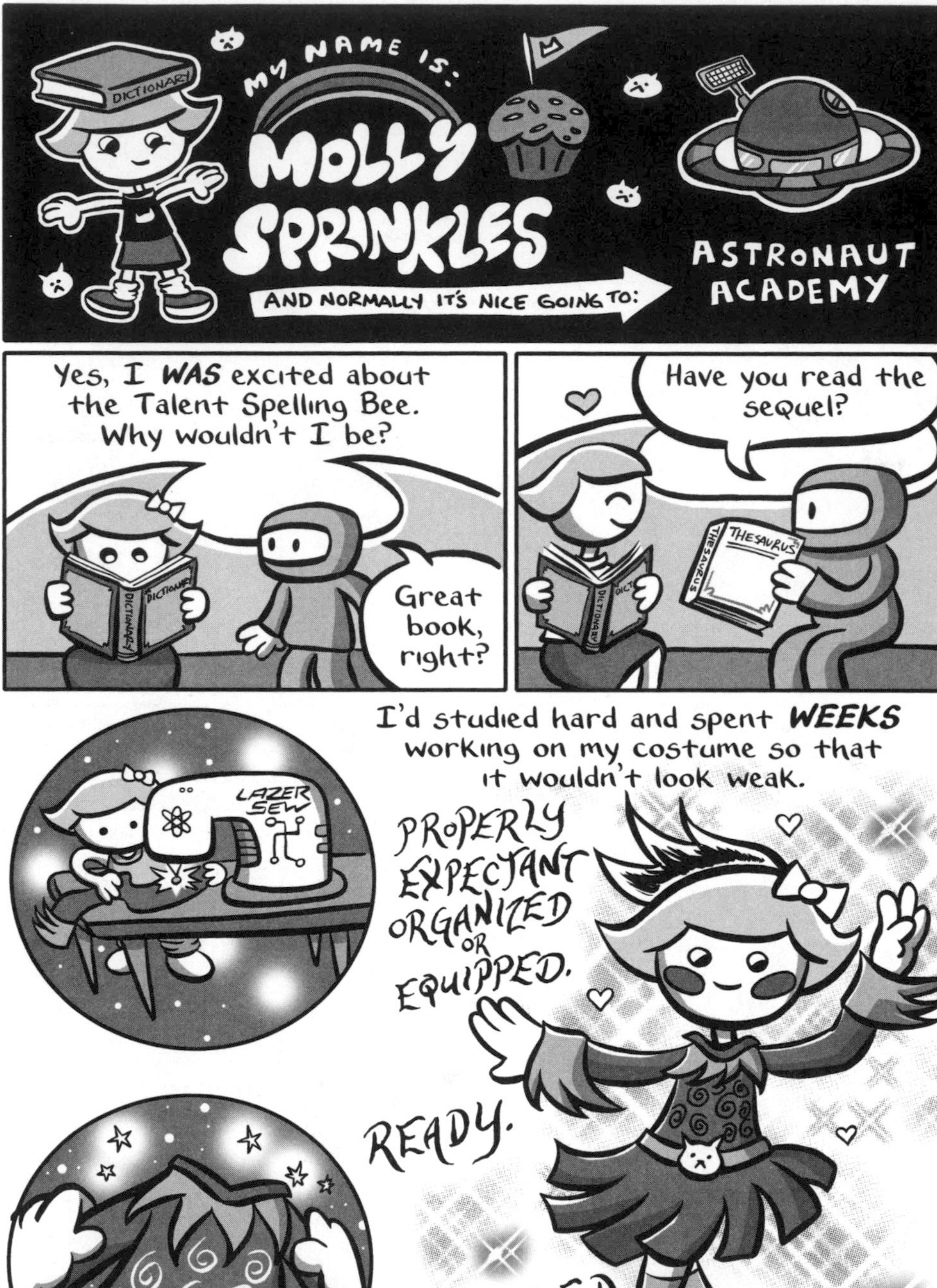
DICTIONARY
MY NAME IS:
MOLLY SPRINKLES
AND NORMALLY IT'S NICE GOING TO:
ASTRONAUT ACADEMY
Yes, I WAS excited about the Talent Spelling Bee. Why wouldn't I be?
DICTIONARY
Great book, right?
Have you read the sequel?
THESAURUS
DICTIONARY
I'd studied hard and spent WEEKS working on my costume so that it wouldn't look weak.
LAZER SEW
PROPERLY
EXPECTANT
ORGANIZED
OR
EQUIPPED.
READY.
P-R-E-P-A-R-E-D

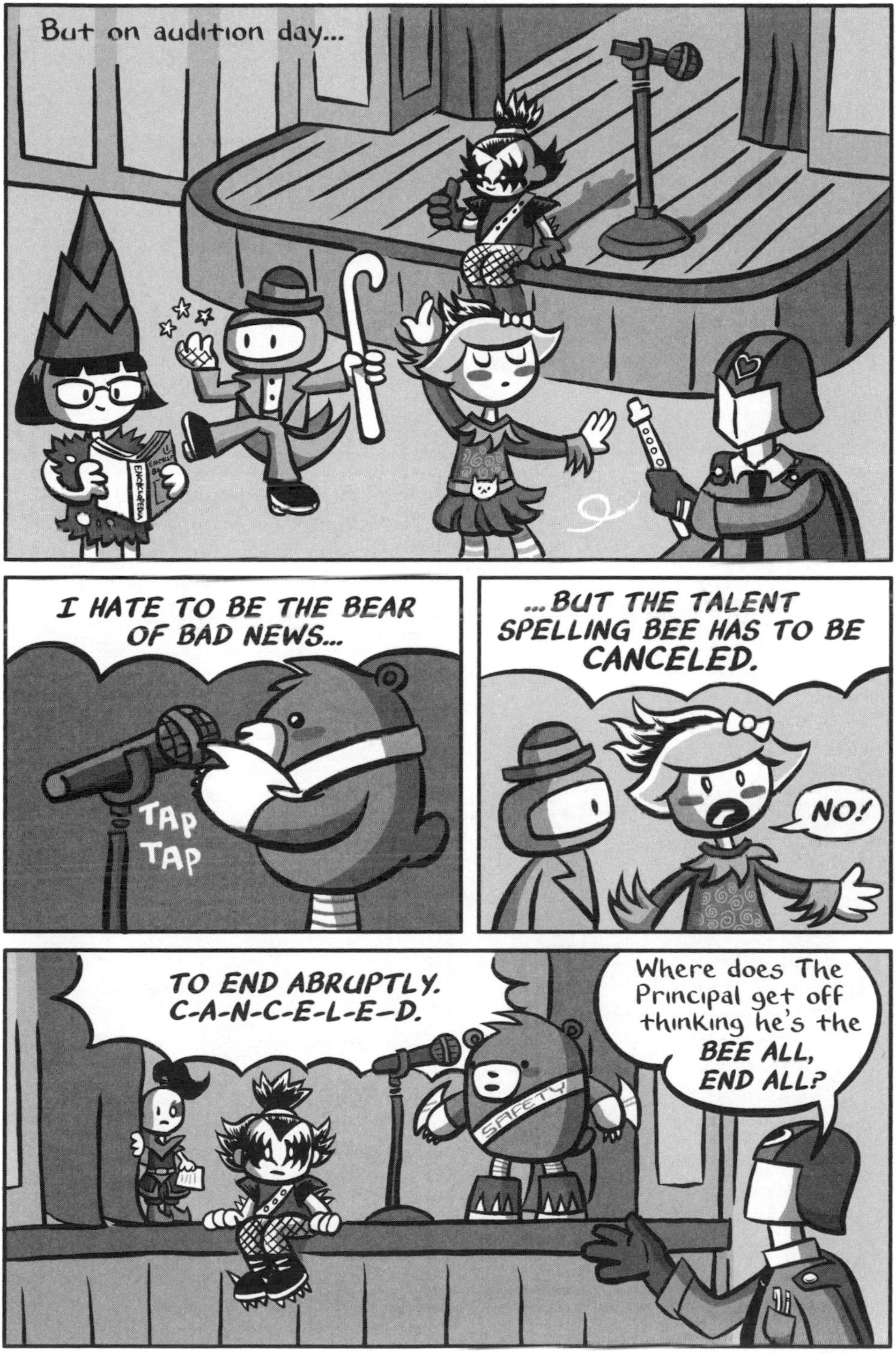
But on audition day...
I HATE TO BE THE BEAR OF BAD NEWS...
TAP TAP
...BUT THE TALENT SPELLING BEE HAS TO BE CANCELED.
NO!
TO END ABRUPTLY. C-A-N-C-E-L-E-D.
Where does The Principal get off thinking he's the BEE ALL, END ALL?

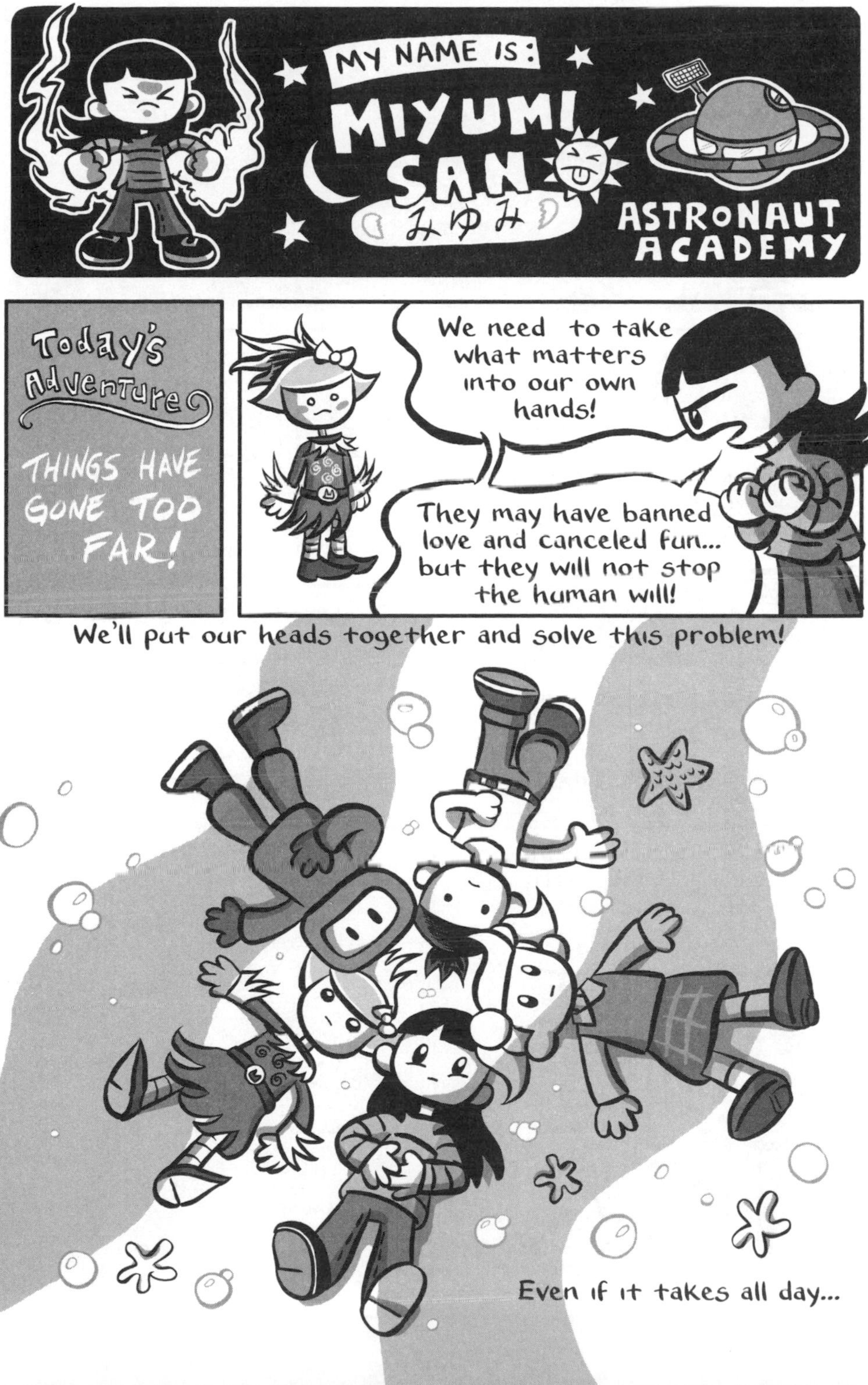
MY NAME IS:
MIYUMI SAN
みゆみ
ASTRONAUT ACADEMY
Today's Adventure
THINGS HAVE GONE TOO FAR!
We need to take what matters into our own hands!
They may have banned love and canceled fun... but they will not stop the human will!
We'll put our heads together and solve this problem!
Even if it takes all day...

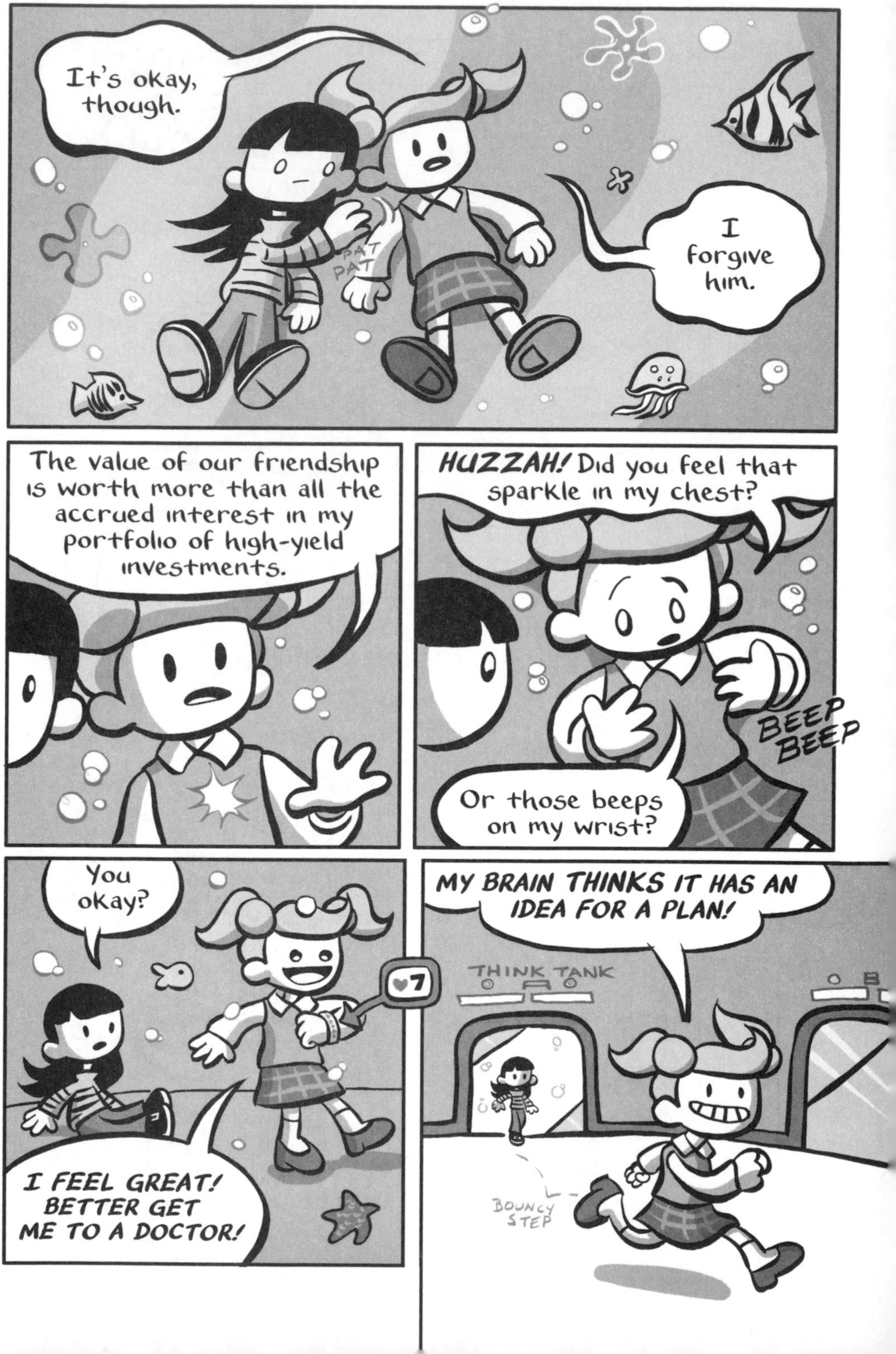
It's okay, though.
PAT PAT
I forgive him.
The value of our friendship is worth more than all the accrued interest in my portfolio of high-yield investments.
HUZZAH! Did you feel that sparkle in my chest?
BEEP BEEP
Or those beeps on my wrist?
You okay?
7
I FEEL GREAT! BETTER GET ME TO A DOCTOR!
MY BRAIN THINKS IT HAS AN IDEA FOR A PLAN!
THINK TANK
BOUNCY STEP

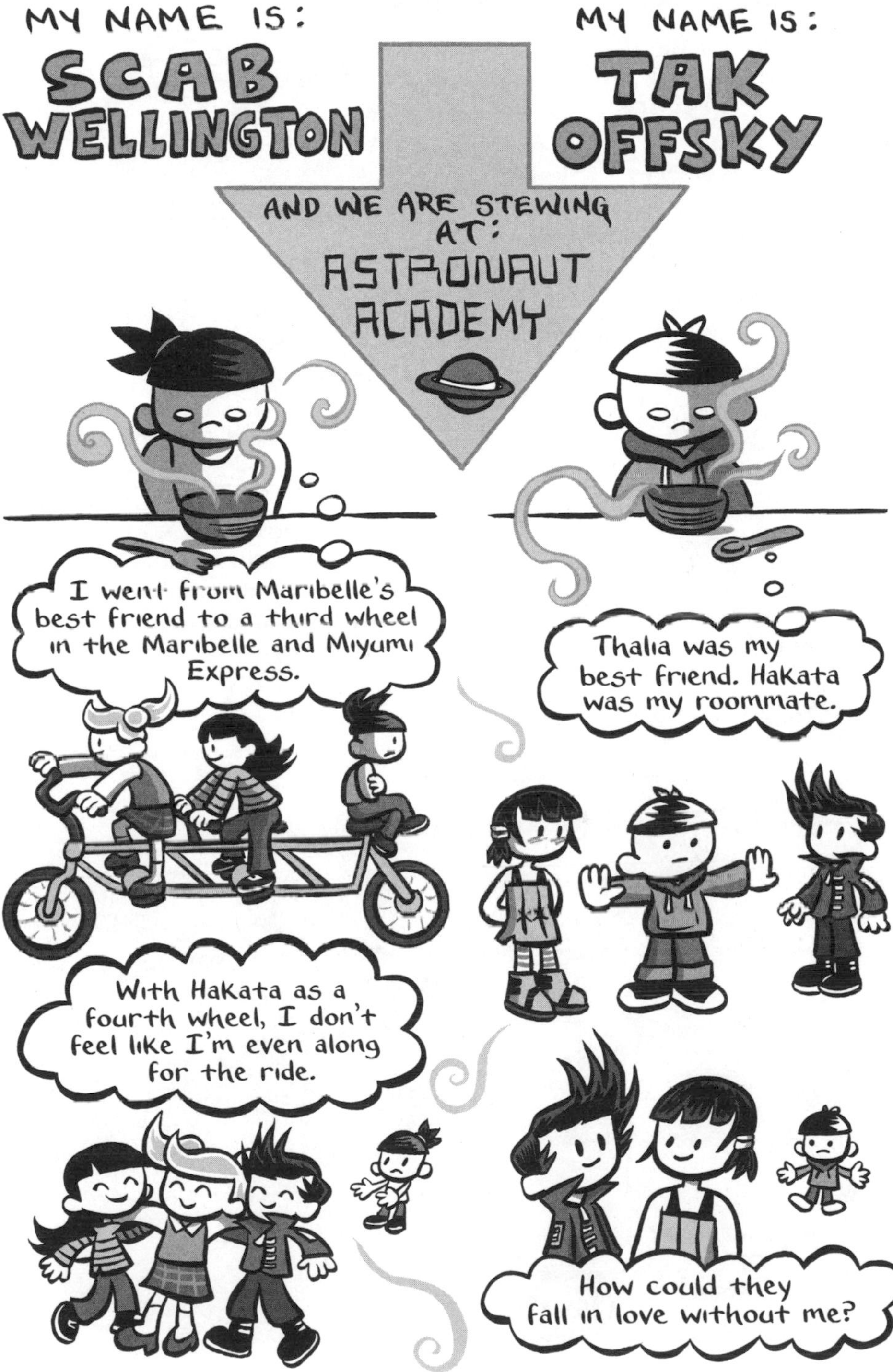
MY NAME IS:
SCAB WELLINGTON
MY NAME IS:
TAK OFFSKY
AND WE ARE STEWING AT:
ASTRONAUT ACADEMY
I went from Maribelle's best friend to a third wheel in the Maribelle and Miyumi Express.
Thalia was my best friend. Hakata was my roommate.
With Hakata as a fourth wheel, I don't feel like I'm even along for the ride.
How could they fall in love without me?

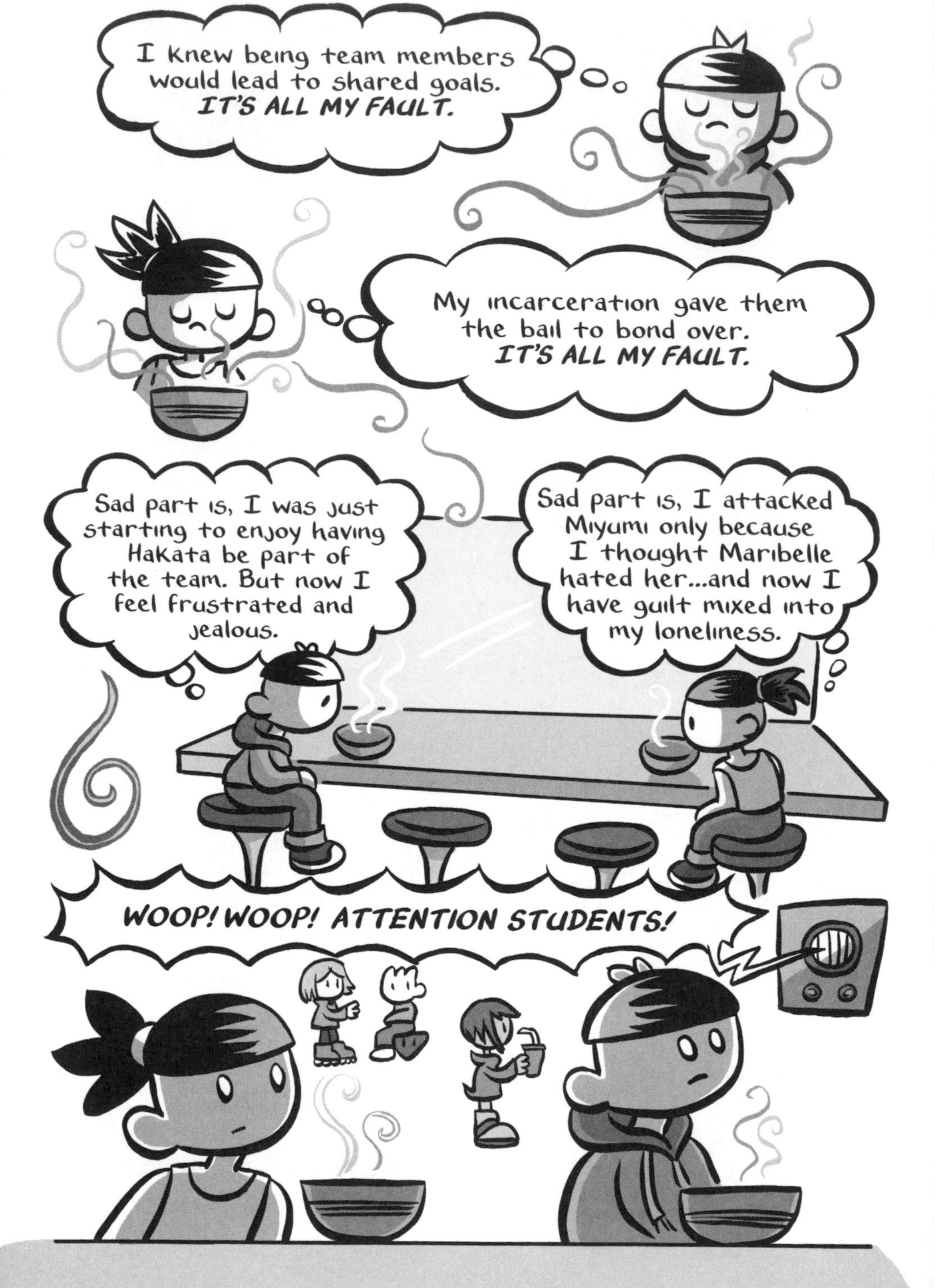

I knew being team members would lead to shared goals. IT'S ALL MY FAULT.
My incarceration gave them the bail to bond over. IT'S ALL MY FAULT.
Sad part is, I was just starting to enjoy having Hakata be part of the team. But now I feel frustrated and jealous.
Sad part is, I attacked Miyumi only because I thought Maribelle hated her...and now I have guilt mixed into my loneliness.
WOOP! WOOP! ATTENTION STUDENTS!

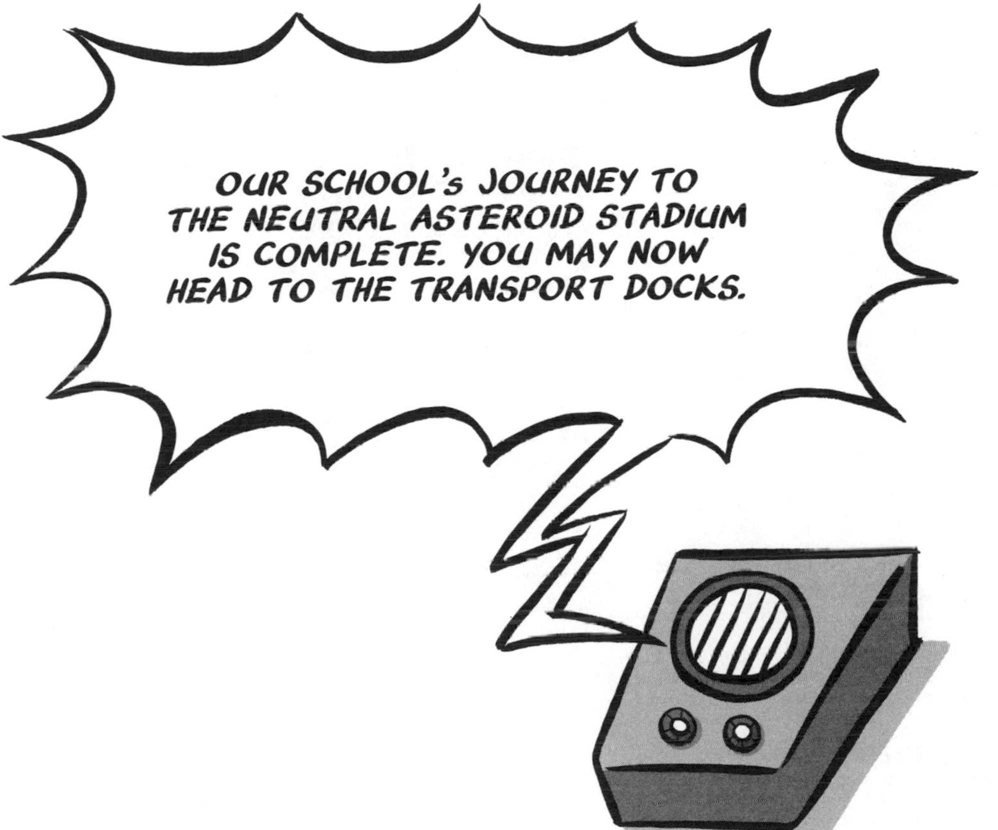
OUR SCHOOL's JOURNEY TO THE NEUTRAL ASTEROID STADIUM IS COMPLETE. YOU MAY NOW HEAD TO THE TRANSPORT DOCKS.

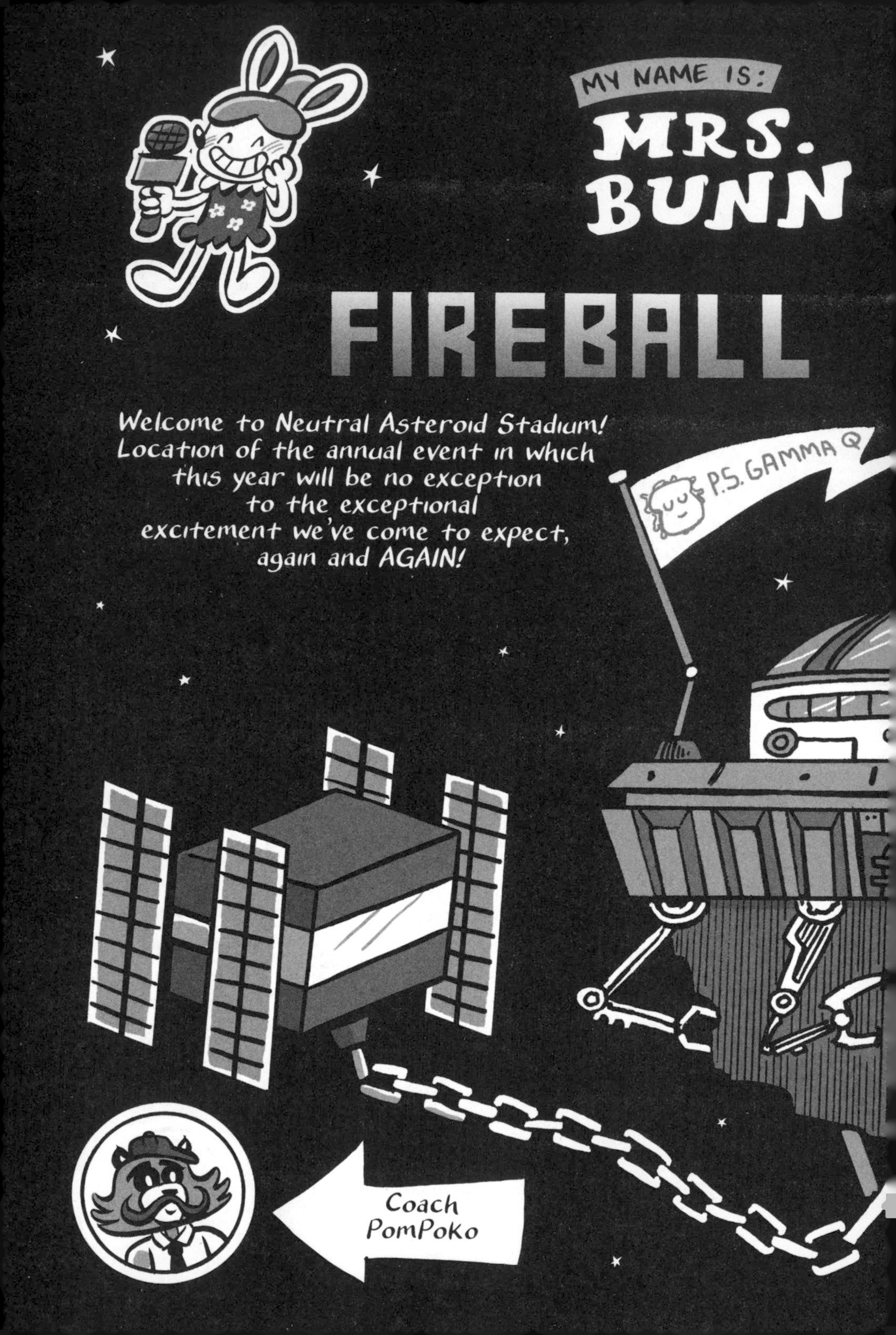
MY NAME IS:
MRS. BUNN
FIREBALL
Welcome to Neutral Asteroid Stadium! Location of the annual event in which this year will be no exception to the exceptional excitement we've come to expect, again and AGAIN!
P.S. GAMMA Q
Coach PomPoko

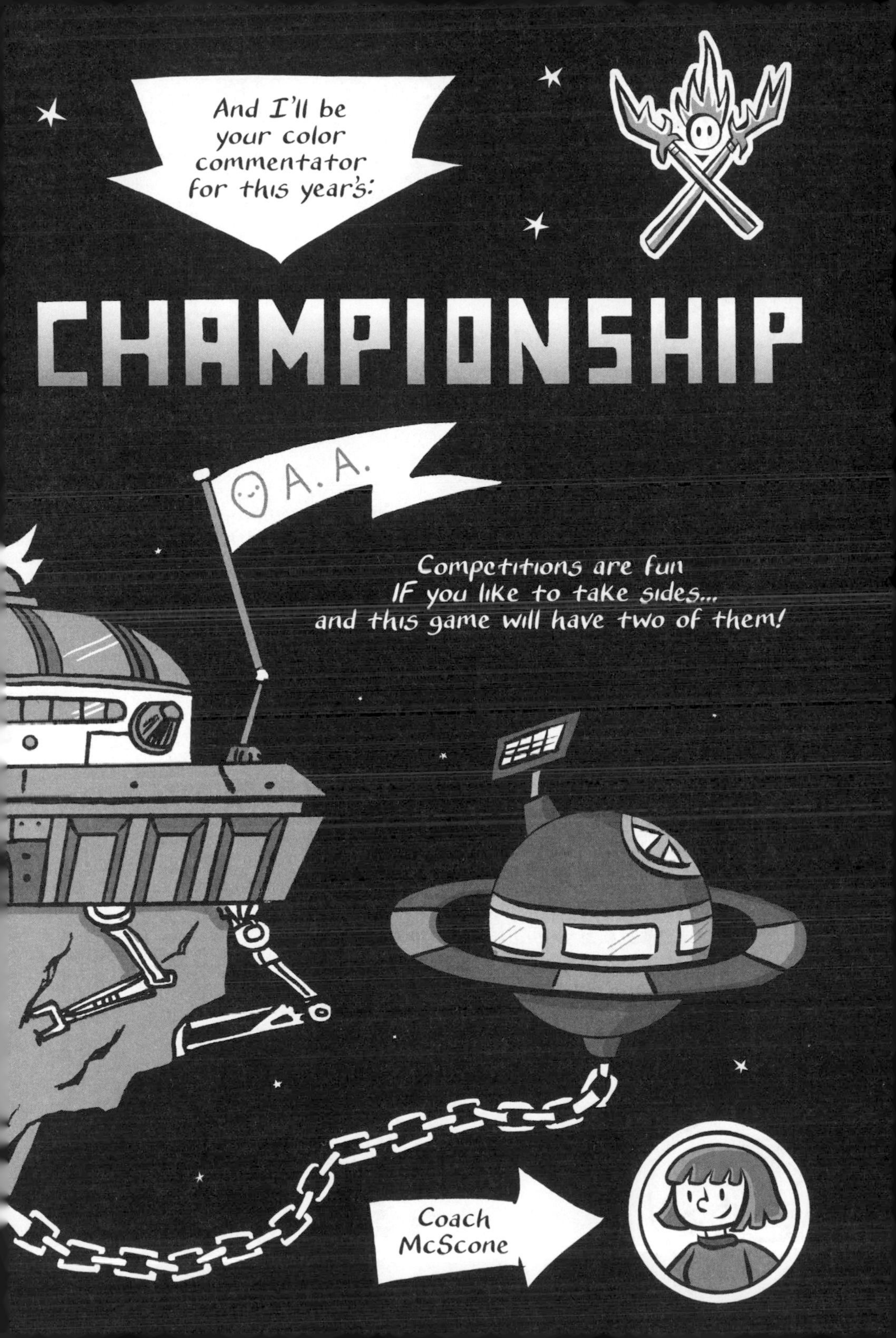
And I'll be your color commentator for this year's:
CHAMPIONSHIP
A.A.
Competitions are fun IF you like to take sides... and this game will have two of them!
Coach McScone

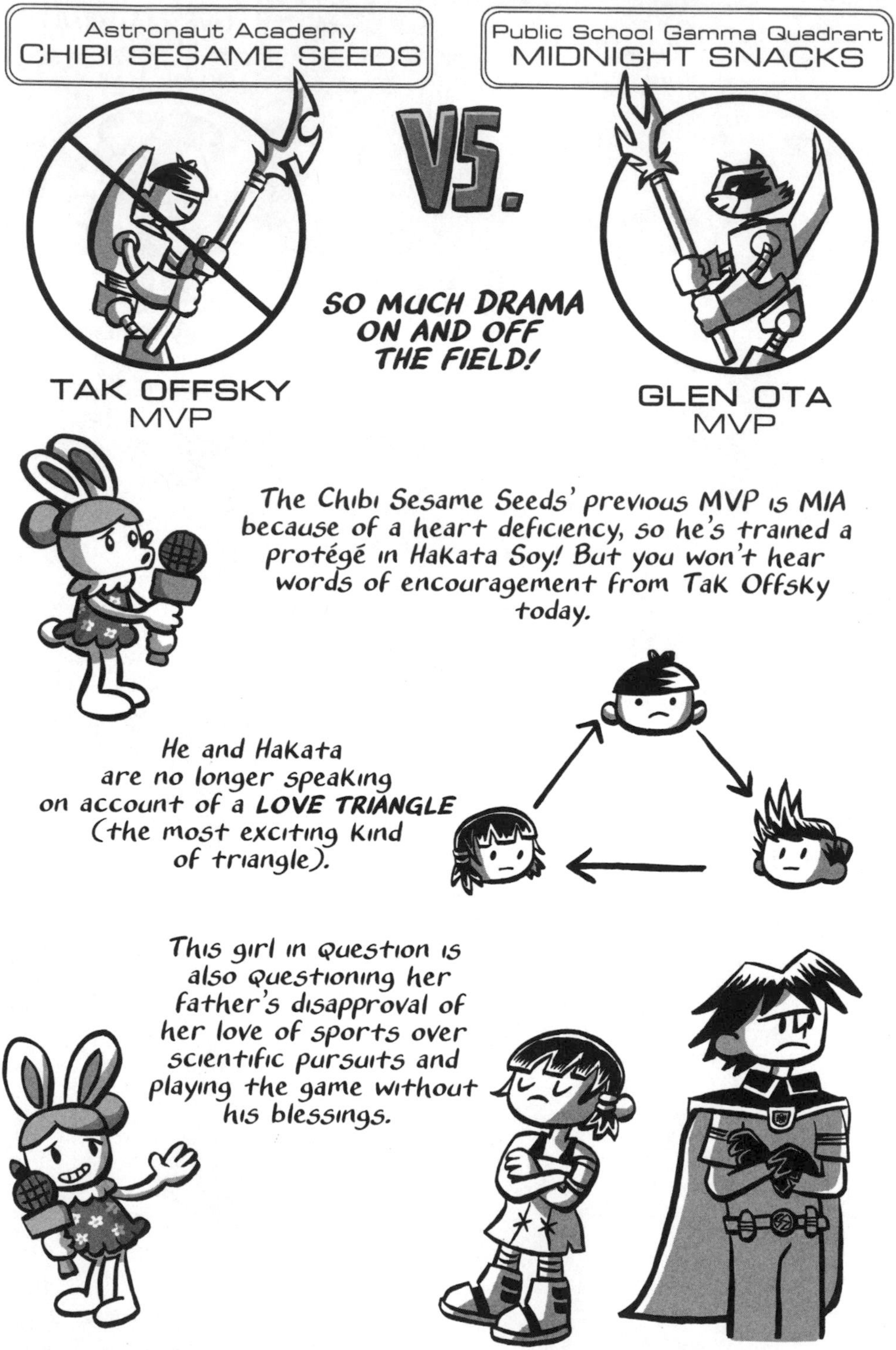
Astronaut Academy
CHIBI SESAME SEEDS
Public School Gamma Quadrant
MIDNIGHT SNACKS
VS.
SO MUCH DRAMA ON AND OFF THE FIELD!
TAK OFFSKY
MVP
GLEN OTA
MVP
The Chibi Sesame Seeds' previous MVP is MIA because of a heart deficiency, so he's trained a protégé in Hakata Soy! But you won't hear words of encouragement from Tak Offsky today.
He and Hakata are no longer speaking on account of a LOVE TRIANGLE (the most exciting kind of triangle).
This girl in question is also questioning her father's disapproval of her love of sports over scientific pursuits and playing the game without his blessings.

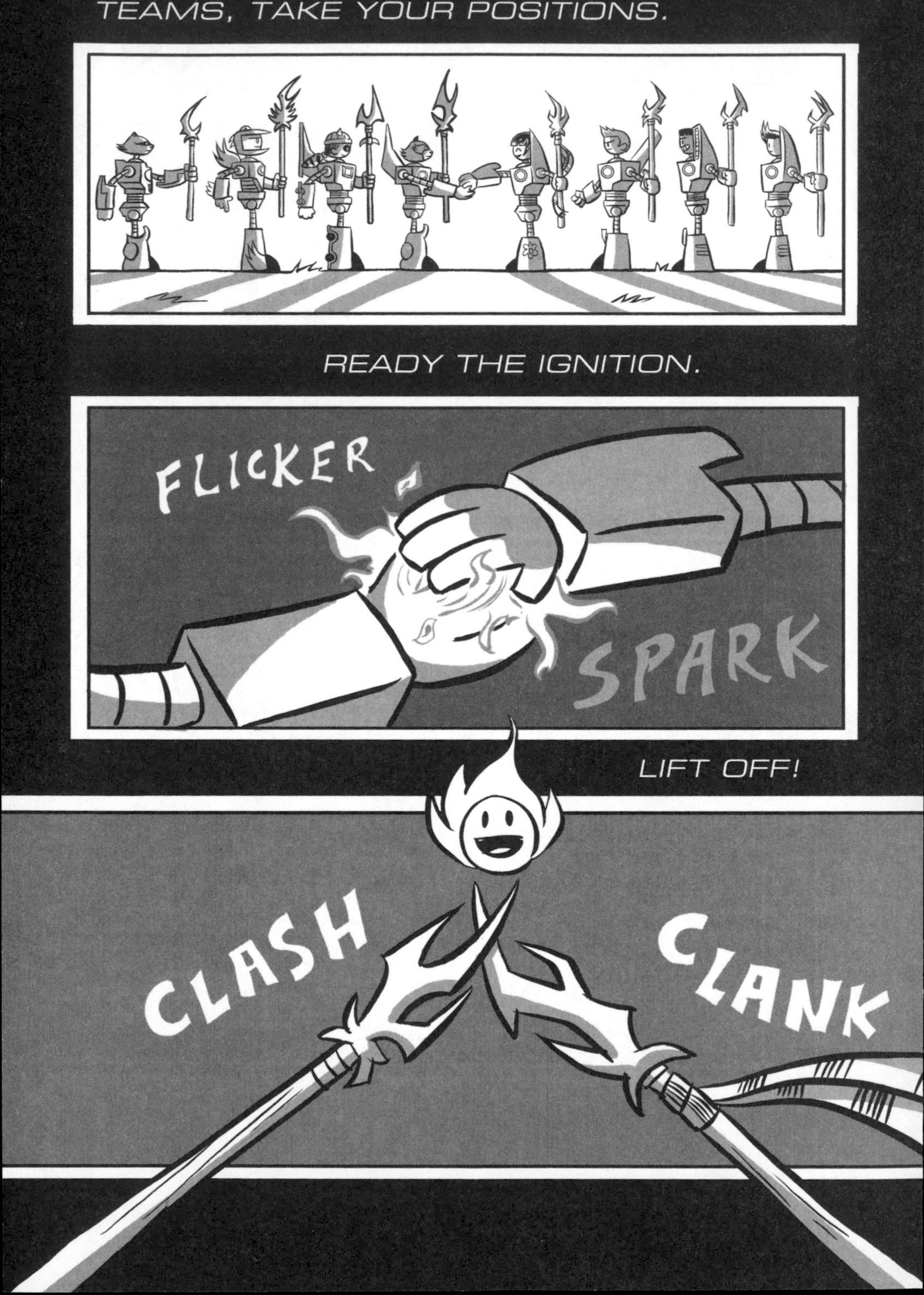
TEAMS, TAKE YOUR POSITIONS.
READY THE IGNITION.
FLICKER
SPARK
LIFT OFF!
CLASH
CLANK

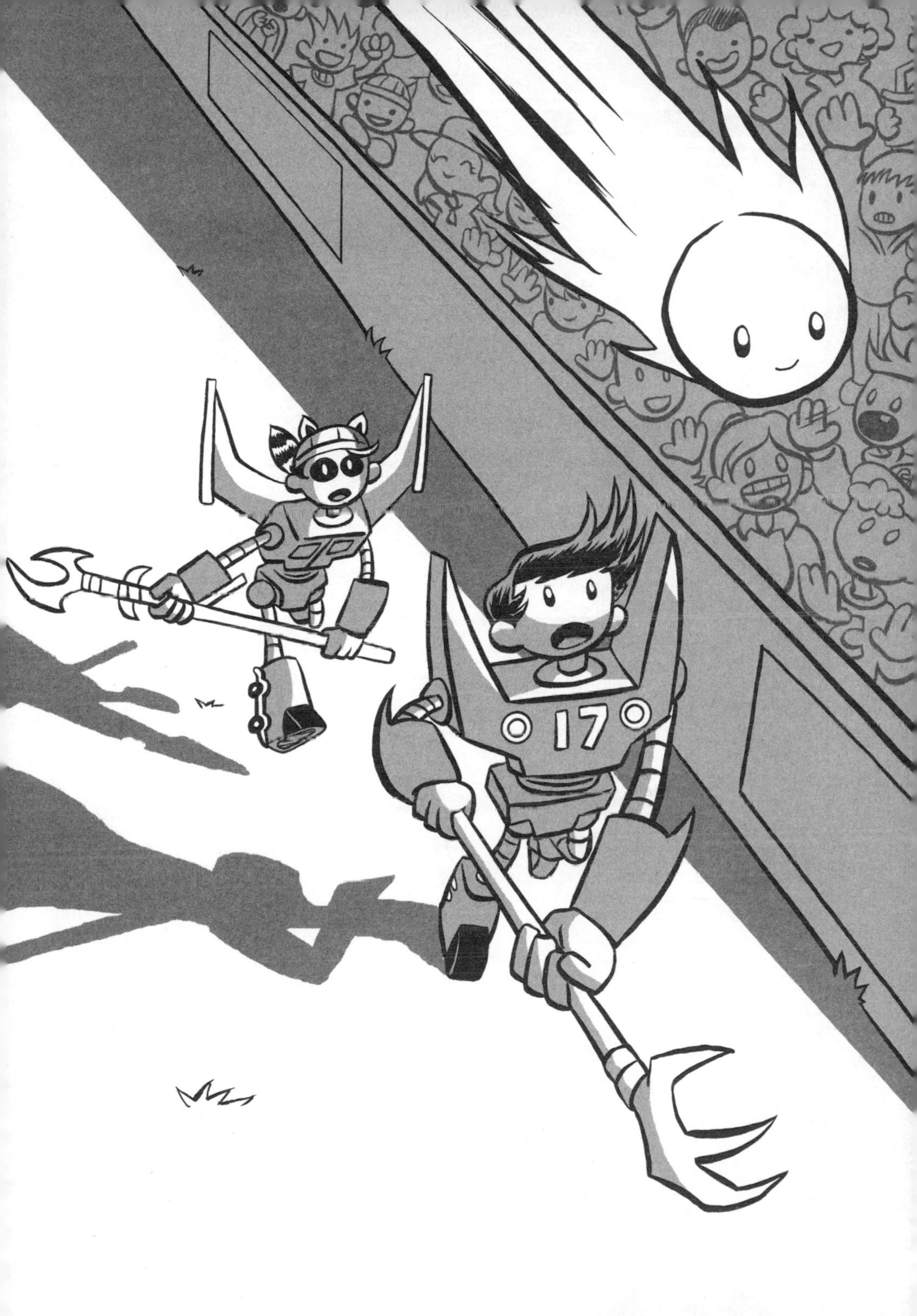
17

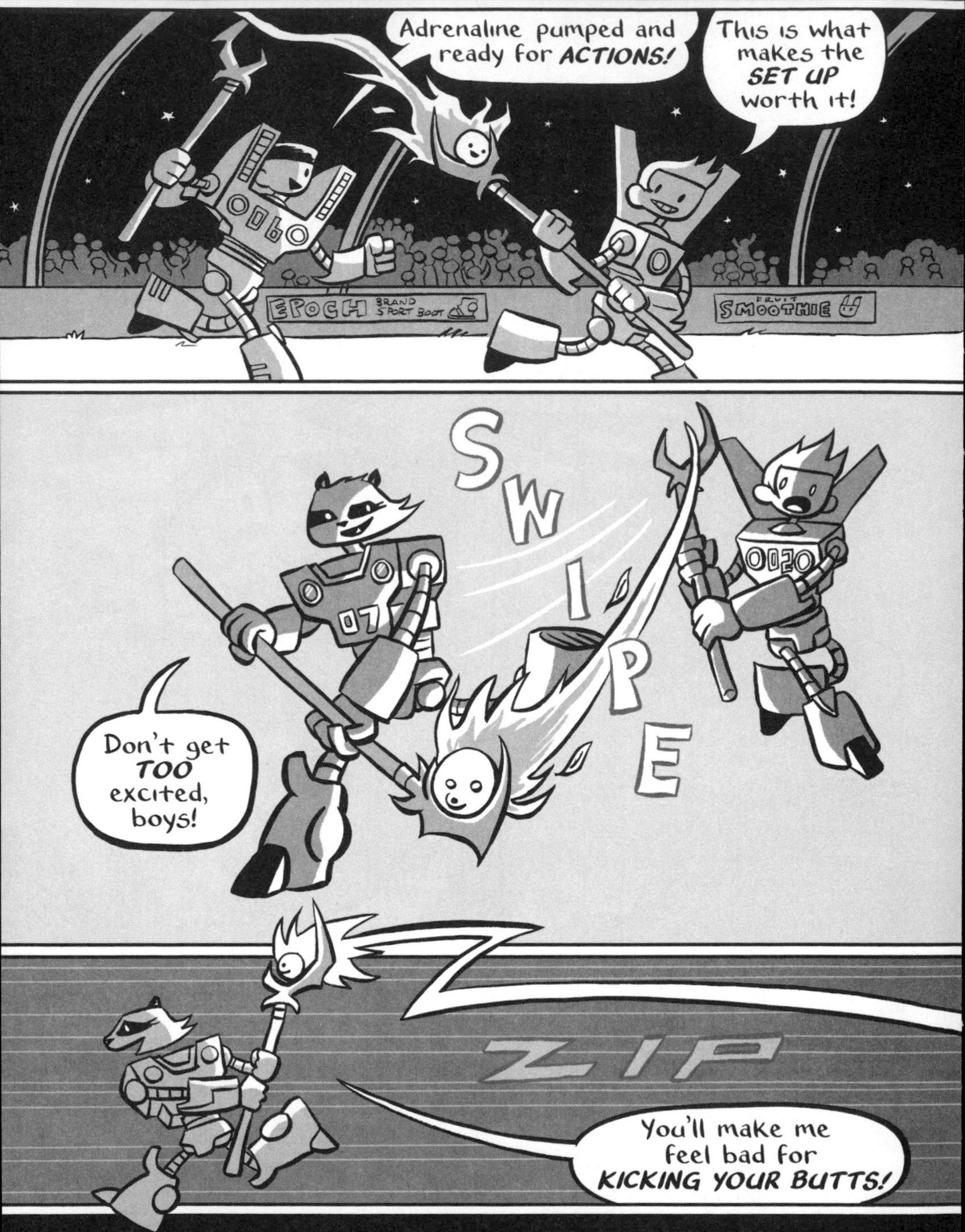
Adrenaline pumped and ready for ACTIONS!
This is what makes the SET UP worth it!
EPOCH BRAND SPORT BOOT
FRUIT SMOOTHIE
SWIPE
Don't get TOO excited, boys!
ZIP
You'll make me feel bad for KICKING YOUR BUTTS!

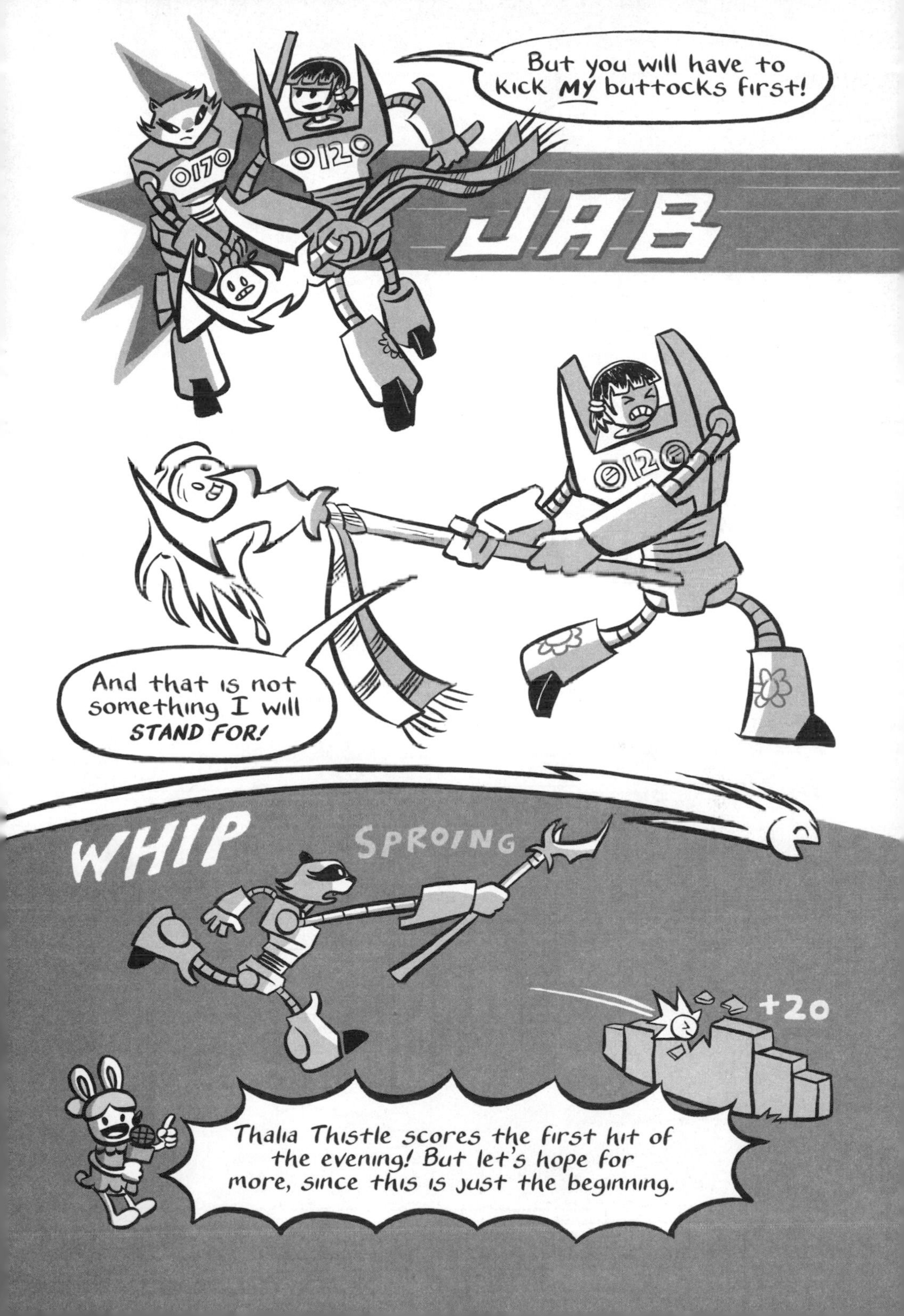
But you will have to kick MY buttocks first!
JAB
0170
0120
And that is not something I will STAND FOR!
WHIP
SPROING
+20
Thalia Thistle scores the first hit of the evening! But let's hope for more, since this is just the beginning.

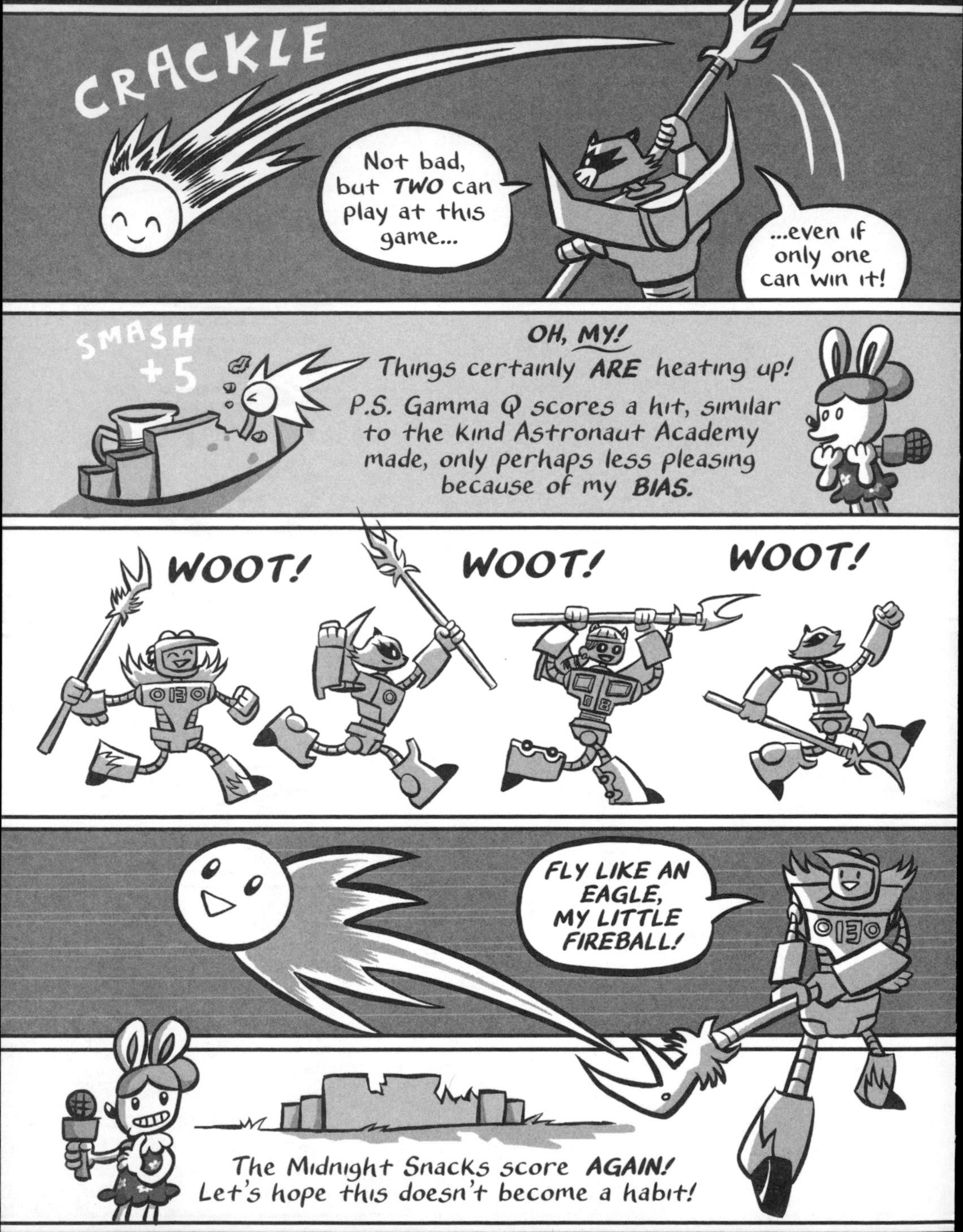

CRACKLE
Not bad, but TWO can play at this game...
...even if only one can win it!
SMASH +5
OH, MY! Things certainly ARE heating up!
P.S. Gamma Q scores a hit, similar to the kind Astronaut Academy made, only perhaps less pleasing because of my BIAS.
WOOT!
WOOT!
WOOT!
FLY LIKE AN EAGLE, MY LITTLE FIREBALL!
The Midnight Snacks score AGAIN! Let's hope this doesn't become a habit!

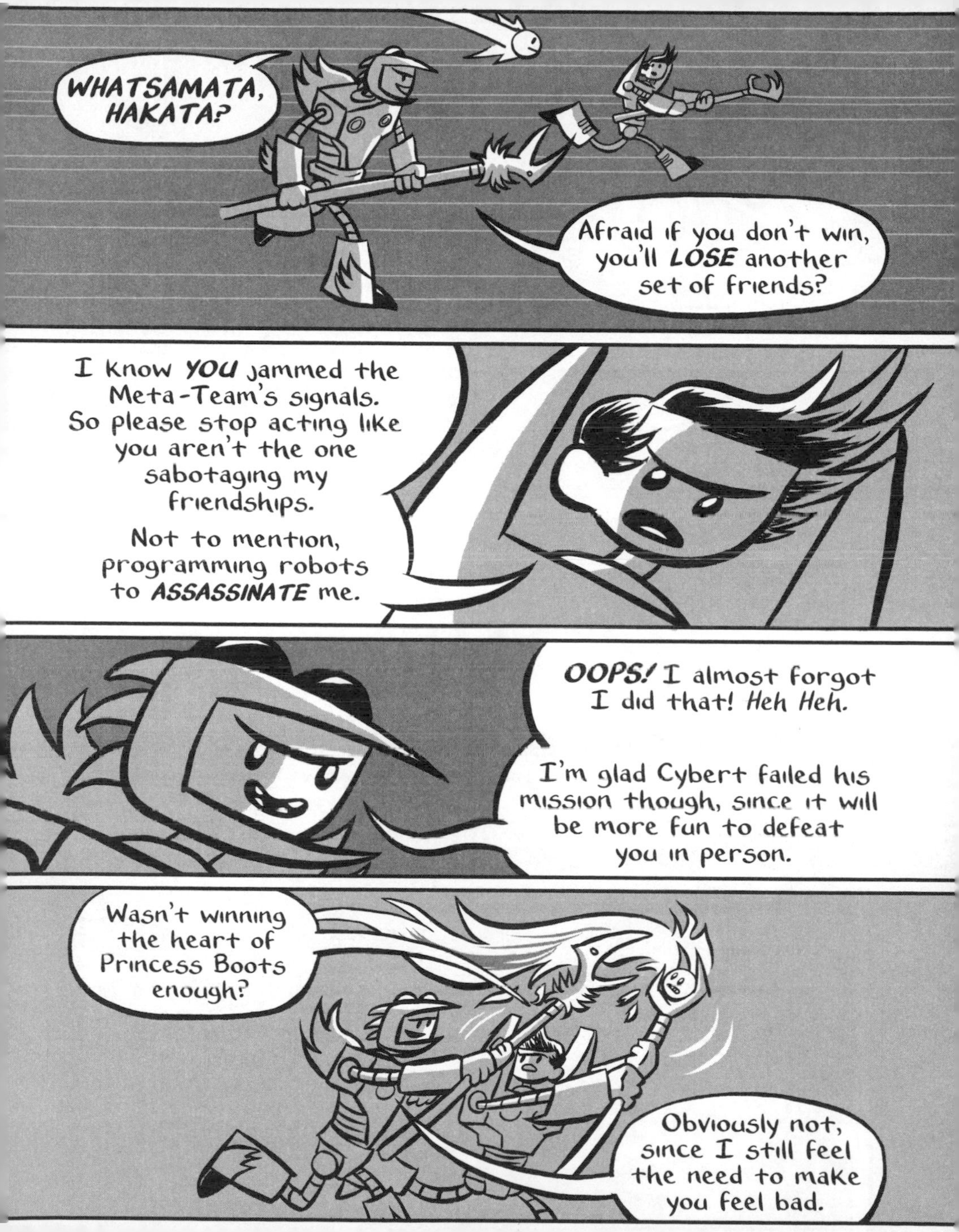
WHATSAMATA, HAKATA?
Afraid if you don't win, you'll LOSE another set of friends?
I know YOU jammed the Meta-Team's signals. So please stop acting like you aren't the one sabotaging my friendships.
Not to mention, programming robots to ASSASSINATE me.
OOPS! I almost forgot I did that! Heh Heh.
I'm glad Cybert failed his mission though, since it will be more fun to defeat you in person.
Wasn't winning the heart of Princess Boots enough?
Obviously not, since I still feel the need to make you feel bad.

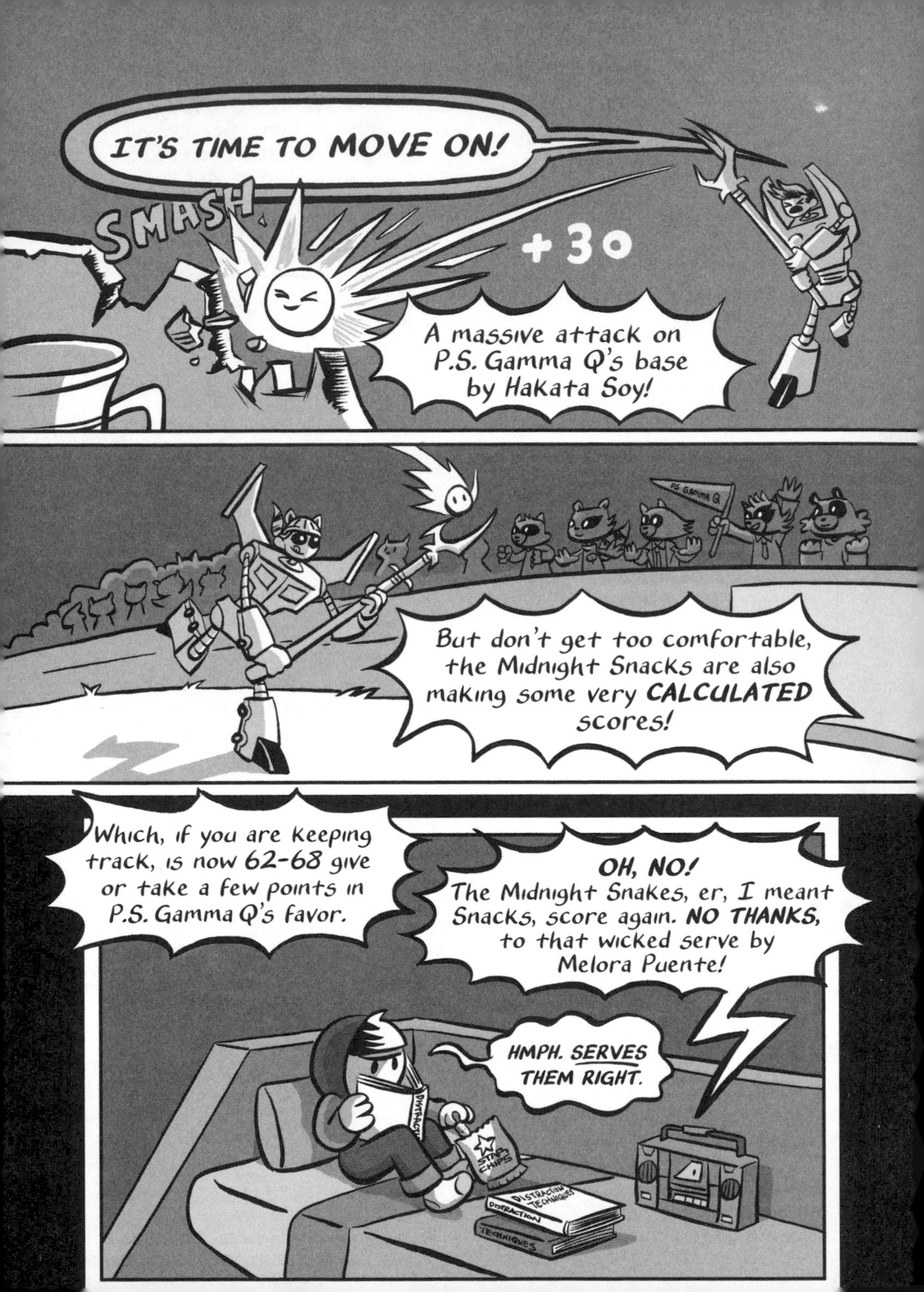
IT'S TIME TO MOVE ON!
SMASH
+30
A massive attack on P.S. Gamma Q's base by Hakata Soy!
PS GAMMA Q
But don't get too comfortable, the Midnight Snacks are also making some very CALCULATED scores!
Which, if you are keeping track, is now 62-68 give or take a few points in P.S. Gamma Q's favor.
OH, NO! The Midnight Snakes, er, I meant Snacks, score again. NO THANKS, to that wicked serve by Melora Puente!
HMPH. SERVES THEM RIGHT.
STAR CHIPS
DISTRACTION TECHNIQUES
DISTRACTION TECHNIQUES

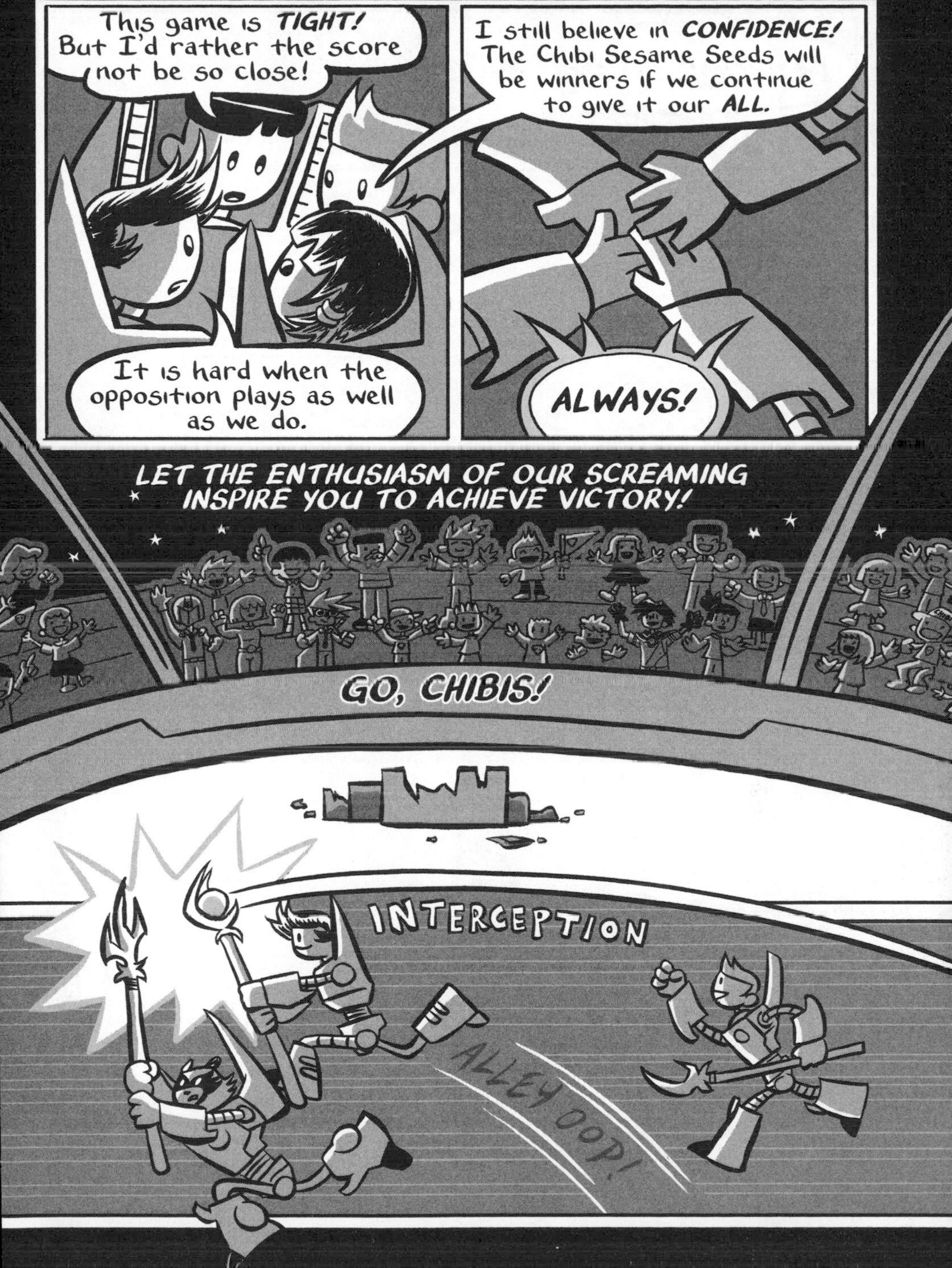
This game is TIGHT! But I'd rather the score not be so close!
It is hard when the opposition plays as well as we do.
I still believe in CONFIDENCE! The Chibi Sesame Seeds will be winners if we continue to give it our ALL.
ALWAYS!
LET THE ENTHUSIASM OF OUR SCREAMING INSPIRE YOU TO ACHIEVE VICTORY!
GO, CHIBIS!
INTERCEPTION
ALLEY OOP!

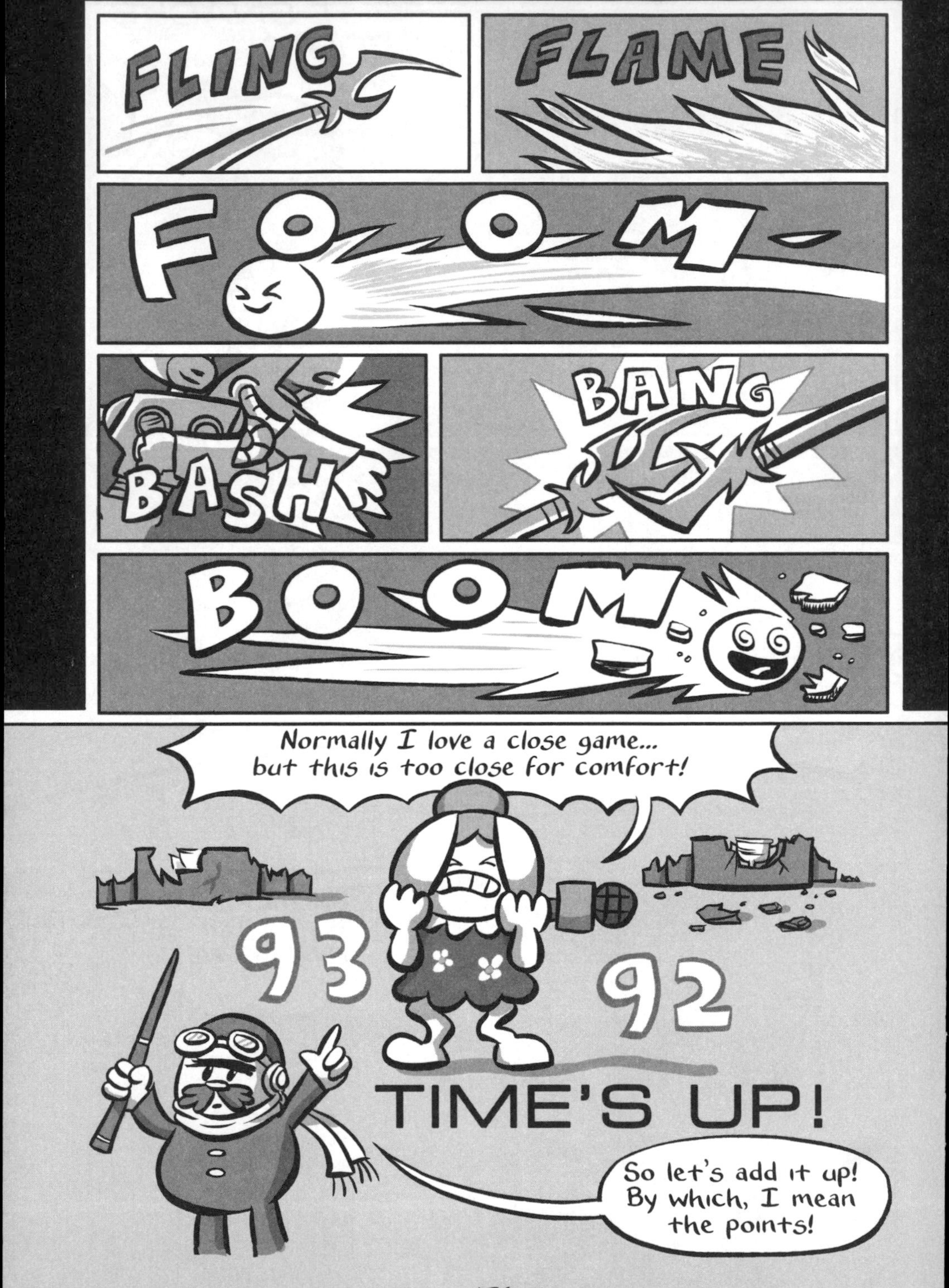
FLING
FLAME
FOOOM
BASH
BANG
BOOOM
Normally I love a close game... but this is too close for comfort!
93
92
TIME'S UP!
So let's add it up! By which, I mean the points!

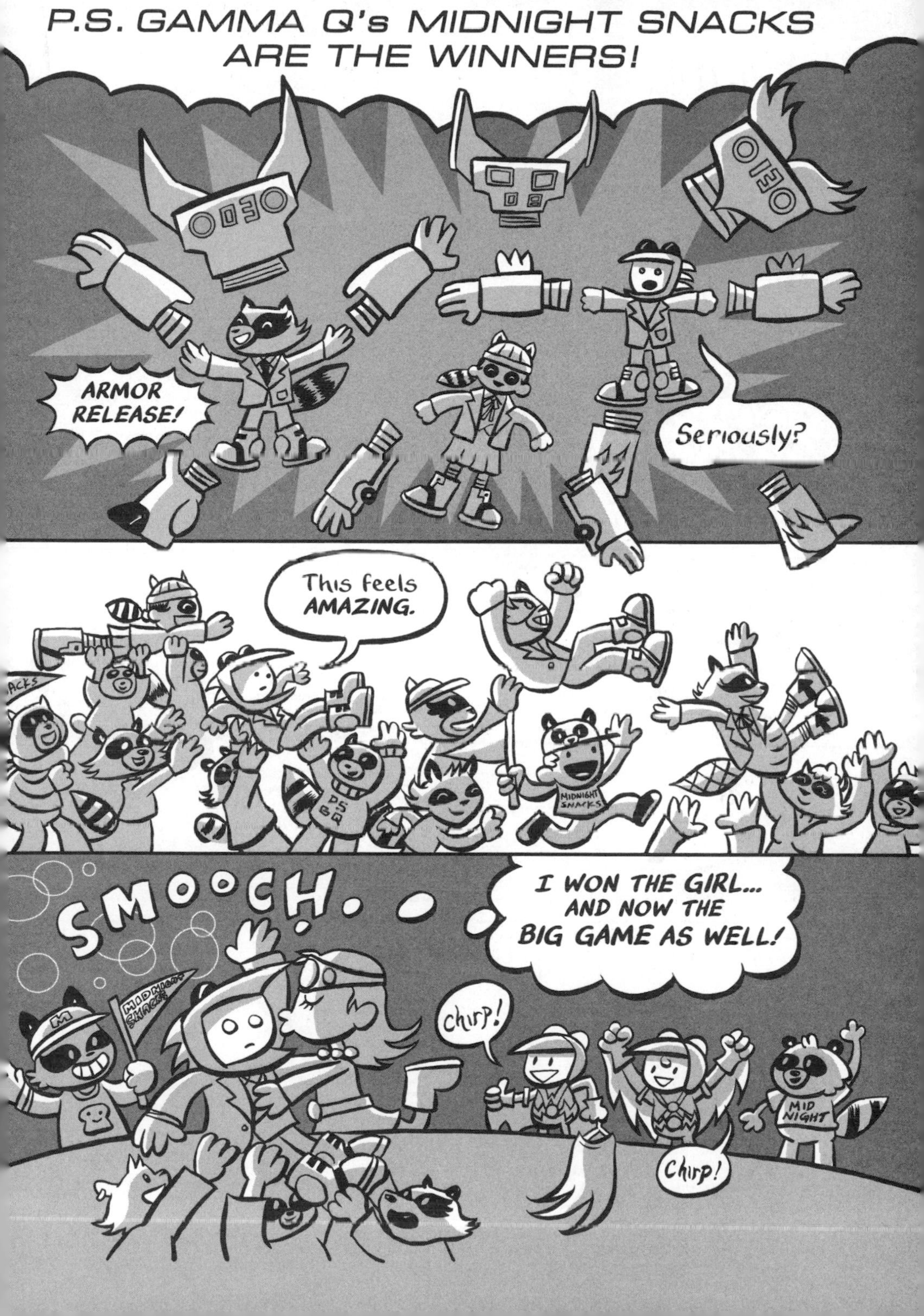

P.S. GAMMA Q's MIDNIGHT SNACKS ARE THE WINNERS!
ARMOR RELEASE!
Seriously?
This feels AMAZING.
MIDNIGHT SNACKS
PS GQ
SMOOCH.
I WON THE GIRL... AND NOW THE BIG GAME AS WELL!
MIDNIGHT SNACKS
chirp!
MID NIGHT
Chirp!

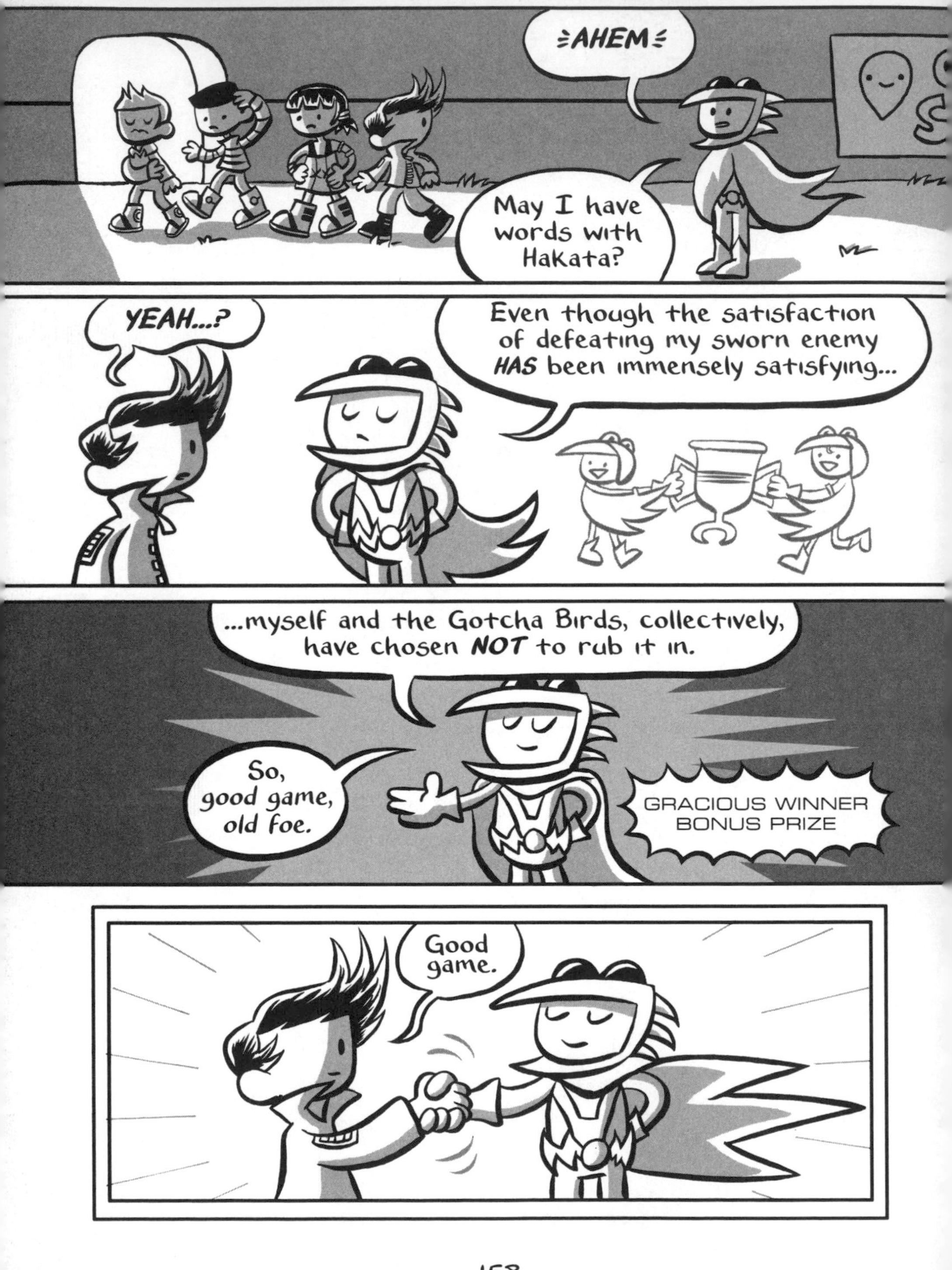

AHEM
May I have words with Hakata?
YEAH...?
Even though the satisfaction of defeating my sworn enemy HAS been immensely satisfying...
...myself and the Gotcha Birds, collectively, have chosen NOT to rub it in.
So, good game, old foe.
GRACIOUS WINNER BONUS PRIZE
Good game.

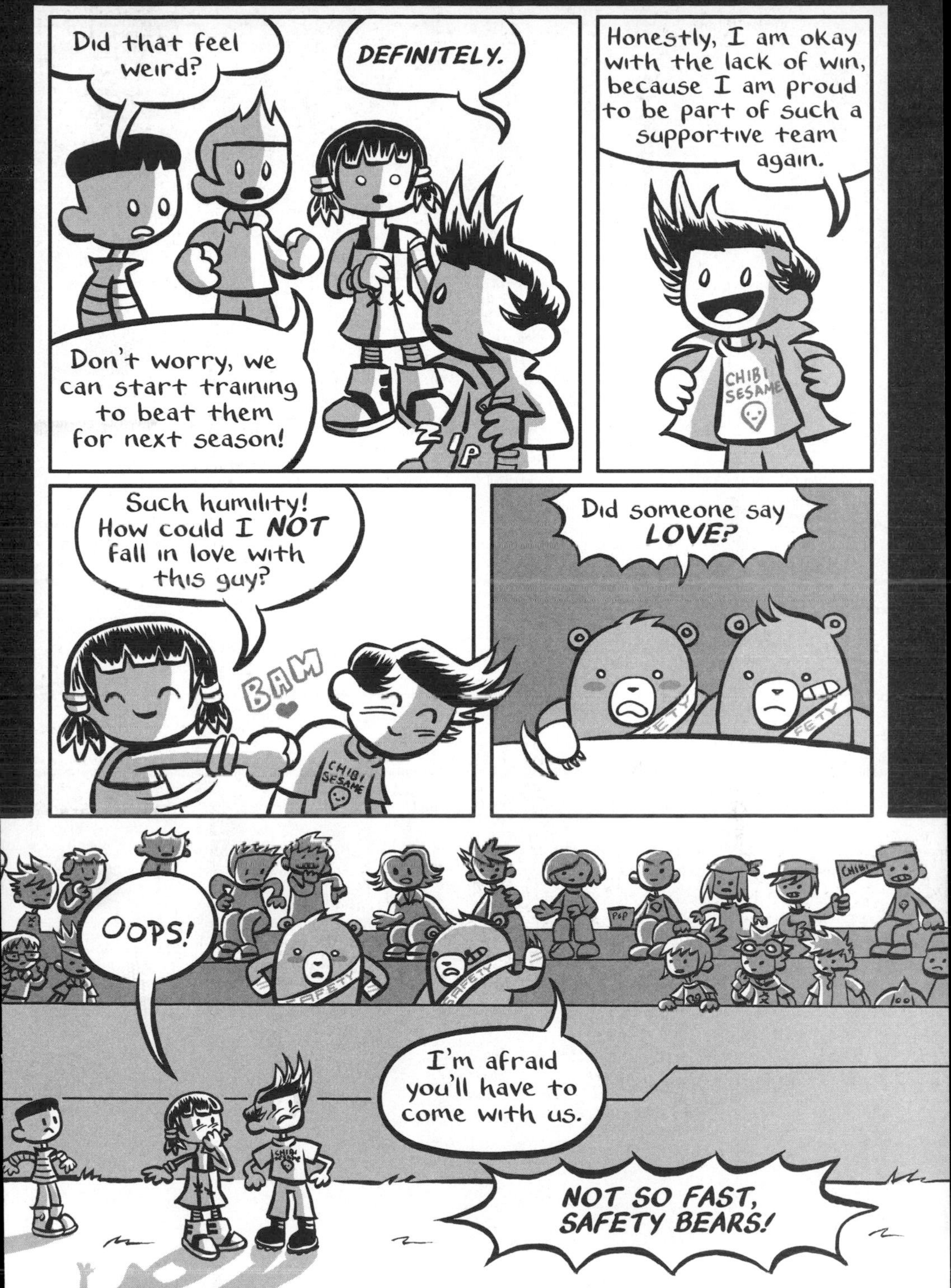
Did that feel weird?
DEFINITELY.
Don't worry, we can start training to beat them for next season!
ZIP
Honestly, I am okay with the lack of win, because I am proud to be part of such a supportive team again.
CHIBI SESAME
Such humility! How could I NOT fall in love with this guy?
BAM
CHIBI SESAME
Did someone say LOVE?
OOPS!
I'm afraid you'll have to come with us.
NOT SO FAST, SAFETY BEARS!

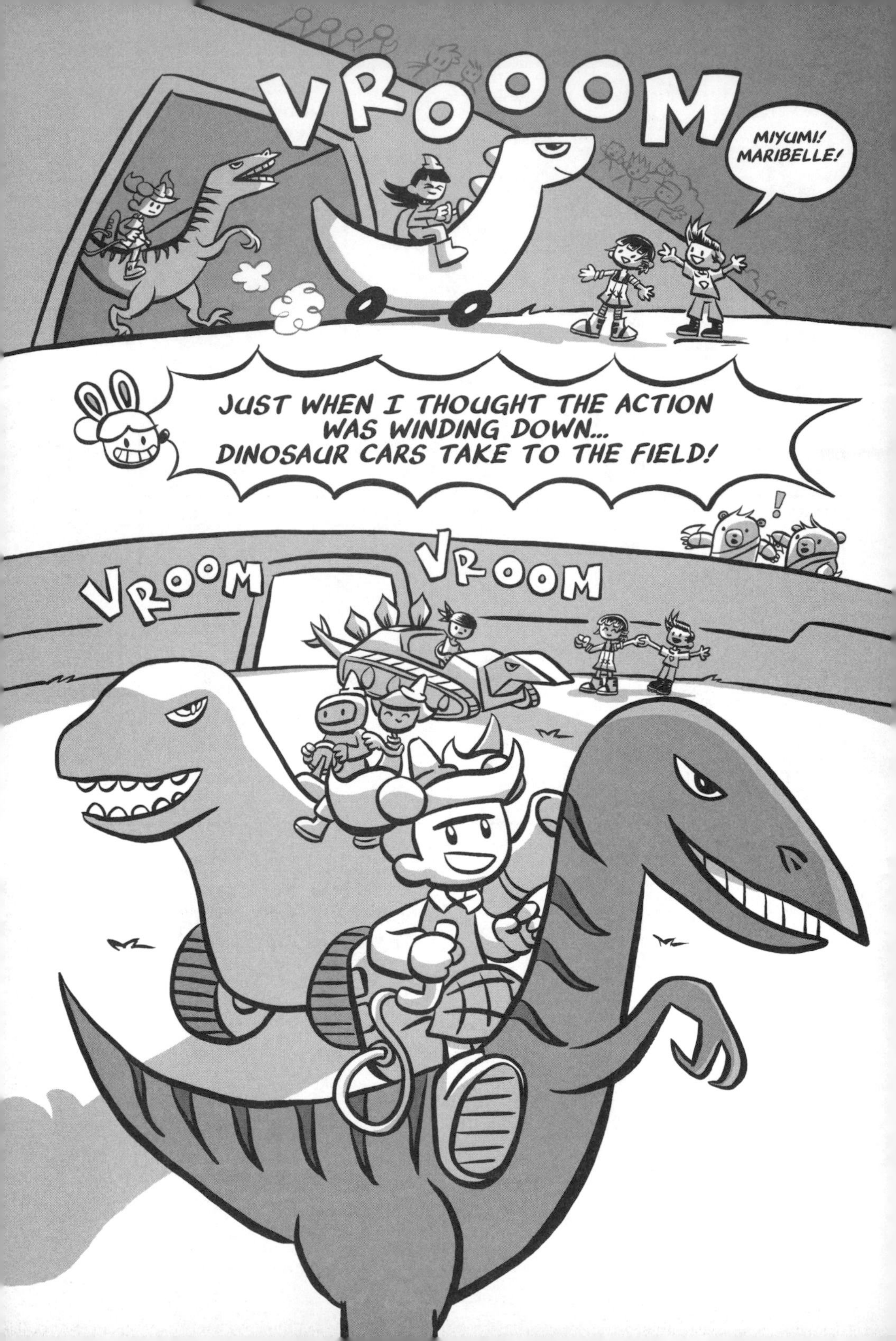
VROOOM
MIYUMI! MARIBELLE!
JUST WHEN I THOUGHT THE ACTION WAS WINDING DOWN... DINOSAUR CARS TAKE TO THE FIELD!
!
VROOM
VROOM

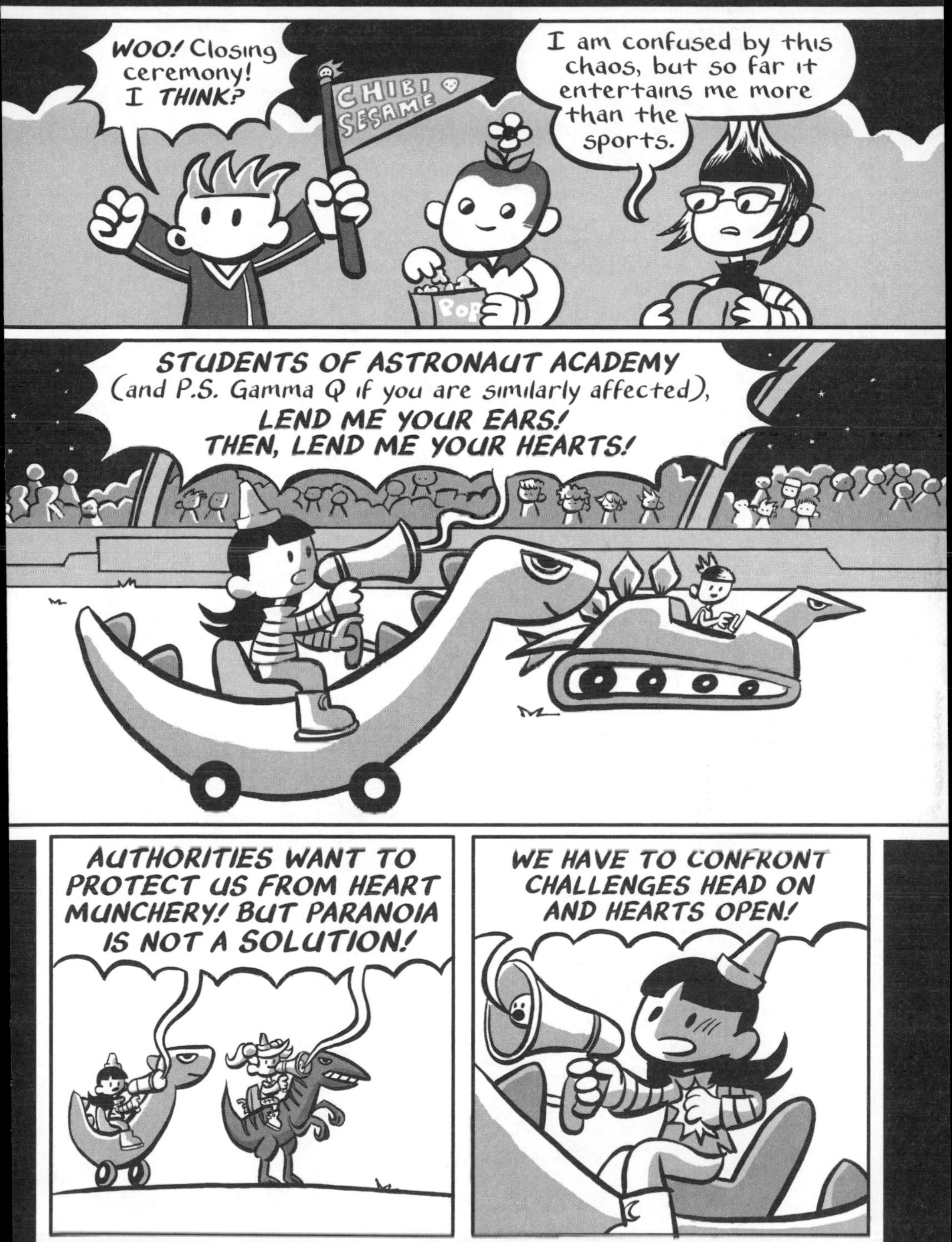
WOO! Closing ceremony! I THINK?
CHIBI SESAME
I am confused by this chaos, but so far it entertains me more than the sports.
POP
STUDENTS OF ASTRONAUT ACADEMY (and P.S. Gamma Q if you are similarly affected), LEND ME YOUR EARS! THEN, LEND ME YOUR HEARTS!
AUTHORITIES WANT TO PROTECT US FROM HEART MUNCHERY! BUT PARANOIA IS NOT A SOLUTION!
WE HAVE TO CONFRONT CHALLENGES HEAD ON AND HEARTS OPEN!

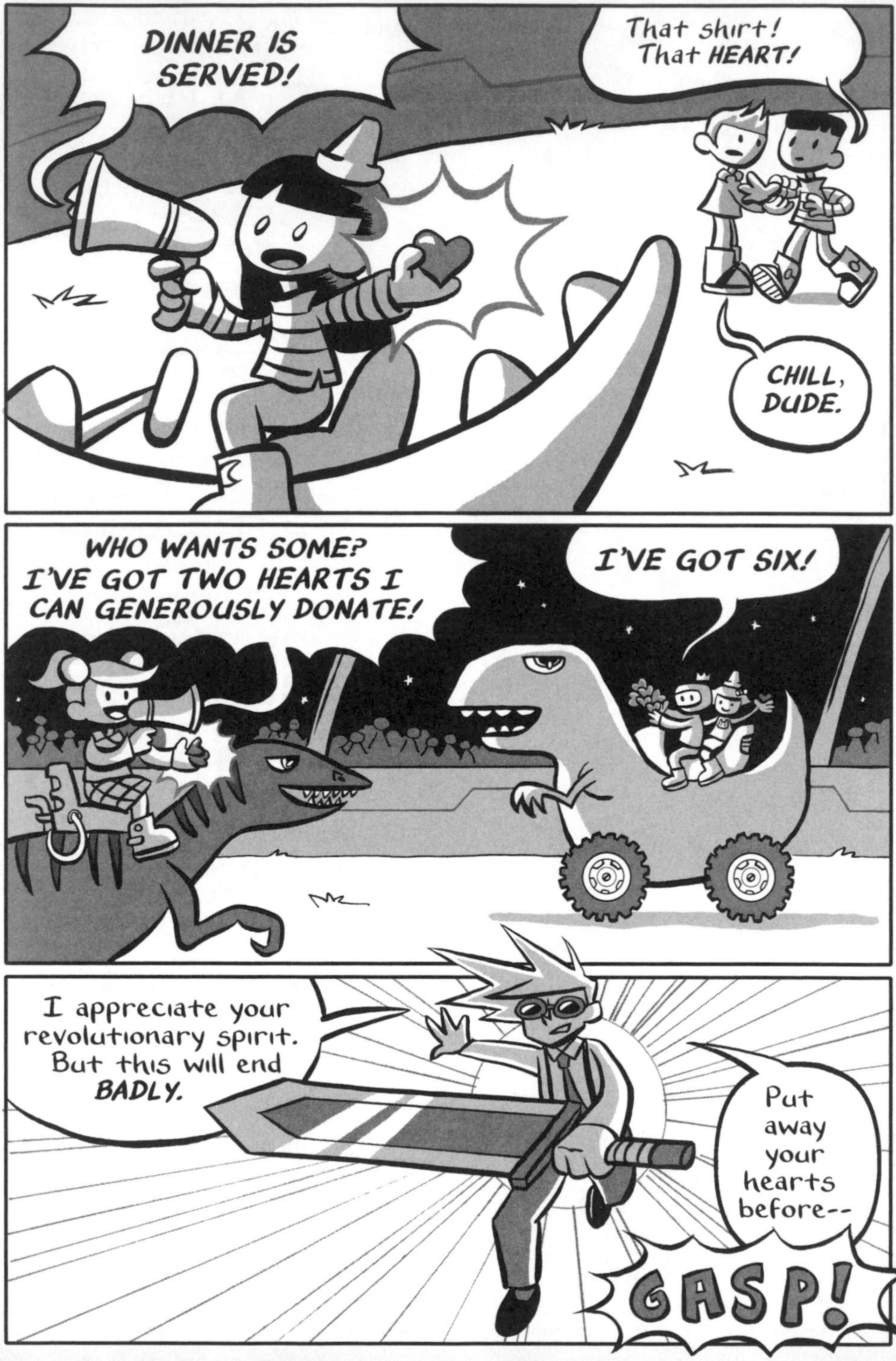
DINNER IS SERVED!
That shirt! That HEART!
CHILL, DUDE.
WHO WANTS SOME? I'VE GOT TWO HEARTS I CAN GENEROUSLY DONATE!
I'VE GOT SIX!
I appreciate your revolutionary spirit. But this will end BADLY.
Put away your hearts before--
GASP!

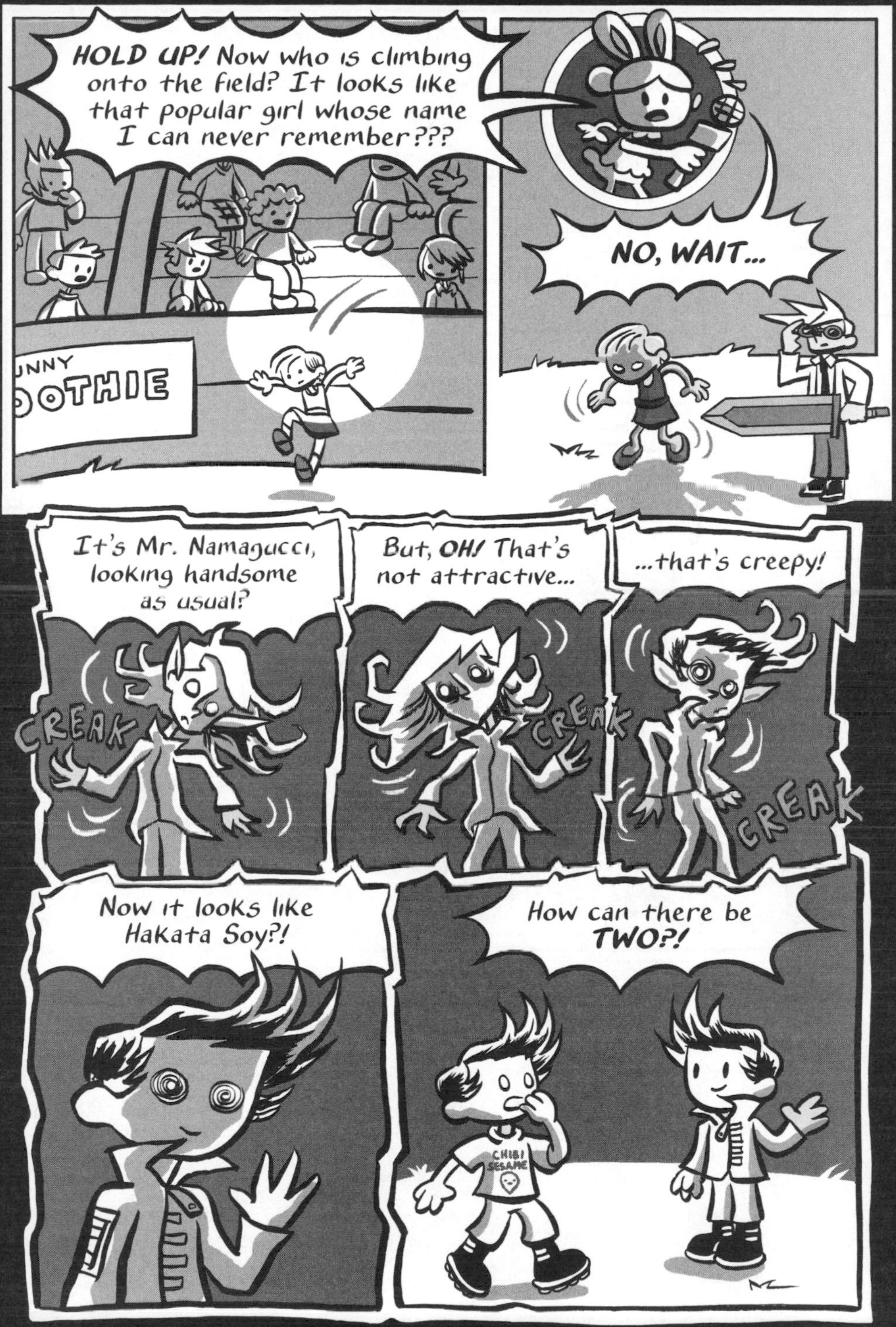
HOLD UP! Now who is climbing onto the field? It looks like that popular girl whose name I can never remember???
UNNY
OOTHIE
NO, WAIT...
It's Mr. Namagucci, looking handsome as usual?
CREAK
But, OH! That's not attractive...
CREAK
...that's creepy!
CREAK
Now it looks like Hakata Soy?!
How can there be TWO?!
CHIBI SESAME

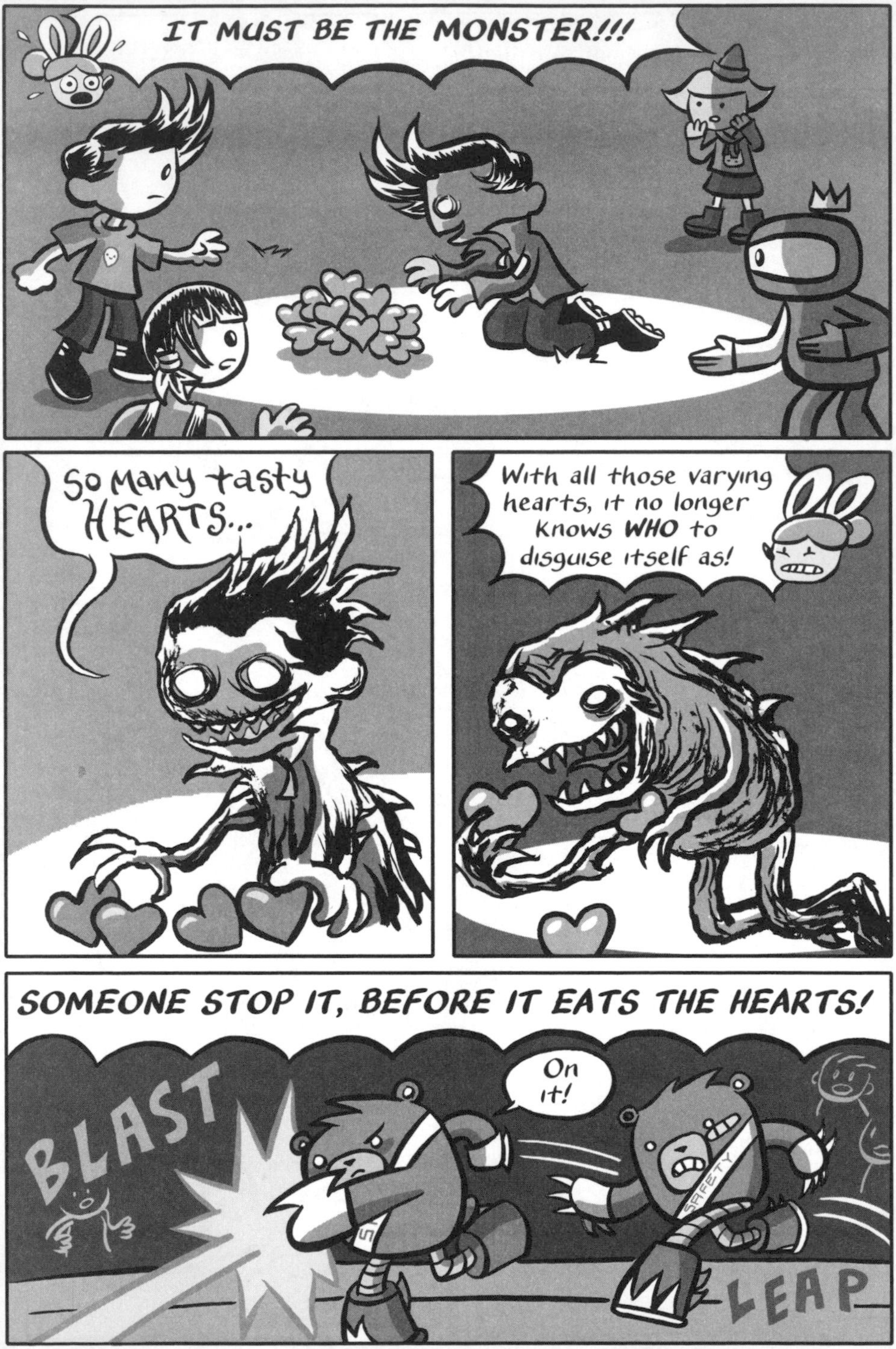
IT MUST BE THE MONSTER!!!
So Many tasty HEARTS...
With all those varying hearts, it no longer Knows WHO to disguise itself as!
SOMEONE STOP IT, BEFORE IT EATS THE HEARTS!
BLAST
On it!
SAFETY
LEAP

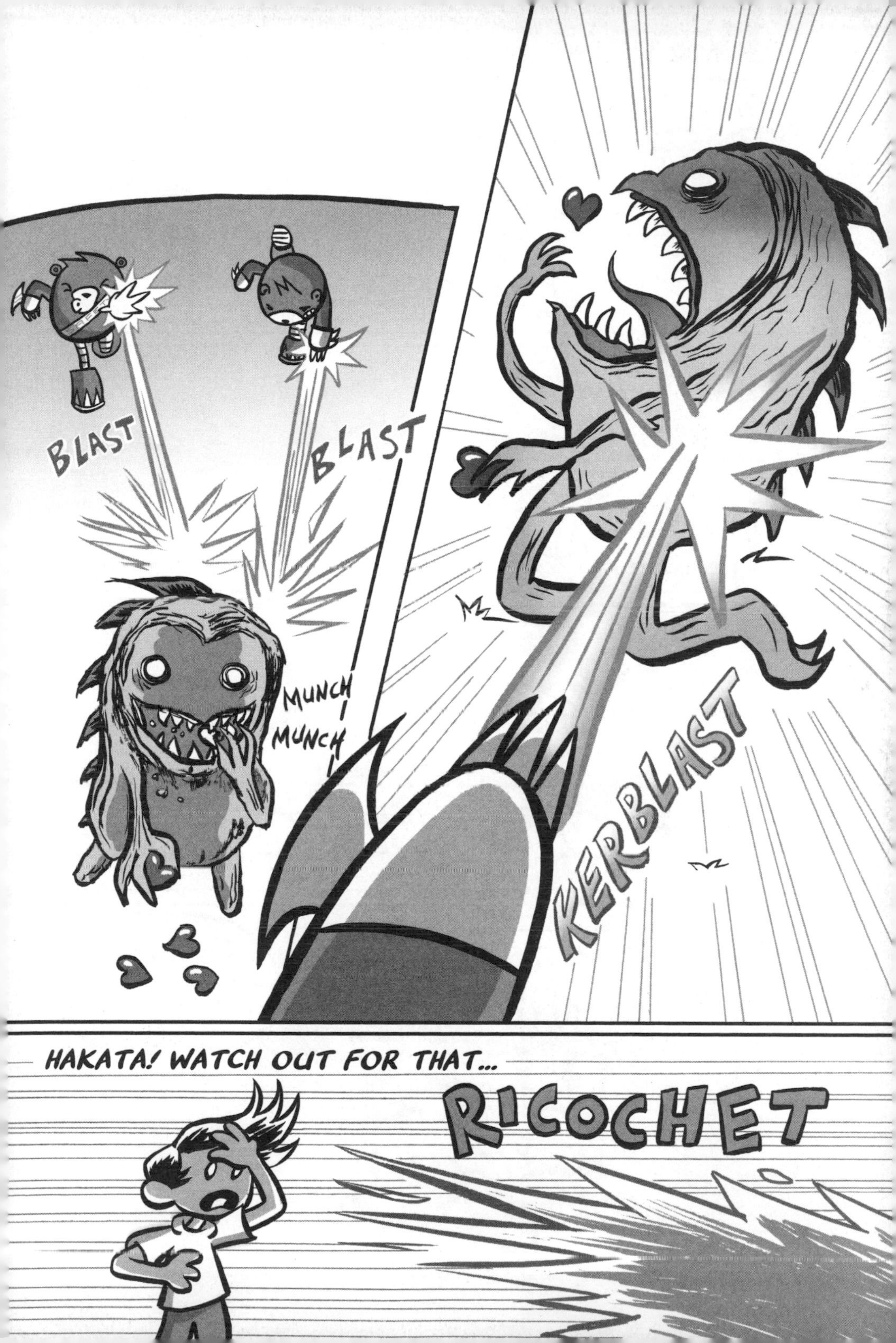
BLAST
BLAST
MUNCH MUNCH
KERBLAST
HAKATA! WATCH OUT FOR THAT...
RICOCHET

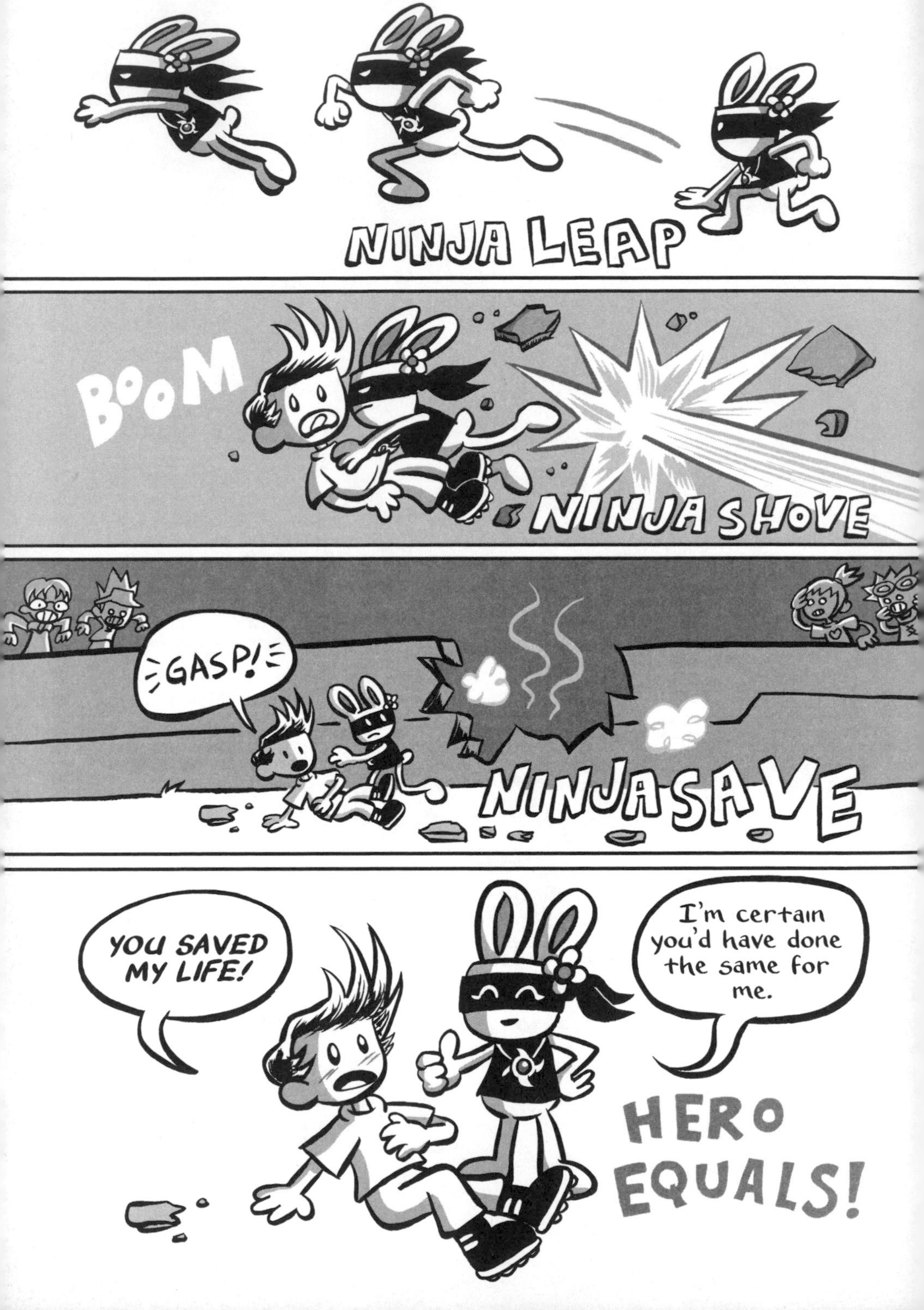
NINJA LEAP
BOOM
NINJA SHOVE
GASP!
NINJASAVE
YOU SAVED MY LIFE!
I'm certain you'd have done the same for me.
HERO EQUALS!

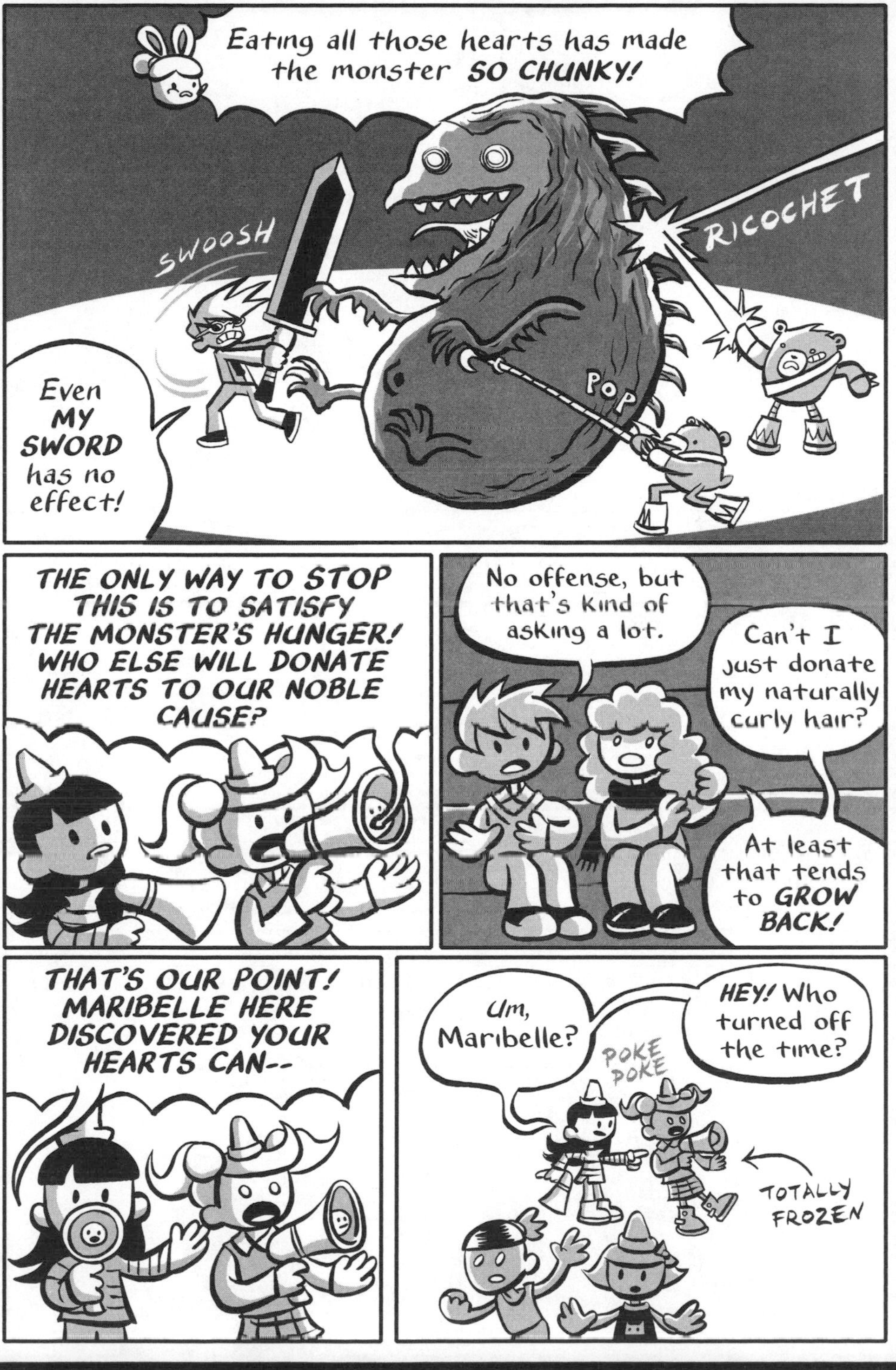
Eating all those hearts has made the monster SO CHUNKY!
SWOOSH
RICOCHET
POP
Even MY SWORD has no effect!
THE ONLY WAY TO STOP THIS IS TO SATISFY THE MONSTER'S HUNGER! WHO ELSE WILL DONATE HEARTS TO OUR NOBLE CAUSE?
No offense, but that's kind of asking a lot.
Can't I just donate my naturally curly hair?
At least that tends to GROW BACK!
THAT'S OUR POINT! MARIBELLE HERE DISCOVERED YOUR HEARTS CAN--
Um, Maribelle?
HEY! Who turned off the time?
POKE POKE
TOTALLY FROZEN

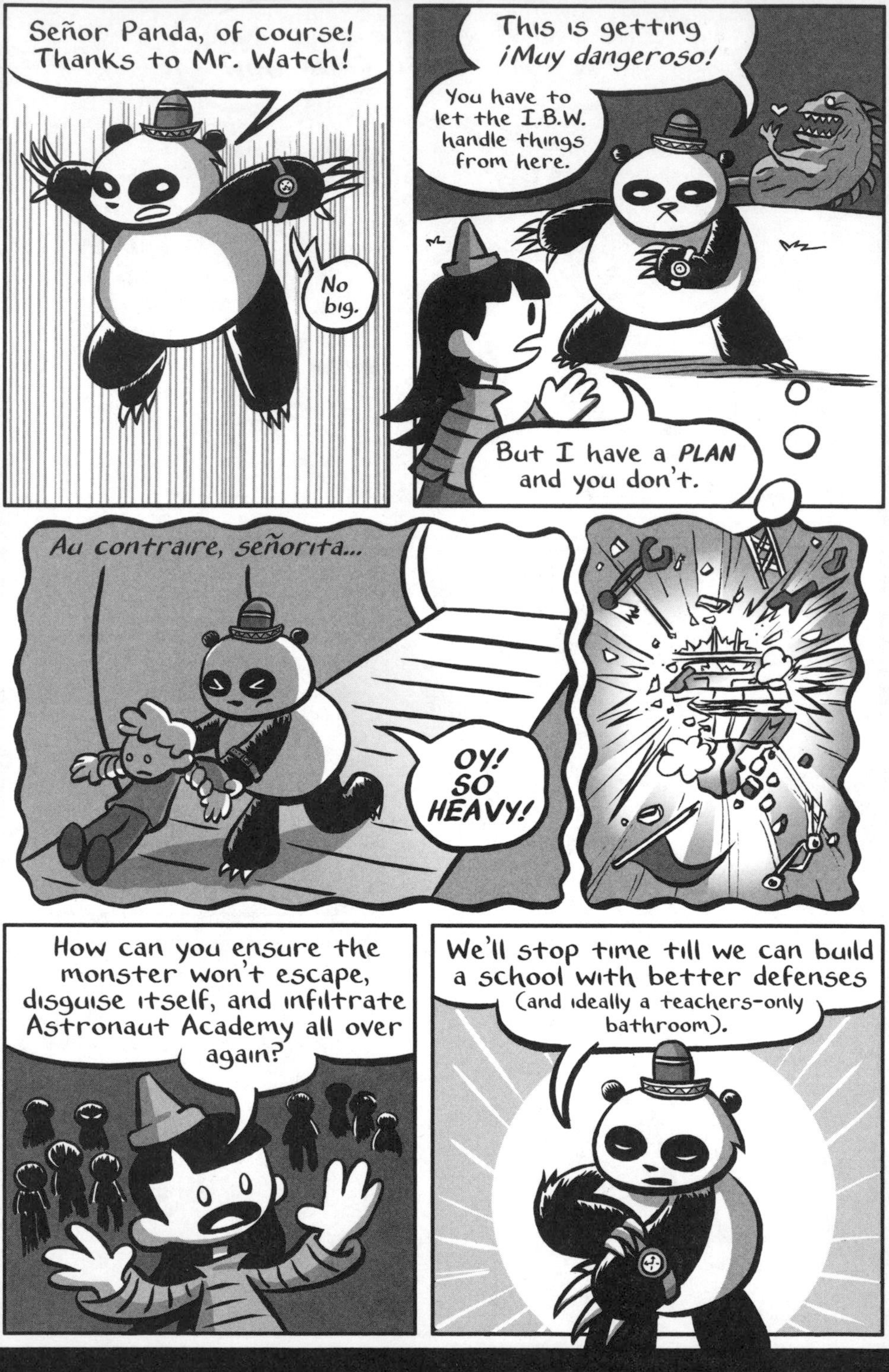
Señor Panda, of course! Thanks to Mr. Watch!
No big.
This is getting ¡Muy dangeroso!
You have to let the I.B.W. handle things from here.
But I have a PLAN and you don't.
Au contraire, señorita...
OY! SO HEAVY!
How can you ensure the monster won't escape, disguise itself, and infiltrate Astronaut Academy all over again?
We'll stop time till we can build a school with better defenses
(and ideally a teachers-only bathroom).

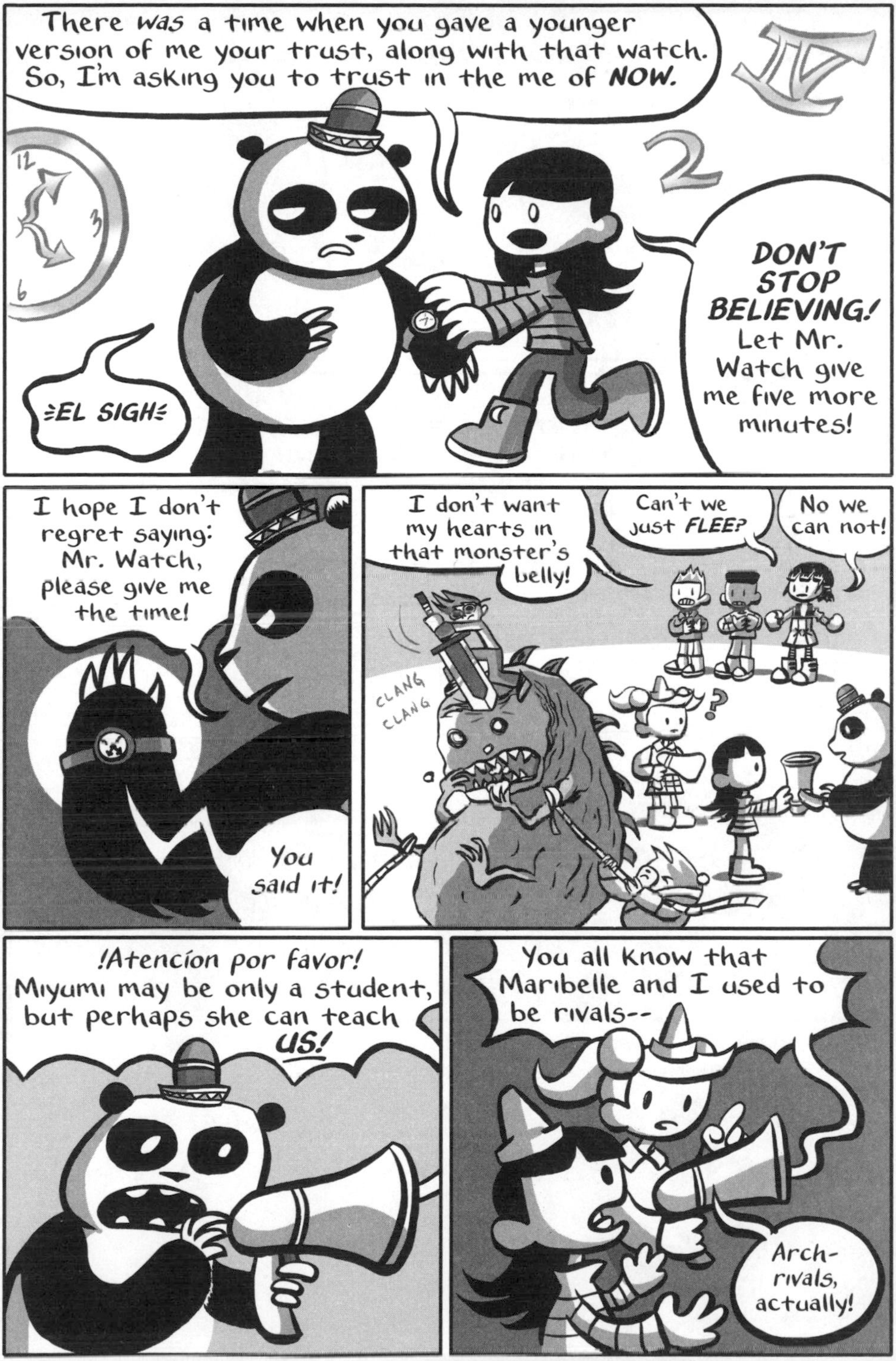

There was a time when you gave a younger version of me your trust, along with that watch. So, I'm asking you to trust in the me of NOW.
≶EL SIGH≶
DON'T STOP BELIEVING! Let Mr. Watch give me five more minutes!
I hope I don't regret saying: Mr. Watch, please give me the time!
You said it!
I don't want my hearts in that monster's belly!
Can't we just FLEE?
No we can not!
CLANG CLANG
!Atencion por favor! Miyumi may be only a student, but perhaps she can teach US!
You all know that Maribelle and I used to be rivals--
Arch-rivals, actually!

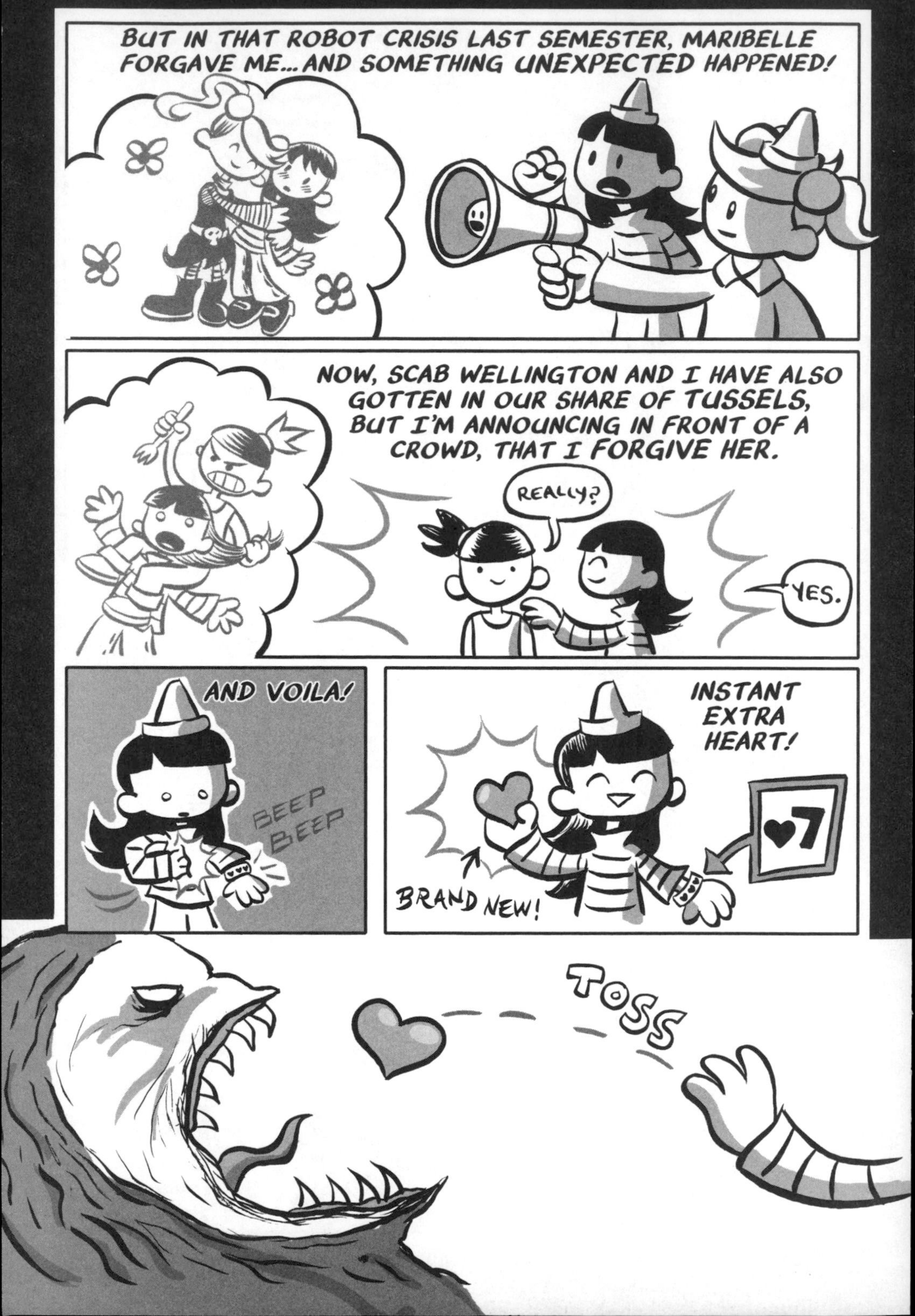
BUT IN THAT ROBOT CRISIS LAST SEMESTER, MARIBELLE FORGAVE ME... AND SOMETHING UNEXPECTED HAPPENED!
NOW, SCAB WELLINGTON AND I HAVE ALSO GOTTEN IN OUR SHARE OF TUSSELS, BUT I'M ANNOUNCING IN FRONT OF A CROWD, THAT I FORGIVE HER.
REALLY?
YES.
AND VOILA!
BEEP BEEP
INSTANT EXTRA HEART!
BRAND NEW!
7
TOSS

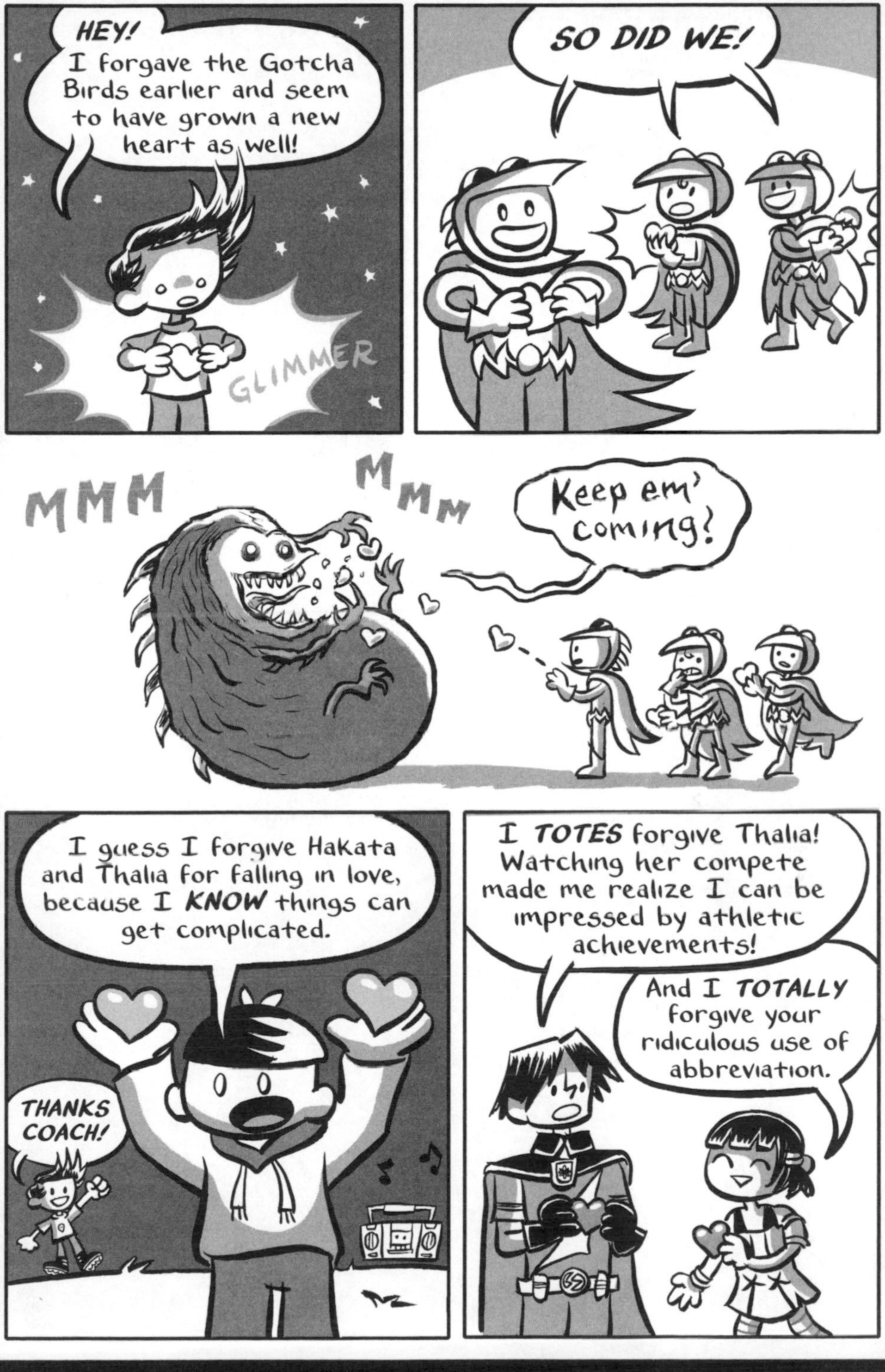
HEY!
I forgave the Gotcha Birds earlier and seem to have grown a new heart as well!
GLIMMER
SO DID WE!
MMM
MMM
Keep em' coming?
I guess I forgive Hakata and Thalia for falling in love, because I KNOW things can get complicated.
THANKS COACH!
I TOTES forgive Thalia! Watching her compete made me realize I can be impressed by athletic achievements!
And I TOTALLY forgive your ridiculous use of abbreviation.

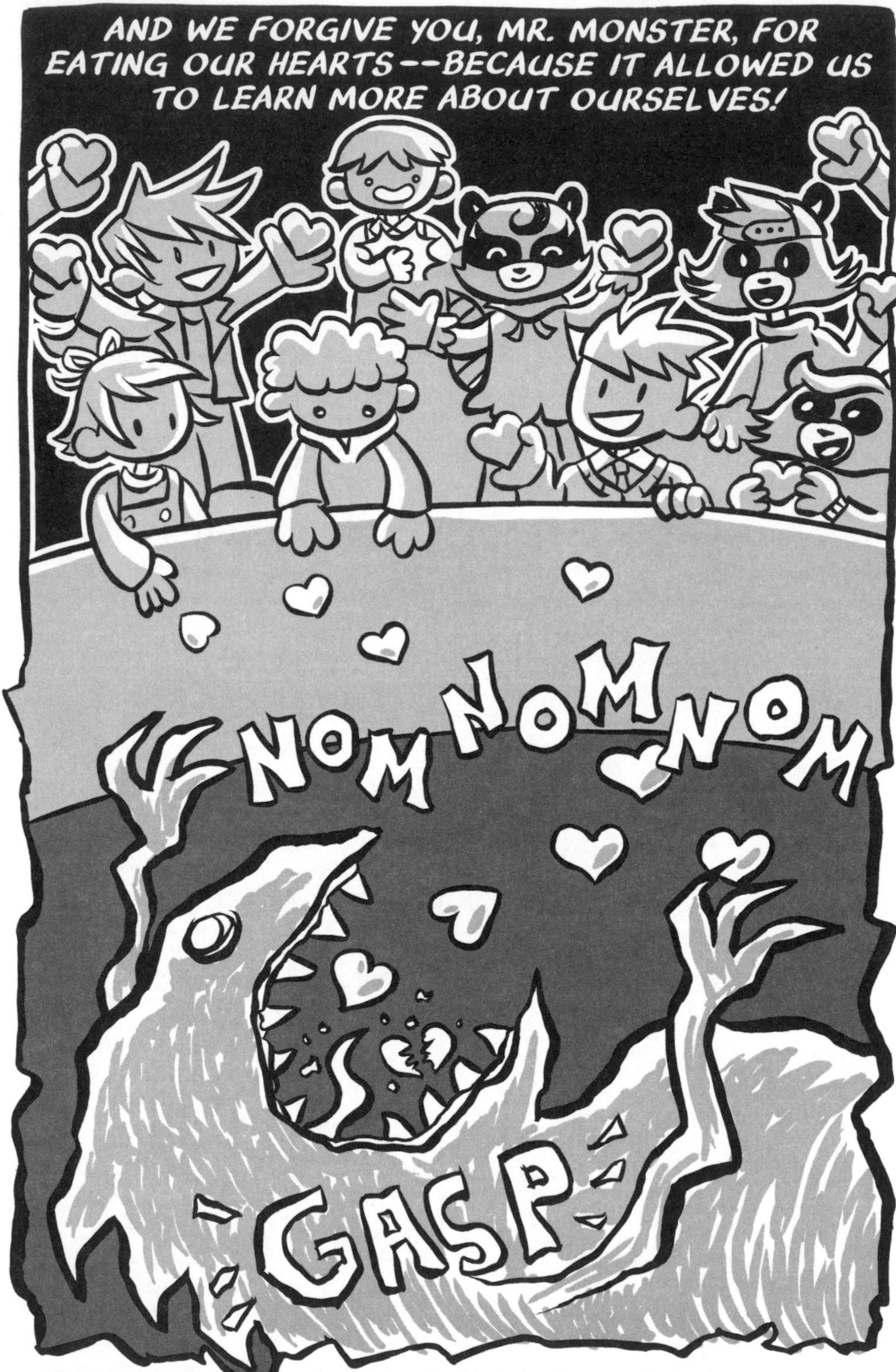
AND WE FORGIVE YOU, MR. MONSTER, FOR EATING OUR HEARTS--BECAUSE IT ALLOWED US TO LEARN MORE ABOUT OURSELVES!
NOM NOM NOM NOM
GASP

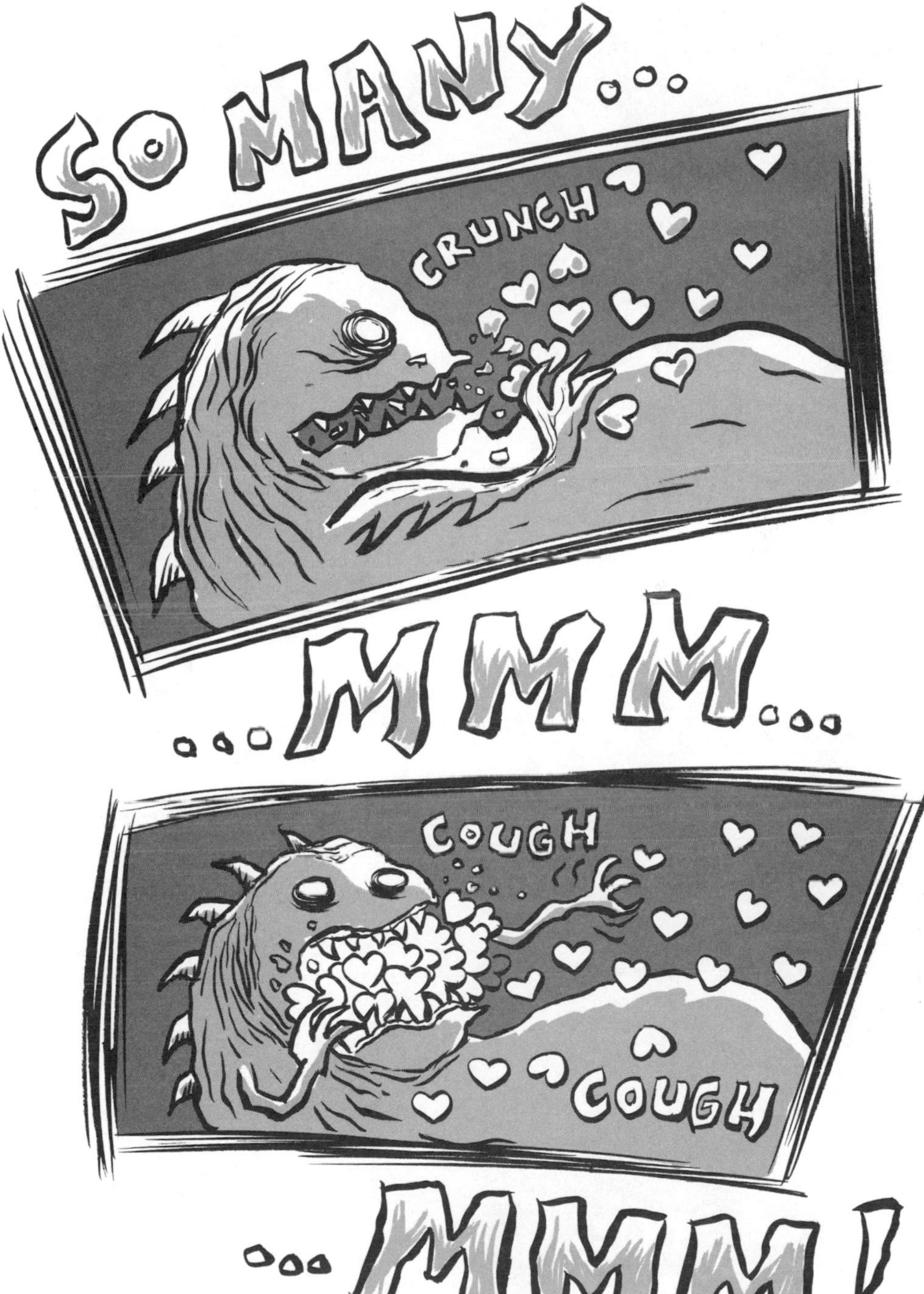
SO MANY...
CRUNCH
...MMM...
COUGH
COUGH
...MMM!

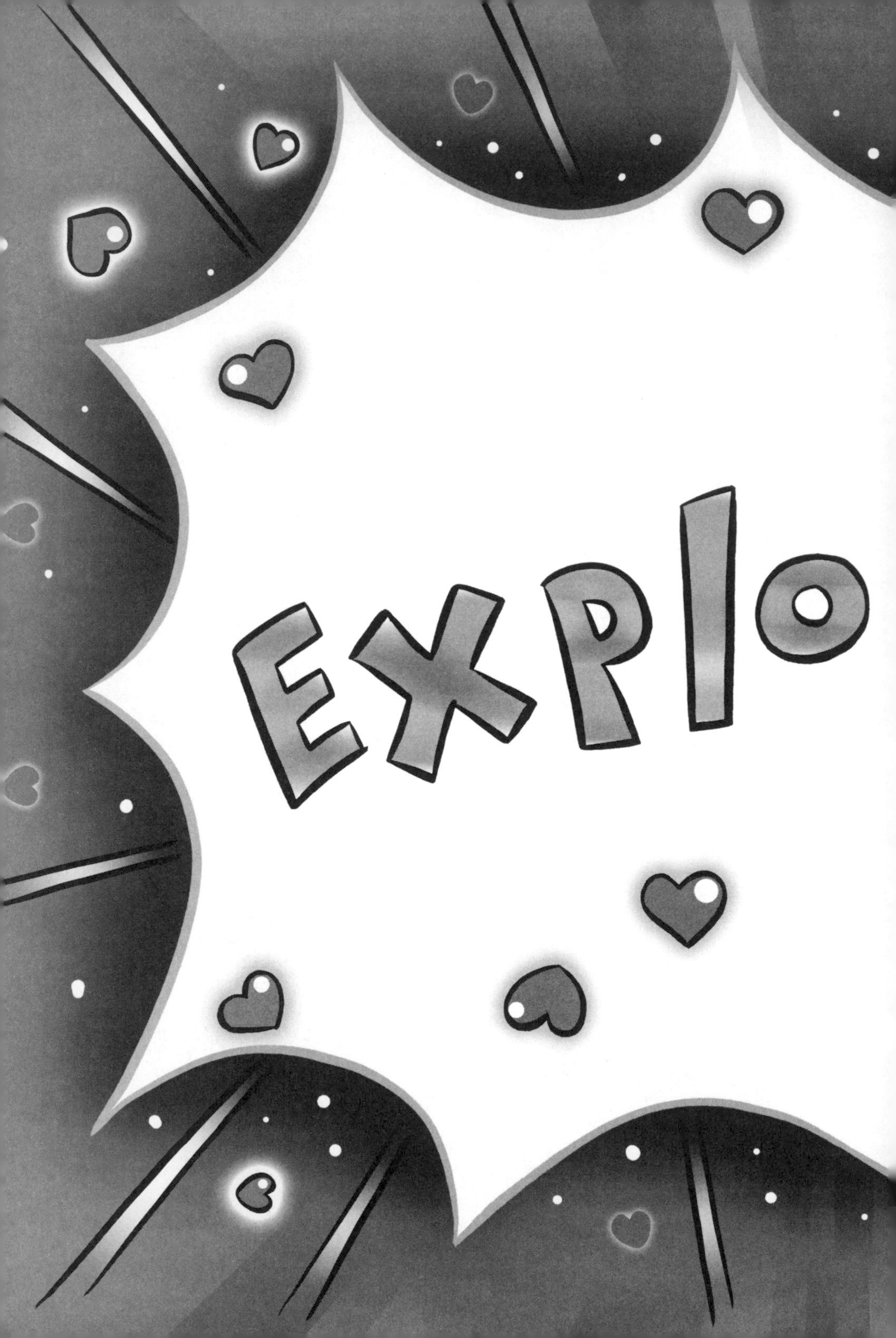
Explo

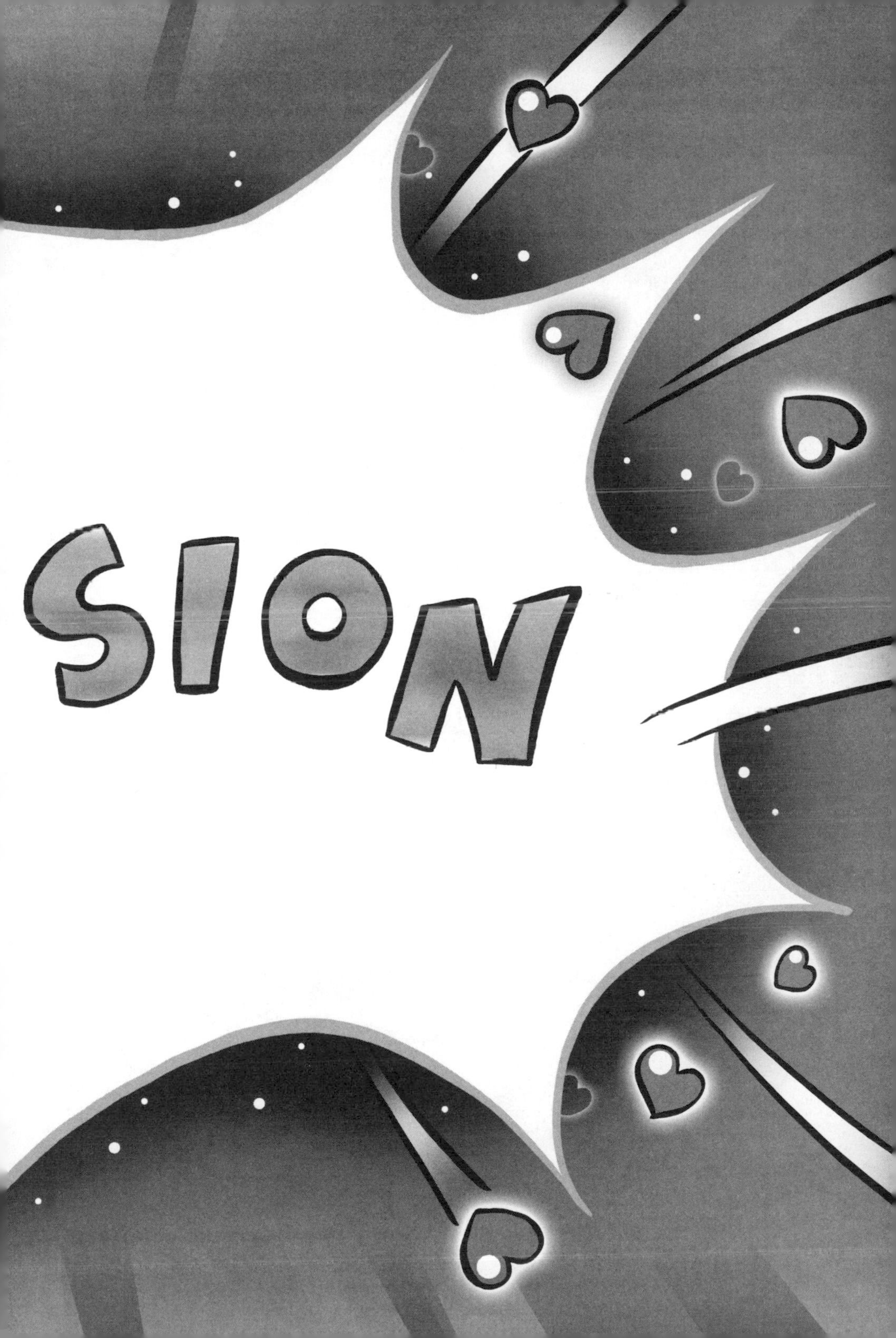
SION

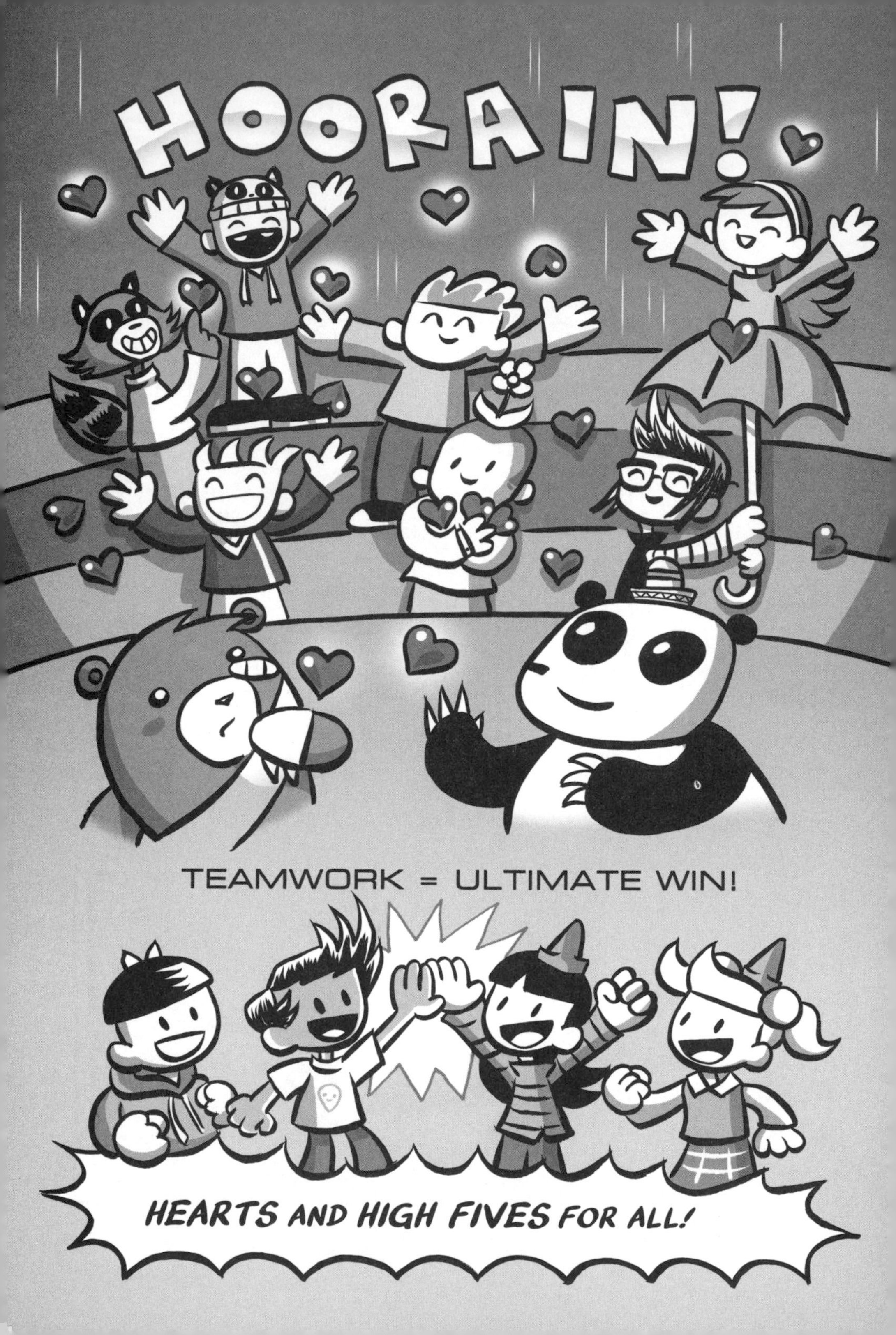
HOORAIN!
TEAMWORK = ULTIMATE WIN!
HEARTS AND HIGH FIVES FOR ALL!

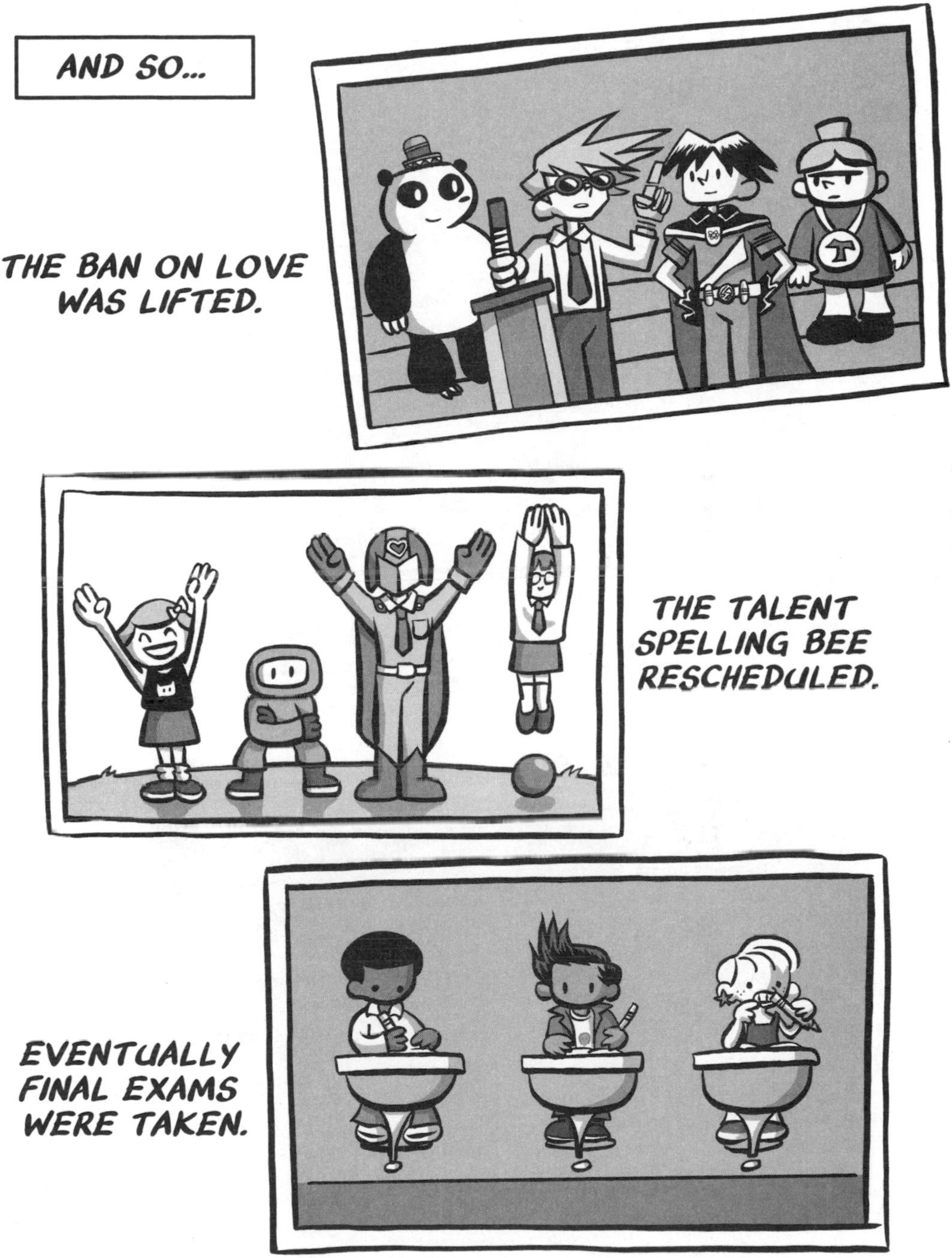
AND SO...
THE BAN ON LOVE WAS LIFTED.
THE TALENT SPELLING BEE RESCHEDULED.
EVENTUALLY FINAL EXAMS WERE TAKEN.

BUT FIRST...
THERE WAS A DANCE PARTY!
(As is customary for the end of dramatic conflicts.)

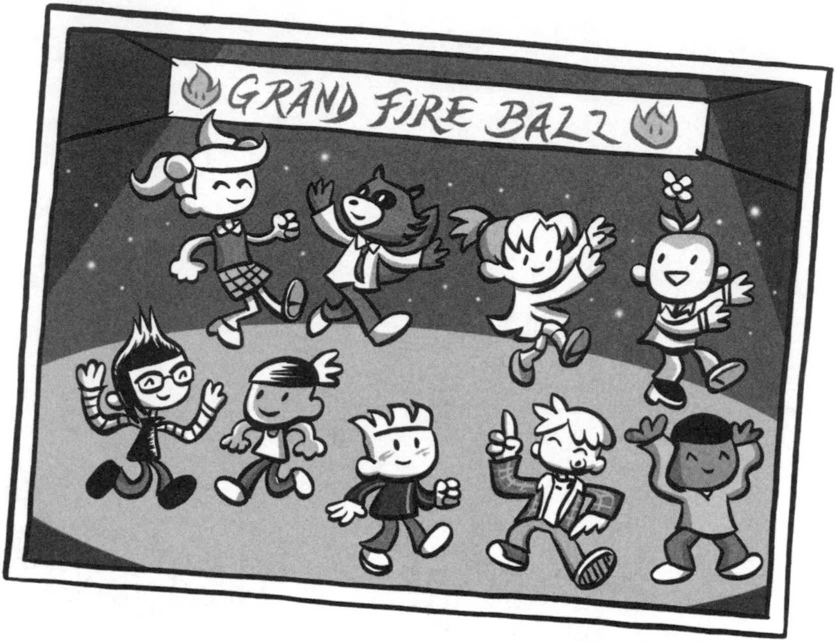
GRAND FIRE BALL

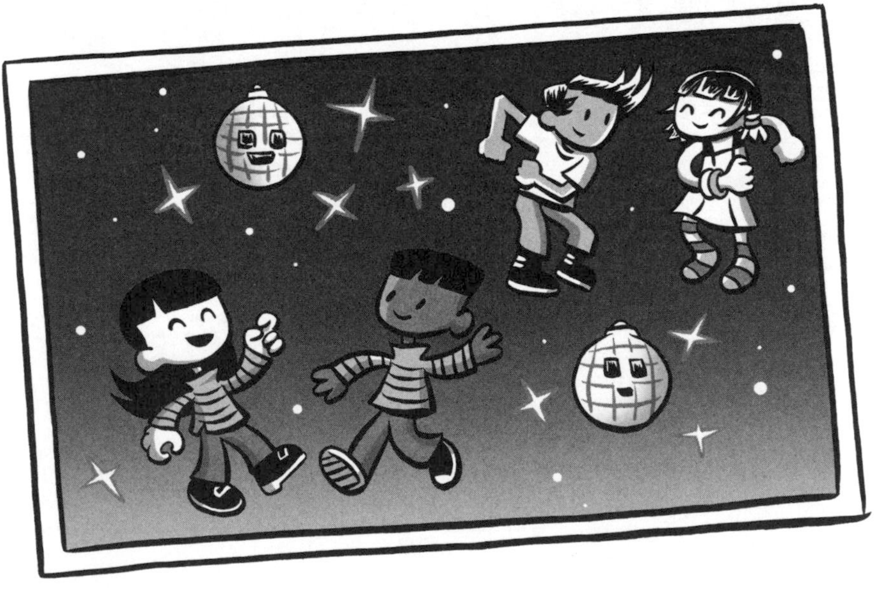

EVEN THOUGH A LOT OF RIVALRIES ENDED...

...NOT EVERYONE WAS READY FOR FRIEND REQUESTS.

BUT NO ONE KNOWS WHO OR WHAT
THE FUTURE CAN HOLD!

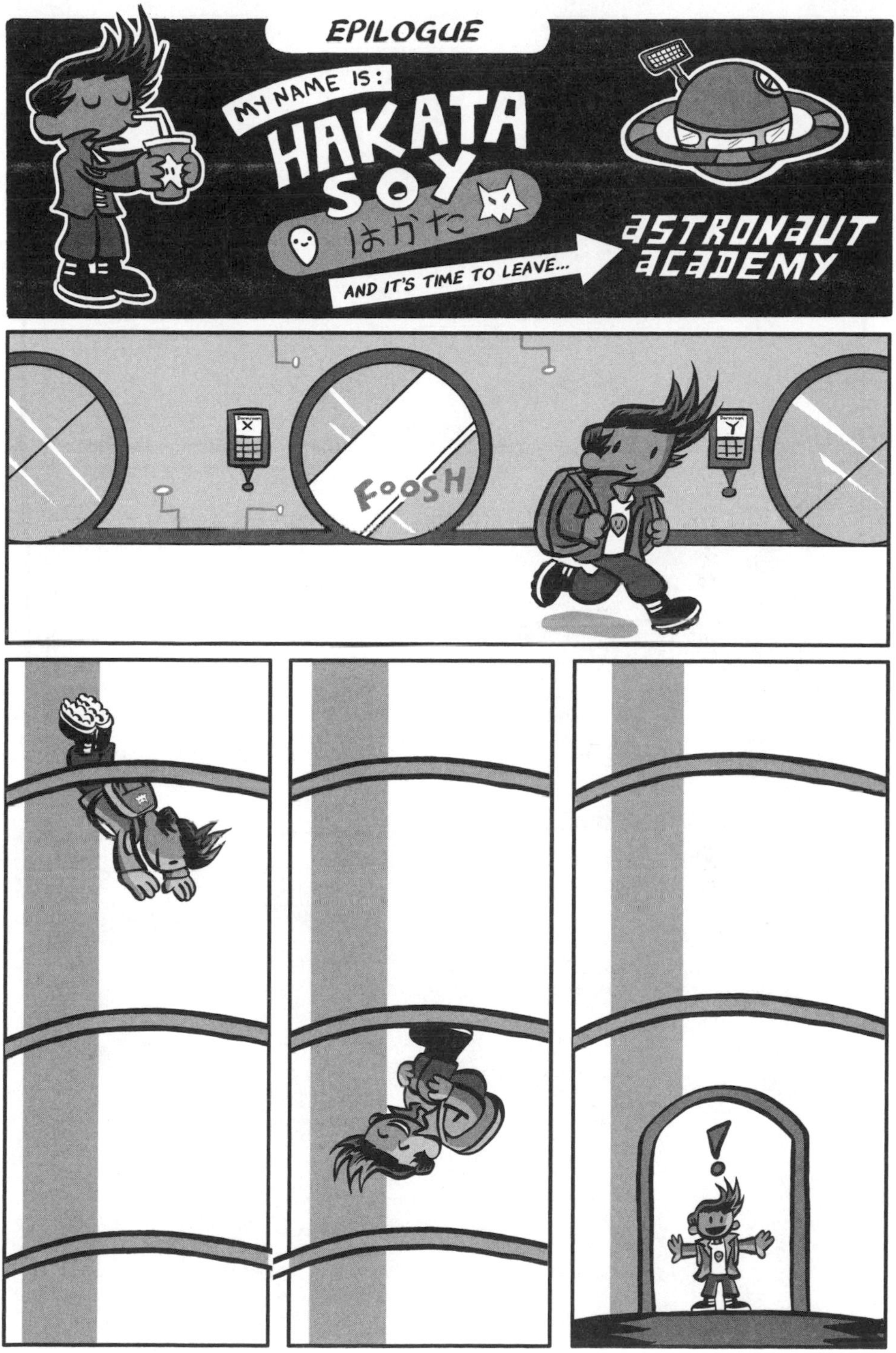
EPILOGUE
MY NAME IS:
HAKATA SOY
はかた
AND IT'S TIME TO LEAVE...
ASTRONAUT ACADEMY
X
Y
FOOSH

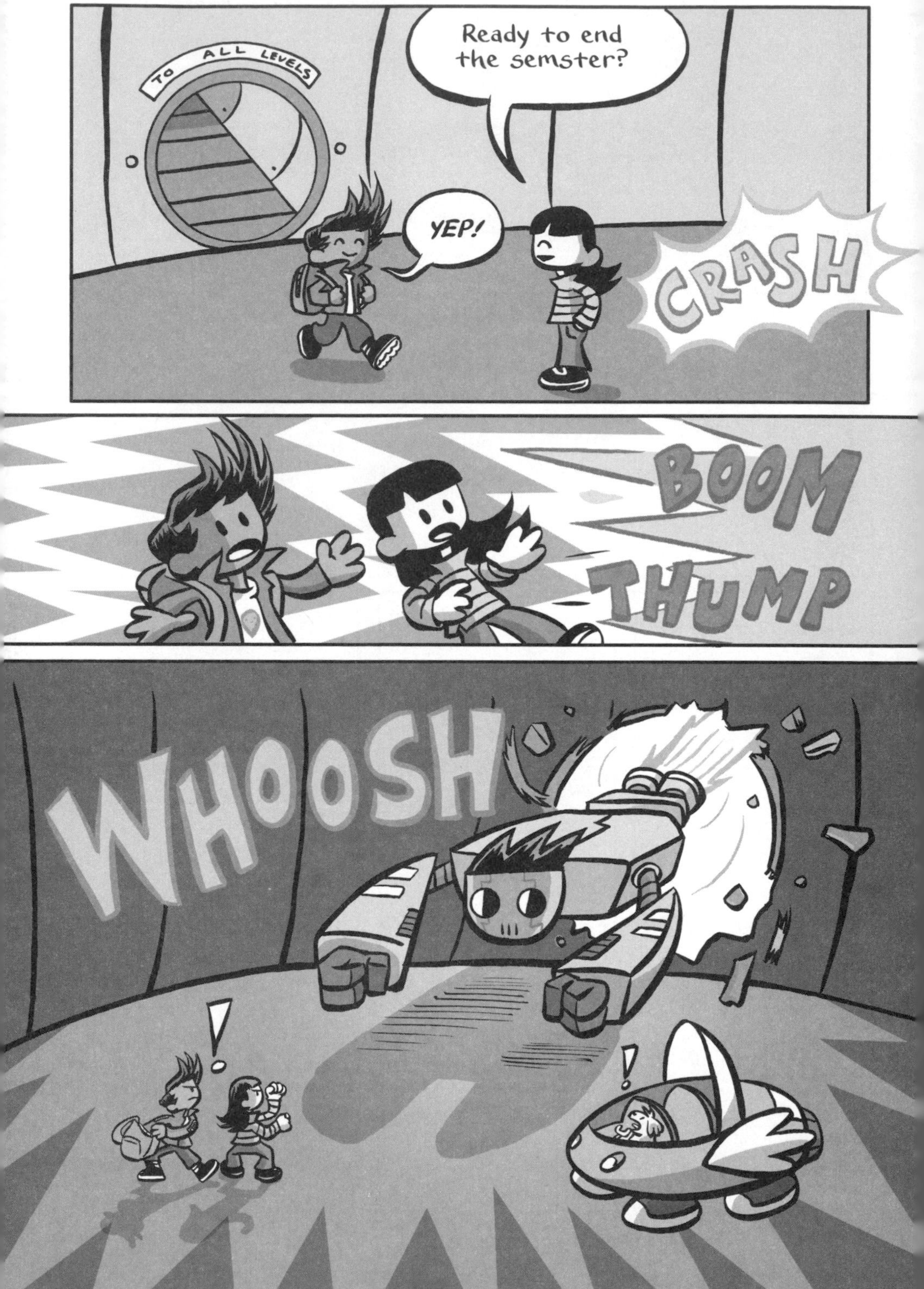
TO ALL LEVELS
Ready to end the semster?
YEP!
CRASH
BOOM
THUMP
WHOOSH
!
!

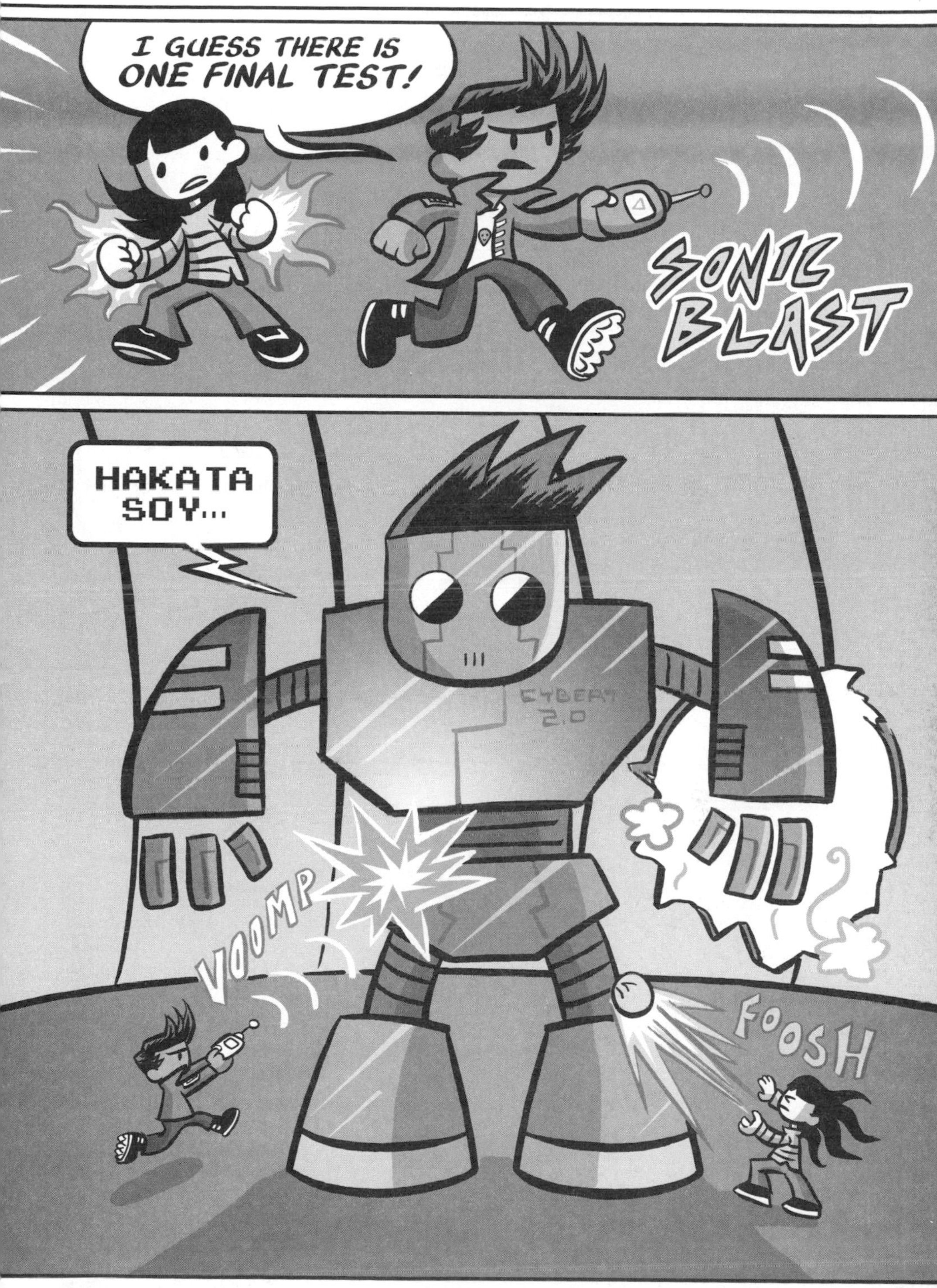
I GUESS THERE IS ONE FINAL TEST!
SONIC BLAST
HAKATA SOY...
VOOMP
FOOSH

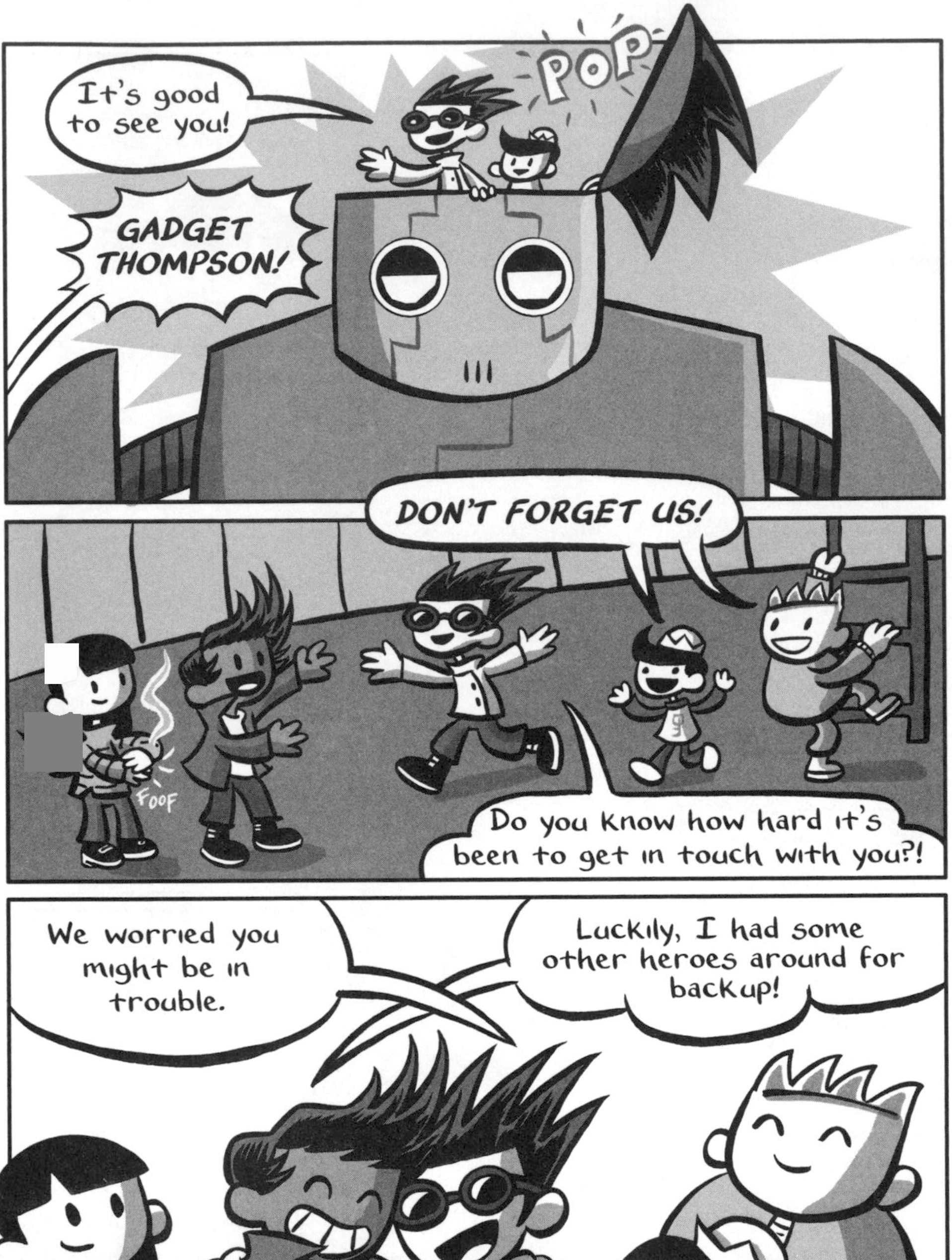
It's good to see you!
POP
GADGET THOMPSON!
DON'T FORGET US!
FOOF
Do you know how hard it's been to get in touch with you?!
We worried you might be in trouble.
Luckily, I had some other heroes around for backup!
Cool!

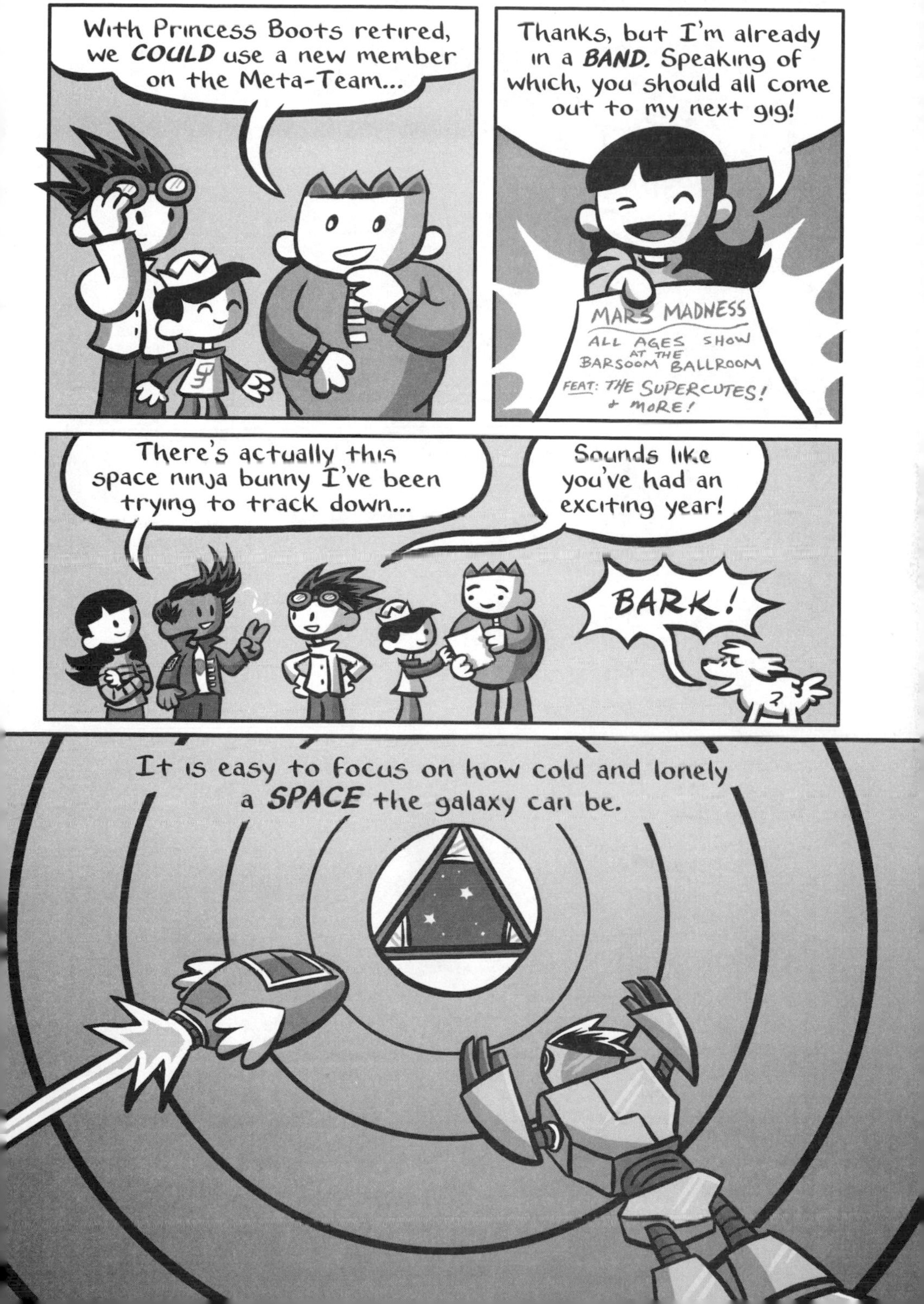

With Princess Boots retired, we COULD use a new member on the Meta-Team...
Thanks, but I'm already in a BAND. Speaking of which, you should all come out to my next gig!
MARS MADNESS
ALL AGES SHOW AT THE BARSOOM BALLROOM
FEAT: THE SUPERCUTES! + MORE!
There's actually this space ninja bunny I've been trying to track down...
Sounds like you've had an exciting year!
BARK!
It is easy to focus on how cold and lonely a SPACE the galaxy can be.

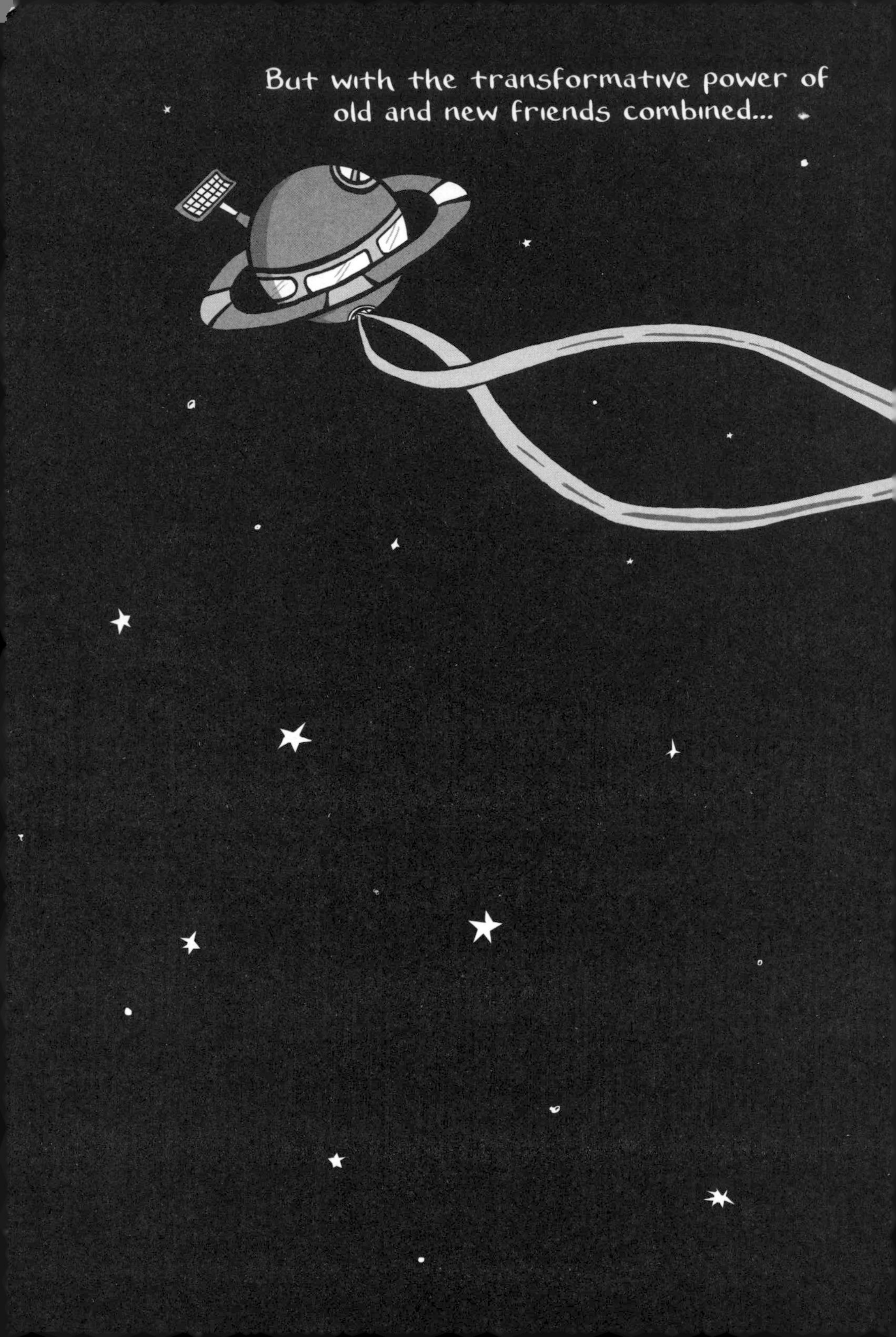
But with the transformative power of old and new friends combined...

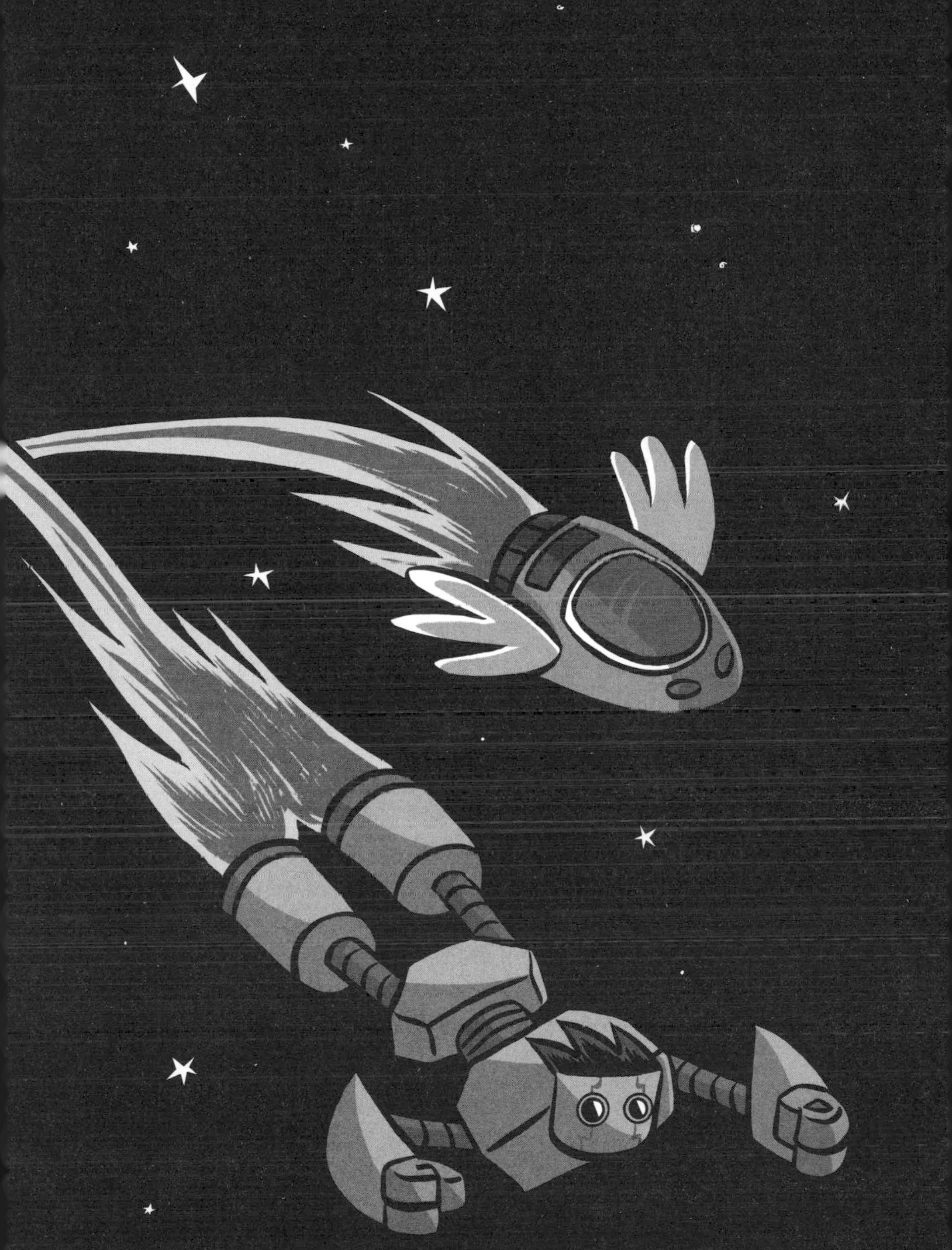

...I feel as though I am just getting **WARMED UP!**

making astronaut academy

by dave roman

Sketch Book

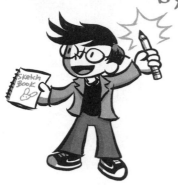

Ideas can come at any time, so I always keep a sketchbook and pencil close by.

PANDA HAT
CHA CHA CHA
oops!
MIYUMI
SECRET AGENT

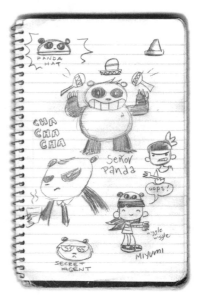

I love designing new characters and imagining how they might interact with each other.

Prelude ??

1) Middle
2) Beginning
3) END!
4) Epilogue

SHOULD THIS GO FIRST?

I organize my various ideas by making lists and a story outline.

I write the "script" as a series of rough layouts called thumbnails.

OBVIOUSLY MR PANDA HASN'T STUCK TO THE SILLYBUS. BUT TRUST ME WITH THE AUTHORITY THAT COMES FROM BEING SLIGHTLY OLDER HE KNOWS WHAT HE IS DOING.
BUT WHAT IF I FAIL MY FINAL EXAM?
OH! DON'T WORRY BECAUSE I ALREADY TOOK THEM FOR YOU.
YOU TOOK MY SPANISH TEST FOR ME?
YEP! IT'S IN YOUR FUTURE!
I'D FEEL VIOLATED IF WE WEREN'T THE SAME PERSON.
BUT SEÑIOR PANDA DOESN'T CARE ABOUT PROFICIENCY EXAMS OR MOCK LESSONS!
He only cares about WHO is taking them.
GULP
Because he's not a real SPANISH TEACHER!
SENT By the I.B.W.!
That Panda is a NARC!

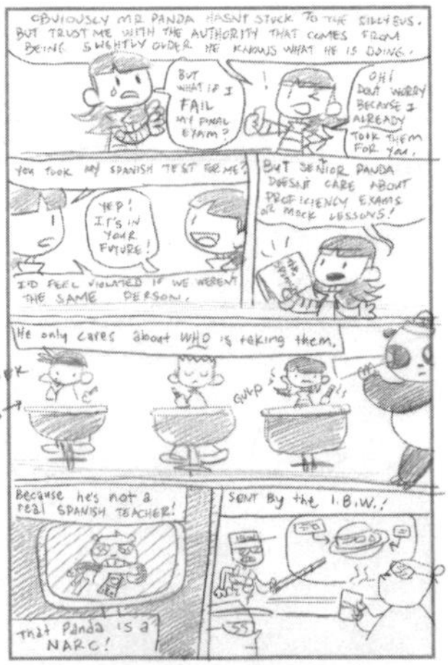

My editor will read the early draft to give feedback and request revisions before I move on to the final art.

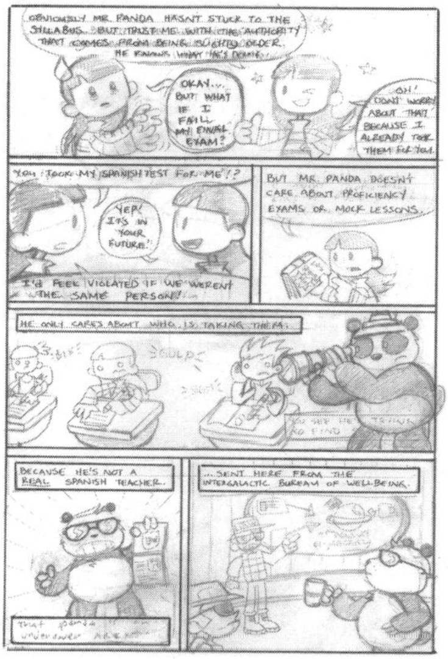
OBVIOUSLY MR. PANDA HASN'T STUCK TO THE SYLLABUS. BUT TRUST ME WITH THE AUTHORITY THAT COMES FROM BEING SLIGHTLY OLDER. HE KNOWS WHAT HE'S DOING.
OKAY... BUT WHAT IF I FAIL MY FINAL EXAM?
OH! DON'T WORRY ABOUT THAT BECAUSE I ALREADY TOOK THEM FOR YOU.
YOU TOOK MY SPANISH TEST FOR ME!?
YEP! IT'S IN YOUR FUTURE!
I'D FEEL VIOLATED IF WE WEREN'T THE SAME PERSON!
BUT MR. PANDA DOESN'T CARE ABOUT PROFICIENCY EXAMS OR MOCK LESSONS.
HE ONLY CARES ABOUT WHO IS TAKING THEM.
SGULP
SIGH
BECAUSE HE'S NOT A REAL SPANISH TEACHER.
...SENT HERE FROM THE INTERGALACTIC BUREAU OF WELL-BEING.

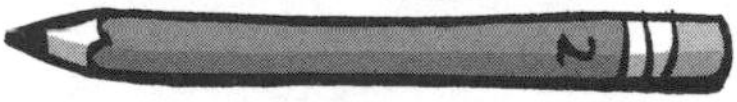

The pencil art is drawn on thick Bristol board which can handle lots of erasing!

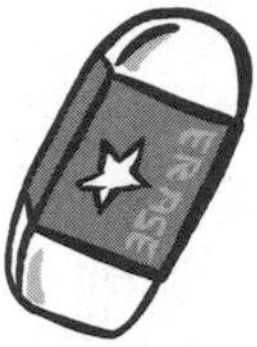
ERASE

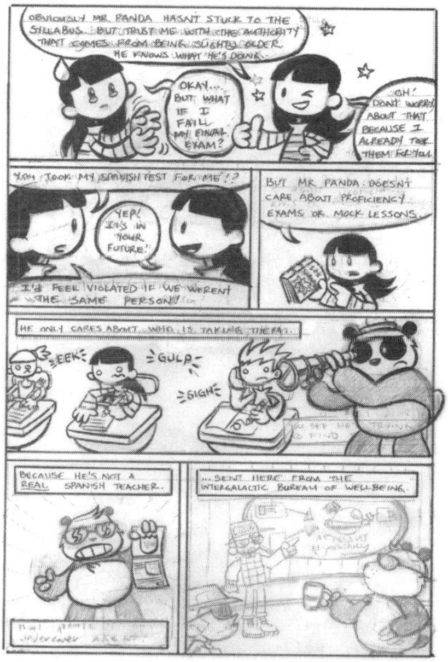
OBVIOUSLY MR. PANDA HASN'T STUCK TO THE SYLLABUS. BUT TRUST ME WITH THE AUTHORITY THAT COMES FROM BEING SLIGHTLY OLDER. HE KNOWS WHAT HE'S DOING.
OKAY... BUT WHAT IF I FAIL MY FINAL EXAM?
OH! DON'T WORRY ABOUT THAT BECAUSE I ALREADY TOOK THEM FOR YOU.
YOU TOOK MY SPANISH TEST FOR ME!?
YEP! IT'S IN YOUR FUTURE!
I'D FEEL VIOLATED IF WE WEREN'T THE SAME PERSON!
BUT MR. PANDA DOESN'T CARE ABOUT PROFICIENCY EXAMS OR MOCK LESSONS.
HE ONLY CARES ABOUT WHO IS TAKING THEM.
EEK
GULP
SIGH
BECAUSE HE'S NOT A REAL SPANISH TEACHER.
...SENT HERE FROM THE INTERGALACTIC BUREAU OF WELL-BEING.

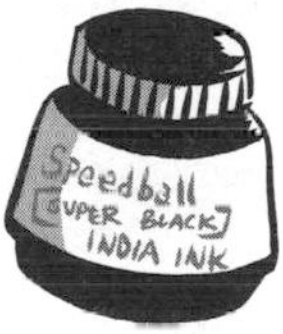
Speedball
SUPER BLACK
INDIA INK

India ink is used to create dark, permanent lines. I apply it with a watercolor brush capable of various line weights.

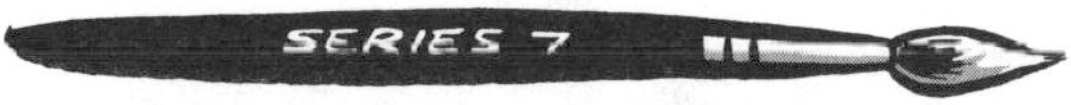
SERIES 7

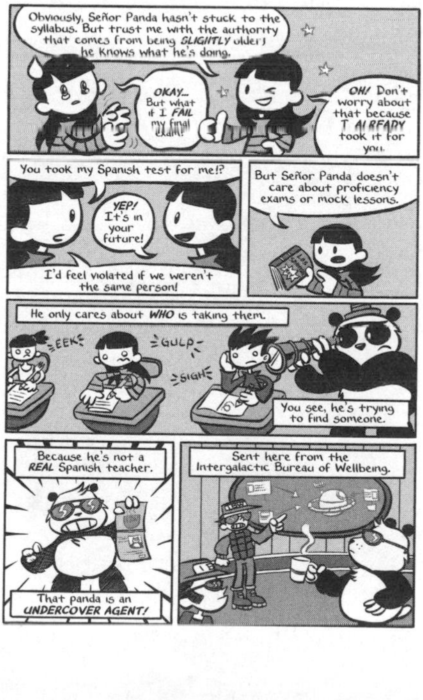
Obviously, Señor Panda hasn't stuck to the syllabus. But trust me with the authority that comes from being SLIGHTLY older! he knows what he's doing.
OKAY... But what if I FAIL my final exam?
OH! Don't worry about that because I ALREADY took it for you.
You took my Spanish test for me!?
YEP! It's in your future!
I'd feel violated if we weren't the same person!
But Señor Panda doesn't care about proficiency exams or mock lessons.
He only cares about WHO is taking them.
EEK
GULP
SIGH
You see, he's trying to find someone.
Because he's not a REAL Spanish teacher.
Sent here from the Intergalactic Bureau of Wellbeing.
That panda is an UNDERCOVER AGENT!

The inked pages are scanned into a computer where I add the gray tones and final lettering.

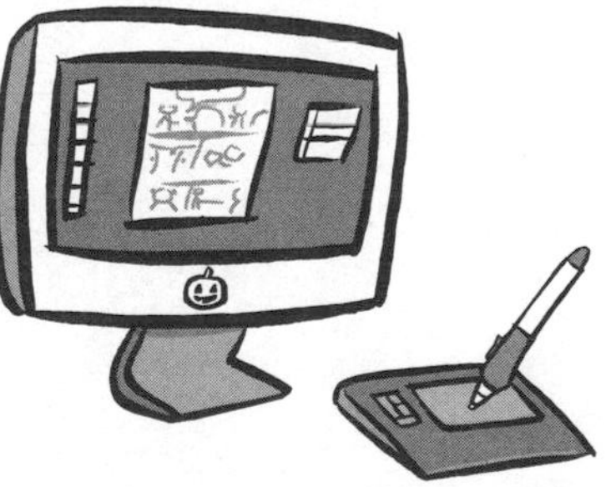

Then I send the files to the publisher and start the process all over again!

First Second
New York

Production assistants: Gale Williams and Megan Brennan
Additional gray color assists: Ma. Victoria Robado (Shouri),
Charles Eubanks, and Craig Arndt
Technical support: John Green
Life support: Raina Telgemeier

Copyright © 2013 by Dave Roman
Published by First Second
First Second is an imprint of Roaring Brook Press,
a division of Holtzbrinck Publishing Holdings Limited Partnership
175 Fifth Avenue, New York, New York 10010
All rights reserved

Cataloging-in-Publication Data is on file at the Library of Congress.
ISBN: 978-1-59643-621-3

First Second books are available for
special promotions and premiums.
For details, contact: Director of Special Markets,
Holtzbrinck Publishers.

Interior book design by
John Green

FIRST
EDITION

First edition 2013

Printed in the United States of America by
RR Donnelley & Sons Company, Harrisonburg, Virginia

BY ART
WE LIVE

1 3 5 7 9 10 8 6 4 2